Please Leave in Book

CA
CH
HE
KI
LH
LU
M/C
PA
PE 10/17
RI
SB
SO
TA
TE
TI
TO 02/12
WA
WI

Garden of
Secrets Past

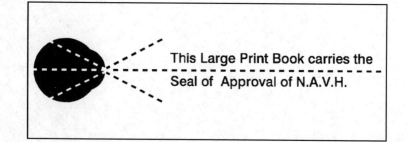

This Large Print Book carries the
Seal of Approval of N.A.V.H.

GARDEN OF
SECRETS PAST

ANTHONY EGLIN

THORNDIKE PRESS
A part of Gale, Cengage Learning

GALE
CENGAGE Learning

Detroit • New York • San Francisco • New Haven, Conn • Waterville, Maine • London

GALE
CENGAGE Learning™

LIBRARY OF CONGRESS CATALOGING-IN-PUBLICATION DATA

Eglin, Anthony.
    Garden of secrets past / by Anthony Eglin.
        p. cm. — (Thorndike Press large print mystery)
    ISBN-13: 978-1-4104-4158-4 (hardcover)
    ISBN-10: 1-4104-4158-X (hardcover)
    1. Kingston, Lawrence (Fictitious character)—Fiction. 2. Botanists—Fiction. 3. Historic gardens—Fiction. 4. Murder—Investigation—Fiction. 5. Family secrets—Fiction. 6. England—Fiction. 7. Large type books.
    I. Title.
    PS3605.G53G37 2011b
    813'.6—dc22   2011031064

Published in 2011 by arrangement with St. Martin's Press, LLC.

Printed in the United States of America
1 2 3 4 5 6 7 15 14 13 12 11

For my friend, artist Bob Johnson

ACKNOWLEDGMENTS

Sturminster Hall, the fictitious garden and house in *Garden of Secrets Past,* is modeled in part on the National Trust historic estate at Shugborough, in Staffordshire.

When I first visited Shugborough fifteen years ago, to film a one-hour documentary for the British Tourist Authority, I came away with lasting memories of its illustrious heritage and the picturesque garden and park with its eight monuments scattered throughout the landscape. Like most, I was intrigued with the Shepherd's Monument and its mysterious inscription: a conundrum that has baffled some of the world's cleverest minds for two hundred and sixty years. It was this stone edifice with its marble relief that inspired the beginnings of *Garden of Secrets Past.* Save for this one ancient monument, all other parts of the story are fictional, as is the cast of characters.

All the code sequences described in the book are accurate, and for that I owe thanks to Simon Singh (famous for his book *Fermat's Last Theorem*), gaining valuable knowledge from his authoritative *Code Book* (Doubleday, 1999). I am also fortunate to have had the help of the American Cryptogram Association, which showed me how to encipher the code hidden in the lines of Gray's *Elegy*. If errors were committed in interpreting and explaining how the codes functioned, *mea maxima culpa*.

A special thanks to Peter Norback, whose Top Tag Pet ID provided a most ingenious hiding place for cryptic messages.

Once again I'm indebted to DC Claire Chandler, Hampshire Constabulary, for coming to my rescue with invaluable advice on UK police procedural matters.

I am deeply grateful, as with past books, for the critical advice and editing skills of Dave Stern, John Joss, Roger Dubin, and my wife, Suzie. Your collective support, direction, advice, and keen eyes have breathed added life to my story and given it that all-important final polish.

At St. Martin's Press/Thomas Dunne Books, a heartfelt thanks to Associate Publisher and Executive Editor Pete Wolverton for his steadfast support, guidance, and patience through five books now. Also a thumbs-up to Anne Bensson for her able assist with the final edit. And lucky me to have the remarkable talents of copy editor Cynthia Merman to add the finishing touches.

My last, but not least, thanks go to all my readers, many of whom have written expressing the pleasure that my stories have given them. I can't ask for more than that.

PROLOGUE

Staffordshire, England

"Twenty-seven, twenty-eight, twenty-nine — thirty." Pippa took in a deep breath and yelled as loud as her six-year-old lungs would allow. "Ready or not, here I come!"

She and her brother, Timothy, who was nine, had been playing hide-and-seek for an hour. She was now tiring of it, and hungry too. When they'd started the game, she would run off eagerly searching for Timmy. Now she dawdled, scarcely bothering to look around, knowing that finding him was more a question of luck than anything else; he was just too clever in discovering sneaky places to hide.

The sun had reached its zenith. The breeze that had ruffled her frock and stirred the leaves in the ancient trees was now no more than a sometimes sigh. When they'd first arrived at the garden with their parents, she'd welcomed the sun's warmth; now she

11

tried to escape its intensity by walking under the trees and sidling along the shady side of the massive rhododendron bushes. All week she and Timmy had been praying that their picnic wouldn't be rained out, and now she would welcome a passing shower.

She'd had enough, she decided. A few minutes more and she would call out, to let him know. In any case, they'd agreed that this was the last game; afterward they would return to the shade of the huge copper beech where, by now, Mum and Dad would have a picnic lunch spread out on the familiar tartan blanket. More than anything she wanted that cold glass of lemonade.

The grounds at Sturminster Hall, like many English estates that opened their gates to the public for a modest charge, were made to measure for picnics and families with children. There was no shortage of diversions and hiding places to be discovered in its fifteen hundred acres of historic gardens and parkland. Intimate enclosures adjacent to the big mansion, most surrounded by soaring hedges of yew and holly, offered nooks and crannies aplenty. Arched openings in the dense hedges led to other gardens: a water garden, a rose garden with sturdy arbors and pergolas hidden under a deluge of a thousand blossoms, and a brick-walled garden that boasted the finest herbaceous borders in the land. Farther on, woodland walks opened to rolling meadowland where venerable oaks, beeches, and spreading horse chestnuts cast dappled shadows on the grazed grass. Winding languidly through the estate, the shallow, reed-edged River Swane provided a boundless supply of frogs, tiddlers, newts, tadpoles, and sometimes elvers. During school holidays and weekends, many of them ended up as short-lived trophies, in jam jars with holes punched in the lids.

A breath of warm air teased Pippa's straw-colored hair as she continued her half-hearted search. Now and then, she purposely scuffed the toes of her sandals in the dry grass so that Timmy might hear her coming. For all she knew, she might already have passed him by. She stopped alongside a row of towering shrubs cloaked in a blanket of white and purple flowers, and gazed around. This was silly, she said to herself. Pointless. She would never find him. Setting off again, she entered a grass clearing with a curving backdrop of trees. A few paces away, rising up to the sky, was a scary-looking old stone monument many times her height. Framed in its rough-hewn surround was a picture carved on a grayish-white panel. She gazed at it for several seconds. It must be very old, she thought. She couldn't make out what the robed people in the picture were supposed to be doing, but it *was* pretty. As she turned away from it, eager to be on her way, to make one last futile effort to find Timmy, she saw the man. A dozen more steps and she would have tripped over him. She stopped in her tracks and let out an impulsive gasp, quickly stifling it with her tiny hand.

He was stretched out on the grass on his stomach, one arm splayed, his face turned away. Why would he be wearing a woolly jacket on such a hot day? she wondered. She stared at him for a moment, relieved that she hadn't awakened him from his nap, then crept past him as quickly and quietly as she could. About to go on her way, she paused to glance back at him. A shiver ran through her slender frame, and her heart started racing. His open eyes were staring up to the sky, and there was a dark reddish stain on his temple. She looked away, screamed, and ran as fast as she could, leaving a sandal behind.

ONE

Three weeks later, London

Lawrence Kingston's seven-room flat on Cadogan Square in the Royal Borough of Kensington and Chelsea would reveal few, if any, surprises to a first-time visitor who already knew something of the man. No abstract or postmodernist art, no plasma TV, high-tech gadgets, or sports memorabilia, nothing jarring or eccentric, nothing at odds with his personality, his days in the halls of academia, or his inerrant taste. Kingston's pied-à-terre was the result of an endogenous process that had resulted in less a visual impression than a feeling, where comfort and livability trumped all else. What, to the uneducated eye, appeared to be a haphazard arrangement of furniture and furnishings, was, in fact, an intuitive marriage and placement of antiques, Oriental carpets and collectibles, a paradoxical blend of the timeworn and the elegant that

15

interior-decorating consultants, no matter how skilled or how astronomical their budget, would find impossible to replicate.

On a drizzly late afternoon in June, settled in this sanctuary of quiet and familiar trappings, Kingston sat in his leather wingback, reading *Country Life,* an empty bone china teacup and saucer at his elbow. While many retirees were at a loss to find things to do on a rainy afternoon, Kingston rarely faced that quandary. To the contrary, he invariably had too many things to occupy his mind and his time. His circle of friends was quite small and he liked it that way. If he really found the need for company, he could always rely on Andrew, his friend and neighbor.

In the midst of an article on antique roses championing the romantic qualities of the Moss rose, *Rosa* William Lobb, his concentration was disrupted by the familiar sound of the letterbox flap snapping closed. He took his cup and saucer into the kitchen, then went along the hall to get the post. As he flipped through the half dozen or so letters and flyers on his way back to the living room, his eyes came to rest on a small, hand-addressed envelope. The ivory-colored paper was of fine quality, the kind used for special invitations. Placing the rest of the

16

post on the coffee table, he opened the envelope and slipped out the one-page folded letter. Like the envelope, it, too, was written in longhand. Immediately he noticed that it wasn't signed. Now he was really curious. He read it.

Dear Dr. Kingston,
We are acquainted, but for reasons I'll explain later, I prefer to remain anonymous for now.
No doubt you'll question why I'm writing in this clandestine fashion. I'll come straight to the point. About three weeks ago, a crime took place on my property, which has left me deeply disturbed. As if the deed itself were not enough, a subsequent disclosure, related to the incident, has given rise to all manner of speculation as to its implications — too complex to explain in a brief letter.
These last weeks have been unnerving and vexing, and I'm deeply troubled that both my standing in the community and my business affairs may suffer adversely as a consequence. The police have been investigating the crime but have yet to come up with suspects or leads. Frankly, I am not satisfied with their progress, so I have decided to take steps to get to the

17

bottom of it myself.

Aware of your reputation as an independent crime solver, I wish to retain your services to conduct a separate inquiry. Furthermore, I am prepared to pay, within reason, whatever it takes to put the matter to rest. Accordingly, I am requesting that we meet at 3 p.m. on Tuesday, June 8th, at the address below, to discuss the matter in further detail.

This is of paramount importance to me, and you are my last resort. I hope you will not let me down.

21 Chesterfield Street, London W1J

Kingston read the letter a second time, then placed it beside him on the sofa. He stared into space, thinking about the imponderability of it all. Who wrote it? What was the crime? What was the mysterious "subsequent disclosure"? If he and the writer were, indeed, acquainted, then why the secrecy? No point wasting time pursuing that line of thought, he decided. In Kingston's case, the word "acquaintance" would cover countless people, many of whom he could no longer remember and a few he'd prefer to forget. The address offered no clues. He wasn't familiar with Chesterfield Street but knew that the W1 postal code placed it somewhere

18

in London's West End. He glanced down at the letter. He knew little about handwriting analysis, but judging by the larger-than-normal letters and assertive strokes, it was an educated guess that it had been written by a man. He pulled on his earlobe, a habit. What else was contained in the letter that could divulge more about the writer? Referring to his "property" suggested that he owned more than just a semi-detached. Perhaps the man was a landowner of sorts. That would explain his "standing in the community" comment. All the above, plus the fact that he was prepared to pay a tidy sum for Kingston's services, indicated that he was a man of means. Last, was the proposed meeting time and date — no alternatives — take it or leave it? Whoever wrote the letter was confident in the knowledge that his was a gold-plated proposal, and he wasn't prepared to take no for an answer from Kingston.

Kingston went to the bookshelf and pulled out a well-thumbed *AA Route Planner*. Chesterfield Street, he quickly discovered, was in Mayfair, a ritzy area of London behind Piccadilly. If this was the man's residence, it supported his earlier contention that the man was well-off. Kingston had visited that neighborhood twice — on both occasions to purchase model lead soldiers from Tradition on Shepherd Street — and remembered it as a mixed-use neighborhood. It could easily be just an office address. He figured that there must be many hundred in that part of Mayfair.

He put the book back in its place, crossed the room to the window, and looked out. Gazing abstractedly at the rain-smudged scene of passing cars and pedestrians hurrying with slanted umbrellas aloft, he thought about the letter. Dwelling further on it and trying to unearth more about the writer was pointless. He could find out simply by showing up on Tuesday. He had nothing whatsoever to lose, and even if it resulted in his deciding to turn down the offer, it should certainly prove to be an interesting encounter, if nothing else. He had to admit, though, that if anything had tipped the scales, it was "I am prepared to pay whatever it takes." It wasn't that he had grave concerns about the torpor of his balance sheet but, as with most fixed-income retirees, his net worth had shrunk considerably over the last annus horribilis. Prior to the meltdown of the financial institutions, the housing crisis, and the resulting collapse of the markets, he'd come to rely on a steady stream of interest income from his savings and investments, to supplement his two pensions. For the time being, those days were gone. So the prospect of a new stream of income, most likely a generous one, was a blessing he wasn't going to dismiss lightly.

He turned away from the window with an inexplicable feeling approaching ebullience, a sense of optimism that surprised him. So much so that he found himself wishing that tomorrow was Tuesday and not three days away.

TWO

Kingston sat in the back of the cab on his way to 21 Chesterfield Street. For the occasion he'd decided to wear his navy double-breasted blazer with a white shirt and University of Edinburgh striped silk tie — dignified but not too formal.

As the cabbie navigated the hurly-burly of traffic at Hyde Park Corner, headed toward Park Lane, Kingston gazed out of the window, admiring the magnificent Wellington Arch in the center of the roundabout. It was originally built to provide a grand entrance to London, and he never tired of seeing it. London had been his adopted home now for more than ten years. As each year passed, he had come more and more under its spell and — even he would admit — more in love with it. When friends asked about his infatuation, he would smile and quote George Bernard Shaw: "A broken heart is a very pleasant complaint for a man in London if he has a comfortable income."

Not that his transition from a married life in the country to one of a silver-haired bachelor in London had been without its ups and downs — far from it. Thinking back, he was surprised that it hadn't taken much longer to get over the grief of losing his beloved wife, Megan, who had been killed in a boating accident on a lake in Switzerland, over twelve years ago. Moving from Scotland after her death, he had quickly come to terms with the vicissitudes and advantages of urban life in one of the world's most populated capitals. It took almost a year of agonizing and self-doubt before he could summon the courage to let go of the house near Edinburgh; it had been the home that they'd shared lovingly for more than thirty-five years, where they'd raised their daughter, Julie, and realized their dreams. Several years ago, at age twenty-four, Julie had taken a job with Microsoft in Seattle. In the passing years she had become an independent and very successful single woman. He made a mental note to drop her an overdue e-mail when he returned.

To Kingston it was as much the country acre of land with mature garden, a small orchard, and a sizable kitchen garden as the house itself that had come to mean so much to him. For almost as long as he could remember, he had cultivated and had come to memorize every square inch of soil there and had nurtured its every plant, shrub, and tree from seeds or cuttings.

On the sultry day in late August, after he'd handed over the keys to the new owners, he'd taken a walk through the garden for the last time. Being alone with his memories, knowing that he would never again see his garden as he had created it, was more than he could endure. Afterward, he'd had to sit in his car for ten minutes, near tears, until he'd regained his composure enough to drive.

The poignant memory melted as quickly as it had come, as he noticed that they'd pulled up to the Mayfair curb. At the same time he heard the cab driver open the sliding window separating the two of them and announcing a cheery, " 'Ere we are, guv." He got out, paid the cabbie plus a generous tip for such a short journey, and glanced at his watch. It was ten minutes to three.

With time to spare, Kingston stood on the pavement for a moment, admiring the pristine cut-stone building, with its black iron railing across the front and on the balconies above, elegant yet unpretentious. As he ascended a short flight of steps leading to the portico entrance, he spotted the name JARDINE'S engraved on a small plaque on the brick wall to the right of the shiny black door. To most, it would offer no clue as to the owner or tenant, but Kingston already had an idea who it might be. He pressed the doorbell below the plaque and waited. Hearing the buzzer, he gripped the polished-brass doorknob, pushed the door open, and entered. Inside, his suspicions were confirmed. There was little doubt in his mind that it was a gentlemen's club. Thinking back to the letter, this made perfect sense. What better place for an influential client to impress his guests?

Kingston had a vague recollection of the club by name and reputation, but that was about all. He would later learn that it was established in 1796. Its primary purpose was to provide a "home from home" for the gentleman of the time, most typically disinclined toward matters domestic. Still considered one of London's most exclusive clubs, it had retained most of its original bylaws and rules of conduct, at the same time moving prudently with the times by providing expanded facilities and services, and relaxing what for two centuries had been stringent membership requirements, even permitting — which is not to say welcoming — women as members, but only whenever and wherever.

As the tall door closed silently behind him, he embraced the hallowed establishment, crossed the Oriental-carpeted floor, and approached the elderly concierge hunched behind a Regency desk.

The man looked up over his glasses, a benevolent smile on his wizened face, as Kingston approached. "Good morning, sir. How may I help you?" he asked, in a voice that went with his years.

"Dr. Kingston. I'm here to meet one of your members — so I've been instructed," he added.

"Ah, yes. He's expecting you, Doctor. You'll find him in the reading room. Down the main corridor, second door on the left, sir."

Kingston entered the thick-carpeted reading room, closed the door quietly behind him, and surveyed the interior, looking for signs of recognition from any of the half dozen or so members slumped in armchairs, lost in reading or, in one case, napping. As yet, none had looked up or seemed even to be aware of his presence. Now and then the rustle of a newspaper or a polite cough interrupted the churchlike hush as Kingston continued to glance around. He was beginning to feel like an interloper, thinking about making a graceful retreat, when someone in the farthest corner by the window lowered his magazine, stood, and waved him over.

Kingston started across the room but still didn't recognize the individual. It wasn't until he was close to the gray-haired, elegantly dressed man that the penny dropped. For a moment his steps faltered. *Good God,* he almost muttered out loud. *Of all people, not you!* He pulled himself together and reached out diffidently to shake Lord Morley's outstretched hand.

Kingston had sworn that he would never again have dealings with the man. Francis Morley — Lord Morley — was the sixth earl of Ramsbury, a member of one of Britain's most distinguished families. The sudden recollection of his experience with the man brought a bitter taste to Kingston's throat. That Lord Morley would have the audacity to ask him for help now, after all that had passed between them, was beyond Kingston's ken. He was tempted to turn on his heels and leave there and then, but good manners and his sense of curiosity prevailed. He pulled up a chair opposite Morley and sat down.

"Can I get you anything?" asked Morley. "Tea? Coffee? Perhaps something stronger?"

"Thanks for asking, but I'm fine, for now."

Morley gave a half smile. "I appreciate your coming."

"It was shrewd of you to write an anonymous letter," Kingston replied, still not having recovered fully from the shock of coming face-to-face with Morley again, after all these years. "You knew damned well that, no matter how intriguing you might make it, I wouldn't have come if I'd known it was you who'd written it."

Morley leaned back, showing not the slightest resentment to Kingston's stinging rebuke. "I thought it would appeal to your sense of the mysterious, that's all."

Only part of what Morley had said registered with Kingston. The rest was washed away in the onrush of memories and bad feelings that he'd managed to dam all these years. It had happened ten years ago. Morley had hired him to oversee the restoration of a garden he'd purchased in the south of France. Kingston had spent six months on the project, and when the time came for Morley to pay his fee, it got very nasty. Despite his considerable wealth, he had tried to cheat Kingston out of a good share of what was due to him. Rather than pursuing legal action, which he knew would involve a lengthy and expensive court case, Kingston had chosen to walk away from it and take the loss, writing it off as a hard lesson learned and never to be repeated. He'd sworn to himself that the misery and humiliation of those few months in France would never happen to him again. Yet here he was, not only face-to-face with his former antagonist but being offered another job. The man had a lot of gall, Kingston thought . . . He suddenly realized that Morley was speaking again.

"I must say you're looking remarkably well, Lawrence."

"If it's all right with you, Francis, perhaps we could skip the pleasantries and you could explain why you invited me here. Given how disgracefully I was treated on the last job, what could possibly make you think that I'd repeat the same mistake?"

"That was then and this is now, Lawrence," Morley said, his expression showing no signs of remorse or guilt. "I know I treated you rather shabbily at the time and

— I know you may find this hard to believe — I've regretted it ever since. You see, things are not always as they seem on the surface. I should never have undertaken such an ambitious and costly project to begin with. My accountant at the time either neglected or chose not to tell me how precarious my financial situation was. In fact, I was close to bankruptcy, and it wasn't a question of not *wanting* to pay you. It was simply that I had no money."

They looked into each other's eyes for a moment, as if both realizing that dredging up the past was in neither of their best interests. At least Morley had made a halfhearted attempt to explain and apologize, and Kingston would accept it for what it was, with no further discussion. He was eager to move on, to have Morley explain the mysterious "crime" and why he'd been so conspiratorial about it. He leaned back, now eyeing Morley with more interest.

"Tell me about this crime, Francis, and why you think I can help you. Where did it take place, by the way?"

"It happened in the garden at Sturminster, the family home. Have you been there?"

"Once — many years ago."

Sturminster, Kingston knew, was one of

29

Britain's preeminent landscape gardens. It had been the seat of the Morley family for more than three hundred years, and its fifteen hundred acres of parkland included a magnificent house, extensive gardens, and recent restoration of an old walled kitchen garden — a showcase of organic and bio-dynamic vegetable gardening — plus a working farm, all open to the public.

Morley leaned back but didn't appear fully at ease. "No point in beating about the bush. The crime I referred to in the letter is a murder." He paused, as if waiting for the word to sink in. "It goes without saying that it has left us all in a state of shock."

"That's understandable."

"I doubt we've had more than a half dozen murders in the entire county in the last hundred years, and now one shows up right on our bloody doorstep."

"Tell me about it."

Morley nodded and took a long breath. "About a month ago, a young girl — only six years old — discovered a dead man's body in the park. He's been identified as William Endicott. A professor at the Institute of Archaeology and Art, in Wolverhampton."

"I'm surprised I haven't seen it in the paper or on TV."

"It was reported in the local papers when it happened but, as I said in my letter, the police have exhausted all their leads. Although their investigation is ongoing, they've no idea who might have wanted Endicott dead and why."

"I'm sure you didn't go to all the trouble of enticing me here to tell me about an unsolved murder. There must be more. In your letter, you said you're dissatisfied with the police investigation? Something that they're not doing or overlooking?"

Morley nodded. "The murder is why I wrote to you, of course, but there's more to it. First and foremost, let me stress that I want to have it resolved and put behind us as quickly as possible."

"And you want me to help solve this crime? To conduct this inquiry of yours?"

Morley nodded again. "I do. Because you're experienced in these matters, you're persistent, and, frankly, I can't think of anyone even remotely more capable of solving it than you."

"Really? What makes you think that I could succeed when the police have made no headway? And surely you must know that most murder cases aren't solved overnight; they often take years."

"I know all that, Lawrence. Let me explain. As far as the police are concerned, we've given them our full cooperation from the start and will continue to do so. Inspector Wheatley, the senior investigating officer, is highly experienced, very bright, and quite thorough. But it's my belief that someone with your track record, conducting a separate inquiry without the constraints and bureaucratic rules and regulations imposed on official police inquiries these days, could bring results and do it more quickly. Before lifting a finger, they have to fill out a damned form. You must know how it is."

"An independent inquiry will still require liaison with the police. Frankly, I don't think you'll gain much by hiring me."

Morley shifted in his seat and looked at Kingston for a long moment. "There are other reasons."

Kingston noted a subtle change in Morley's tone. "I'd be curious to know what they could possibly be," he said.

"The first is your knowledge of and interest in gardens. I'm sure you're aware that Sturminster is among the largest, most historic, and important gardens in the country."

"Of course," said Kingston with a concealed smile. "But surely you're not suggesting that we're looking for a killer from the plant world?"

"This is a serious matter," Morley snapped.

"What other reasons, then?"

"It may sound odd, but it has to do with your experience with codes."

"Codes?" Kingston was speechless.

"Yes." Morley's look was supercilious. "Correct me if I'm wrong, Lawrence, but weren't you involved with codes of some kind in the past? I seem to recall your having mentioned it at one time, when we were in France. Something to do with your army career, I believe. And there was that case where you found your missing professor friend. Didn't that involve solving some kind of cryptic message?"

"Yes, but I don't see how —"

"Our monuments — the mysterious monuments in Sturminster's garden."

Kingston vaguely remembered having read about the eight ancient monuments dotted throughout the estate garden and parkland.

Morley interrupted his thoughts, sparing him the embarrassment of an uninformed reply. "One of them — the Arcadian monument — bears a mysterious inscription of ten letters, thought to be a code of some sort. They were chiseled on the monument in the middle of the eighteenth century, and their meaning is unknown today. It's baffled some of the greatest minds of our time."

"You're implying that the murder could be connected in some way to that monument, the inscription?"

Morley took a moment before replying. "I haven't ruled it out. And neither have the police. But that's not all."

Kingston squinted, perplexed. "What else?"

"There's a second code as well — at least it's presumed to be a code — found on the dead man's body."

"*Another* code?" Kingston was becoming mildly irritated with the way Morley was doling out teasing morsels of information, as if he were reeling in a stubborn fish. Perhaps he should tell Morley that it wasn't having the effect he might be hoping for. It started to remind him of the old days, too, which was disconcerting.

"That's correct. When the forensics chaps examined the body, they found a torn scrap of paper in the man's pocket. Written on it, in longhand, was a series of letters, over a dozen. Since it's the only piece of real evidence so far, the police have focused on it believing that it could be part of a coded message. They actually brought in a specialist from GCHQ, the government communications agency, to look it over. They're the chaps —"

"Yes, I know about them. SIGINT, signals intelligence."

"Of course you'd know that code breaking is one of the many specialties in their bag of tricks?"

"Indeed," said Kingston. Along with MI5 and MI6, GCHQ was a key player in Britain's intelligence gathering and national security going back before World War II. In his long-ago army days he'd attended courses on intelligence and information systems and had visited GCHQ.

Morley continued. "Wheatley e-mailed me the GCHQ findings, but I must confess that I found their explanation almost unintelligible — if you'll pardon the pun — a lot of mumbo jumbo about ciphertexts, keywords, algorithms, and so forth. Anyway, the upshot was that only if the matching piece of paper were found could they possibly read anything into the sequence of letters."

"Did they conclude that it was part of a coded message?"

"They didn't count it out."

"What about the police?"

"Wheatley told me that they were going to withhold the information — for now, anyway — and asked us to do likewise."

"I'm not surprised. The press would be all over a story like that."

"Indeed they would," said Morley, nodding. "They've been all over us as it is."

"You've had adverse publicity?"

"I'm afraid so."

"I assume it's already having a negative effect on attendance?"

"At first, attendance went up. But it's been dropping ever since."

"Understandable. In the beginning, these things bring out all the thrill seekers and the morbidly curious, just the kind you don't want."

"Exactly. The fact that a small child discovered the body doesn't help either. We get hundreds of thousands of visitors every year, and many are families with young children."

"So there's been a substantial drop in revenue?"

Morley nodded. "Our family admission is thirty pounds, so if we lose fifty a day — well, you can do the math. And that's on top of the free fall in income we've had with this bloody awful economy."

A moment of silence fell, punctuated only

by the dulcet chime of a long-case clock, on the far side of the room, striking the half hour.

Morley spread his hands and exhaled. "Well, Lawrence, that's about the size of it. I don't expect your answer right away, of course. I'm sure you'll have a lot more questions." His eyes searched Kingston's face, as if hoping to find the glimmer of a positive reaction.

"I understand your reasons and determination to have this unfortunate matter resolved. I'll even go as far as saying I sympathize with you, but this time I think I'll pass."

Morley looked offended. "Surely you're not going to turn down five thousand pounds a month, guaranteed for six months, plus all expenses. Are you?"

Kingston was dumbstruck. He hadn't for one moment been thinking of such a large amount of money. Also, if his assignment could be limited, perhaps to six months, with an option to continue or quit, it changed the whole picture. He knew his answer was already too long in coming but guessed that Morley would take it as a good sign and would be patient.

"Let me think about it, Francis," he said at last. "Twenty-four hours. Okay?"

"All right, Lawrence. In the meantime, I'll have Simon — Simon Crawford, our general manager — put together a package, with a time line, names, copies of police reports, et cetera, detailing everything concerning the case thus far. I know the board will be pleased to learn that we've had this conversation."

"You're assuming I'm going to say yes, then?"

"No. I just thought it would give you a better understanding of what has happened and what the police have done so far, that's all; help you make the right decision."

"Very well."

With the tacit understanding that the meeting was over, the two stood. Morley picked up his magazine and newspaper and looked at Kingston as if he'd like to continue the dialogue but knew it would serve no purpose.

Kingston met his gaze, knowing that this was the appropriate and perhaps last chance to voice what he'd been mulling over for several minutes. How Morley received the sine qua non could well influence Kingston's decision.

"Before we part company," he said, "I'd like to say one thing further. It's based on our past experience working together.

Before I can even consider your offer, I would insist on a sizable advance on your proposed fee and would also require an escape clause written into the agreement, should things not work out as we expect. Without those conditions, Francis, there will be no point in any further discussion."

After a few seconds, Morley nodded. "I'm willing to accept your terms." He reached in his coat pocket and pulled out an expensive-looking wallet. He extracted a card and handed it to Kingston, looking deep into his eyes. "I don't want to sound melodramatic, but you're my last resort. I hope you won't let me and Sturminster down."

"Thanks," Kingston replied, dutifully glancing at the card, slipping it into his own wallet. "I'll keep that in mind."

Ten minutes later, Kingston was on a number 11 bus headed for Chelsea and his flat. Squinting out the window through the light rain at the gray buildings of Great Scotland Yard, former headquarters of the Metropolitan Police, he thought back on their conversation. What struck him most was that Morley had seemed like a different person from the one that he'd previously crossed swords with and had come to regard with disdain. How much of it had been an act? he wondered. While it was expected that Morley would apply a certain amount of pressure to persuade Kingston to take the job, it bothered Kingston that he'd been almost too assertive. Morley couldn't have made a better pitch if his life had depended on it. Bringing up the money at the end was a trump card, and Morley had played it well.

He glanced out the window again, watching the snarl of Knightsbridge traffic and the shoppers scurrying along the pavement in the rain, under the shelter of Harrods' green awnings. He had no illusions about the disruptive changes in his life that would result should he accept the job. He'd lived through it all before. That included the usual rollicking he'd certainly get from Andrew, his bachelor neighbor and close friend, who lived three doors from Kingston on Cadogan Square. Andrew was independently wealthy, having sold his software company just before the dot-com bubble burst. He was not at all happy with Kingston's investigative dabbling and was always harping that it was too dangerous for Kingston's advancing years. Andrew also owned a small Georgian house on the banks of the Thames in Bourne End, where the two often spent weekends, entertaining. His "country estate," he called it.

The circumstances of this case were different, though. Aside from the money, it was not only a serious commitment but there was also a moral aspect to it that ran contrary to Kingston's character and code of ethics. He'd been taught a painful lesson once; why would he consider accepting a job from someone whom he knew to be arrogant and deceitful?

The Sloane Square bus stop was fast approaching. He made his way to the back of the bus. He'd promised Morley an answer by tomorrow afternoon. Plenty of time to think on it, he said to himself, stepping off the bus.

THREE

Three days later, Staffordshire
"Shortly after that, the police arrived. I believe you know the rest of the story, Doctor."

Simon Crawford folded his arms and leaned back. He and Kingston were seated on carved mahogany chairs in the manager's office that more resembled a gracious living room than workspace. When Kingston had sealed the deal with Morley — with a fat advance and the provision that he could drop out at any time after two months with

41

no forfeiture — it was agreed that the first step would be to set up a meeting between Kingston and Crawford. Morley had explained that Simon Crawford had acted as Sturminster's liaison with the police from the start and, outside of them, knew more about the case than anyone.

Crawford had spent the last ten minutes briefing Kingston on the events that had taken place on the day that William Endicott's body was found. On arrival he'd given Kingston a canvas satchel filled with documents, police reports, clippings, and copies of pages taken from a number of Sturminster's library books, items that he and Morley had deemed relevant to the case.

When they'd met, Kingston had pegged Crawford as midsixties and indubitably ex-military. His attire was impeccable: suit and shirt, pressed and starched, perfectly knotted striped tie. He had the right bearing to carry it off, and the clipped manner of speech. His features certainly fitted the bill too: short hair peppered with gray, ruddy-cheeked complexion, and a toothbrush mustache. His account of the day of the murder had been clear and concise. He was in the main house meeting with suppliers, he'd said, when he'd received a mobile call from Albert, one of the gardeners, saying that an agitated man, who'd been picnicking in the garden with his family, was reporting that his young child had just discovered what appeared to be a dead body in a clearing near one of the monuments. Telling the gardener to stay put with the father, and that he was on his way immediately, he hurried out of the house and within two or three minutes had joined them. The visitor led them to the spot near the Arcadian monument where, sure enough, the body lay. Crawford said that he'd then made a cursory visual examination of the body — knowing better than to touch anything — concluding that the man was dead. He called 999 and reported the incident, telling the gardener to round up a couple more staff members on the double and return to the scene. While the gardener was gone, he waited near the stranger's body, taking stock of the immediate area, observing nothing out of the ordinary. When the men returned, within a matter of minutes, he instructed them to keep the area secure until the police arrived. He then turned his attention to the family who were nearby, packing their picnic gear, preparing to leave. At his insistence, knowing that the police would want to talk to them, he took the four of them to the house where, under the care of two staff members, one a former nurse, they were made comfortable in one of the drawing rooms until they could give their statements. That done, he returned to the scene to rejoin the men guarding the area, where they all waited until the police arrived. In answer to Kingston's only question, Crawford was emphatic in asserting that no one else had been near or touched the body between the time he first saw it and when the police arrived at the scene.

While Crawford answered a phone call, Kingston gazed around the elegant room thinking of the incongruity of it all. Here, amid the beauty of the fastidiously redecorated room with its fine woodcarving, coved ceiling, marble fireplace, and satinwood cabinetry, they were discussing a man's murder. Even in its day it must have cost a fortune, he contemplated. He still hoped he'd made the right decision in accepting Morley's offer. In the end the temptation of taking on such an unusual and intriguing challenge and the financial reward had outweighed his misgivings about Morley's character. If things were to go sour this time, he could always bail out early.

"Sorry about that," said Crawford. "Another damned reporter. Where were we?"

Kingston flashed an ambiguous smile.

44

"Would you mind if I asked a couple of questions? Sooner or later I'm sure I'll be able to talk with the police, but getting your perspective and learning more about your involvement would be a helpful start."

"Not a problem. I'm happy to pass on everything I know."

"Thanks. It's appreciated." Kingston pulled his chair a few inches closer to the desk and leaned back. "This Endicott chap, what's known about him?"

"All the usual stuff, according to Inspector Wheatley. But apparently nothing that throws any light on why he was murdered or by whom." He paused. "You've been informed that Wheatley is the policeman heading up the case, I take it?"

"I have. Lord Morley told me. How did the inspector describe Endicott?"

Crawford didn't answer right away. Instead, he looked up at the ceiling for a moment, pursing his lips, before looking back at Kingston. "Name is William Clarke Endicott, fifty-nine years of age, bachelor," he said, as though he'd memorized it. "Until six months ago he was employed by the Institute of Archaeology and Art in Wolverhampton. He taught courses in Greek and other Middle Eastern antiquities — archaeological subjects, that sort of thing."

45

He paused, running his fingers across the edge of the leather-topped desk. "What else?" he muttered to himself. "For what it's worth, he has an elderly mother who lives in an assisted-living home in Rugeley — a small town about fifteen miles south of Sturminster. Umm . . . no other living relatives and what few friends he had were mostly colleagues from the institute. From all accounts he had no hobbies to speak of, except travel, which he did quite a lot, mostly to places of archaeological interest. No surprise there."

"Hmm. Any criminal record?"

Crawford shook his head. "No."

"Where did he live?"

"In Little Cherwyn. It's a small village near Cannock. Owned a bungalow with no mortgage."

"Which would suggest that he wasn't hard up."

"Possibly. Though according to Wheatley, it looked like he never spent a penny on the place — the inside was a mess."

"How far is the village from Sturminster?"

"No more than ten miles, maybe less."

"Not far from home."

"Right."

"What about his car?"

"It was parked in his garage, apparently."

"So someone drove him to Sturminster?"

"Or he cycled or walked."

"Doubtful he'd walk ten miles."

"I agree."

"No bicycle's been found, I take it?"

Crawford shook his head. "If it had been left somewhere on the grounds, it could easily have been stolen."

"How about cause of death?"

"Skull fracture. Fatal blow to the head." Crawford smiled. "You're really testing my memory, Doctor. I can see now why Morley thinks so highly of you."

"One blow or more than one?"

"I don't know. You'll have to ask the police."

Kingston nodded. "Of course. I'm sorry. Not too many more questions. If that's all right with you?"

"No need to apologize. Fire away."

"Have the police established an estimated time of death?"

"Yes. It was approximately twelve hours prior to the time that the body was discovered."

Kingston glanced at the clock across the room, figuring the lapse in time. "So that places it sometime before midnight?"

"Correct."

"So he was either killed in the park then

or could have been killed elsewhere and dumped on the grounds later."

Crawford nodded. "Either one. Although it wouldn't be easy smuggling a body onto the grounds at night."

"Security?"

"Right. Ours might not be up to Buckingham Palace standards but it's up-to-date technology and up until now has proved remarkably efficient. There's pretty much round-the-clock patrolling, too, of course."

"What about the weapon?"

"They haven't found one as yet."

"I suppose you wouldn't know if the pathologist detected anything about the wounds that would help identify the murder weapon."

Crawford shook his head. "Sorry, I wouldn't. It's all in the police report."

Kingston scratched his temple. "What about your security people? Nothing from them?"

"No. They reported nothing unusual during the days and nights in question. That doesn't mean to say the murder couldn't have taken place during visiting hours or, like you said, his body been dumped here during the daytime. Obviously I can't elaborate on our security systems, but suffice it to say that we have fifteen hundred acres and it's impossible to monitor every inch of it, twenty-four/seven."

A gap in the conversation followed while Crawford took another phone call. Kingston took the opportunity to gather his thoughts and ponder whether he'd overlooked anything he'd wanted to ask. He was finding Simon Crawford hard to read. On one hand, he was being cooperative and reasonably friendly; on the other, Kingston was starting to have a hard time with the terseness of his answers. Was he always like this, Kingston wondered, or just eager to move things along and get the meeting over with? As he was contemplating this, he looked across the desk to see that Crawford was off the phone.

"Sorry again. I've told them to hold all calls." Crawford turned to face Kingston again.

"Just a couple more questions," said Kingston, deferentially.

"Go ahead."

"Have the police found anything at all to connect Endicott to Sturminster?"

"As far as I know, not a damned thing. I know for sure that they've interviewed not only the staff but everyone we know of who's had anything to do with the estate in the past couple of years or so — and that includes me, Lord Morley, and members of the board of directors. They've also interviewed contract workers and most of the estate's regular suppliers and tradesmen. In that regard, I must say that Wheatley's people have been extremely thorough."

"Morley mentioned there was a scrap of paper found on the body, with letters on it. A kind of code, perhaps?"

"Right. What about it?"

"Have you seen it?"

Crawford hesitated, then nodded. "I've seen a copy. It's just a series of capital letters, a dozen or more perhaps, on copier-type paper." He smiled. "No watermarked personal stationery, if that's what you're wondering."

"In ink?"

"It was a photocopy."

"Of course, I was forgetting. What did you make of it?"

"Nothing at all, frankly."

"Any chance of getting a copy of it?"

"Of course. I can't see why the police would object. They have the original. It's now an exhibit."

"Thanks. That could help."

Crawford scratched a reminder note on the pad at his elbow and kept what looked to be a real gold pen between his fingers.

Kingston continued. "According to Lord Morley, GCHQ took a look at it and submitted a report. Could I get a copy of that too?"

"You can. I have a copy on file. Morley tells me you know something about codes?"

Kingston nodded. "Back in my army days, I attended an intelligence course at Joint Services Intelligence, in Ashford. I've also visited GCHQ."

Crawford made a feeble attempt to suppress a smile. "Now why wouldn't I have known that?" he said.

Kingston shrugged off the jibe. "With only a dozen or so letters it would be impossible to know if it's truly part of a code. It could be a lot of things — password, PIN, combination to something, perhaps."

"I'll get you a copy of Harry Tennant's report. He's the chap who looked at it."

"Thanks."

"As a thought, you might want to have Morley or Wheatley put you in touch with Tennant. At least you'll be able to understand what he's talking about. That's more than I could."

"Thanks, I'll do that. If it turns out to be part of a coded message, it would be reasonable to assume that the code would be a simple one, unless the other piece of paper has substantially more letters."

Crawford nodded. "So I've been told. But unless we find the other half, all this code malarkey means absolutely nothing."

"You're right, of course," Kingston replied with a slow nod. "That said, if it does turn out to be a coded message, it begs the important question that no doubt you've all thought about, Simon: What is it that could be so important, so confidential, as to require such secrecy? And did Endicott know what it was, or was he attempting to find out?"

"We've considered all of that."

Crawford's uncrossing his legs and body language hinted that their conversation could be ending.

"I have one last question," said Kingston. "It's rhetorical, but permit me to ask anyway. I take it nothing was found at the crime scene that the police might have considered significant? Anything out of place, anything to indicate that the assault might have taken place elsewhere? Was there —"

"According to Inspector Wheatley," Crawford interrupted, a frisson of impatience in his tone, "when he gave us his last briefing, all regulation procedures were conducted to the nth degree, right down to fingertip searches by forensics. And he was emphatic that nothing was found at the scene that would be considered out of the ordinary." He paused, leveling his eyes at Kingston. "Unfortunately, there were no cigarette butts or train tickets next to the body," he said with a vestige of a smile.

"That's too bad," Kingston said.

The talk moved on to more mundane matters: the weather, of course, and British sports cars. Crawford had earlier admired Kingston's restored Triumph TR4 and, as it turned out, owned a Jaguar XK120. Before long Crawford suggested that they get some fresh air and visit the purported crime scene, where the body was found. While they were gone he would arrange to have the copies made.

As they were leaving the house, an Audi convertible drove up and pulled into the parking place next to Kingston's TR4. A young man with lank blond hair, wearing a sweater and jeans, stepped out and walked toward them. Ignoring Kingston, the man pulled Crawford aside, saying he wanted to have a word. Kingston thought nothing of it, instead turned away to admire the splendid view from the top of the entrance steps. Immediately below, a long, narrow bed of pink floribunda roses gave way to a sweeping terraced lawn, divided in the center by a wide gravel path. Each lawn was edged on the path by symmetrical rows of eight-foot-high pyramids of golden yew, twelve in all, clipped to perfection. Beyond, centered in the path, was a fountain depicting a boy with a swan. Past that, lay the river and open grazing land.

Kingston heard Crawford speak and turned in time to see the young man enter the house. "Sorry about that," said Crawford. "That was Julian, one of Lord Morley's nephews." Kingston noted that Crawford's expression was distant, as if he was reflecting on his hurried exchange of words with Julian. Then Crawford clapped his hands and said, "Well, let's go, shall we?"

Short of Crawford's pointing out the exact spot and describing the man's injury and body position, the tranquil scene, as Kingston had suspected, proved to be of little interest. Glancing at his watch, he was starting to think about the drive home and wondering if he should suggest taking a break for lunch before leaving, when Crawford spoke up once more. "We should look at a couple of the monuments before you go. You know about them, I take it?"

Kingston nodded. His recollection of the monuments — sometimes called follies — in the garden at Sturminster had been vague until Morley's question the other day had jogged his memory. Eight of them, Francis had said. Such monuments were a typical design embellishment in large estate gardens of the period, he knew. They were often whimsical, even eccentric, using ancient Greek and Roman architecture for inspiration. When he was teaching at Edinburgh University, he'd included a short discourse on the idiosyncratic garden features in his lectures. He showed examples of English garden follies in a slide show, then explained that while they'd been around for more than four hundred years, the fad had a renaissance in the mid-eighteenth century, when they started popping up in almost every other garden of England's grand country houses. His students invariably became more interested when he further explained how the trend was escalated by young men of means who took a year or two — often more — out of their postgraduation lives to travel around Europe on the "grand tour" in an effort to broaden their horizons and learn about language, architecture, geography, and sociology. Most returned to England where, in later years — many of them having inherited the family estate — they built their own re-creations of Gothic ruins and renditions of ancient temples that are now scattered with seeming abandon about the landscapes of many English country estates.

"Our monuments?"

Kingston was jolted back to the present. "Somewhat," he replied, turning toward Crawford. "I seem to recall a story about them in one of the garden magazines, *Gardens Illustrated,* I believe, but that was a long time ago."

"Let me show you a couple, then." Crawford gestured over his shoulder and headed down a small gravel path that led between two of the most enormous rhododendron bushes that Kingston had ever laid eyes on. On the other side of the rhodies, they came to a small glade with a curved backdrop of dark conifers. Centered in front of the spruce, cypress, and yew was a curious-looking structure as high as a small house and almost as wide.

"This is the Arcadian monument," said Crawford, as the two walked up close to it. "One of eight situated throughout the garden and the park." Crawford stood silently to one side, watching as Kingston gazed up at the monument.

Supported on either side by two carved Doric columns, the lichen-stained stone entablature across the top was decorated with rustic carvings. Together they formed a strange-looking rough-hewn arch that was the setting for the centerpiece white-marble slab on which the likeness of a painting — which Kingston would later learn was by Poussin — was carved in relief. His eyes then rested on the inscription carved below the pastoral scene, the sequence of ten Roman letters: D. O.U.O.S.V.A.V.V. M. He noted that the beginning D and the ending M were wider spaced, separated from the other letters.

Lost in thought, pondering the letters and the incongruity of the elegant marble against the crude stone arch, he suddenly realized that Crawford was speaking.

". . . the last of the monuments to be built, about 1750, so it's believed — they were all designed by one man, Matthew Seward. It's been suggested that the separated D and M could be initials or stand for the Latin *dis manibus* — sacred to the dead. This was found commonly on Roman tombs, dedicating the soul of the departed to the spirit world. Only problem is that here the two letters don't stand together."

"Yes, I see that," said Kingston, finally taking his eyes off the chiseled lettering. "And no one knows what the letters signify?"

"No. For three hundred years, cryptographers, historians, mathematicians, scholars, you name it have all tried to solve the riddle, with no success. It's even rumored that Darwin and Dickens tried but gave up. We even invited a few of the Bletchley Park experts who'd cracked the Nazis' Enigma code during the war — not many of them left, you know — to see if they could decipher it. It was part of a public-relations stunt that backfired, a few years ago. Turned out to be a royal disaster."

"Why was that?"

"Well, for one thing, Poussin was rumored to be a Grand Master of the Knights Templar."

"I see what you mean."

"The press had a heyday with it. If the place had burned to the ground, we wouldn't have had more coverage. Before we knew it, every Grail hunter and curiosity seeker in Christendom descended on us — people camping, caravans, camera crews. Everywhere you turned it was utter chaos."

"People interested in code solving?"

"More like people interested in the treasure."

"Treasure?"

"You don't know the story of the missing money, the Morley feud?"

Kingston shook his head. "Why would I?"

"You're right. It's an old Staffordshire legend about Sturminster and the two brothers who founded the estate back in the seventeen hundreds. It's rumored that while Admiral James Morley was making history and amassing a huge fortune with his sea victories of the Seven Years' War, his brother, Samuel, was secretly salting away, for his own purposes, a large share of the moneys contributed by James — funds intended exclusively for the expansion of Sturminster. Much of the money was unaccounted for, and to this day there are those who believe it was hidden somewhere on the estate by Samuel Morley."

"I can see why the monument would be so intriguing — solve the code, find the treasure."

"Intriguing? That's putting it mildly. Some of those people are fanatical. They caused considerable damage to the gardens and to the Arcadian monument, sad to say."

"I can appreciate why you wouldn't want a repeat of that."

Crawford nodded. "Right. That's why the police have been downplaying the code thing."

"Makes sense." Kingston paused, thinking. "These letters," he said, pointing at the inscription. "Is there any similarity to those found on Endicott's person?"

"The piece of paper? None whatsoever."

Kingston simply shrugged. He wondered why Morley hadn't mentioned the legend.

"Follow me," said Crawford. A few paces behind Crawford, Kingston was gazing around to see if there was any way a car might have been driven close to the monument. The answer came almost immediately when they crossed a narrow dirt track, wide enough for a vehicle, that ran past the back of the clearing. Kingston estimated that anyone passing by on that road would be barely fifty feet away from the spot where the body was found. As he was visualizing the possibilities, he heard Crawford talking again and hurried to catch up. "I'll show you a couple of other places of interest on the way back to the office. But first, you must see our famous yew tree." Soon they encountered another grassy clearing where Crawford pointed out another monument, this one much smaller, mounted with a large stone globe. Perched on top of the globe, a sphinxlike marble cat stared down. "This is Amunet's monument," he said. "It's named after the admiral's favorite Siamese, said to have accompanied him on voyages."

"The admiral being James Morley," Kingston said.

"That's correct. I'm not certain if it's ever been established whether he knew that his brother was stealing from him or, if he did, at what point he found out. We do know that eventually they never talked to each other again and James Morley stopped visiting Sturminster — hence the feud rumor."

Continuing, they passed another monument, this time considerably larger and farther away. It resembled a smaller version of a classical Greek temple. "That's the Athenian temple," said Crawford. "The design is based on the Temple of Hephestus in Athens. It's amazingly accurate in detail."

Five minutes later they were standing under one of the largest trees Kingston had ever seen. Crawford, who had now assumed the practiced mantle of tour guide, pointed out that it was reputedly the largest in England, with a spread of 525 feet in circumference. At charity garden parties during the war, an admission charge was made to view the tree, he added.

Their next stop was the walled vegetable garden. As they walked the gravel pathways that divided the spacious raised beds, filled to capacity with every kind of vegetable imaginable, Crawford launched into a rambling commentary, describing how it had been restored to its 1805 glory days when it had enjoyed a reputation as one of the most ambitious horticultural centers of its kind, employing what at the time were considered revolutionary gardening techniques. The garden, he droned on, was now a showcase for organic and biodynamic agriculture, a farming approach that looks upon the maintenance and furtherance of soil life and other ecological factors to provide high-quality crops, more nutritional food for human beings, and better feed for livestock. Pausing now and then along the way, he pointed out displays that showed how soil improvement could be achieved by implementing various methods: applying sufficient organic manure and compost, using earthworms to enrich and revitalize the soil, proper crop rotation, working the soil, protective measures, using cover crops, and with diversified crops rather than monoculture. To Kingston, it sounded as if Crawford had memorized it by rote, oblivious to the fact that he was preaching to the choirmaster.

Back at the house, Crawford picked up the copies of the reports from the police and GCHQ that had been made and gave them to Kingston. On their way out, they took a detour to the rococo decorated library, where Crawford described its beginnings when it housed the admiral's personal collection of books, antiquities, and ephemera collected on his voyages abroad. He further explained the methodology of how the volumes were stored, pointing out certain shelves by subject category.

"Oh, and here's something Francis thought you might find interesting." Crawford took a large volume from a nearby shelf and handed it to Kingston. "It's considered the definitive history of the Morley family. Written by William Oxbridge-Bell, the noted historian. Though I should warn you, it's quite a slog."

"Thanks," said Kingston, taking it.

Crawford glanced at his watch. "I have a meeting with an American television production company at two. Much as I hate to, Lawrence, I must wind up our meeting for now. It was a pleasure to get to know you and I hope that I've been able to give you a clearer picture of the case as far as Sturminster is concerned. Don't hesitate to call me if you have questions. Please feel free to come back at any time," he said with a fleeting smile.

Kingston was relieved that a lunch wasn't planned. Another hour or more with Crawford, even if it was only small talk, was not what he would have preferred. "Thanks again," he said. "You've given me a lot to think about, and I can now see why Endicott's death is so perplexing."

After exchanging cards, they left the library and a minute later stood at the colonnaded entrance to the grand mansion. After good-byes and a quick handshake, Kingston walked to his TR4 and lowered the satchel of documents behind the driver's seat. He slipped behind the wheel and, with a quick wave of farewell to Crawford, who was watching from the flagstone steps, took off down the tree-lined driveway.

FOUR

Ten minutes after leaving Sturminster, Kingston sat at the bar of the Red Lion in the village of Longdon Green, studying the chalkboard menu, a half pint of best bitter in front of him and the Morley family book on the stool next to him. He'd spotted the thatched pub on his way up, keeping it in mind should he feel the need for something to eat before driving home.

Few customers remained in the saloon lounge. The lone waitress had left for the day, leaving a stout, balding man behind the bar — whom Kingston had pegged as the landlord — to serve the stragglers and resume what all bartenders turn to in moments of inactivity and with no one to chat up: polish the glasses. Sid's jovial face — his name had been uttered several times since Kingston's arrival — was as round as a soccer ball, set with a large, disjointed, and veined nose and a smile on his florid face that seemed permanent. A half dozen framed black-and-white photos on the wall behind the bar depicting rugby players readily explained the nose.

"So what's it to be?" he asked, catching Kingston's eye.

"The ploughman's, please," Kingston responded.

"Right you are," he replied, scribbling the order on a pad. In a few seconds he was back behind the bar refilling a customer's beer glass. That done, he turned his attention to Kingston. "Looks like more rain's on the way," he said.

Kingston nodded. "It was starting to spit when I drove in. As long as that's all it is, I don't mind."

"Got a long drive?"

"London."

"Long enough."

A thought hit Kingston. It was more than likely that Sid would know something about Sturminster. The estate was only minutes

65

away, and it was a sure bet that some of the staff frequented the pub — perhaps Crawford or, even better, Morley himself.

"I was just up at Sturminster," he said. "Beautiful place."

"That it is. Are you a gardening sort?"

"You might say that. But it was business related this time."

Sid nodded. "Once in a while we do luncheons, birthday parties, and the like for the staff. We've catered events up there too."

"You probably know Simon Crawford, then?"

"I do. Met him several times. Decent sort."

"Yes, he seems to be. I met him for the first time today."

Kingston took a sip of beer, wondering if he should tell Sid a white lie about his reason for being at Sturminster or just tell the truth. He needn't have worried.

"You know about the murder, then?"

"I do," Kingston replied with a quick nod.

"Rum business, that one. Something not right about it, if you ask me."

"Why do you say that?"

"When it happened, it was all over the news. Then bang — suddenly not a word."

"It's probably because the police have no leads, no suspects. There's been nothing to report." He paused to sip his beer. "Any people from Sturminster who are regulars?"

"A few, yes."

"They must have some opinions about the case. Do they discuss it all?"

"They did at first. That was all everyone talked about for days. You wouldn't believe some of the theories and rumors that were flying around. Not so much anymore, though; people seem to have forgotten about it. It's back to business as usual. Understandable, when you think about it."

Kingston sighed. "Symptomatic of the times, I'm afraid. Nothing shocks or offends that much anymore. If it does, the anger won't last for long, simply because, around the corner, there'll be another calamity or horror story to capture our attention."

"You've got it right there," said Sid, who turned away to answer the ringing phone.

Kingston welcomed the break, mostly because it gave him time to weigh his next question. He saw no reason why bringing up Morley's name now should appear out of place. He couldn't afford to appear too inquisitive, though, or Sid would rightfully question his motives.

The lunch would take awhile, so he propped up the book on the bar and started to read. It soon became clear that the early history of the Morleys was a sweeping saga, even compared with other illustrious and better-known English families of the time, such as the dukes of Wellington and Marlborough. Whereas the latter made history on the battlefield, James Morley — who started his naval career in 1712 as a fourteen-year-old volunteer aboard the frigate HMS *Carnelian* — carved his reputation and amassed his considerable fortunes through his exploits and victories on the high seas. His naval prowess, the efficiency of his eventual administration of the admiralty, and his many strategic reforms left an enduring mark on the British navy, his repute overshadowed only by that of Admiral Horatio Nelson.

Though James Morley had never owned the estate at Sturminster, it was solely through his endeavors and financial support that its creation was made possible. While he was engaged in naval warfare and exploration across the globe, furthering the expansion of the British Empire and later embarking on an epic four-year journey circumnavigating the world, his older brother Samuel was busy at home, developing the old family seat at Sturminster. Samuel had inherited the estate from their father in 1720. From that moment on he had dedicated his entire bachelor life to its expansion. Systematically, over thirty years, Samuel Morley had purchased freeholds, leaseholds, and copyholds of the other tenants of the manor, which included two substantial villages, a corn mill, a paper mill, and various tracts of undeveloped land. As he'd bought up the properties, he'd demolished the cottages and other structures on them. Thus, what had once been a densely built-up area was transformed piecemeal into fifteen hundred acres of open parkland, which Morley gradually converted into a model landscape by large-scale planting of trees and shrubs and erecting the eight Grecian-inspired monuments that came to distinguish Sturminster. During this time he also had a new, larger, and grander house built.

None of this would have been possible if not for the constant stream of money provided by brother James from his ever-growing war chest. Ironically, during those many years the seafaring James Morley rarely visited Sturminster. The reason for that had not been mentioned in the book, so far. Kingston wondered why.

As he was thinking on it, Sid reappeared.

"Your lunch will be here in a couple of minutes. Sorry for the delay. Bit short-handed back there today." He gestured to the book. "Reading up on the Morleys?"

"Yes. Between you, me, and the gatepost, I'm about to start working with Lord Morley on a project. I should really say 'for him,' because I doubt he'll be directly involved."

"You're probably better off."

"Why's that?"

Sid stopped polishing and shook his head. "Blokes who work at the estate have come in and dropped a few comments. Nothing firsthand, though." He paused, as if debating whether he should leave it at that or continue. "Word has it that he throws his weight around a bit — you know, 'the big I am.' He also has somewhat of a reputation for being tightfisted. Other than that, he appears to be typical of that sort, if you know what I mean."

Kingston nodded slowly.

In the silence that followed, he decided to take the plunge and hope that Sid didn't find his next question out of place or too nosy. "I take it you wouldn't know much about the Morley family, then?"

Sid gave him a strange look, his smile erased. "The family?" he said, haltingly. His smile returned right away. "Oh, I think I see what you're getting at. The never-ending Sturminster feud and the money that was supposed to have been nicked?"

Kingston was taken aback but quickly gathered his senses and nodded. "I'd heard the rumor. The reason I asked, though, was more curiosity than anything else."

"I wouldn't be the one to ask about that. Tristan Veitch is your man. You need to talk to him."

"A local?"

Sid nodded. "Last I heard he was living over near Abbot's Broomfield by the reservoir. I'm told he's a bit of a recluse, a cantankerous old bugger."

"What's his line of work?"

"He's sort of a self-appointed historian for this part of the county. Most of it related to Sturminster and the Morleys, of course. The history of the family is quite a saga, by the way."

"So I'm gathering," Kingston said, nodding at the book. "I'd like to meet this Veitch fellow. Any idea how I can contact him?"

"He's probably ex-directory, but you might want to give the *Post* a call. That's our local paper. They publish historical articles of his from time to time."

At that moment, a lady wearing an apron appeared with Kingston's ploughman's lunch spread out on a wooden board. She placed it on the bar and vanished as quickly as she had arrived.

"Well, I'll quit wittering on and leave you to enjoy your lunch," said Sid. "Another Worthington's?"

Kingston nodded. "Please," he said, feeling chuffed with his good fortune and his decision to stop at the Red Lion in the first place. Slicing into the generous wedge of Stilton, he was already thinking about meeting Tristan Veitch.

Driving back to London, he gave thought to what he had learned from his meeting with Crawford. The skimpy background on William Endicott was a modest start but hardly thought provoking. The only thing that had struck him as remotely significant was Endicott's job at the institute. According to Crawford, the professor's specialty was Greek and Middle Eastern archaeology, and the Sturminster monuments were all Grecian-inspired. Coincidence? Maybe, but it could also suggest that architecture could be the common denominator that somehow linked Endicott to Sturminster and perhaps the murder. The connection was flimsy, but the institute would be on his list of places to check out.

As for the GCHQ report, after he'd had

the chance to read it and had studied the copy of the scrap of paper found in Endicott's pocket, he would probably take Crawford's advice and compare notes with Tennant. It would seem unlikely, however, as Crawford had contended, that either would amount to much, until the missing piece of paper showed up — if it ever did.

Of everything that he'd learned or seen during his brief time at Sturminster, the Arcadian monument had interested him most. With its primitive, rough-hewn stone surround, it oozed a feeling that was otherworldly and unsettling. In stark contrast, the monument's centerpiece had the exact opposite effect. The aesthetic beauty of its pastoral scene, delicately sculpted from white marble, was clearly meant to serve as a counterpoise, to imbue a sense of harmony and repose in those contemplating it. Then, looking more closely at it, spotting the presence of a sarcophagus in the elysian depiction, the symbolism became clear: Even in paradise, death exists. As if all that weren't enough, there was the cryptic inscription. He wondered if Matthew Seward, the monument's creator, had added it of his own volition, or had someone else been responsible? If the latter were the case, it would seem logical that it would have been one of the Morley brothers, who'd commissioned it in the first place, who would have conceived of adding the baffling inscription.

He could now appreciate more than ever why the Arcadian monument had provoked so much interest over the centuries and had attracted such a cultlike following of would-be code breakers and theorists. As far as the murder was concerned, it was easy to understand why it would be natural for people to jump to the conclusion that the monument had something to do with the crime. With the body discovered a stone's throw from the monument and, on top of that, the code angle — two code angles, no less — it had all the makings of a sure thing. Though he still had reservations about it having a direct connection to the murder, he certainly wouldn't dismiss the possibility of it having *some* connection, no matter how tenuous. He made a mental note to look at the other monuments more closely the next time he returned to Sturminster.

Stuck in heavy commuter traffic on the A446 in a steady rain that had started soon after he'd left the pub, Kingston could do little but twiddle his thumbs and watch the raindrops bouncing off the TR's bonnet. His radio had gone on the blink several days ago and wouldn't be fixed for another week.

He glanced momentarily at the ugly hole in the dashboard. Why was it so devilishly hard to get anything repaired or serviced these days? he wondered. Surely it hadn't always been like this. He was reminded once again — it happened with growing frequency of late — how much England had changed in the last few decades, and not for the better, to his way of thinking.

It wasn't until he was rounding Marble Arch, close to home, that he remembered Mrs. Tripp, his doughty and talkative house-cleaner. "Damn," he muttered. "That's all I need." Nothing short of Armageddon would keep her from her appointed rounds. At the stroke of nine every Friday, the doorbell would ring and there she would be, planted on the doormat like a garden gnome, with her cheery countenance and cliché-ridden greeting. When possible, he tried to make plans for Fridays. Not so much to be out of her way as to avoid her chronic and trivial jabbering. After a three-year drubbing, he had developed an impenetrable but polite self-defense system. There was no question in his mind that she was beyond cure.

When Kingston arrived at his flat at five thirty, she was still doing the ironing.

She glanced up when he entered. "There you are, Doctor. I hope you're all right? I've been worried stiff about you. You've been gone all day," she bleated, shaking her head.

"I'm fine, Mrs. Tripp." He glanced at his watch. "It is getting late, you know. Perhaps you should call it a day and go home?"

"Don't you worry yourself, Doctor," she said breezily, continuing to iron. "I'll just finish up here then I'll be out of your hair. In any case, Arthur's not coming home until later this evening. He's going to one of his bridge club meetings. Oh, and I put the post on the coffee table for you."

Kingston nodded. "Thank you. If you need me, I'll be in the living room." He started for the door, but he knew that she wasn't about to let him escape that easily.

"Did you read that story this morning, on the front page of the *Mail*?"

"I didn't," he replied, hand on the door-knob. "I don't read the *Mail*."

"Gave me the willies, it did — about these Satan worshippers in Russia, I believe it was. Killed three people, then cooked them. Can you imagine? Goths, they called them. I got sick to my stomach when I read it. I don't know how . . ."

"Mrs. Tripp, I can understand your revulsion, but there are things I must attend to, so if you'll pardon me, I'll say good evening and go do some catching up."

"Of course. I understand, Doctor. I'll see you next week then?"

"You will," he said with a disguised sigh, before closing the door behind him.

In the living room, he placed the satchel on the floor next to the couch and picked up the post from the coffee table. Nothing of interest save a postcard from his friend Andrew depicting a large brown spotted trout on one side and a terse message — as usual — on the other:

Lousy weather, otherwise having a good time. Hope you're staying out of trouble while I'm gone. I'll treat you to lunch at the Anchor when I get back.

Cheers,
Andrew

An hour later, after a light dinner — with a notepad, pen, and a glass of Côtes du Rhône by his side — he placed the contents of the satchel on the coffee table. Slowly and deliberately, he started to read. Some, like transcripts of conversations with the police — written by Simon Crawford, from memory, as notated — he read twice to make sure he wasn't missing anything that was unclear, contradictory, or ambiguous. In a few cases he made notes of statements and time lines that he would cross-check later.

When he'd finished, almost two hours later, he was left with a vague sense of disappointment. He certainly now had a clearer picture of everything that had happened on that terrible day at Sturminster and the days that followed, but the documents had revealed nothing new. The police did indeed seem at a dead end. There was no new information that would help expand his inquiry.

He returned the papers to the satchel and took his wineglass back to the kitchen. He'd been planning to read more of Morley's book before retiring but had concluded that the last two hours had been more than enough reading for one night. Though he'd rather not admit it, he needed a break, even if it was only a short one. An hour or so catching up on the news and sports on the telly should do the job, he decided. He nodded off in less than fifteen minutes, in the middle of the national weather report.

FIVE

Andrew, back from his fishing trip, took a long sip of wine and glared at Kingston. "For Christ's sake, Lawrence! What the hell's wrong with you?" His voice was loud enough to cause embarrassment, not only to Kingston but to surrounding diners as well. "The minute I turn my back you go and do something —" He rolled his eyes and shook his head. "I have to say it — plain *stupid!*"

Lunch at the Anchor had started pleasantly, Andrew talking at length about his fishing trip, which sounded a little too hohum for Kingston's tastes. After ten minutes or so, the conversation had drifted, for no good reason, to an exchange of thoughts — a mutual commiseration of the growing scandal over politicians' expense accounts and mass cabinet resignations that was dominating the headlines daily. It was then that Kingston had chosen to tell Andrew about Lord Morley's letter and their meeting, finally breaking the news that he'd agreed to help in the Sturminster murder case.

After Andrew's initial outburst, Kingston had summarized his trip to Staffordshire and given a short account of his meeting with Simon Crawford, with emphasis on the Arcadian monument, which he knew would appeal to Andrew's sense of the abstruse.

Andrew had sat in an undisguised funk and listened without comment, but he was not finished, not by a long chalk. "I'm gone ten days — only ten days — and in that time you've visited the scene of a bloody murder, met with Lord what's 'is name, and agreed to join in a half-assed investigation. I give up!" He spread his hands and shook them in frustration.

Kingston knew better than to try to persuade Andrew that not only was he doing the right thing but that he *wanted* to do it, too. He'd tried that tack before and it hadn't worked. So why bother now? Nevertheless, it was heartening to know that Andrew thought enough of their friendship to make such a fuss about his sanity and well-being. Instead, he made an attempt to change the subject. "Isn't your Bourne End open garden weekend coming up soon?" he asked, taking a last sip of coffee.

Andrew sighed. "You haven't listened to a word I've said, have you?"

"I have, and your disapproval is duly noted. When is it?"

"When is what?"

"The garden tour."

"It's the eleventh of next month. And I hope you can make it this time."

Last year, despite promising to help Andrew host his Sunday open garden — an annual village event featuring a dozen or so local gardens — he was forced to renege at the last minute because of an unexpected turn in the plant-hunting murder case that had dragged him up to Wales.

"Don't worry, I'll make it this time. I've been meaning to come and see the garden anyway. A visit is long overdue. I haven't even seen your new rose garden yet, nor those pricey urns you got from France."

"I know."

From his tart reply and crotchety look, Kingston knew that Andrew wasn't ready to give up on the Sturminster business.

"So," said Andrew, followed by a long moment of thought, "if, as you say, the case is bogged down, what's your plan?"

Kingston couldn't resist an indulgent, if fleeting, smile. "It's a stalemate now, but I doubt for long. There'll be a break in due course. There nearly always is. New evidence surfaces, something in the victim's background sheds new light on the case, a change-of-heart informant comes forward, perhaps an unexpected find that's been tucked away for years in one of the crevices of the Morley family closet — or even better, someone finds the missing part of the code. It may take longer than we would like, but something will surface, mark my words. In the meantime, we must work with what little we have."

Andrew shook his head. "Somehow I didn't think you'd be moping around the house, feather-dusting your bibelots, for long."

"I wasn't planning to, Andrew. I plan on visiting the institute where Endicott worked. Perhaps have a talk with his mother — see if the police missed anything there. And then there's a gentleman named Tristan Veitch. A historian of sorts."

"A historian?"

"He specializes in the history of Staffordshire, particularly the area surrounding Sturminster. I'm told that he also knows a lot about the Morley family."

"The family? Why do you want to know about them?"

"Apparently they've been feuding for centuries."

"And you think this might have something to do with the murder?"

Kingston hadn't thought about it that explicitly before, but now hearing Andrew put it so bluntly . . .

"Possibly. Yes," he said, somewhat unconvincingly.

"And you're going to step right into the middle of it? You do know that family disputes often come to a bad end, don't you? Even the police don't like to go on domestics."

"I'd hardly consider a meeting with a cantankerous historian to be life threatening."

"Have it your way." Andrew folded his arms and looked away.

"If you're so worried, why not come with me?"

Andrew shook his head. "No way," he said curtly.

"You wouldn't have to do anything. Just sit quietly and take notes. I'd enjoy the company."

"You're not going to persuade me, Lawrence. You can try 'til you're blue in the face. I want no part of it. You can stick your neck out if you want, that's your business, but I'm not that thick-skulled, and I'm sure you get my drift."

At that moment the waitress arrived and placed the bill folder on the table, judiciously between them, then departed with a polite "thank you, gentlemen." Andrew was quick to grab it, which brought no protest from Kingston who knew, by now, better than to argue. In any case, Andrew had offered to treat earlier.

After leaving what appeared to Kingston to be an unnecessarily large wad of bills for such a modest lunch — even taking into account the stiff price tag of the Pouilly-Fumé — they walked out of the dining room and in a couple of minutes were leaving the Anchor's car park in Andrew's red Mini Cooper. On the road out of the village, Andrew slipped into third gear and glanced at Kingston. "I suppose I'm going to have to accept the fact that you're not going to change," he said with a sigh.

"I'm not so sure about that. To be honest, if it weren't for the money I wouldn't have accepted the assignment. And I can drop out anytime I want. I'm not doing it just for the challenge, if that's what you're thinking."

"Lawrence, I hate to say this, but the only time you'll give up playing detective is if and when you meet another Megan. Someone whose life is more important to you than your own."

Kingston put a hand to his mouth and faked a yawn. "Seems to me we've been over this ground before," he said, looking out the window to avoid Andrew's gaze.

At least a mile had whizzed by before Kingston spoke again. "Andrew, I have no information, evidence, or explanation whatsoever for making this prediction, but I have a suspicion that this case will eventually prove to be much bigger and more far-reaching in scope than any of us realize. If it makes you feel better, it could be my last hurrah."

"When pigs have wings!"

SIX

The next morning Kingston rose early. During breakfast he read and reread the police reports and some of the other material that Crawford had given him. There was no question that, to date, the police had conducted a thorough examination, seemingly having left no proverbial stone unturned. Nevertheless, reading between the lines it was evident that they had no idea who might have killed Endicott, and they appeared to have no leads whatsoever.

The correspondence from GCHQ was much as Crawford had described — brief and to the point: Only if the matching piece of paper were located could it be determined if codes were involved. In summation they suggested that the letters were probably a combination or password of some kind.

Breakfast finished and the dishes put away, Kingston, following Sid's suggestion, called the *Midlands Post* to inquire about

Tristan Veitch. Though they couldn't give Kingston the number, they agreed to pass on a brief message to the historian letting him know that Kingston wanted to contact him regarding matters concerning Sturminster.

He had better luck finding Mrs. Endicott, the murdered man's mother. Even though he couldn't recall the name of the village where Crawford had said she was staying, it didn't take long. An Internet search located the assisted-living house Kingston was looking for in the village of Rugeley. From the picture, Richmond Court more resembled a manor house than an assisted-living home. He printed the page and set it aside. He didn't plan to phone, though. He would learn much more if he could talk to Mrs. Endicott face-to-face. As had been his practice with similar circumstances in the past, he called Richmond Court to make sure that she was still a resident there, and after learning that she was, asked what would be an appropriate time to stop by to see her. He was told that the best time would be early afternoon, sometime after two P.M.

That afternoon, Kingston rounded Richmond Court's circular driveway and parked in a designated area on the side of the house. Stepping out of the car, he paused to admire the lovely old house and its spacious and peaceful surroundings: salubrious, as well they should be, he thought.

The front door was ajar, so he entered but rang the brass doorbell anyway. Inside, with nobody in sight, he stood in the parquet-floored entrance hall admiring the room before deciding to go in search of someone in charge. Soon he heard the clip-clop of heels coming from a hallway on his left. Odd that, in a rest home, the woman wouldn't be wearing quieter shoes, he thought. A smiling young lady, dressed in a dark suit, approached to greet him.

"Good afternoon, sir. Welcome to Richmond Court. You've certainly brought a lovely day with you. I'm Patricia Wilkinson, service administrator."

Kingston beamed back, suddenly realizing that she might think that he was a prospective client inquiring about future care for a relative or friend. "Good afternoon," he replied, adopting an avuncular tone. "My name is Kingston," he said, handing her his card in a manner where she was not likely to miss his name and title.

"Nice to meet you, Doctor. How may I be of help?"

"I'm an acquaintance of William Endicott.

You're aware, I'm sure, of his unfortunate death recently."

She looked suitably solemn and nodded. "I am, yes."

"I would like if possible to have a few short words with Mrs. Endicott, who I understand is one of your residents. I don't want to disturb her unnecessarily, but I'm only in the Stafford area for a brief time. Knowing I would be within a few miles of Richmond Court I decided that, rather than talk to her on the phone, I'd do it in person. It's always so much more pleasant."

"Let me talk to her. I don't think it should be a problem at all. She welcomes visitors, actually. It shouldn't take long," she said, flashing a Colgate smile and turning on her heels. In two minutes she returned, asking Kingston to accompany her to the terrace where, she said, Mrs. Endicott was reading.

The wisteria-covered, Yorkstone terrace — past its bloom, sadly — stretched the width of the house and faced out to a freshly mown lawn, edged on all three sides by perennial borders. Kingston was impressed. Ms. Wilkinson did the introductions, then made a polite exit, leaving them alone. Kingston pulled up a wicker chair underneath the sun umbrella and sat facing a smiling Mrs. Endicott. She was a small

Dresden-like woman with meticulously coiffed hair dyed a henna color, wearing a cream-colored knitted shawl over a silk blouse. Unlike many women of her age — he guessed to be early eighties — who were prone to apply the rouge, lipstick, and powder like war paint, her makeup was applied sparingly and with obvious care. Her eyes were a periwinkle color and still had plenty of sparkle in them. He smiled, noticing the folded tabloid paper and Montblanc pen on the low table next to her. It was the *Guardian*'s racing form. An encouraging start, he thought.

"So, Doctor," she said, "what brings you here? You knew my son?"

If he closed his eyes, he could have been listening to a woman half her age. She had none of the speech patterns associated with advancing age. "I didn't," he replied, "but I would like to offer my condolences."

"Thank you," she said quietly, with a quick nod.

"I never met your son, but I was friends with a man who I believe did."

"Patricia said you were a doctor." She smiled, playfully. "Are you here to give me a mental checkup?"

Kingston chuckled. "Goodness, no. I'm not that sort of doctor."

"What are you here for, then?"

"I've been hired, among other things, to look into the death of your son. To find out why he was killed and for what reason."

"Surely the police are doing that. At least it gives me comfort to think that they are."

"They're working on it all the time, I can assure you."

Her eyes widened slightly and looked directly into his. "Are you a private detective?"

He smiled. "Not exactly, but close enough. I'm really a retired professor of botany, but somehow I keep getting roped into either helping the police or being retained by private individuals — as in this case — to assist in investigations."

"So you want to ask me questions, I take it?"

On the drive up, Kingston had been concerned that she might be too infirm, or possibly suffering from dementia, to be willing or even able to carry on an intelligent conversation. He needn't have worried. Time had neither dulled her quickness of mind nor blunted her humor; she was even volunteering information.

"If that's okay. I don't want to take too much of your time."

"That's the one thing that I've plenty of

90

now — time, memories, and bad dreams." She forced a wan smile. "I don't expect you to understand this, but there are still times when I get up in the morning, spend time in front of the mirror, then put on some nice clothes, convinced that William will be arriving around ten o'clock to take me out for the day, like he used to." She pulled a handkerchief from the sleeve of her blouse and brushed her nose with it. "I'll do my best to answer your questions, Doctor, but I would prefer that we not dwell on my son's death."

"I understand," said Kingston tenderly. "I know the police will have asked you many of the same questions, so I apologize in advance if I burden you by repeating any of them."

For the next fifteen minutes he ran through a list of questions that he'd more or less memorized, making sure that he sprinkled them with pleasant banter and the occasional witticism, which she seemed to enjoy. Running out of questions, he was starting to accept the inevitable: that his trip would prove worthless. It hadn't been a complete waste of time, though. He'd gained a certain satisfaction from being with her. He even felt a twinge of sadness that someone so bright and full of life should be

91

confined in a social backwater, with a prescribed circle of friends, mostly not of her choosing, and with probably few stimulating mental challenges.

The sun was warm on Kingston's back, so he shifted his chair to one side to be farther under the umbrella. At the same time, a woman in a pale blue duster arrived, asking whether they would like cold drinks. The interruption presented him with an excuse to leave, which he was thinking of doing anyway, but Mrs. Endicott insisted that he stay and have a drink — a "grown-up" one, if he preferred. "They make a wonderful Pimm's Cup," she added.

With their drinks on the table — Kingston had declined the Pimm's offer, instead settling for a mineral water with lemon — they continued talking. The easygoing conversation segued from one subject to another, often finding common ground. She'd started by commenting about the quality of the food at Richmond Court and how she'd had a hand in working with the kitchen staff to improve it. This led to several amusing anecdotes about a series of cooking classes she'd once taken in Lyon, a city with two dozen Michelin stars and almost two thousand restaurants that Kingston had visited three times. That prompted her to recommend the movie *Julie & Julia,* which he had not yet seen. They moved from movies to books, surprised to find that they had similar tastes in contemporary fiction. In fact, in the past year they'd both read the most recent novels by Ian McEwan, Sebastian Faulks, and Ken Follett.

After a short break in the conversation, while the staff lady refreshed their drinks, Dorothy — as she now insisted on being called — asked about Kingston's years as an academic. He gladly complied, telling about his days at University of Edinburgh teaching botany; the all-too-early death of Megan; their travels, describing the house and garden there and raising Julie; how she'd immigrated to the United States and his subsequent visits to Seattle; his transition as a bachelor from Edinburgh to London — trying to keep it brief. Only when he'd finished, did she speak.

"Being a botanist, you must have had a wonderful garden in Scotland. Do you have one now, in London?"

"A very small one. Not much more than a handkerchief-size lawn surrounded by a few shrubs, a couple of large camellias, and some vines, all enclosed by a brick wall. It doesn't get enough sunshine for roses, I'm afraid. The garden in Scotland was another matter entirely. It wasn't that large, mind you — about a half of an acre — but it contained an amazing variety of plants, shrubs, and trees, lots of roses, clematis, hardy geraniums, lavender, hellebores. I wish I had some pictures to show you."

"It must have been wrenching to leave it all behind."

"It was. Believe me."

"William and Danielle had a nice garden," she said, as if the memory was dear to her.

"Danielle? I thought your son was a bachelor?"

"He was divorced several years ago. They used to live near Cannock. Lovely old timbered house, called Birchwood."

"Danielle was the gardener, then?"

"Oh, no. It was Will's garden."

Kingston was thinking back to his interview with Simon Crawford. He was sure that Crawford had commented that, according to Inspector Wheatley, Endicott's bungalow looked as though he'd never spent a penny on it. Wouldn't that apply to the garden, too? he wondered. As he was pondering the conflicting statements, he was aware that Dorothy was looking at him with a frown.

"It was just a guess," he said. "You know,

with William busy at the college all the time."

"Actually, Danielle wasn't interested in the garden that much — hardly at all, in fact. It used to irk Will sometimes that she couldn't even remember to water it during hot spells when he was gone. She wasn't what one would call a homebody."

"Did William care for the garden on his own, or did they have a gardener?"

"He did nearly all of it himself. A man came in every now and then, for spraying and maintenance, but Will wasn't a checkbook gardener. He actually won some awards."

"Really?"

"For dahlias." She glanced up to the umbrella, frowning. "Come to think of it, I don't recall having seen those among his belongings."

"It must have been nice for you to have been able to spend time there."

"It was. Most of that time, after my husband died, I was living in a small house in Wolverhampton. No garden to speak of, so I really looked forward to the weekends at Birchwood. I'll say one thing in Danielle's favor — she was a wonderful cook."

Kingston glanced surreptitiously at his watch. He'd stayed much longer than he'd anticipated and doubted that he was going to learn anything more related to the case. "Well, Dorothy, I'd better be on my way. I'm planning to make a stop on my way home, so I don't want to leave it too late. I thoroughly enjoyed our chat, and I'll make you a promise. The next time I'm in Staffordshire, I'll give you a ring and come and see you again."

"That would be lovely, Doctor," she said with a little smile.

Kingston stood, leaned over, and placed his large hand over one of hers. "Good-bye for now then, Dorothy," he said, returning her smile.

"I'm so glad you came," she replied.

At the open French doors to the terrace, he stopped and turned back to her. "Next time, maybe you'll give me a couple of tips for Ascot week," he said.

She smiled. "I'd be happy to."

When Kingston returned home, there was one message on his answerphone. To his surprise it was Tristan Veitch.

"This is Tristan Veitch, Dr. Kingston. I'm aware of your reputation, so I presume you must be calling about the Sturminster murder case. Curiously

96

enough, I'm most eager to talk to you about it — and about a lot of other things as well. I rarely leave the house these days and have been out of sorts lately — flu, possibly — so if you would come up here, I'd appreciate it. I can't go into details, but it's critical that I see you as soon as possible. Meet me at my house tomorrow at noon, if you would. The address is the Tiled House, Mulberry Lane, Abbot's Broomfield. Take the B5013 east out of Rugeley. Believe me, you'll want to talk to me."

Veitch went on to give further directions. This was more than Kingston could have hoped for. Why was Veitch so keen to see him, and why the hurry? What did Veitch know about Endicott's murder, he wondered, and what were the "other things" he'd mentioned? "Interesting," he muttered.

SEVEN

When the phone rang at eight thirty the following morning, Kingston's first thought was that it might be Andrew wanting to know if the trip to see Mrs. Endicott had proved worthwhile or — miraculously — if he'd changed his mind about joining Kingston on his next investigative inquiry. He'd been wondering how long it would be before Inspector Wheatley called him, but the call still came as a surprise. Maybe it was the early hour.

"Dr. Kingston?"

"Yes."

"This is Inspector Wheatley, Staffordshire police. I'm calling about the Sturminster murder case. Lord Morley has informed me that you've been hired to conduct an independent inquiry into the murder."

"That's correct."

"We have no problem with that. That's a matter between the two of you. However, the purpose of my call is to advise you that you are bound by law to share with us any information related to the case that you might acquire."

"Of course. It's been agreed that Lord Morley will pass on any information that falls into my hands. I'll be reporting to him on a regular basis."

While the inspector sounded cordial, Kingston knew from experience that the police — understandably so — were not generally enthusiastic about having members of the public meddling in police affairs, and that this was simply a shot across the bow. As things progressed, he knew that collaboration with the police would be as essential to his own investigation as it was to theirs.

"As you may know," Kingston continued, "I've worked with the police —"

"No need to explain. We're all too aware of your reputation, Doctor. Let me give you my phone number — direct line — where you can reach me."

Kingston grabbed the pen by the phone. "Ready," he said, writing down the number.

"You make sure that Morley keeps in touch with us, that's all. We'd like to know immediately about anything you might uncover, not after the fact."

"I know the procedure, Inspector, and you have my word on it."

The call ended abruptly, leaving Kingston a little surprised that Wheatley hadn't asked more questions.

Thinking on the conversation, Kingston wished now that he'd asked if they had any more leads. As the days passed it would become critical to find out just how much the police knew, even if only to avoid unnecessary duplication and possible embarrassment with Morley. With Francis's name coming up, Kingston thought about calling him, or Crawford, just to check in, but decided it was premature and, in any case, he really had nothing to report at this time. Perhaps after his meeting with Veitch — if it proved of value — he would call them.

From everything he'd learned so far about the case, knowing too that the police had apparently reached a dead end, the only possible line of investigation open to him was to continue probing into the seemingly prosaic life of William Endicott. He thought about calling the institute where Endicott had worked to learn about his academic life, but time was getting short and he decided that, time allowing after his chat with Veitch, he would stop by the institute unannounced, hoping that the dean or someone in charge would see him.

He didn't want to be late for his appointment with Veitch. There seemed to be no questioning the veracity and earnestness inherent in Veitch's message, but Kingston hoped that he wouldn't end up being saddled for hours with an octogenarian historian wanting to talk about events hundreds of years in the past.

"Damn!" Kingston muttered. He was on the Edgware Road, heading out of London in a steady drizzle, and had just realized that he'd left Veitch's directions on the kitchen table. Too late to turn back now; he would just have to rely on his memory, which was still remarkably good, certainly compared to Andrew's, who was younger by ten years. With the village of Abbot's Broomfield as small as it had appeared on the map, he figured it shouldn't present a problem. He could always inquire if his memory failed him.

The village was tiny indeed, nothing more than a sprinkling of cottages set back on either side of the narrow road that curved for little more than a hundred yards through the tree-lined high street. Not a pub, post office, or shop in sight. So much for making inquiries, thought Kingston. It took a second pass through the near-deserted hamlet before he spotted the unmarked, one-car-wide lane that Veitch had said to look for. "The house is a quarter mile in but easy to miss," he'd cautioned. Even at that, driving at a snail's pace, Kingston almost overshot it. The house was completely shielded behind high walls of dark-leaved pittosporum, the only clue of habitation being a nearly invisible weathered picket gate set in the hedge. Kingston parked alongside the hedge, got out, and stretched his legs. The skies were cement and brooding, but least it had stopped drizzling. He passed through the gate, closing it behind him. Ahead was a handsome, if small, Victorian redbrick farmhouse with a gray slate roof. The arched doorway was flanked by two large bay windows with shiny white frames. In the absence of a knocker or doorbell — at least Kingston couldn't see one — he rapped on the door with his knuckles. In a few seconds, it opened halfway to reveal a tall, slender woman with long ash blond hair, simply but tastefully dressed all in gray. An attractive woman, but whether it was a trick of the light or not, her face appeared to have the same gray hue as her clothing. Expecting Veitch, Kingston was taken aback momentarily.

"You're Dr. Kingston?" she said in a colorless voice, saving him the introduction.

"I am. Mr. Veitch is expecting me," he replied with a half smile.

The woman stood motionless, hand gripping the edge of the door, her expression and body language offering no suggestion that she might invite him in. After an unusually long pause, she said, "Yes, he told me to expect you."

Immediately Kingston sensed that something was amiss. Though only a few words, something in how she'd said them raised doubt, a suspicion that bad news wasn't long to follow.

"I'm sorry," she said at length, stepping out onto the porch.

Now he could see that her face was pale and she looked troubled.

"I'm Amanda Veitch. My brother was taken to the hospital about an hour ago. I wanted to call you but couldn't place where Tristan had put your number. I suppose it wouldn't have made much difference anyway; you'd probably have left by then. He'd said you were coming up from London."

"I'm awfully sorry to hear that," said Kingston somberly. "In your brother's phone message yesterday he mentioned that he hadn't been feeling well. Thought he might be coming down with the flu."

She shook her head. "It was nothing like that."

"Then my showing up on your doorstep is the last thing you need right now," Kingston replied. He was beginning to feel uncomfortable having this kind of stilted exchange with a woman he'd just met, about an unexplained ailment that had afflicted her brother, a man whom he'd yet to meet.

"I'm just sorry you had to drive all the way up here to find out."

"That's of the least concern. I'd best be on my way, you have far more important things to attend to." He reached in his jacket pocket and pulled out his wallet, extracted a card, and handed it to her. "Perhaps you'd be kind enough to call me when your brother is discharged and has fully recovered," he said.

"I'll do that," she said, unsmiling. With that, she turned and went back into the house, closing the door without a backward glance.

Sitting in the car, Kingston stared at the Triumph shield badge on the steering wheel, absorbing the bad news about Tristan Veitch. His knee-jerk reaction of disappointment had vanished before he'd even reached the car. Though Veitch was a stranger, Kingston was reminded that the poor man's illness was not a moment for self-pity.

He glanced at his watch. Wolverhampton was nearby, and there was plenty of time left in the day for a visit to the institute where Endicott had taught. He took out his *AA Road Atlas* from the glove compartment and studied it for the quickest route. Satisfied, he turned the key in the ignition and the engine coughed into its satisfying rumble. He started down the lane.

Kingston's visit with the dean of the Archaeology and Art Institute, an attentive and forthcoming man, lasted no more than fifteen minutes. He learned nothing whatsoever to suggest that Endicott was anything more than an above-average teacher, generally liked by the faculty and students, that he had no unusual traits or habits, had an excellent attendance record and, by and large, preferred to keep his private life to himself. The only snippet of dubious information that surfaced was that there had been complaints by several female staff members that Endicott was given to the occasional sexist comment and a trifle too easygoing with his hands. This Kingston already knew, though, having read it in the police report.

Navigating his way out of Wolverhampton, he thought back on the events of the day and how disappointing things had turned out — two more dead ends. Though he'd never met the man, he was beginning to understand how Inspector Wheatley must feel. He smiled, reminded of a humorous comment he'd once read: "I live on a one-way street that's also a dead end. I'm not sure how I got there." How he remembered these things eluded him. They did come in handy every once in a while, though, even if only to put a more cheerful spin on life. Andrew always cringed when Kingston used them. Andrew, yes — he could hear his now all too familiar "playing detective" bellyaching when they next spoke.

An hour later, the sight of Hyde Park Corner ahead made him feel better. A couple of pints and dinner at the Antelope would improve his frame of mind no end.

When the phone rings at the crack of dawn or late at night, it usually triggers an involuntary alarm that the person calling is either in a foreign time zone or, worse, is the bearer of bad news. Such were Kingston's thoughts as he picked up the phone at six fifteen the following morning. At least he was up. He'd just retrieved the *Times* from the doorstep and was waiting in the kitchen for the electric teakettle to boil.

"This is Kingston," he said curtly, trying to disguise his displeasure.

"It's Amanda Veitch, Doctor. I apologize for calling at this hour, but I have no choice. I'm calling from Stafford Memorial Hospital," she said, a noticeable tremble in the telling words. "I've been here all night with Tristan." Her voice trailed off for a moment, then she continued, seemingly having regained her composure. "He wants to see you."

Kingston smiled. From the minute he'd picked up the phone he'd been expecting bad news; now this lucky turn of events. Veitch must be on the mend and Kingston would get his interview after all.

"Today? Is he well enough?"

"The doctor doesn't think so, but Tristan's insistent." Another pause followed, this time longer. "They're saying he might not have long to live," she blurted. "So if Tristan is to get his wish, you'll have to get up here as quickly as you can."

Kingston's short-lived burst of optimism evaporated as he searched for words of comfort. None came. "I can leave within the next ten minutes or so," he replied. "Where's the hospital?"

"It's Stafford Memorial on the A34 on the north side of town. He's in critical care."

"Don't bother with directions. I'll find it." He glanced at his watch. "If the traffic co-operates, I should be able to make it a little after eight. You'll be there, I take it?"

"I will. I'll wait for you in the reception area."

Entering the hospital an hour and twenty minutes later, Kingston saw no sign of Amanda. The only person in the reception area, other than an elderly man sitting alone in a corner reading a book propped up on his walker, was a woman who was talking to the receptionist. She must have caught sight

107

of him out of the corner of her eye because she turned and started walking toward him. It wasn't until she was close that Kingston recognized her as Amanda. Even then it was hard to picture her as the woman he'd met only the day before. This time she was dressed smartly, wearing a navy pea coat with a camel-color skirt, a scarf wrapped stylishly around the collar of her white blouse. Her hair was different, too, tied up in a neat chignon. And this time she wore makeup. Given the gravity of the circumstances, she looked remarkably composed.

"Good morning, Doctor," she said with a weak smile. "Thank you for coming."

"The news is very sad. I'm sorry."

She pursed her lips and nodded. "You'd best not waste time." She nodded to the far corner of the lobby. "Take the lift over there to the second-floor critical-care ward B, room five. They're expecting you, so ignore the sign and just go in." She brushed a stray hair from her brow and fixed her hazel eyes on Kingston. "If it's all right with you, I won't accompany you. I've been up most of the night and desperately need a cup of tea and a sandwich — at least something. I've hardly eaten a thing since yesterday. I'll wait for you in the cafeteria."

"Of course. I'll see you in a while, then."

He headed for the elevators.

When Kingston entered the room and saw Tristan Veitch, he knew immediately that the man was suffering from something far more serious than the flu. He was propped up in bed, eyes closed, breathing laboriously, aided by the oxygen line to his lungs through a nasal feed. All around, a battery of medical instruments, monitors, and other devices flickered, hummed, and beeped ad nauseam as they controlled and tracked his condition and vital signs. Kingston stood at the foot of the bed, faintly disturbed by the scene: alone with a stranger whose days, even hours, could be numbered, he was having serious doubts about being there at all and wondering if he should say anything — even where to start. As he was about to speak, Veitch's eyes opened slowly, as if he'd somehow known that his visitor had arrived that very moment.

"Dr. Kingston," he mumbled in a scratchy near whisper, as his heavily lidded eyes swiveled slowly to meet Kingston's.

"Yes."

"Please. Sit down."

Kingston dragged a nearby chair purposefully close to the side of the bed. He didn't want to risk missing anything that Veitch had to say. "Thank you for seeing me," he said. "To be truthful, I'm not sure that I should be here in the first place."

"Let me be the judge of that," Veitch wheezed.

Kingston thought it a feisty remark for someone who was deathly sick. It occurred to him then that perhaps Veitch hadn't been told just how serious his condition was. "Of course." He nodded.

"Are you working with the police this time, too?" The question was the last thing Kingston expected. It meant that Veitch knew about him, which wouldn't be that surprising. He wondered whether Veitch knew he was working on the Sturminster case.

"No, I'm not."

"It doesn't matter."

"But how did you know who I was, why I wanted to talk to you?"

"When the *Post* called and said you'd left me a message, your name sounded vaguely familiar. Then I remembered reading about you in the papers. Historians tend to have good memories, you know — aided by a quick Internet search, of course." He paused, as if needing to regain his breath before continuing. "The famous Professor Kingston . . . Sturminster . . . the murder: It wasn't hard to put two and two together to realize why you were calling."

"And you wanted to see me?"

"Yes."

"You said you were anxious to talk about the murder? William Endicott?"

Veitch nodded. "I am."

"For the record, have you discussed any of this with the police?"

"No."

"May I ask why?"

"It doesn't matter." Veitch inhaled deeply, his chest rattling. "Everything's changed now. There's no longer reason for me to remain silent. People need to know what I know."

"About the murder?"

"About the Morleys. Isn't that what you wanted to know? Your timing was perfect, Doctor." He reached to the bedside table for a water glass and took a long drink. Veitch obviously knew about the case, but then he would, living a stone's throw from Sturminster.

"It's too complicated to tell you everything that I've uncovered — you'll find out for yourself when you read my drafts."

"Your drafts?"

"Yes. I want you to look at what I've written, what I've discovered. It's all there. I've made all the connections, the relationships," he rasped, sucking in air.

Kingston was surprised to see a fleeting, conceited smile cross Veitch's lips. "Unscrambling some of it wasn't easy, but we did it," he croaked. "The cover-ups, the people, the places — high places, I might add. It's much bigger than I ever imagined." The man was rambling, his eyes bright and feverish.

"Slow down a minute," said Kingston. "What did you unscramble? Are you talking about codes, the scrap of paper the police found on Endicott's body? What —"

"Codes . . . right." Veitch nodded and continued his rant. "I'm talking about damning information — unspeakable crimes that, if made public, would expose Sturminster's glorious history as a sham. Crimes that would cause irreparable damage to the legacy of the Morleys."

A fit of raspy coughing stopped Veitch at that point, long enough to make Kingston wonder if he should call a nurse. The coughing spell finally over, Veitch lay back on his pillow, eyes closed, breathing laboriously and irregularly. Kingston took the opportunity to stand and stretch his legs. The metal chair was small and uncomfortable. As he stared at the steady undulations of the ECG monitor's glowing wavelength pattern, Kingston's mind was in overdrive trying to fathom the implications of what Veitch had just told him and what it might have to do with Endicott's murder.

Finally, Veitch looked up. "Where was I?" he mumbled.

"You said you'd uncovered some damaging evidence concerning the Morley family that would also cast aspersions on Sturminster's reputation."

"Damaging! God, that's an understatement. These were heinous crimes. You've heard that old saying, 'Follow the money'? Well, that's what we did."

"What money?" asked Kingston, noting the plural "we" again.

"What money? That's a good one." Veitch clutched the edge of the blanket, his expression even grimmer than before. "I wasn't going to let them stop me. The story of a lifetime." His voice was becoming weaker, but he struggled on. "One of the most egregious misdeeds in our history, Kingston. When it all comes to the surface — when people realize who was implicated . . . the staggering amount of money involved . . . the crimes committed . . ." He sank back into the pillow, trying to regain his breath.

Kingston heard voices in the hallway. A second later the door opened and a woman

113

entered the room.

"Well, Mr. Veitch. And how are we doing today?" It was a woman's voice, pleasant but authoritative. Kingston got up and turned to face a young woman. She was darkly complected and not much more than thirty years old, by his reckoning. The nurse with whom he'd talked earlier stood a few paces back.

"I'm Dr. Chandra," she said. "And you must be Dr. Kingston."

"Yes. I'm a friend of the family."

"I know. Amanda Veitch told me you were coming. She told me that it was very important that her brother see you. Normally, we allow only family members in critical care, but in a few cases we bend the rules."

"Thank you for that. I'm most grateful to have had the chance to talk with him."

Kingston tried to smile, to stay calm, hoping she would allow him to continue his conversation with Veitch for a few more minutes.

Dr. Chandra, however, was having none of it.

"It's time for you to leave, I'm afraid. If you'll excuse me," she said, brushing past him to the side of the bed.

About to leave, Kingston took a last glance at the hollow-cheeked Tristan Veitch. As the doctor started to tend to him, he held up a scrawny hand, as if to say *Wait a moment,* and stared across at Kingston.

"You must come back, Doctor," he said. "I have to tell you the rest. Just be careful, that's all."

"I will." Kingston nodded, then left the room.

As the lift descended, Kingston's mind was a kaleidoscope of thoughts, emotions, and questions, all clamoring for attention. Veitch clearly knew something about Endicott's murder — he'd said so in his phone message and again just now — yet he'd spent most of the time talking about evil things concerning the Morleys that had happened over two hundred years ago. Why was that? Another thing worried Kingston. Veitch appeared to be in bad shape, and it could become a question of time. He had to talk to the man again and very soon.

For now, trying to evaluate everything Veitch had divulged would have to wait. He had the rest of the day to do that. In less than a minute he would be with Amanda again. What, if anything, should he tell her? One question now became paramount: How long was Veitch expected to live? He knew that the question was blatantly self-serving and that by asking it he could be accused of being callous, but suddenly it had become crucial. Obviously, Veitch had put all his highly incriminating evidence to paper. As an experienced writer and historian, it was almost certain that it was well documented and perhaps backed up, too. If the right moment presented itself, perhaps he could risk asking Amanda if he could take a look at Veitch's work.

The lift *dinged* and he stepped into the reception area, now much busier. One way or another, whatever it took, a follow-up meeting with Veitch had to be arranged as soon as possible, even if it meant staying in Stafford overnight. To make that happen would take Amanda's cooperation, which he knew could be a touchy issue. He'd known her for only twenty-four hours and though up until now she'd been willing to help him, he knew that from now on he had to be careful what he said and what he asked of her. The sixty-four-thousand-dollar question: How much did she know about her brother's activities?

Twice Veitch had used "we" when describing his activities. Did that mean he was working with someone or, given his unstable condition, had it been just a slip of the tongue? Was his collaborator Amanda? A possibility. In any case, if someone had been

116

working with him regularly, she would surely have known it.

Heading for the cafeteria, he thought back to his conversation with her only yesterday and the dreadful finality of those last few words when they'd talked on the phone: "He might not have long to live." Until now, she'd been more than accommodating to his intrusion into her life at the worst possible time. She had enough to worry about and uncertainty to deal with as it was. To add more could jeopardize their fragile relationship, and he certainly wanted to avoid that. Less important was another unanswered question that had been nettling him since they'd first met. Under normal circumstances, he would have never dreamed of asking it, but if he happened on the right moment, he would take the risk: What was the nature of her brother's terminal illness?

Entering the sunlit cafeteria, he spotted Amanda sitting by a large window reading a magazine, an empty plate, coffee cup, and saucer on the table. Hearing him approach, she looked up and put the magazine aside. "How is he?" she asked, her eyes tired and reddened from lack of sleep and anxiety.

"Quite talkative, actually," he said, pulling up a chair and sitting across from her.

"I'm glad, for your sake."

"He spoke for about ten minutes. Then the doctor arrived, so I had to leave."

"Was it Dr. Chandra?"

"Yes."

"Did she give you an update?"

Kingston shook his head. "No. She did mention that you'd talked to her about letting me see Tristan, though. Thank you for that."

"Was he able to help? To give you the kind of information you were hoping for?"

"Yes, he was. Frankly, I wasn't expecting quite as much. I was surprised at how lucid he was."

"That's good."

"This project he'd been working on — the one involving the Morley family — had he told you about it? Did you know what it involved?"

The slightest flicker in her eyes told Kingston all he needed to know. She looked away for a moment, fidgeting with a jade ring on her right hand. After what seemed a long time, her eyes came back to meet Kingston's. It was a wistful look that he'd not expected. "In many ways, Tristan is a secretive man," she said. "He's been that way since he was a child. You never knew what he was up to until he — and only he

118

— was satisfied that, whatever it was, it was finished to his liking. When he made those balsa-wood models of his — airplanes, mostly — it was always behind closed doors or when no one was around. Only when they were finished would he be willing to show them to any of us. He can be the most generous person in the world when it suits him, particularly when it comes to material things. But with ideas, projects, ambitions, and the like, he doesn't much like to share. It's as if he's afraid that someone might come along and criticize, shoot holes in his ideas or, worse, steal them. So, in answer to your question, I know a little, but there's probably considerably more that I don't." She looked down. "I'm going to miss him," she said softly, a slight waver in her voice.

Kingston was touched by the poignancy of her answer. He caught himself just in time, as he was about to reach out and place a hand on hers. "I realize that you hardly know me, but if there's anything that I can do to help you through this bad patch, please say so. Whatever it might be, don't hesitate to ask."

"That's kind of you and I appreciate it," she answered, regaining her composure. "Are you headed back to London now?"

"I think so. When I left Tristan, I sensed

that he wanted to tell me more, but that may have to wait. If it's all right with you, perhaps I could come back and see him again, if he's willing."

"I don't see why not."

"There's another possibility. I have a friend who lives near Tamworth. Since I'm up here anyway, I could call him and see if he can put me up for the night." He smiled. "Or perhaps more aptly, put up with me for the night. If so, I could come back tomorrow."

"That's entirely up to the doctor and Tristan. I have no objection to your seeing him, if that's what you're asking. As long as it's what he wants and it's not affecting his well-being or peace of mind, why would I?"

"I'll let you know, then. Perhaps you could give me a phone number where I can reach you."

"Sure." She took a miniature leather-bound pad from her handbag, tore off a page, jotted down her number and address, and handed it to Kingston. "That's my mobile," she said. "I hardly ever use the house phone anymore."

"Thanks." Kingston folded it once and slipped it into his shirt pocket.

Amanda rose and so did he. "Thank you for coming and for your kind offer of help," she said. "I hope you'll understand my not wanting to stay longer but, as you know, it's been a dreadfully long twenty-four hours."

"I understand fully."

"Thank you. I'll go up and say good-bye to Tristan and then head back home. They say there's a nasty storm coming in this afternoon, so traffic could be a mess on the Stafford stretch of the motorway. You might want to take an alternative route."

"I will, thanks."

Kingston walked with her to the lifts, close to the main entrance. Silently waiting, they both stared up, ritually, at the lighted floor indicator descending. Knowing that the doors would open at any moment, he turned to her. "Amanda," he said, realizing that it was the first time that he'd addressed her by her first name.

She lowered her eyes and looked at him. "Yes?"

"I've been curious about something. It's really none of my business and if you prefer not to answer, I'll understand."

She looked at him quizzically. "What is it?" she said, after a moment's thought.

"What is the nature of your brother's illness?"

The lift door opened and she stepped in and turned to face Kingston. "The doctor isn't certain yet, but she thinks Tristan might have been poisoned," she said.

Before he could respond, the doors had closed.

EIGHT

That night, Kingston stayed at the James Hotel in Lichfield, about twenty miles from the hospital. The "friend" in Tamworth that he'd mentioned to Amanda was, in fact, a septuagenarian uncle of Megan, whose name was Clive. Clive was a confirmed bachelor, an intolerable blowhard who'd spent his life passing himself off as an expert on everything. While Megan was alive, an uneasy truce had existed between him and Kingston, but the mere thought of spending an entire evening having to listen to Clive pontificating had never been in question. That aside, he had no idea if Clive still lived in Tamworth and had no wish to find out. The James suited him fine.

After leaving the hospital yesterday morning, he'd sat in the TR wondering how he should interpret Amanda's answer to his question. Poisoning suggested all manner of possibilities, ranging from accidental food poisoning to a premeditated act committed with intent to kill. What kind of poison was another issue altogether. Many poisons were readily available on the open market, some of the most lethal belonging to the animal and plant worlds, as Kingston knew only too well. But Amanda had said, "He might have been poisoned," which, if taken literally, left no doubt as to her meaning. He'd hoped he would be proved wrong, but there was plenty of reason for suspicion. If Endicott's murder was related to Veitch's discoveries, then it wasn't unreasonable to conclude that the same person or persons responsible for Endicott's death wanted Veitch out of the way, too.

Putting on his seat belt, he'd been reminded how quickly it all happened. Now that the gravity of the events was starting to sink in, he was already beginning to have mixed feelings about having taken on the inquiry. He'd dismissed that thought, reminding himself that Veitch's startling information about the Morleys had given the case a new twist, maybe a break of sorts, much more than he'd ever hoped for when he'd knocked on Veitch's door the day before. On the other hand, Veitch was now apparently near death; possibly poisoned by someone or someones who would stop at nothing to prevent his discovery about the Morley family from becoming public. There had been times during murder investigations that he'd worked on in the past, when his life had been in jeopardy, but in all those cases there had been physical confrontation of one kind or another. This case was different. He'd barely started and already he was uneasy about what he could be getting into. If he continued digging, would he also become a target? After thinking about it briefly, he'd concluded that now was not the time to worry about it and that further speculation was pointless. Until he received more information from either Amanda or the hospital and had the chance to give it a lot more thought, he would forget his misgivings.

Under ominous darkening skies, he'd considered whether or not to drive back to London. In the end, the storm had made the decision for him. As he'd been studying his road map, deciding which road to take out of town, the wind had picked up, hurling leaves and debris roof-high across the car park. Then it had started bucketing down. The idea of driving back to London was a nonstarter. What remained of the day called for a warm and comfortable refuge where he could sit with a drink by a cheering fireplace, savoring the prospect of a good meal and a good night's rest, with uninterrupted time to absorb and analyze everything that had taken place in the last twenty-four hours — hence the James Hotel.

At breakfast the next morning in the hotel's conservatory Garden Room, Kingston thought about the day to come. During the night, the storm had passed and the skies outside were now cloudless and atypically blue, even though it was summer. Earlier, while shaving, courtesy of the toiletries kit the hotel provided, he'd made up his mind that the first order of the day would be to figure how he could wangle another talk with Tristan Veitch. He might get permission simply by phoning critical care, dropping Dr. Chandra's name, saying that he was Dr. Kingston and was on his way to revisit the patient in room five. That would be plan B; first, he must talk to Amanda. The last thing he wanted was for her to feel that he was being indifferent to what she was going through or uncaring of her brother's plight, by taking advantage of the situation to further his own goals. As it was, he hadn't been completely forthcoming about his reason for showing up in the first place. Sooner or later he would have to tell her what that was, but only when he felt the time and place were right.

By eight forty-five, after a satisfying break-fast and three cups of coffee, he was back in his room, the slip of paper bearing Amanda's phone number in hand. He looked at his watch one more time. A reasonable enough hour to call, he decided. After what must have been close to ten rings — he was about to put down the phone — she answered.

"It's Lawrence Kingston," he said, trying not to sound overly cheerful.

"I was hoping you'd call, Doctor. I left a message on your answerphone last night."

Something was wrong, he knew. Her words had come quickly, with an edge of agitation. "What is it?" he asked.

"The house has been ransacked."

"Good Lord! When was this?"

"While I was gone yesterday. When I got back, the place was a terrible mess. I called the police right away. They were here for several hours. They're coming back this morning to check for prints and whatever. A neighbor stayed with me last night."

"Was it a burglary? I mean, are items of value missing?"

"Not really, at least none of my jewelry, small antiques, the usual things that are stolen. My laptop's gone but it was really old, so that's no great loss. Tristan's study was hit the worst. They took his computer and iPhone, and the police say that other electronic devices could be missing, going by the cords and cables that remain. They weren't methodical. They just trashed the place. Books all over the place, file drawers emptied, a horrible mess. Drawers in the living room were emptied, too, but the police say it was clear that Tristan was targeted, that they were looking for something of his."

"Did they ask you what that might be?"

"They asked the obvious: Did he keep valuables in his study, large amounts of money, valuable paintings, collections of any kind, guns, anything worth stealing? Had I noticed any strangers in the neighborhood lately or had people done work on the house recently? That sort of thing."

"What about the project that he'd been working on? The one we talked briefly about yesterday?"

"It started off as a project, but over the last several weeks it became more like an obsession. I've never seen Tristan get so wrapped up in any of his work before. Not only that, he had this nagging worry — almost paranoia — about it being stolen or somehow lost. He was almost afraid to leave the house."

"Weren't you concerned that what he was writing about could be libelous or even place him in some kind of jeopardy?"

"Those thoughts had crossed my mind. Yes. Every time I broached the subject he always said he would tell me in due course." She paused briefly, then continued, a tinge of anger in her voice. "It's the reason he was poisoned, isn't it? That damned project of his." Another pause. "The burglary — that too. They're all somehow connected."

"It certainly looks that way. What other reasons could there be? There's the timing, too." Though Amanda was probably right, Kingston knew that further conversation on this path would lead nowhere. Not only that, if it were to continue, it would be difficult to avoid having to explain the circumstances that had led to his involvement and the most likely reason why her brother was in the hospital. "As I said before, if there's any way that I can help, I want you to ask. Whatever it is."

"I'll keep that in mind, Doctor. Coping with Tristan being deathly sick was one thing, but this is much more. And it frightens me."

"I can well understand. Just promise to call me if matters get worse."

"I will. Thank you. I have to wait here for

the police and I don't know how long that will take. I was planning to see Tristan later today, but I doubt that's going to be possible now. Perhaps it's just as well, though. Telling him about the break-in would be out of the question. The last thing he needs. First off, he'd be worried sick about me, being home alone. If you weren't in London, I might ask you to go in my place."

"I'm not in London. I stayed up here last night, in Lichfield, because of the storm."

"Really? Then if it doesn't interfere with your plans, perhaps you could check in on him and call me later to let me know how he's doing. You'll have to explain that I couldn't get away today, of course. Just tell him that I had to wait for someone to look at the roof because of storm damage, something like that."

"I'd be more than happy to visit him, Amanda. I'll go this morning before driving back home."

"Good. When we hang up, I'll ring the hospital and let them know you'll be coming in my place. You'll call me later?"

"I will."

Kingston put down the phone, sat on the edge of the bed, and stared at the books on the bedside table, contemplating this disturbing development. The morning sun beaming through the rustling leaves of the silver birch outside the window conflicted with his mood, as it projected playful patterns on the white stucco. He'd long ago stopped concerning himself with the fickleness of the English weather, but for a brief moment it struck him as unjust that such awful news should be accompanied by such a cheerful display of nature.

The white-haired receptionist looked up as Kingston approached the hospital's entry desk. "May I help you, sir?" she asked.

"I'm Dr. Kingston. I'm here to visit Mr. Veitch, in critical care. I'm given to understand his sister called earlier this morning, granting permission."

"Yes, Doctor," she replied, moistening her lips. "Dr. Chandra asked to speak with you when you arrived. I'll see if I can locate her." She reached for the phone.

Kingston turned away, gazing around the reception area. He was hoping against hope that Veitch was feeling well enough to continue where he'd left off. Shortly, he heard the receptionist call his name.

"She's on her way down, Doctor."

He'd been half expecting, for obvious reasons, that Dr. Chandra might want to talk to him about his visit with her patient, but a nagging doubt now persisted, leading him to wonder if the reason for her breaking away to talk to him was to explain why seeing Veitch today was not in the cards. Another thought crossed his mind: As happened often, she could be under the impression that he was a medical doctor. He hadn't told Amanda or anyone else anything to the contrary.

Another minute or so passed, then he saw Dr. Chandra step out of the elevator and head toward him. As she got close, she gestured for Kingston to walk with her across the lobby. "I have bad news, I'm afraid," she said with no inflection. "Mr. Veitch died a short while ago."

For what seemed a long time they stood, bound by an uneasy silence, her eyes never leaving Kingston's. Finally, he spoke.

"That is bad news. Does his sister know?"

"Yes. I spoke with her. She said you were coming."

"I should give her a call, then."

She smiled grimly. "We had hopes of saving him, but we got to him too late, I'm afraid."

"Amanda . . . his sister said you thought it might have been poisoning?"

"It certainly looks that way. I can't say for

131

sure, though. We don't have the lab report yet."

"A copy would go to the police, I presume?"

She gave a thin smile. "I think I know what you're getting at, Doctor. Foul play? Right?"

Kingston shrugged. "Curious, that's all."

"Unfortunately, this is a sensitive area that ultimately rests with the hospital's legal department and the police. All we do, as standard procedure, is to determine if poisoning is the cause of death. If it is, then it's the pathologist's job to determine what kind of poison. Unless foul play is obvious, we are not bound to report it as a possible homicide. That's for the police investigators to determine."

"I understand."

She pursed her lips briefly, then said, "Sorry."

Kingston took a deep breath and exhaled. "I'll be on my way, then. Thanks for taking the time to tell me personally. I appreciate that."

She nodded and smiled sympathetically. They shook hands, then she turned and headed back to the elevators.

NINE

Two and a half hours later, Kingston swung his garage door closed, locked it, and set the ADT security alarm. Two years earlier, his TR4 had been stolen from his rented Waverley Mews garage and he'd gone to great lengths to make sure it wouldn't happen again.

From a traffic standpoint, the drive back from Stafford had been uneventful. With dry weather and no road works or accidents, he'd had plenty of time to relive and try to sort through the shocking events of the last twenty-four hours, and to start shaping a tentative course of action for the hours and days to come. The first priority, when he got back to his flat, would be to call Amanda to offer his condolences. He sensed that it could be another difficult conversation for both of them.

He knew that more prying into her brother's activities or raising the question of another visit without good reason would be a breach of etiquette and would run the risk of ending the relationship there and then. Nonetheless, he also realized that if his inquiry was to continue, he had to find a way to examine Tristan's study, sooner rather than later. Whether he achieved that would depend on her frame of mind when they spoke. He hoped that she would be willing to cooperate. Another option, of course, was to tell her everything, including what her brother had divulged in the last few hours of his life. That would be his last alternative, he decided.

He went through the post and checked his answerphone. The first message was from Amanda. It wasn't until he heard twenty seconds or so that he realized it was the call she'd left earlier, to tell him that the house had been ransacked. There were no other messages of importance.

There was little doubt in his mind now that the break-in was related to Veitch's investigation into the Morley family and the potentially explosive material he'd unearthed. So the burglars would certainly have cleaned the place out, taken all of Tristan's manuscripts, records, notes, phone records, et cetera, anything and everything that could point to complicity or guilt. The fact that they'd taken his computer and iPhone confirmed that. Nevertheless, they'd perhaps overlooked something. If that something existed, Kingston intended to find it, no matter how insignificant or minuscule. "The truth, if it exists, is in the details," was one of the few proverbs he'd been known to use with any frequency.

If premeditated poisoning was the cause of death, it raised a lot of burning questions: Why was Tristan poisoned and by whom? When and what type of poison? How was it administered? Was it acute or chronic, that is, administered over a period of time? Considering all that, one possibility hadn't escaped him. Much as he found the thought repellent, it couldn't be dismissed. Had Amanda played a role? He wanted to rule out the thought summarily but knew that could end up being a mistake. From what little he knew of her and the way she had exhibited genuine concern and caring for her brother, she would seem the last possible suspect. However, having dealt with more than one murderer — two of them women, in fact — he knew better than to take things at face value, to assume anything. The police, he knew, had their own ways of looking at these things, too. The first people to come under scrutiny were usually family members or friends, particularly in husband-and-wife situations or sibling relationships like theirs.

Kingston went into the kitchen to make a pot of coffee, still thinking about how he could bring her around to the idea of his visiting her without making it seem self-serving or appear that he was intruding in her personal life. If she got the impression that he was inquiring solely for his own benefit, she could easily take it the wrong way, and that would be the end of his just-begun investigation — for the time being, anyway. Waiting for the coffee to percolate, he stared out the window into the small garden below where the clematis, Perle d'Azur, was putting on a flamboyant show on the south wall facing him.

He turned his thoughts to Veitch and his shocking indictment of unnamed members of the Morley family and the "staggering amount of money" involved, which would be in keeping with the rumor about money that Samuel Morley had embezzled from his brother. If everything Veitch had said was true — and Kingston had no reason to doubt the veracity of the historian's claims — one or more of the Morley clan was complicit in crimes of conspiracy, larceny, and, by the sound of it, much more. Question was, which of the Morleys? Had Veitch meant those in the distant past, or present-day members? Either way, it was starting to look as if he would be knocking on Morley's door for a chat much sooner than he thought. That he was unaware of crimes of this magnitude seemed impossible, and yet

he'd sworn that there was no truth whatsoever to the rumor.

Kingston sat on the sofa, a mug of coffee
at his side, and dialed Amanda's number.
This time she was quick to answer, and he
was pleased that her voice seemed normal.

"Hello, Amanda," he said softly but firmly.
"I'm calling to offer my condolences. Dr.
Chandra told me this morning, at the
hospital. I just got back home, as a matter
of fact. Are you okay?"

"I am. Yes. Thanks for asking. The truism
is undeniable, though: No matter how much
you try to prepare yourself for this kind of
news, when it happens it's as if you'd done
nothing. In a perverse way, Tristan's study
being ransacked has turned out to be a good
thing of sorts. At least it's given me something meaningful to do today."

"Is your friend, your neighbor, still staying
with you?" Kingston asked, trying not to
sound too inquisitive about the break-in so
early in the conversation. She'd raised the
matter of Tristan's study, though, and he
was wondering how he could keep her on
the subject without making it sound contrived.

"No. She had to get back to her shop."

"The police returned, I take it?"

"Yes, they did. They spent the better part

of two hours questioning me."

"Has cause of death been established?"

"No. They haven't received the coroner's postmortem report yet."

"Did they offer any theories, motives, why someone would have wanted to harm him?"

"They didn't. No answers, just questions."

"Did they ask about Tristan's line of work?"

"They did. They wanted to know everything about him: what he'd been working on, what projects and assignments, if anyone was employing him, if he was collaborating with anyone or he'd met with anyone at the house or elsewhere in recent weeks. They also wanted to know if I knew anything about his work or had been assisting him in any way. I didn't, by the way, and I wasn't helping him either."

Kingston was thinking about asking if the police had mentioned Endicott's name, when she cut in.

"The police inspector was curious about you, why you wanted to meet with Tristan and what took place at the hospital. I told him that Tristan had asked to see you and that's all I knew. Then I realized that I knew virtually nothing about you. You've never told me what you do or why you called Tristan in the first place. Are you mixed up in this somehow?"

"No, I'm not, Amanda. Let me explain why I wanted to talk to him. I'm a retired professor and occasionally —"

"You don't have to explain your background. Inspector Wheatley told me all about you, and your reputation, your 'inclination to meddle in police matters.' "

Kingston nodded to himself. That answered his earlier question.

"So why did you want to see Tristan?" she asked.

"About three weeks ago, the patriarch of a well-known Staffordshire family retained me to conduct an inquiry into a suspicious death — a murder, in fact — that had taken place on their property." He paused. "You might as well know the name of the family in question — it's Morley."

"Really? Sturminster?"

"The same. To begin with, I needed to learn, independently, all about the family, both past and present. By a stroke of luck, I found out that Tristan was a historian who, so I was told, probably knew more about the Morley family than anyone else in the county. That's why I called him and how I ended up on your doorstep. That's it, plain and simple. It turns out now that Tristan was working on a story that if published might result in a potentially devastating criminal investigation of the Morley dynasty, one that could rewrite the history books. He told me this at the hospital. He was convinced beyond doubt, it seemed, that members of the Morley family were guilty of capital crimes. I got the impression he also realized that if word got out about what he'd uncovered, the consequences could be very serious indeed. The people concerned wouldn't hesitate to take extreme measures to prevent that from happening."

"So that's why Tristan wanted to see you at the hospital?"

"It is. He must have sensed that it might be his only chance to tell me."

A lengthy pause followed, which implied that she was weighing his explanation.

"I was going to tell you all this, Amanda, but I decided it could wait, at least until after the funeral service," he said. "If there's to be one."

"I see."

"I only wish it were different, particularly piled on top of everything else. But you deserve to know the truth."

When she still didn't answer, Kingston was starting to wonder if she might be too upset to continue and want to end the conversation. He decided not to wait any longer and simply ask, point-blank, if he could pay her a visit.

"I'm returning to Staffordshire to visit my client in a couple of days," he said. "If it wouldn't be an imposition, and providing you feel well enough, of course, I'd like to spend a couple of hours with you, so we can talk this over."

"Don't you think you should be telling all this to the police?"

"I will, of course. But it's important that I talk with you first."

"What purpose would that serve? It seems that you've told me everything already."

"Not everything, Amanda."

"Look, Doctor, I'm satisfied, for now anyway, that the police are doing all they can to get to the bottom of this and, for the time being, I think it best that we wait until we have more information. You've been kind and considerate, and when this is all over, perhaps we can meet again."

"I understand. I know how difficult it must be for you right now. I respect your wishes and hope, too, that one day we can get together. Good-bye for now."

Kingston lowered the phone and stood, thinking how he could have handled the call better, not at all happy with her unfavorable decision. The one narrow avenue of investigation that he'd pinned his hopes on was now blocked, which meant that the only remaining line of inquiry was through Lord Morley. In the coming hours he must focus on how to break the news of Veitch's accusations to Morley, what to tell him and what to hold back. In an aberrant way, he was looking forward to that confrontation.

Kingston's phone call to Morley, at nine the next morning, was directed to Simon Crawford. Morley, he said, was in Paris on a business trip and would be returning on Friday, five days hence. Kingston said that he'd come across information relevant to the murder, stressing that it was important he meet with Morley as soon as possible. Crawford seemed genuinely encouraged by the news and assured Kingston that he'd pass on the message to Morley the moment he returned.

In the kitchen, with a fresh cup of tea, Kingston turned his thoughts to the next couple of days and what he would do with himself. He knew, without looking at his calendar, that he had no commitments, nothing that demanded his attention. A phone call to Andrew would doubtless elicit an invitation to lunch or an event of some sort. It usually did. Maybe he should suggest a visit to Andrew's garden at Bourne End, an overnight stay. He hadn't seen it for a long while and he really should make an effort to help Andrew shape it up before the Open Garden event. The more he thought about it, the better the idea sounded. At least the weather had taken a turn for the better. The last couple of days had been clear and sunny — but just in case, he'd check the forecast. Andrew would want to know about his trip to Stafford, too. That would be another slanging match, he knew.

His phone call was picked up by Andrew's answerphone. It was his usual succinct message, so Kingston had no idea when he might expect a call back. Having recently returned from his fishing trip, it was doubtful that Andrew had wandered far from home, he assumed.

It wasn't until six thirty that evening that the phone finally rang. Kingston was in the kitchen with a glass of Sancerre, readying dinner: salmon fish cakes. He no longer needed Jane Grigson's classic recipe; he knew it by heart. He wiped his breadcrumb-daubed hands with a cloth, went into the living room, and picked up the phone.

"Hello, Andrew," he said, trying to sound jocular.

"This isn't Andrew." A long pause followed. "Is this Dr. Kingston?" It was a woman's voice. Then he realized. It was Amanda.

"Amanda. I didn't expect to hear from you so soon."

"I'm calling to say I've changed my mind."

Her lackluster voice was the same one he remembered from the day they'd first met. "In what way?"

"I've been thinking a lot about what you told me yesterday. I was up all night and I've thought of little else since. That's not the only reason, though. I got a call this morning from Inspector Wheatley — the results of the postmortem, the toxicology tests. The police are convinced now that Tristan was poisoned intentionally."

"I'm sorry to hear that. Did they say what kind of poison?"

"Yes. It was aconite."

"Aconite?"

"Yes. I wrote it down. I've since looked it up. It comes from a plant."

"I know. *Aconitum.* It's beautiful and grows all over the world, but it's also one of the deadliest, if not *the* deadliest, plants."

"This changes everything. All along, I'd been hoping that it was an accident or something else entirely. Now this. It keeps going from bad to worse and I no longer know what to think or where to turn."

They spoke for another five minutes and it was agreed that Kingston would return to Staffordshire the next day to talk things over and attempt to make sense out of Tristan's untimely and highly suspicious death. When he'd suggested conducting a thorough search of the house and outbuildings, looking for anything the burglars or police might have missed that might reveal more about Tristan's research, she'd raised no objection. Staying overnight was no problem, she'd said. She also added that Tristan kept a well-stocked wine cellar, which was music to Kingston's ears. When the conversation ended, he was left with the impression that she was now willing to help however she could to find her brother's killer.

TEN

Off the top of his head, Kingston knew that *Aconitum* — also known as monkshood, from its hood-shaped blossoms — was a common plant that grew in the wild and was used extensively in horticulture for its bright blue flowers that, in many ways, resembled delphinium. Worldwide, there were over two hundred species of the genus, most, but not all, blue, and every part of the plant was poisonous. The poison is from the toxic alkaloid aconitine, which is concentrated mainly in the root. Kingston remembered reading that as little as 2 mg of aconitine could cause death in an adult male within four hours, and that one-fiftieth of a grain can kill a sparrow in seconds. It had always amazed him to see it growing willy-nilly in gardens all over Britain. Most nurseries nowadays caution gardeners about its toxicity and advise that it not be grown in areas where children might be present and to keep it in the background of borders. Even handling the plant improperly can cause poisoning.

He wondered how the aconitine had been administered to Tristan. He went into his small office and woke up his Mac. Within minutes he had more information on aconitine than he could have imagined. He found that in some cases of premeditated poisonings, a tincture of aconitine — an alcoholic extract — had been mixed into a drink, usually whisky or other strong liquor, making the taste of the poison unnoticeable. This raised another question. If Tristan was reputed to be a recluse, then the odds that he was poisoned at home were far greater. So how had someone slipped him the drink or poisoned his food? And who?

Another five minutes on the Web and he'd read all he wanted to know. It was timely, because the cordless phone next to him started ringing. He picked it up, responding with a simple "Hello."

"Dr. Kingston?"

Kingston recognized the slight northern accent. "This is he."

"Inspector Wheatley. I'm calling concerning the recent death of Tristan Veitch. You're still working for Lord Morley, I take it?"

"I am."

"I'm sure that by now Amanda Veitch has told you that we've interviewed her both concerning her brother's death and the break-in and burglary at their house."

"She has, yes."

"She tells us that four days ago you contacted her brother about a project you were working on, and subsequently he left you a phone message requesting you to meet him at their house. Is that correct, so far?"

"It is. Except that the meeting never took place. By that time he'd been taken to the hospital."

"Quite. After that, at his request, you visited him in Stafford Memorial."

"I did."

"By rights, because you're a material witness in a criminal proceeding, I should have you come in for a formal interview. But for reasons of expediency, and to save you a long trip, I decided to forgo the formality and question you on the phone. I must inform you that our conversation is being recorded, of course."

"I appreciate the special treatment, Inspector. I'm happy to cooperate."

"Excuse me a moment, Doctor."

Kingston waited while the inspector conferred with someone in the background. In a few seconds, he was back. "I know it was you who first called him, but I want to get this straight. It turned out that he was glad that you'd called and wanted to talk to you anyway. Quite a coincidence, I'd say. Is this pretty much what happened?"

"Yes, it is."

"On this phone message, did Mr. Veitch tell you why he wanted to see you?"

"It was all rather vague. As you know, he was a historian and was working on a story about the history of Sturminster and the Morleys. It seemed he'd uncovered some sordid criminal acts that had taken place in the eighteenth century. It involved the Morley family at the time."

"Was he aware that you were conducting

an inquiry for Morley, or that you'd been involved in investigative work before?"

"He said he knew of my reputation, that's all."

"Tell me what happened when you arrived for the appointment."

"Very little. His sister, Amanda, met me at the door. She told me that she was Tristan's sister and that he'd just been taken to the hospital. I apologized for arriving at such a bad moment, gave her my card, and left. It all happened in a couple of minutes."

"Had she been expecting you?"

"Yes. Her brother had told her I was coming."

"What was her state of mind at the time?"

"She was visibly upset. Genuinely so, I'd say."

"Did she say why he'd been hospitalized?"

"No. She didn't."

"How did you manage to visit Tristan Veitch in critical care at the hospital, alone?"

Kingston had to think for a moment. "The morning after I met Amanda Veitch, she called me at home saying that her brother was in critical care and wanted to see me. The doctor had told her that Tristan didn't have too long to live, and if I still wanted to see him, I'd best leave right away. I met her at Stafford Memorial later that morning and was able to spend about ten minutes with Veitch."

"She said you returned to the hospital the next day."

"That's correct. After I'd seen Veitch that day, I was planning to go back home, but a bad storm came in and I decided to stay overnight in Stafford instead of driving back down."

"To London?"

"Right."

"Where did you stay?"

"The James Hotel, in Lichfield." Kingston realized by now that the reason for the cross-examination was that the inspector was making sure that Kingston's version of events agreed with whatever Amanda had told him.

Wheatley had not finished. "So why did you return to the hospital?"

"Amanda asked me to see Tristan in her stead."

"When was that?"

"The morning before I left the hotel to return home."

"About what time?"

"About, let me see . . . about nine o'clock."

"She called you?"

"No, I called her. She'd been trying to

reach me at home. She didn't know that I'd stayed in Stafford overnight and said she'd been calling to tell me the house had been ransacked and that she'd left a message on my machine. She asked me if I would visit Tristan in her place that morning. She was conscience stricken, but for obvious reasons couldn't or didn't want to leave the house. She asked me to tell Tristan that she would try to see him later that day."

"So when you finally got home, was there a message from her on your phone machine?"

Kingston was beginning to realize that this was no provincial copper he was talking to. "There was, yes," he replied. "The date and time recorded verified what she'd said."

"Good. Couple more questions and that's it — for now, anyway."

"Fine," said Kingston.

"When you saw Veitch at the hospital, what did you two talk about? Did he tell you anything about his work, anything that might suggest that he knew someone would want to send some kind of message — or worse?"

Kingston had to think quickly. This was the question he'd hoped wouldn't be asked.

"He was in bad shape. I could tell that trying to say even a few words was stressful for him. He told me that he was working on a book. I got the impression that it was an opus of sorts, a big deal. Thinking about it, it made sense because he was probably more accustomed to writing articles for the local paper, historical societies, and such."

"What was the book about? Did he tell you?"

"Somewhat. It was to be a definitive history of Staffordshire, with the focus on people who had contributed to its development and progress throughout the centuries, as opposed to the usual facts and figures, that is."

"Not exactly Ian Rankin, though?"

"Hardly."

"Anything more?"

Kingston knew that if he tried to gloss over what Veitch had told him he could have a lot of explaining to do later and could even end up facing a charge of withholding evidence in a homicide case. He was walking a thin line and he knew it.

"There was, actually," Kingston said at length. "I found it interesting, for obvious reasons. As I mentioned earlier, he said that he'd stumbled on information related to Sturminster that was at odds with what has been recorded historically. It dealt with what he called the missing money legend, some nefarious activities that supposedly took place back in the 1700s. If his research were to be proved correct, he said it would rewrite the history books. When the names of the people implicated were made public, and the staggering amount of money involved was revealed, the repercussions would be beyond belief. Those were his exact words, as far as I recall."

"If he was referring to the legendary Morley family feud over the admiral's missing money, that's hardly new information. Every county in England has its share of questionable history and legends, and ours is no exception. He wouldn't be the first by a long chalk to suspect that there's a small fortune buried somewhere on Sturminster's land."

"I got the impression that it was far more than 'suspect.' He was a historian, after all, and as such he would know of every legend, myth, and fable passed down through the ages or in the books."

"Even if what he said is true, Doctor, with all of his manuscripts, papers, and notes, and his computer gone, it's doubtful that we'll ever know for sure what he'd found out. All I know is that someone poisoned Tristan Veitch, and people don't usually do that unless there's a very compelling reason.

Like I said before, I'd appreciate it if you'd keep me in the loop on new information you run across. I'm aware of your reputation and I'm sure that, going forward, we can work together on an amicable basis. I'm sure Lord Morley would want it that way."

They exchanged phone numbers and e-mail addresses, and the conversation ended on a cordial note.

Kingston felt that he'd acquitted himself quite well. He certainly hadn't dodged any questions. He'd made no mention of the fact that Veitch had intimated that he knew something about Endicott's murder or that he had more or less confirmed that codes of some kind were involved in his investigation. In both instances Veitch's admissions had been vague, to say the least. In any case, if he had told the inspector, it would have opened a floodgate of questions for which there were no factual answers. Despite all that, he had a nagging suspicion that the real reason for Wheatley's call was to substantiate Amanda's version of what had happened. Was she considered a credible suspect in her brother's death?

ELEVEN

Under a Wedgwood-blue sky, a warm still-ness all around, and with the distant chimes of church bells faint on Kingston's ear, the Victorian house at Abbot's Broomfield presented a much more cheering welcome than on his first visit. Even the weathered brick appeared richer and warmer. It was now Amanda's house, or so it would seem, and he hoped, as he approached the front door just before noon, that she hadn't had a change of heart since their phone call, that she really would hold to her promise. As an admittedly indulgent afterthought, he was also curious to inspect Tristan's wine cellar. Heeding her offer, he'd packed a small overnight bag.

Amanda greeted him with the sunniest smile he'd seen from her and ushered him into the living room. She was more self-assured and at ease than before. As when they'd met at the hospital, she was dressed stylishly, this time in a dark gray twinset that looked like cashmere, and tan chinos. With a single strand of iconic pearls at her neck and her hair tied back, Kingston was thinking that she could pass as the old Amanda's winsome twin sister.

The room was deceptively large, contradicting the house's outward appearance. It had a low-beamed ceiling and walls painted an ecru color with shiny white trim. The furniture, predominantly European antiques, was offset by an eclectic mix of furnishings collected from various travels around the world, or so it appeared, though Kingston couldn't imagine either of them as world travelers. Two walls were taken up with bookcases and a third had wide French doors that led to the garden. When he'd arrived and Amanda was getting coffee, he'd glanced outside and had been impressed that the garden, like the room, was considerably larger than he'd expected, well planted and clearly well cared for. He would ask her for a tour later.

With coffee, served in Blue Willow pattern china cups, they sat on either side of a glass-topped coffee table. This required that Kingston stretch out his legs to one side. After an exchange of pleasantries and the obligatory chat about the weather, the conversation quickly turned to the harrowing events of the past days. Kingston knew that rehashing it all was as much cathartic as anything else, and he doubted that it would shed any new light on the case. He was more interested in asking her about Tristan, trying to find out more about him and taking a look at the study and other parts of the house, where Tristan might have hidden some of his work material or backup data. Not to mention the wine cellar. He must be patient, he knew.

They talked for the best part of an hour. To begin, she'd listened silently and with no emotion to Kingston's account of his conversation with her brother at the hospital. In turn, she'd told him what little she knew about the project that he'd been working on, his daily routine, and what he did when he wasn't working. Most of his contact work was done by phone or e-mail, she said. Rarely did anyone visit him personally. That's why she'd been mildly surprised when he'd told her that Kingston was coming to see him. In answer to an obvious question from Kingston, she maintained that, as far as she knew, Tristan hadn't been involved in any arguments or disagreements, or had had any money problems of late. And she would certainly have known if he had, she added. Soon, they got into the poisoning issue. Right off, she swore that she'd never heard of aconite until Dr. Chandra had mentioned it. She'd also lain awake at night, she said, racking her brain as to who could have committed such a monstrous act. Tristan had few acquaintances and even fewer friends, and she'd eliminated, as extremely unlikely suspects, other people who had been at the house in recent weeks. These included their gardener, a cleaning woman who came in every other week, the meter man, the postman — a regular for at least five years — and a plumber who'd done work for them in the past. As far as outside contacts were concerned, there were virtually none. In answer to Kingston's questions, she said that he hardly ever ate out and, on the occasions he did, it was always with her. There were two pubs within walking distance, but he frequented neither of them. Though he collected wine, he wouldn't be called a drinker by any stretch of the imagination. And he didn't belong to any clubs or special interest groups. Despite all this, she was firmly convinced that the poison was administered somewhere other than their home.

That subject exhausted for the time being, Kingston proceeded to tell her what he'd read about aconite. The symptoms of ingesting aconite, he said, become evident quickly; the initial signs were gastrointestinal, which included nausea and vomiting, which would suggest that the poisoning had taken place within the last week. The only other possibility he could think of was that the poisoning had been carried out over a longer period of time, using much smaller doses.

As she answered his questions, he watched surreptitiously for slight signs that could suggest that she was not being truthful or was attempting to avoid a direct answer. Nothing she said, however, gave him reason to suspect so. If anything, she appeared relaxed and much more confident than at any other time since they'd first met. As they talked, Kingston found his mind wandering off in another direction. He was thinking ahead, wondering if there were other ways Amanda could help in his investigation. The thought was self-serving, but it also offered a dividend that he hadn't overlooked: Having Amanda as a sort of partner in crime would increase the chance that their friendship would continue, at least for a while, anyway. As he was observing her, pondering the thought, a timer went off in a nearby room.

The buzz brought him back to his senses. A voice inside him was saying, *Don't start something you know you won't finish.*

Amanda rose, announcing matter-of-factly that lunch would be ready in about five minutes. For Kingston this was an unexpected surprise. She also asked if he would like to stay overnight, saying that it was no bother for her. Pleased despite himself that she'd raised the subject, he agreed, saying that he'd brought his overnight bag, just in case.

The perfectly poached quenelles with a tarragon cream sauce that arrived on the table minutes later, with no fanfare or fuss, were accompanied by a bottle of chilled Vouvray, leaving him to wonder where she'd learned to cook so well and if she'd practiced all these years on Tristan. He realized more and more that his first impression of her on that solemn first day couldn't have been more off target.

Though she'd never asked about his personal life, Kingston found himself talking freely about his teaching days in Edinburgh, the loss of his wife, and the successful career of his daughter. Whether or not it was the wine, she had managed to put aside the misery and perplexities of the last few days, surprising Kingston by raising personal matters of finance, the house, and the quandary she faced now that Tristan was gone.

"It's a lovely house," said Kingston, wanting to ask questions but containing his natural curiosity.

She nodded. "Growing up here, I've

always adored it, and living here over the past few years I've grown to appreciate it even more. It holds so many fond memories, but now, of course, those I'm sure will be overshadowed forever."

"You'll stay for a while, though, won't you?"

"Absolutely. It's far too early to make that kind of decision. Good thing is that I can take my time. I doubt that I'll be going back to work now."

"What was your occupation?"

"Special education — I was a teacher."

"For students with learning disabilities?"

She nodded. "Behavioral, physical, developmental."

"I know how demanding teaching can be, let alone with special-needs children."

She paused as if lost in the past. "When Mum died, Tristan and I thought seriously about selling the house, but neither of us fancied the idea of living alone anymore and he was the one who suggested we share it. In the beginning we had our ups and downs, but we soon developed our own living patterns, as it were, and I must say it turned out to be both an agreeable and a practical arrangement."

"You were never married, then?"

"Yes, I was, but my husband died a week

after our third anniversary. Killed in a motorway accident."

"I'm sorry," he said. "We share something in common."

She nodded and looked away briefly but said nothing.

"What about the garden?"

She gave a half smile. "You mean do I have a green thumb?"

"Well, it is quite large and it's going to take up a lot of your time."

"I'll hire a gardener, I guess. I'm not going to let it run down, if that's what you mean."

She was talking about how Tristan took care of the flowers while the kitchen garden was her territory, when she suddenly changed the subject. "Would you like to take a look at Tristan's study?" she asked.

"I would. Yes."

"Do you really expect to find anything now, after the police have been through it with a fine-tooth comb?"

He shrugged. "It's a long shot, I know, but having done a lot of research and writing in my time, I know that many people keep duplicate copies of important papers — these days, electronic backup files. It may be wishful thinking, but I'm just banking on Tristan having done the same." He paused, scratching his forehead. "It's not so much a question of whether he did or didn't, really. The all-important question is: Between the burglars and the police, did they leave anything for us to find?"

Amanda nodded over her shoulder toward a door behind them. "His study is down the hall, last room on the right. You go ahead. I have things to do in the kitchen and phone calls to return, so take your time."

Kingston thanked her and headed down the hall.

The room was roughly twelve feet by twenty feet. On the wall facing him, a small pair of French doors led to the kitchen garden: a series of raised beds filled with a goodly selection of vegetables and herbs. The wall on his left was floor-to-ceiling shelving, filled to the gunnels with books of all kinds. The rest of the room was a hodge-podge of furniture: side-by-side oak filing cabinets, a smallish table piled high with books and papers, a glass-front bookcase, and a large leather-topped desk whose surface was mostly empty save for a Cornishware jar filled with pencils and pens, three framed photos, a coiled power cord, a USB cable, and a mouse pad — vestigial evidence of Tristan's computer. He reminded himself to ask Amanda what make it was. It was immaterial, he concluded. Behind the desk, a small table held an HP all-in-one printer and a modem. If Tristan had used an external hard drive, it too was gone, and there were no CDs to be seen either. He turned his attention to the books. Not surprisingly, many were historical, not only local but also national and histories of world countries. The remainder was an assortment of biographies, reference, DIY, and gardening books. Fictional works were few, only older works or classics. Remembering that Amanda had said that "books were strewn all over the place," he decided it was unnecessary to take all the books out to see if Tristan had hidden anything behind them. If any had been left on the shelves, the police would have done that, he assumed.

He picked up one of the photos. It was of Amanda, in her twenties, he guessed. By the looks of the staging, it had been taken in a photo studio. Striking a modellike pose, in a simple black dress and a natural smile, she looked exceptionally beautiful. The second photo pictured a fortyish man standing proudly alongside a blue vintage car. Was it Tristan? Kingston wondered. Not enough of the car showed for Kingston to determine what make or model, but what little showed of the bonnet ornament appeared to be an eagle or bird of some kind with spread wings. The last photo was of two children who could have been twin girls about age eight, by Kingston's naïve guesswork. Glancing around the room, he suddenly realized what was missing. There were no stacks of papers, folders, and the like anywhere, not even a memo or scratch pad. He pulled open the closest file-cabinet drawer. It contained perhaps a dozen hanging folders. A quick glance at the tabs revealed that they were all personal or house related: insurance, maintenance, garden expenses, taxes, pension, and so on. Nothing work related, which came as no surprise. A quick assessment of the remaining file drawers had similar results. Two had been cleaned out entirely.

Kingston went to the other side of the desk and pulled open the top center drawer. Inside, it looked like every other top drawer he'd ever seen: a jumble of paper clips, more pens and pencils, computer cables tied with rubber bands, an open roll of Polo mints, cough drops, what appeared to be a gold cigarette lighter, and other odds and ends. Five minutes more, rummaging through more drawers and two small cupboards, Kingston reluctantly concluded that nothing of interest remained in Tristan's study, not as far as his investigation was concerned, that is.

When he entered the kitchen, Amanda looked up from writing. "Find anything?" she asked.

He shook his head. "No. Between the burglars and the police, they certainly did a thorough job."

"I don't think the police found much. I didn't see them hauling any boxes out. At least they left the few pictures."

"A nice one of you."

"Thank you. I had it taken for Mum and Dad's anniversary. It was supposed to be the two of us, but Tristan got a bee sting in the garden a few days before the photo was to be taken and his face swelled up."

"That's a shame. Was that Tristan in the photo with the old car?"

"No. It was a friend of his. I forget his name."

"I have a thing for old cars. Do you know what it was?"

"I really don't know. It was beautiful. A lot older than your nice car, though."

Kingston nodded. "Are there any other places in the house where he might have stored papers, files, electronic storage devices?"

She smiled and shook her head. "Not

really. In any case, I wouldn't know an electronic storage device if it bit me." She put aside her pen and notepad and stood. "Would you like to see the garden?" she asked.

"I would, very much."

He followed her through the well-equipped kitchen into a tiled-floor mud-room, which doubled as a pantry. They passed a row of coats, scarves, and odds and ends hanging from wooden pegs on the wall, then through a Dutch door that led to the garden.

As soon as they crossed the threshold, an overpowering fragrance stopped Kingston in his tracks. He didn't need to look around to locate the florescent source. Symmetrical beds, cut out of a lawn half the size of a football field, were stuffed with a confection of mixed perennials in muted shades of mauve, lavender, and pink. Crowning the rectangular pools of color, tumbles of white shrub roses — Iceberg, he guessed — looked like clumps of snow. The garden was enclosed on his left and right by high hedges of yew and holly, underplanted with what appeared to be Nepeta and English lavender. A flagstone path traced the hedge around the perimeter. The garden was contained at the far end by a ten-foot-high wall of honey-colored brick, smothered with a marriage of climbing roses and clematis. The harmonious scene was embellished with several Chippendale-design teak benches, old garden ornaments and statuary and — the icing on the cake — a circular reflecting pool with a central fountain. He turned to Amanda. "Tristan did all this?"

She nodded. "Most of it. Yes."

Kingston smiled. "The Constant Gardener?"

She nodded. "An apt description. We have a gardener who comes in to help, one day a week now, but Tristan created the garden many years ago and has maintained it all this time, up until a year ago when he started to get back problems. It's going to be expensive to keep it up, though."

"If I lived closer, I would offer a hand."

"I'm sure I'll work something out," she said, as they started their walkabout.

After lingering in the garden for a half hour, Amanda suggested that they return to the house. There were things to do in the kitchen and his room that required her attention.

As they passed through the mudroom, Kingston's shoulder brushed against the rack of coats and something fell to the floor.

He stooped and picked it up. It was a dog collar. Two leashes dangled from the next peg. "You have a dog?" he asked.

Amanda stopped and turned. "We did. A Jack Russell. Winston died about a year ago. I kept his collar and leashes, thinking that one day we'd get another dog, but that never happened. I may reconsider that now, though."

"A dog around the house would be good in a lot of ways."

She nodded. "Tristan and Winston were practically inseparable, and though he never said it outright, I don't think he ever really wanted another dog to take Winston's place."

Kingston hadn't been listening closely to what Amanda was saying, because the unusual ID tag on the collar had caught his attention. Not more than an inch long, it was enclosed in a clear plastic case. On it was printed a logo, TOP TAG PET ID, and above that, *Insert into USB Port.* Around the center of the plastic case were several nicks and scratches.

"Well, I'll be damned," he muttered.

Amanda frowned. "What is it?"

"I've never seen a pet tag like this before. It's a miniature flash drive. It copies and stores information from a computer. In this case, it's Winston's CV, I assume?"

"Oh, that thing. Tristan saw it advertised in a magazine and thought it was a brilliant idea. He was always into gadgets and the latest electronic gizmos. I prefer the old-fashioned metal tags myself."

"These thing can hold a lot of information, though."

"That's what he said."

"Do you mind if I borrow it?"

"Be my guest, though I find it hard to believe you're interested in Winston's vaccination record."

He smiled. "I'm not. I just want to check it out, that's all. I'll make sure you get it back."

By now, Kingston had talked himself into believing that the flash drive could well have been Tristan's secret hiding place to back up his incendiary files. With Tristan's computer and Amanda's laptop gone, he had no way of finding out if he was right. If there was any way of leaving right now without appearing heedless and ungracious, he would take it, but that was out of the question. He had no choice but to wait until he returned home to open it.

Around five in the afternoon, Amanda disappeared without explanation, reappearing several minutes later carrying a bottle of wine, two wineglasses, and a corkscrew. "Here," she said, placing them on the coffee table, close to Kingston. "I thought we'd have this with supper tonight. I think it'll go with what I'm throwing together." She hesitated, brushing fingers across her forehead. "I always left that decision with Tristan, of course. Anyway," she said, starting to leave again, "if you need me for anything, I'll be in the kitchen for about a half hour. In the meantime you might want to open that — to see if it's still okay," she added with an ingenuous smile, leaving the room.

Kingston picked up the bottle and studied it. Now he knew why she'd questioned its being "okay." It was a 1978 Gevrey-Chambertin Burgundy.

The rest of his stay with Amanda was far more pleasant than he'd anticipated. The wine cellar hadn't disappointed either. Kingston had figured that Tristan's collection was close to a thousand bottles, many dating back to the 1980s and quite a few Bordeaux and Burgundy reds going back as far as the 1950s.

Considering all she'd been through in the preceding several days and the fact that they'd known each other for such a short time, there wasn't a single awkward moment between them and no moments where cracks had showed in her self-control in holding back the anguish and sorrow that must surely be roiling close to the surface of her thoughts. On top of that, she'd gone to the trouble to cook two meals for him. How many women who had just lost a loved one would even consider doing that? he marveled. Perhaps it was also a way to help her forget, even if only for a brief time. He decided that she'd either been putting up a brave front or wasn't self-pitying. He preferred to believe the latter. What was even more encouraging — though she hadn't said it in so many words — was that from now on she was willing to help him in whatever way she could to track down those responsible for her brother's death.

TWELVE

Shortly before noon the following day, Kingston arrived back at his flat, impatient to see what was on Winston's tag. It was a long shot, he knew, but if Tristan was as much a geek as Amanda believed he was — given the scratches on the plastic casing suggesting that it had been opened a number of times — there was an outside chance that he'd used the tag to store additional information, if that were feasible. After all, once the dog's data were entered, there would seem little need to open it frequently.

Kingston inserted the Pet Tag's USB connector into one of the ports on his Mac. In seconds a message appeared on the screen. Atop a page of computer hieroglyphics, punctuated with the word *Microsoft,* were the words THIS PROGRAM CANNOT BE RUN ON DOS. He had no idea what it meant in technical terms but figured that the Pet Tag inventors had decided arbitrarily either to market it to Windows users only, or had conducted a focus-group study, concluding that dog-loving Mac owners were not worthy of such innovative technology. There was a simple answer, though: Andrew. As former owner of an IT company, he'd be able to sort it out. Kingston picked up the phone.

Andrew, being Andrew, seized on Kingston's request as another opportunity to have lunch. This suited Kingston because it was as good a time as any for him to tell Andrew everything that had happened during his time in Stafford. Andrew's response had been as expected: exasperation followed by resignation. Three hours later, the two arrived back at Kingston's flat where Andrew opened his laptop and inserted the Pet Tag.

"Well, we know it works," said Andrew. A window had appeared on the screen showing a columnar template with Winston's name and contact information. Scrolling down revealed more spaces showing his medical records, food and dietary requirements, vet and grooming information, and more.

"Let's see what else is on here," he said, fingers jiggling on the touch pad.

Seconds later, the screen was filled with dog photos.

"Good grief," said Kingston, "it's even got Winston's holiday pictures, by the looks of it."

For a few moments they continued to view the on-screen information in silence.

Kingston wanted to move on, to find out what else the tag contained, but he bit his tongue and watched Andrew tinker with the program and mutter to himself, technical jargon mostly. After a minute of this, Andrew glanced at Kingston. "It looks as though you may be partly right," he said, going back to the touch pad. "I think it's possible to add text copy into the program." A few wordless seconds passed. "Even better," said Andrew. "Not only that, it can be done so that it's hidden. Unless you know where to look for it, it can't be seen by anyone nosing around your pet's bio. Clever."

"Is there anything hidden on this one?" Kingston asked, his hopes building.

"Let's see."

Kingston sat on pins and needles while Andrew tapped away at the keyboard with impressive speed and dexterity.

He stopped suddenly and rolled his chair back. "Voilà!" he said with a grin.

Kingston moved closer to the screen. His heart skipped a beat. He was looking at a page of single-spaced text. Even at a glance he could tell that it was what he'd been hoping for: details of Veitch's research. Andrew scrolled down through page after page of typed and scanned handwritten notes.

"This page deals with the construction of the monuments," Kingston said.

Andrew scrolled some more.

"Correspondence between the admiral and his brother, by the looks of it."

Andrew kept scrolling.

"Stop there," said Kingston. "This is a letter from the architect, Seward, stating how many men he plans to hire to build one of the monuments. Amazing."

Andrew was grinning as he watched Kingston, whose eyes were glued to the screen. "I have to give you credit, your idea wasn't as nutty as I thought," he said.

"Sometimes you get lucky," said Kingston, leaning back.

Andrew sighed. "If I'd been smart, I'd have let you believe that it stored only the dog's ID. If nothing else, it might have given you pause to at least reconsider aborting this obsessive and risky hobby of yours."

Kingston ignored both the unintentional pun and the admonishment, and thanked Andrew for his effort. After printing the entire thirty-plus pages of Veitch's notes and copying them onto a CD, Andrew departed, but not before reminding Kingston once more of his commitment to attend Andrew's Open Garden at Bourne End.

For the next three hours, Kingston immersed himself in reading, organizing, and trying to piece together a coherent picture of what perhaps had led Veitch to reach his startling conclusions. He was encouraged initially by the volume of information but soon discovered that it was merely an accumulation of disparate data, facts, and observations assembled from various sources. None of it was chronological or in any particular priority. It was as if it had been compiled over a lengthy period: a sporadic scribbling of thoughts, speculative ideas, place-names, biographical references, Web sites, anything and everything that Veitch thought relevant about the Morley family from its beginnings in the early eighteenth century.

Despite several handwritten references to the "cover-up" and the "money trail," there was no hard evidence or documentation, however tenuous, to substantiate financial malfeasance of any kind. Neither was there any evidence of criminal intent by any Morley, save for a reference to the perpetual rumor alleging grand theft by Samuel Morley: that while his legendary admiral brother James was making history and amassing a huge fortune with his great sea victories of the Seven Years' War, Samuel was secretly salting away, for his own purposes, a goodly share of the moneys contributed by James, funds intended exclusively for the expansion of Sturminster. One entry alluded to allegations that much of that money was unaccounted for and likely hidden somewhere on the estate by Samuel Morley. Conspicuously absent was mention of the coded message that Veitch had given a nod to, or anything whatsoever to suggest that he had started, was in the middle of, or had completed a book or full-length treatise on the supposed exposé. This led Kingston to believe that if Veitch *had* started to write the story, he must have considered it either insufficiently developed or too premature to warrant mention when the notes were compiled. It also struck Kingston as odd in another way: If Veitch had intended all along to use the exposé for profit, a book would be the logical way to go. Why hadn't he mentioned it?

Nearing the end of the document, Kingston was becoming reconciled to the idea that it wouldn't provide anything like the evidence he'd hoped for: nothing even close to the incriminating information to which Veitch had alluded with such conviction on his deathbed. For all Kingston knew, he might have stored these notes on the Pet Tag months or years ago. It might have been an experiment that he'd later abandoned because of insufficient information or hard evidence. The more he thought on it, anything was possible.

It wasn't until page twenty-three that something incongruous caught his attention. It was at the end of a two-page section describing the succession of Morleys over the years. Scrawled in barely decipherable handwriting was a list of a dozen and a half names — first and last — some crossed out, including a few with the Morley surname.

The list offered no clues as to the identity of the people, if they were living or dead, how they might be connected — if they were — or why Veitch had singled them out and chosen to include them in the first place. One name jumped out at him: Julian Heywood. Could it be the same Julian he'd met at Sturminster, with Simon Crawford? Kingston remembered Crawford saying that the young man was Francis Morley's nephew, but that didn't mean they shared the same surname. He leaned back and considered the implication. If they were one and the same, it didn't necessarily mean that some of the names on the list couldn't be from past generations. But what if all of them were alive and well today? That would certainly work in Kingston's favor.

While it was hardly a game changer, at least it was something tangible to go on. It could also have bearing on his meeting with Lord Morley. On top of dropping the bombshell about Veitch's allegations, he must now divulge this new information. While it was only a list of names, Veitch must have had good reason for noting them. Perhaps Morley might have some thoughts on the matter. How many of them would he be able to identify? Kingston wondered.

Following the family history pages and the

list of names, Kingston was perplexed to find five pages devoted to biographical notes of several notable persons living when Samuel Morley was developing Sturminster. Highlighted were Sir Robert Walpole, described as Britain's first prime minister; his son Horace Walpole, member of Parliament, playwright, and novelist; Thomas Gray, one of the most important poets of the eighteenth century; and a passing reference to the architect Matthew Seward. Kingston knew a little about the first three but not Seward, though the name sounded familiar. Then he remembered where he'd heard it. Crawford had said that it was Matthew Seward who had designed the monuments at Sturminster. Why Veitch had thought it significant to mention these men in his notes puzzled him. He read the first page about the life of Robert Walpole and, finding it dull, he decided to read the rest of the notes in the morning.

He put the pages aside and thought about his upcoming meeting with Lord Morley. According to Crawford, Morley was returning from his trip the day after tomorrow, so Kingston could expect a call soon. He poured himself a Macallan with a splash of water and reflected on Veitch's words at the hospital. If everything he'd said was true, casting a net in the murky waters of the Morley family could bring interesting things to the surface, even if not fish of the predatory kind. Forearmed with this potentially explosive information, his meeting with Morley was going to assume an entirely different tone. It would be illuminating to see how he would respond to Veitch's accusations, true or not. On top of that, it would be interesting to observe his reaction when presented with Veitch's list of names and told that it was Kingston's plan to interview if not all, most of those on the list who were still alive.

Kingston was up with the dawn chorus of birdsong on Thursday. Chelsea was obviously nothing like the English countryside in that respect, but Cadogan Square's plentiful greenery offered refuge to a sizable population of songsters. In addition to the ubiquitous blackbirds and sparrows, he'd spotted a growing number of gabbling starlings, finches, linnets, and the occasional house martin. Somewhere he'd read that in recent years the number of birds in and around London had increased. That rare tidbit of environmental news had pleased him no end. As a scientist, he was all for saving the planet but was beginning to tire

of the incessant drumbeat of climate change
and end-of-the-world hysteria.

Having been gone, on and off, for the better part of a week, chores needed tending to
and shopping had to be done. The refrigera-
tor shelves had empty spaces that he hadn't
seen for weeks, he was out of milk and
bread, and his hall-closet wine cellar was
getting low on reds. Over breakfast he spent
a half hour trying to finish the *Times* crossword, with middling success. Most of that
time was spent on one clue that he finally
realized was a devilishly concealed anagram.
The clue was: *He has no plans to purchase
my pub and leisure complex.* The jumbled
(complex) twelve letters of *my pub* and *leisure,* when rearranged, provided the answer:
impulse buyer.

Putting the puzzle aside, he took another
look at the five pages of Veitch's notes on
influential eighteenth-century men to determine whether anything further could be
read into them or figure out why Veitch had
included them.

Rereading the section on Robert Walpole,
it looked as if Veitch had copied it from a
Web site — probably had, Kingston concluded. The last time he'd read anything
related to that period in Britain's history
was when he was in gray-flannel shorts

behind a desk with an inkwell and stained fingers. It did remind him, however, of one worthless tidbit that he'd learned about the man when in college: Walpole was partial to Bordeaux wines, in particular Lafite and Margaux, which he ordered direct from the chateaux in France in sixty-three-gallon casks known as hogsheads.

The passage started with Walpole's early life and career when, in 1702, he entered politics. In the years to follow, he was appointed secretary of war and, later, treasurer of the Royal Navy. Kingston stopped, jotted down this last piece of information, and continued.

Soon thereafter, Walpole was convicted falsely of corruption and spent several months in the Tower of London. After his release, he served sequentially as paymaster, first lord of the treasury, and chancellor of the exchequer. Nearing the height of his power, he was called upon to salvage the financial wreckage resulting from the South Sea Bubble — the collapse of the stock market manipulation that eventually ruined many British investors.

Before continuing, Kingston reflected briefly on what he'd just read. Walpole had been mentioned more than once in Oxbridge-Bell's tome, as had Matthew

Seward — reminding him that while he'd been engrossed with the incidents of the past several days, he'd forgotten all about the book. He made a mental note to finish and return it when he met Morley. But why had Veitch included such textbook historical facts on Walpole? The only connection Kingston could make, a marginal one, was that he had served twice in governmental positions of power, including that of treasurer of the navy. Had he and Admiral James Morley been friends? From memory, Kingston recalled that Morley had started his naval career in 1715, or thereabouts, so it was possible chronologically. If not close friends, they would certainly have known each other. Also, as chancellor of the exchequer, Walpole would have controlled the purse strings and must have wielded considerable influence as to how the spoils of war were apportioned. Kingston tapped his pencil on the table and looked across the room. Then Veitch's words came to mind: "Follow the money." Was this why he'd researched Walpole? Kingston wondered.

He returned to the papers to learn what had piqued Veitch's interest in the bio of Walpole's son Horace. Here Kingston was on more familiar ground, having once read a lengthy article that described Horace Walpole's checkered life as a dilettante and man of letters, and his brief career in politics. He read on, skipping parts that he felt were extraneous.

Horace was born in 1717. At ten, he entered Eton College, the six-centuries-old independent public seat of learning for boys, once referred to as "the most famous public school in the world." From Eton he went on to King's College, Cambridge. After university, he embarked on the grand tour of the Continent with his friend poet Thomas Gray, whom he had met at Eton. Immersing themselves in the social life, they traveled extensively throughout Europe. Like many peripatetic young men at the time, Walpole was smitten with the ancient culture and archaeological sites of Rome and the ruins in Greece. About this time, he also started to develop an interest in early Greek and Roman forms of secret writings and early cipher devices now known as cryptography, from the Greek *kryptos,* meaning hidden or secret. Kingston stopped reading and stared into middle space. At last a reference to cryptography — albeit flimsy — but what did it mean? Reminded again that Veitch could have compiled the notes a long while ago, all Kingston could extrapolate from the mention was the possibility that Veitch could have later obtained further evidence to circumstantiate that Horace Walpole had been brought in to decipher the code on the Arcadian monument and that it did, indeed, have something to do with the age-old legend of Sturminster and Endicott's murder as well. After clearing his muddled mind for a moment, Kingston went back to reading.

Returning to London in 1741, Walpole embarked on a career in politics. When his father died four years later, he received a large inheritance that enabled him to purchase a fanciful castlelike villa on a forty-acre estate in Twickenham called Strawberry Hill. Here he began the monumental task of doubling its size and adding extensive gardens and landscaping. Walpole went about filling its rooms with an eclectic collection of furnishings, antiquities, and works of art, and building a special library to house his huge collection of books, historical prints, and poems and plays.

Kingston leaned back, shaking his head. Even though he was skimming Veitch's notes, he was already tiring of historical facts on eighteenth-century politicos. Nevertheless, he read on, not wanting to risk missing something salient.

Suffering from gout, Walpole left England

for France for a cure and stayed several years. During this time, he published his essay *On Modern Gardening,* about the origin and evolution of the Augustan style of garden design where classical ornament and allusion to early Roman landscapes were part of the theme. While in France, his perhaps closest friend, Thomas Gray, died. During Walpole's lifetime his main literary efforts had been his correspondence with his friends, among them Gray, Sir Horace Mann, and Matthew Seward. Walpole died in 1797, at his house in London. His quotation, "The whole secret of life is to be interested in one thing profoundly and in a thousand things well," was a fitting commentary for a man of so many talents.

Though encouraged by the nugget of information on Walpole's knowledge of cryptography, Kingston had had enough of a history lesson and decided to take a break. He could do with a cup of tea. In the kitchen with the notes, waiting for the electric kettle to boil, he thought about what he'd read. What had been Veitch's intent when he'd saved all this information? Where was he headed with it? Kingston had hoped — perhaps with undue optimism — to find a common link among Admiral Morley, the two Walpoles, and Thomas Gray. Save for the navy connection between the admiral and Sir Robert Walpole and the cryptography link to Horace Walpole, he had read nothing to support such a connection.

He eyeballed the next section devoted to the life of Thomas Gray — apparently another lift from the Internet. Despite its appearing all-inclusive, Kingston doubted he would learn anything he didn't already know because he'd studied Gray in his own years at college and greatly admired his works, in particular his magnum opus *Elegy*. Kingston could still recite the opening verses. He decided to read on anyway. The tea ready, Kingston carried it into the living room and settled into his wingback and resumed reading.

Thomas Gray, born 1716 in London, was one of the eighteenth century's most important poets. This, Kingston noted, made him older than Horace Walpole by a year. At age fourteen, Gray was sent to Eton at his mother's expense. Eton gave him companionship with other boys, especially those who shared his interests in books and poetry. Here, he made several close friends, including Horace Walpole, Richard West, son of Ireland's lord chancellor, and Matthew Seward.

After Eton, Gray entered Cambridge,

where he studied for four years before leaving to study law at the Inner Temple in London. About that time he was invited to join his friend Horace Walpole on the grand tour. In 1739, they set out.

Much of what followed in the biography echoed Horace Walpole's account of the tour, so Kingston skipped several paragraphs while finishing his tea. He picked up at the point, two years later, when Gray was back in England.

The spring and summer months of 1742 witnessed Gray's first and most prolific period of creative activity. His poetic efforts were many, though some were incomplete. Soon he returned to his old college at Cambridge to study Greek literature and the history of ancient Greece, subjects he continued to study for five years.

The next two sentences piqued Kingston's interest: "Gray's friendship with Walpole was renewed three years later, and thereafter they corresponded frequently. Gray often visited Walpole at Strawberry Hill and Matthew Seward at his country house."

While it was revealing to Kingston that all these lives intersected, it did not help in opening up new lines of inquiry or reading Veitch's mind when he'd composed the notes. He continued reading, anyway.

Walpole admired Gray's poetry and helped to get his works published. Gray's first collection appeared in 1748. It included the lighthearted *Ode on the Death of a Favourite Cat, Drowned in a Tub of Gold Fishes.*

Kingston smiled, took another sip of tea, and read on.

Unknown to most, Gray had been working for several years on a lengthy meditative elegy to be titled *Elegy,* its inspiration drawn from a small church located in the hamlet of Stoke Poges, Buckinghamshire, where Gray had spent considerable time with his mother and aunt. Over time, the poem turned into a memento mori, a meditation and lament for the inevitable fate of all mortals.

Work on polishing the *Elegy* was slow, but it was finally finished and sent to Horace Walpole, who admired it greatly and arranged to have it published. Gray's *Elegy* was an instant success. It remains to this day the most celebrated poem of its century.

After his mother's death, Gray began taking summer tours visiting various picturesque districts of Great Britain. He focused on exploring great houses, ruined abbeys, and ancient monuments, places of interest and scenery of intrinsic beauty. In 1771, at age fifty-five, Gray died at Cambridge and was buried alongside his mother at the church in Stoke Poges.

Kingston glanced at the remaining pages. Only two paragraphs were devoted to Matthew Seward, the architect responsible for the Grecian monuments at Sturminster. Because of his devotion to Greek architecture and the years spent in Greece, he had earned the name Matthew "Athenian" Seward. One paragraph referred to some of the monuments' design and construction features, another mentioned Seward's fixation on accuracy in replicating Grecian architectural details, his complaints about the workmen, and his shabby treatment by Morley's staff.

He came finally to the last three pages. The first page listed a sketchy bibliography and the following two, miscellaneous notes of no apparent interest. Kingston put them aside, deciding to look at them later. The line about ruined abbeys and ancient monuments had sparked his attention. Many hundreds of old monuments existed in private gardens, parks, and other public areas throughout England. He'd seen many in his travels, not the least those at Sturminster. He was trying to recall when they were built. He thought Simon Crawford had said that the last, the Arcadian monument, was built around 1750. If so, it would be reasonable to expect that Thomas Gray would likely have seen them, since he was still journeying through the English countryside until a year before his death. At that time, the monuments would have been approximately twenty years old. Their age would not have met Gray's criteria in antiquity, but since he'd specialized in Greek literature and history at college, their anachronistic Greek Revival architecture would certainly have attracted his attention.

Kingston leaned back and stared at the ceiling molding, trying, one more time, to figure what had been in Veitch's mind when he'd assembled the notes; going back over the profiles of the four men, each important in his own right; grasping at wispy historical straws to determine why Veitch had determined their relationships significant.

Placing Thomas Gray at Sturminster during the time of the Morley brothers was a good start. His friend Horace Walpole could have accompanied Gray on one or more visits. Walpole's father was prime minister and had been treasurer of the navy, so it would be reasonable to conclude that he and Admiral James Morley would have known each other. Ergo, presumably each had visited or stayed at Sturminster during the important years of its development. Likely, too, they'd all gathered, at one time or another, at Horace Walpole's house, and Seward's too, no doubt. But what exactly did it all prove? He'd give it a rest and look at it again later. He checked his watch, surprised to see that it was almost twelve thirty. With half the day gone, he decided to give his overworked brain cells a rest and go about stocking the larder, do laundry, and take care of unpaid bills. He had to call Andrew, too, to discuss arrangements for the garden event at Bourne End.

Morley's call came in the late afternoon. He was eager to know the nature of the "important" information Kingston had uncovered, but Kingston insisted that to explain it fully would require a face-to-face meeting. Grudgingly, Morley agreed to meet with Kingston at Sturminster the coming Tuesday.

Though there were still plenty of household chores and personal matters to take care of, he decided to spend the evening taking a second look at Veitch's list of names, doing a Google search of each one, and finishing the remaining few pages that he'd left unread that morning. After that he was looking forward to starting a new espionage thriller he'd bought at Waterstone's on his way home from food shopping.

He took out the list, but first — to make sure he hadn't missed anything when he'd glossed over them earlier — took a closer look at the list of reference books, articles, and sources that Veitch had used to compile his notes. One entry, halfway down the list, caught his eye at once: *Winterborne Frieze.* Frieze? Why a frieze? he wondered. Following, Veitch had written: *Found during the renovation of Winterborne Manor. A biblical quotation composed of decorative alphabet tiles below the crown molding of all four walls circling the dining room.* Why had that been of interest? Kingston had seen similar decorative friezes in a few other historical buildings, notably the superb one in the Gamble Room in the Victoria & Albert. It was so long since he'd seen it that he'd forgotten what the letters spelled out, other than it was a lyrical quotation. Continuing, he found another "frieze" notation, a quotation from a poem:

Built like a temple, where pilasters round
Were set, and Doric pillars overlaid
With golden architrave; nor did there want
Cornice or frieze, with bossy sculptures
    graven

194

Milton was scribbled in pencil underneath.

"Curiouser and curiouser," Kingston muttered. Veitch must have thought there was some connection between these friezes and poets and the monuments at Sturminster, but why? And just where was this manor house?

He made a mental note to do a search for Winterborne Manor or a place named Winterborne, though he was convinced by now that everything he'd been reading didn't reflect Veitch's latest findings, that it must have been random stuff that he'd saved from early in his research. After their conversation at the hospital, Kingston had come away convinced that Veitch was not only certain of his allegations but also had sufficient proof to back them up. Nothing whatsoever in what Kingston had read in the notes supported this conviction. On the whole, it had been a disappointing exercise.

THIRTEEN

Tuesday arrived and with it the nicest weather of summer by far. Gone were the sullen drab and drizzly days of the past two weeks. Leaving his flat at nine in the morning, on the short walk to his garage, Kingston couldn't help feeling buoyant about the day to come. The sun was already uncommonly bright, floodlighting the storefronts on the King's Road like a movie set. Glancing up at the band of ultramarine sky daubed with white cirrus bridging the buildings on either side, he anticipated a pleasurable top-down drive to Staffordshire.

He'd spent the weekend with Andrew at his country house in Bourne End, offering suggestions for the garden tour, tidying up the garden, eating and drinking too much, and doing his best to bring Andrew up to speed with the goings-on in Staffordshire. Those conversations never sat too well with Andrew, and they invariably developed into argumentative banter that always led to a temporary but strained détente. In the past, Kingston had adopted a habit of simply smiling when Andrew got overly exacerbated, but of late this only seemed to make matters worse.

Kingston's meeting with Morley was at eleven thirty at Sturminster. As soon as the meeting was over — Kingston was hoping it wouldn't segue into lunch — he planned to detour on his way back to London to look at Winterborne Manor, which he had since discovered was near Banbury in Oxfordshire. As luck would have it, Banbury was on the M40, his route home.

He'd summarized mentally what he would tell Morley, essentially sticking to the chronology of events and bare facts, leaving out irrelevant information like his growing friendship with Amanda and how he'd found Veitch's notes on the flash drive. The latter would only lead to more questions. In any case, as far as the notes were concerned, other than the list of names, nothing in them that he could tell had any bearing on Endicott's murder — far from it. As for the list, he would tell a white lie as to how he came by it. That wouldn't be hard.

The drive through parts of Sturminster's fifteen hundred acres of parkland was always a delight. The contrived but natural-looking style of garden design developed in England at the beginning of the eighteenth century could best be described as gardening on a grand scale. At the time, all over Britain, many formal estate gardens were being torn out and replaced with what is now termed "landscape-designed" gardens. Led by designers Lancelot "Capability" Brown, John Vanbrugh, and William Kent, lands and parks surrounding many of the great houses, frequently hundreds and sometimes thousands of acres, were carefully redesigned and planted, often with full-grown trees, to create sweeping panoramas — a pleasing blend of the formal and the romantic. The topography was invariably reconfigured to create the desired effect. Undulating parkland was punctuated with carefully positioned clumps of trees; rivers were rerouted, serpentine lakes created, elegant bridges constructed; monuments, follies, and large-scale garden ornaments, many in the classical European style, were placed strategically to please the eye. Even sheep and cattle were introduced to the landscape to provide a sense of the rural. On his last visit, he'd seen a large herd of Highland cattle grazing alongside the River Swane.

A young woman who greeted Kingston at the front door escorted him to Lord Morley's study. In many ways, the room resembled Simon Crawford's: exquisite cabinetry, elegant furnishings, and brightly lit by high windows on the wall facing out to the rose garden, now in full sun. Morley got up from his desk when Kingston entered. They shook hands, chatted briefly about trivial matters, and were soon settled in comfortable chairs facing each other.

Morley smiled. "I must say you're being awfully secretive about this information you've uncovered, Lawrence."

"I'm sorry. I didn't want it to appear that way. It's just that what I have to tell you could be construed as unwelcome yet, at the same time, perplexing. In my judgment, too important to explain and discuss in a simple phone call."

"It has bearing on the murder, I take it?"

"I don't know yet. Let's just say that it could."

Morley was no longer smiling. "All right. Go on, then," he said flatly.

Kingston began by telling a trumped-up story of how he'd come across Tristan Veitch by accident. Telling Morley the truth — that it happened while trying to find out about his relatives — wouldn't have gone down at all well, so Kingston had concocted a plausible explanation of how they'd met. It appeared to have worked: Morley accepted his pretext without question. For the next ten minutes Kingston recounted what had happened in the twenty-four hours that he'd spent in Stafford. All this time, Morley sat listening calmly, with no readable expression and no questions.

Kingston had reached the point where he was starting to describe his brief minutes with Veitch at the hospital. He knew it would be the defining moment in their conversation, because Morley was about to learn that the illustrious reputation of his family, his forebears, was about to be brought into serious question, that, for whatever reason, historians, politicians, and others had turned a blind eye to the alleged criminal activity and had somehow managed to keep it a well-guarded secret for two hundred–plus years. On the drive up, he'd tried to visualize how Morley would respond when he broke the news. Now he would know.

Morley listened calmly at the start, his expression and demeanor showing no hint as to what he was thinking. Kingston continued, repeating what he could remember of Veitch's defamatory words, watching Morley's facial expression as he did, curious for his reaction. When Kingston had finished, Morley appeared neither surprised nor affronted.

"I keep forgetting you're new to this part of the country, Lawrence," he said in an avuncular manner — even though Kingston was older by several years. "A rumor, a legend to that effect, has been passed down through the centuries, but no one has ever produced any evidence to give it credibility. It's a bit like the mysterious code on the Arcadian monument. Nothing has ever surfaced to prove that it is a code, but people keep searching for the answer. Same with the missing money rumor." He continued after a brief pause. "The name Veitch sounds familiar. Is he the one who writes occasionally for the paper?"

"Yes, he is. I get the impression that he's well respected."

"Is this all hearsay, or does he have reputable sources and documented evidence to support his allegations? Did you ask that question?"

"I didn't. There was too little time. But it was my impression that there was no question in that regard. He was utterly convinced — convincing too — that what he'd uncovered was factual. Were it not, I seriously doubt he would have summoned me to his hospital bed."

Morley shook his head. "I'll take your word for it, but I still find it hard to swallow that some freelance historian, acting alone, has dug up specious information without offering proof of any kind. He must surely know that there are laws to prevent these kinds of spurious, unwarranted attacks on people's integrity and reputations." He paused, as if thinking on it further. "Why don't you go back and ask the chap?"

"That's not possible, I'm afraid. But anyway, it's irrelevant."

"Irrelevant? Sometimes you talk in riddles, Lawrence. Why?"

"Because Tristan Veitch is dead."

"Dead?"

Kingston nodded. "Murdered, by the looks of it — poisoned."

"Good grief. Why didn't you say so in the beginning? Hasn't this been reported?"

"It happened barely a week ago. I'm told that with poisoning — where foul play is not obvious or the motive cut-and-dried — it takes time to settle the legal and medical conflicts. The hospital staff doesn't want to make mistakes, and they and the police investigators must arrive at a mutual agreement that murder was the intent."

Morley looked flustered. "We should call the police."

"I doubt that's necessary. In any case, I already spoke on the phone with Inspector Wheatley several days ago. I was about to tell you."

"Did you tell him all this?"

"Pretty much everything I knew. As it turned out, there wasn't much that he didn't already know. I believe the real reason for the call was to see if my account of events corresponded with theirs."

Morley nodded. "I told him that we would share all our findings. I'd best make sure we live up to that promise, Lawrence."

"I've been waiting for you to return."

"I understand."

"Let me finish," said Kingston. He continued, telling Morley that the house was ransacked and that all of Veitch's files, everything related to his research, his computer, and his mobile had been stolen, leaving no doubt as to the purpose of the break-in. He then ventured the opinion that it also reinforced Veitch's contention that he was on to something and that something was highly sensitive — incriminating enough, perhaps, to incite murder.

After Kingston had finished, Morley remained stone-faced and silent, clearly weighing the implications of what he'd just heard. Kingston broke the silence.

"There was something else, Francis. I didn't think too much of it at the time, but in my conversation with Veitch, he implied that he was getting help from someone else on his research."

"What do you mean by 'implied'?"

"A couple of times, he used the word 'we.' Obviously, if we can identify that person it would no doubt answer a lot of questions. I realize that it could be just about anybody — it wasn't his sister, by the way, that I'm sure of — but I keep asking myself, what if it had been William Endicott? If he *had* been working with Veitch, he would have been privy to everything that Veitch had uncovered."

Morley's look was quizzical. "I'm not quite sure what you're getting at."

"It could provide a motive for Endicott's murder."

"You really believe that?"

"It's only a theory, but I don't see why not."

"Did you also discuss this with Wheatley?"

"I might have. I can't be sure."

Morley leaned back. "Look, Lawrence, considering that you talked to this Veitch fellow for a mere ten minutes or so, you seem to have placed an awful lot of credence in what he claimed. Not only that, I also think that trying to link Endicott and Veitch in some kind of sinister partnership is stretching it. It appears you haven't a shred of evidence that they even knew each other."

"I'm aware of that, Francis."

"I won't argue with you that it fits neatly into your argument — too neatly, perhaps — but even you must agree that we need tangible proof that they were collaborating."

"That's true," said Kingston, nodding. "I mentioned this in the first place because I want you to know not only everything I've uncovered so far but also what I've extrapolated from those findings — my thoughts in general. In that respect, there's another matter that's come to light. Something that requires your verification — your interpretation, perhaps." He reached into his jacket pocket and withdrew a photocopy of Veitch's list of names and passed it to Morley. "This was found in Veitch's study," he fibbed. "I've no idea what it means in context of the case or why members of your family are included." He shrugged. "It could be nothing, of course."

Morley looked at it carefully for almost a minute.

"Any idea what, if anything, they have in common?" Kingston asked.

Morley shook his head. "I don't. May I keep it?"

"Of course."

Morley frowned. "Curious why just these names were selected."

"I was hoping you might know that."

Morley, obviously lost in thought, said nothing.

"You may have noticed that Julian Heywood's name is included. I mention that because I met him briefly when I was last here. It suggested to me that these could all be relatives who are still living."

"They are. But what the hell does this have to do with anything? Whatever reason this historian fellow had to be interested in my family, I can't imagine it had anything to do with Endicott's murder. Or what happened to Veitch. Lawrence, I want you to focus on what I hired you to do. Is that clear?"

"Francis." Kingston drew a breath, knowing he would have to choose his words carefully or Morley could easily get the wrong idea. "It's not my business to pry into your family's affairs. But if there has been anything family related . . . any incidents that have happened more recently . . . that you might have forgotten to mention, or might have judged insignificant or irrelevant —"

Morley sighed, interrupting. "Just because this fellow possessed a list of names, some of which happen to be family members, you seem to be determined to jump to the conclusion that it may have something to do with Endicott's murder."

"All I'm saying is that Veitch must have assembled the list for a reason. We'll probably never know why, but at least I think we should try to find out."

"If you want my opinion, it's a waste of time."

Kingston looked at Morley, unblinking.

"Believe me, Francis — and I'll say it one final time — the very last thing I want is to delve into matters concerning your family, but when we met at your club, you agreed to give me carte blanche when it came to interviews . . . that I could talk to anyone whom I suspected could provide useful information related to the case, no matter how tenuous."

"I do. That still stands."

"Good. Then with your permission, I'd like to talk with all the people on the list."

"You're a stubborn son of a gun, Kingston. I can't see —"

"Before you raise more objections, Francis, I want to assure you that I have no additional information or motive for wanting to do this other than to learn something about their backgrounds, their interrelationships, and generally get a better understanding of each of them. Everything will be considered highly confidential, of course. I'm doing this for one reason, and one reason only: to find out why Veitch found them of particular interest. If you're able to provide me with brief background on each — those you know — all the better."

"I hate to repeat myself, Lawrence, but I still believe you're placing far too much importance on this damned list. You find it in this Veitch chap's house and you jump to the conclusion that one or more of the people on this list could be implicated in Endicott's murder. Frankly, I find that implausible. If you really want my thoughts on this bloody mess, you could do worse than to look into the past — not this generation of Morleys, but those who created Sturminster."

"I can't convince you, I can see, but I still plan to conduct the interviews. As it is, it's going to take a lot of time and it would make my life a lot easier if I had contact numbers and a brief description of the various members of the Morley family: brothers, cousins, aunts, uncles — that sort of thing."

Morley grunted and glanced down at the sheet of paper, still in his hand. "I still say it's pointless, but I promised you a free hand — so be it. Let me look it over and I'll get back to you by tomorrow."

"Excellent. I grant you, it could turn out to be a wild-goose chase, but one never knows."

FOURTEEN

Kingston left Morley and Sturminster behind, looking in his rearview mirror at the house disappearing among the huge oaks and spreading chestnuts, hoping that their confrontation wouldn't leave any bad feelings. There was no point in dwelling on it anymore, though. Now he needed to focus on Winterborne and what he'd learned on the Internet. He wondered if he should have mentioned it to Morley, then shrugged it off as being of no consequence; after all, he had no idea if the frieze would lead to anything or not.

An hour later, as Kingston drove into Banbury, he was reciting to himself the nursery rhyme that, for centuries, has been memorized by generations of English children.

Ride a cock-horse to Banbury Cross,
To see a Fyne lady ride on a white horse.
With rings on her fingers and bells on her
   toes,
She shall have music wherever she goes.

Banbury, he was aware — having spent many pleasant hours in the romantic rose-filled garden at nearby Broughton Castle — dated to 200 BC when it was believed to have been an Iron Age settlement. He also knew that the "Fyne lady" is generally thought to be a member of the Fiennes family, ancestors of Lord Saye and Sele, owner of the castle.

In the middle of the town, he circled the roundabout and its famous cross, and took the road to Shipton-on-Stour. According to his AA map, Winterborne Manor was about ten miles ahead. Though it was still sunny and warm, it was nearing six o'clock and Kingston was beginning to worry that he might arrive too late. Information that he'd managed to find on the house had been rather sketchy, and phone calls had been intercepted by a short message that offered nothing more. Being the atypically English sort to simply show up and play it by ear, he hadn't given it too much further thought at the time.

Two minutes later, he turned onto the small lane signposted Winterborne Manor, slowing his pace because it was wide enough for only one car. He'd gone about a quarter mile when he pulled to an abrupt stop. Across the road was a high chain-link fence — new, by the looks of it — with a large sign posted next to the padlocked gate. He could see Winterborne Manor through the fence some fifty yards ahead but no signs of activity. He didn't need to get out of the car to read the sign: DANGER. CONSTRUCTION ZONE, ENTRY FORBIDDEN. Underneath, was the name of the builder, architect, and subcontractors. No phone numbers were listed. Cursing, he backed up until he came to a farm gate where he made a three-point turn and headed back to the main road. There, he turned left, back in the direction of Banbury. On the way in, he'd passed a roadhouse a couple of miles from the house. Someone there could surely tell him something about the house. He was ready for a drink anyway.

For a Tuesday evening, the Green Man was surprisingly busy. A handful of customers with drinks were standing near the entrance to what he presumed was the dining room, waiting for a table — a good sign. He was thinking that by the time he got back to Chelsea it would be too late for a full meal so, if the menu looked appealing, he would book a table. He approached the small bar and sat on one of the two empty stools. Next to him, a ruddy-faced, bulbous-nosed gent in a houndstooth sport coat, nursing a whisky, was doing the *Times* crossword. Seeing Kingston, he nodded briefly, took a sip of his scotch, and went back to his puzzle.

Kingston ordered a half of best bitter from the barmaid, a jolly lady who seemed to know most of the customers by their first names. Without his asking, she placed a menu on the bar where he could reach it. She was far too busy to ask about Winterborne Manor, so he sat reading the menu, taking a sly glance to see how his neighbor was doing with the puzzle — not well by the looks of it. Kingston's beer arrived and he told the barmaid that he would like to reserve a table for dinner. At that point, the gent decided to give up on the puzzle. He folded the paper and took a sideways glance at Kingston. "Tough one, today," he muttered, polishing off the last of his scotch and raising a finger to the barmaid for another.

"I know how it is," said Kingston. "If you're like me, one day you romp through it in a couple of hours and the next, you never complete it."

The man nodded in agreement and they slipped into polite conversation.

When Kingston asked about the food, the man said he would rank it "among the best in that part of the county." Kingston then told him what he was doing in Banbury and asked if the man knew anything about the manor house.

As luck would have it, the man, who said his name was Terence, had lived in a neighboring village for twenty-five years and knew a lot about the house and its history.

He said that the Winterborne estate had been in the possession of the Wingate family for the past hundred years or so, and with the passing of the last remaining heir, the house had been sold last year to an American family. As is often the case, they had determined it necessary to make substantial changes to the house, bringing the plumbing, electrical, and heating up to modern-day standards and generally giving the old house a much needed face-lift. He went on to talk, seamlessly and in intimate detail, about the house and the surrounding estate, saying that, over the years, he'd attended several functions and dinners there.

When Terence finally stopped to take a sip of his whisky, Kingston jumped in and asked about the frieze. Terence knew it well, he said. He also knew for the best part what the quotation was and, even better, what had happened to it. When he said that it had been demolished, Kingston's heart sank. "Oh, no!" he blurted out without thinking. It turned out that "demolished" was an ill-chosen word on Terence's part. He corrected himself by saying, "removed, because it was of considerable value." It was composed of foot-square ceramic tiles, each decorated with a letter of the alphabet in bas-relief. Circling the tops of the walls of the dining room, below the ceiling molding, it read, as best he could remember: *Through wisdom a house is built; and by understanding it is established; and by knowledge every room shall be filled with precious and pleasant riches.* It was a quotation from Ecclesiastes, he said.

As to what happened to the dismantled frieze, he wasn't sure; he had a vague recall of its being sold. He supplied Kingston with the name of the builder — the one Kingston had seen on the sign — saying that Mike Kennedy, the owner, would surely know. They chatted for another ten minutes, until a waitress approached to tell Kingston that his table was ready. He downed what remained of his beer, said good-bye to Terence, and left to enjoy his dinner.

The following morning, Kingston made several phone calls from his study. The first was to Kennedy & Sons, Building Services. The owner, Mike Kennedy, was happy to provide what little he knew about the frieze. He was unsure of its age but knew that parts of the house dated back to the early eighteenth century. The owners had asked him to remove the frieze because they were selling it to an antiques dealer in Brighton. He'd been reluctant to do so, though, fearing that the porcelain tiles would be too old and fragile, and he would end up being responsible for any resulting damages. In the end, the dealer came to take a look at it and together they called in an architectural salvage expert to supervise the work. It took two days, he said, but all the tiles were successfully removed with no damage. He made no comment as to why the new owners wanted to sell the frieze. He would have bought it himself, he said, but the asking price was a bit too rich. The antiques dealer's name was Nicolson, and his company was called Artifacts Design. Kingston wrote down the name, thanked Kennedy, and the call ended.

Next, he Googled *Artifacts Brighton* and up popped the listing, first on the page. He picked up the phone again and entered the number. It was one of Artifacts' partners, Trevor Nicolson, who answered. Kingston was just thinking it must be his lucky morning when Nicolson told him that the frieze had been purchased by a client of his in San Francisco. He was wondering what possible questions he could ask next, when Nicolson asked the reason for his inquiring. He seemed satisfied with Kingston's trumped-up answer that he was writing an article about decorative and alphabet friezes, and volunteered that he had several digital photos of the frieze, if that would be of interest. His only caveat in allowing use of the pictures was that, if they were published, Artifacts Design would receive credit.

Fifteen minutes later Kingston received Nicolson's e-mail with six JPEG attachments. A minute later he had the prints spread out on his desk and was admiring the artistic beauty and craftsmanship of the tile work.

No doubt rendered on porcelain, slightly yellowed and crackled with age, each tile — a separate letter of the alphabet — was a work of art in itself. Each letter had its own individual design characteristics, no two alike. Motifs of human figures, animals, serpents, and foliage supported or twined intricately in and out of each letter. The artistry alone was magnificent; that it was painted on tile made it even more remarkable. He took his eyes off them and stared into space. All he had to do now was to figure out why Veitch had chosen to include the frieze among his notes. He let out a long sigh.

He picked up the phone again, this time to call Amanda. For the third time, he lucked out — she answered right away, too. The main reason for his call was to ask her a question about Tristan, but it would also provide the chance to find out how she was faring, without appearing too intrusive.

"You sound quite chipper," he said.

"It's hard not to be cheerful on such a gorgeous day. It must be in the eighties up here. I've spent most of the morning in the garden."

"Wish I could be there to enjoy it with you. It's the customary summer gray here."

She chuckled. "You could tell me what all these flowers and plants are that Tristan planted. I hardly recognize any of them — not that I should."

"I'd be more than happy to. You'll need some hints on how to take care of them, too — pruning, watering, and feeding, that sort of stuff. Nothing too complicated, of course."

"That's settled then. The next warm spell."

He wanted to keep the banter going but didn't want to overdo it, and since they were talking about the garden, the timing couldn't be better. "There's something I wanted to ask you," he said, trying to keep up the lighthearted tone.

"What is it?"

"When you and I walked through your garden, you said that Tristan had created it, and to all intents and purposes had maintained it single-handedly ever since."

"That's right. You made the comment that he was the Constant Gardener. Remember?"

"During those years, did he ever belong to a garden club or exhibit flowers?"

"He did," she said. "I remember his winning a handful of awards for exhibiting flowers. Two small trophies and some ribbons, as I recall. That was quite a long time ago. Why do you ask?"

"It was something Mrs. Endicott mentioned. One more question and then I'm finished."

"Sure."

"Did Tristan grow dahlias at one time? I don't recall seeing any when we were in the garden, not that I was looking for them."

A pause followed. "Yes, he did," she replied, hesitating. "How did you know that?"

"William Endicott grew them, too, and exhibited them."

"I'm not sure that I follow —"

"It could be a coincidence, but I think not. This suggests the distinct possibility that Tristan and William Endicott knew each other. If so, then it's reasonable to infer that it was Endicott who was helping Tristan

218

in his research."

"So you're saying that whoever killed Endicott probably killed Tristan, too. In both cases, to silence them?"

"That's what I believe."

"If you're right, Lawrence — and you may well be — then this gives me even more reason to tell you what I've been meaning to say for a while now."

"What is that?"

"That you should reconsider this investigation of yours. I think you should just walk away from it. Turn all this information that you got from Tristan over to the police and have them deal with it."

"Believe me, I've thought about doing just that, but to live up to the terms of my agreement, I have to discuss it first with Lord Morley. I met with him yesterday, and he gave me the go-ahead to interview certain members of the Morley family."

"That's exactly what I'm getting at, Lawrence. I don't think you should do that. This nasty business could become even more dangerous than it is already, and you're running the real risk of becoming a casualty yourself if you insist on pursuing your investigation. I can't believe that it hasn't occurred to you that whoever committed these two murders is quite possibly either one of the Morley family or is connected to them in some way. You're about to poke a stick in a hornets' nest and I'm very worried, that's all."

Kingston was taken aback by this emotional outpouring of concern for his well-being. Rarely lost for words, he was scrambling to figure a way to respond that would allay her fears without it appearing that he was simply shrugging them off lightly.

"Amanda," he said, trying to play to her feelings, "that thought has occurred to me, and I'm touched that you would think of me that way. I also take your advice seriously. However, I don't think that I've yet reached that point where I'm running undue risks, but if and when I do, I won't hesitate to quit. There's some unfinished business that I want to take care of first, and then I'll decide whether or not to throw in the towel."

"I'm not going to ask you what this unfinished business is; you'd probably prefer not to tell me anyway. All I'm saying is just get it done quickly and then walk away from this dreadful business."

There was no doubting Amanda's sincerity, but she was becoming insistent, her last sentence tantamount to an order. Was there another reason she wanted him to quit? As he was pondering the loaded question, admonishing himself that he was overreacting, she spoke again, apparently determined to have the last word.

"All right," she said. "If I can't persuade you to stop, then please do one thing for me. From now on be extra cautious."

"I will, I promise." It wasn't lost to him that her words were almost identical to her brother's parting words at the hospital.

FIFTEEN

The warm weather of the last few days was holding up, so after lunch and a half hour grappling with the *Times* crossword, Kingston made a snap decision to spend the afternoon outdoors and get some fresh air, rather than mope around the flat becoming more and more worked up about his inability to make tangible headway with the Sturminster murders. As it stood, his only ray of hope, as far as he could see, rested with Veitch's list. He hoped that Morley would come through with the information that Kingston had requested and that the interviews might reveal why Veitch had considered those particular people of importance. Just what that could be, Kingston had no idea.

Where to go? he wondered. London was full of wonderful parks, gardens, and open-air spaces, nearly all of which he'd visited since he'd made the city his home. Which of them would serve his purpose best? Which would allow him reasonable privacy — no children or tour groups — in peaceful and beautiful surroundings with ample space to wander or to simply sit quietly whenever it pleased him? After several minutes' thought, he decided on Syon House, the London residence of the duke of Northumberland and his family. It was a little farther than most, but it was some time since he last visited the two-hundred-acre park facing Kew Gardens on the opposite bank of the Thames, with its imposing house and magnificent conservatory.

Forty-five minutes later, Kingston alighted from the number 237 bus at Syon's Brentlea Gate stop. Wearing his aging straw hat and carrying his jacket, he strolled into the park. Being midweek there were relatively few visitors; even so, Kingston had already chosen to start the afternoon by taking the less-traveled paths, steering clear of high-traffic areas like the Conservatory, the Butterfly House, and the Aquatic Experience.

Walking leisurely and pausing occasionally under the shade of rare and ancient trees —

the estate was originally a fourteenth-century abbey — he was blocking out in his mind all the things that had happened since he'd first met with Lord Morley that day at Jardine's. He was soon realizing that, even though he was making little or no headway with the case, an awful lot had happened in that short space of time, not the least of which had been the death of Tristan Veitch — make that "murder," he corrected himself.

For ten minutes or so, he sat on a weathered bench facing the lake where chartreuse leaves on a row of weeping willow trees dipped to meet the water, making sunlit ripples. One by one, he tried to picture in his mind's eye the several meetings and phone conversations that had taken place during that time, attempting, as best he could, to recall exactly what had been said: Morley, Crawford, Tristan Veitch, Amanda, Dr. Chandra, Dorothy Endicott, Terence at the Green Man, the builder Kennedy, and the chap at Artifacts in Brighton. Had any of them mentioned something that he'd missed or misunderstood — any small discrepancy or slip? If they had, it was eluding him. He looked off into the distance to where the tall columnar statue of Flora broke the horizon like a vertical gray pencil.

With all the tension and disruption of the last several days, there was one part of the puzzle — the slip of paper, the supposed code, found in Endicott's pocket — that, while not entirely forgotten, had been put aside. When Morley first told him about it, the discovery had struck him as an intriguing clue, a likely place to start even if it was only part of a code. But having studied it a number of times now, he'd concluded, as had GCHQ, that as it was, it was useless. Despite this, Veitch had acknowledged that a code or codes of some kind existed. How had he arrived at that conclusion? The other obvious code was the one on the Arcadian monument. But that had remained unsolved for centuries. Was it possible that someone had finally managed to solve it, after all? Horace Walpole came to mind again. Regardless, it raised several questions, first and foremost: What was it that had been of such great importance, so vital or consequential, that someone, or more than one person, had taken preventative measures by encrypting it? That prompted another thought: Could the murderers have already broken either of the codes and were now determined, come what may, to protect that information? Conversely, if they hadn't, did they have credible reason to believe that it concealed information that would incriminate others or perhaps lead to some kind of reward — perhaps the money that Samuel Morley was rumored to have stashed somewhere at Sturminster?

He stared down at the grass verge in front of him, more confused than ever. After a minute or so, he decided to let it go, to stop thinking about the case for the rest of the afternoon. Looking up, he watched a flock of cawing crows take off from the top of a nearby copper beech. "A murder of crows," he muttered.

He donned his straw hat, rose, and started walking toward the Conservatory, the crowning glory of the park. It had been some years since he'd last seen it and it would be a shame not to revisit it while he was here. For no particular reason, he started to think about Amanda, wondering how she was getting along, if she was still managing to cope as well as it had appeared when he was at the house. He was reminded that she'd said nothing about a funeral service for Tristan. During the time they'd been together — with the exception of the brief mention of her deceased husband — she hadn't talked about her family at all, which was understandable, considering the bleak circumstances. It had hardly been the occasion to bring out the family scrapbook. On further thought, he now realized that he could have at least inquired about her well-being this morning, instead of hogging the conversation the way he had, talking mostly about himself. Next time they spoke he must remember to apologize.

An attractive woman walking a terrier approached. It reminded him of the dear departed Winston, to whom, in a round-about way, he owed a debt of gratitude. They exchanged "good afternoon"s and he went back to thinking about Amanda. In some ways, he wished that she lived closer to London. For one thing, he could lend a hand with her garden. He would enjoy getting his hands into the dirt again. Being on the receiving end of her culinary skills raised teasing thoughts, too. Perhaps, when sufficient time had passed, he would ask if she would like to come down to London, to stay for a couple of days. He imagined that she would enjoy that, to get away from the routine and the painful reminders of the recent past. After all, he did have a guest room with its own bathroom. As far as he could recall, in all the time he'd been there, it had been used only two or three times: once when Julie was on a visit from Seattle, and on the other occasions by Andrew —

once when he had locked himself out, and the other when he was having work done on his flat. If it weren't for Mrs. Tripp, he doubted that the towels would ever be changed. He could never understand why she insisted on washing them whether they'd been used or not. That got him to wondering what Andrew would say if Kingston were to announce that he was "entertaining" a lady for the weekend. The Conservatory came into sight and he dismissed the thoughts as frivolous.

An hour later, Kingston was on the top deck of the bus returning home when it came to him out of the blue. He hadn't even been thinking consciously about the code this afternoon, but a thought had just popped into his mind. What if the code Veitch had alluded to was neither the one on the scrap of paper nor that on the Arcadian monument but instead another code entirely? Kingston tried to recall exactly what it was that Veitch had said at the hospital. He remembered that when he'd asked Veitch about the letters on the scrap of paper and mentioned the word "codes," Veitch had nodded in agreement and said "right." That didn't necessarily mean that he was referring to the letters on the paper found in Endicott's possession. He'd said nothing to indicate exactly which code or codes he was referring to.

The more Kingston thought about it, the more plausible it became that Veitch might not have been referring to the fragment. It was only natural that the police, GCHQ, and he too had theorized that the dozen or more letters on the paper could have been a fragment of a code. Now he was becoming even more confused. Another thought struck him. Was that the intent of the mysterious scrap of paper? Had it been planted conveniently in Endicott's pocket, after he'd been killed, making it appear like part of a coded message, with the sole purpose of leading the police off in the wrong direction? If that were so, it presented yet another problem: There had been no mention of codes anywhere among Veitch's notes. Now he was going round in circles. The only reference he could think of that could be construed as involving a code — slender as it was — was the biblical quotation on the frieze. He must take another look at that paragraph when he got back home.

Hanging up his jacket in the hall closet and placing his hat on the shelf above, Kingston went into the living room. The sun was almost over the yardarm and after checking for phone messages he planned to fix himself a stiff drink. The LCD showed two messages. The first was from Andrew, wanting to know if Kingston would like to join him and a couple of friends for an upcoming special gala night of racing at Kempton Park. He went on to explain, in his typical exuberant manner, that in addition to the horse racing, there was live music and entertainment afterward. Kingston thought it might be fun and was ready for a break from the mounting frustration and his worrying about Amanda. Over the last days he'd become aware that it was all now starting to have a detrimental effect on him. He would go, he decided.

The second message was from Simon Crawford. He had some answers regarding the list of people that Kingston had given to Morley. He asked that Kingston call him back on his private number, which he enumerated.

"Answers" was a little too vague for Kingston's liking. He'd been hoping, wishfully, maybe, for something positive, more encouraging. He played the message back to retrieve the number, picked up the phone, and entered it. Crawford answered right away.

"It's Lawrence," said Kingston. "Thanks

for getting back to me so soon."

"Not a problem. Francis has gone over the names but doesn't think he's going to be of much help."

"I thought that might be the case. He probably told you that he's not happy with the idea."

"He did. Anyway, he's done what you requested as far as the family members are concerned. He's jotted notes alongside each name to explain who is who. I'm not sure about the other names. I'll e-mail it in the next five minutes."

"Thanks."

"To set the record straight, I went along with Morley when he suggested hiring you. I still believe it was the right decision. You've worked with him before and you know how impatient he can get. He just wants to see some results."

"I do too, but these things take time. I'll be first to admit that progress thus far has been disappointing. But it's only been a couple of weeks since we started. He must realize that."

"A word of advice, Lawrence. It'll make everyone's life easier if you can wrap up these interviews as fast as possible and get back to the real investigation. Finding out who killed Endicott and why is number one.

One other matter: Morley seems to have this thing about a connection to the distant past. Maybe you should also be trying to find out more about the historical information this Veitch fellow claims to have had. That might prove more productive."

"I plan to do that, of course."

"Good. I'll do my best to keep Francis calmed down, but you know how he is. Oh, there was one more thing. He asked me if I thought *you* might be having second thoughts."

"Second thoughts?"

"About wanting to continue."

"Why would he think that?"

"He didn't say in so many words, but I think he feels that with Endicott's murder and now Veitch's death, you might be wondering if you've taken on more than you'd bargained for, that continuing with the inquiry might now pose even greater danger and you might be concerned for your own well-being. I must say he has a good point."

Kingston was thinking: First Amanda urging him to quit, and now Morley having doubts.

"The thought hadn't crossed my mind, Simon. It would take a lot more than that for me to get cold feet. Besides, nothing yet has happened to make me think that I might become a target or threatened in any way. I want to solve this case and, frankly, threats don't scare me; if anything they would probably spur me on. You might want to tell Francis that."

"I will."

"I'll keep you informed about the interviews, and tell Francis not to worry."

"Good. One last thing, Lawrence, don't go sticking your neck out. The last thing we want is for something to happen to you."

SIXTEEN

Having dispensed with the post — no good news or money — Kingston poured a large whisky and went into his study and turned on his Mac. Crawford's letter was in the inbox. He opened it and clicked on the attachment.

Lawrence

Here's Francis's list. He says that he's been purposefully brief in identifying each person, knowing that it's doubtful you'll contact all seventeen to start with. If you want additional background on any of them, he'll do his best to provide

as much as he can. All ages are guessti-
mates.

In the next day or so, he'll send you
what phone and e-mail addresses he can
gather. Physical addresses you can obtain
when you contact each individual.

I hope that this leads to something that
brings us closer to solving these terrible
crimes.

Simon

Graham Morley: My younger brother.
Barrister. Lives and practices in
Torquay.
Victoria Morley: His wife of 25 years.
Active in local politics and community
issues.
Ethan Morley: Their son, 40. Insurance
broker. Lives outside Birmingham.
Single.
Bridget Morley: Their daughter, 28.
Manages a Bristol restaurant. Single.
Adrian Morley: My cousin. Retired.
Lives in Bath.
Nicole Morley: His wife of 20 years.
Bryce Lytton: My brother-in-law. Part-
ner, Windrush Racing Stables, Lam-
bourn, Berks.
Daisy Morley-Lytton: My sister. Lyt-
ton's wife of 25 years. Antiques dealer.

Julian Heywood: Their son (by Daisy's first marriage), 30. Salesman, Upmarket car dealership, Nottingham.

James Morley-Lytton: Their son, 23. Single. Royal Navy midshipman. Portsmouth.

Vanessa Decker: Supposedly a distant cousin. Living somewhere abroad, as I recall.

Sebastian Hurst: Partner, Windrush Racing Stables.

Oliver Henshawe: Cousin. Leicestershire County Record Office.

Jessica Henshawe: His ex-wife.

Cameron Henshawe: Their son, 29. Something to do with computers.

Molly Henshawe: Their daughter, 23. Graphic designer, London.

Roger Bartram: I believe he's a friend of Sebastian Hurst. Connected to racing in some fashion.

Kingston took a sip of Macallan and went down the list again. It still perplexed him why Veitch had included it in his notes. If Veitch's discovery was all about crimes committed by Morleys of the distant past, why a list of present-day family members? Was it possible that the feud existed to this day? If so, could Endicott — or Veitch, for that matter — have had anything to do with the Morleys? Perhaps with a business or some other arrangement?

Clearly, it would be out of the question to talk to all seventeen people, which wasn't his plan in any case. Coming up with an arbitrary short list of prospects would require careful study of the names to get a clear picture of who was who, their relationships to each other, if any, with ages and places of residence or business taken into consideration but not necessarily a determining factor. He also reminded himself that he wasn't looking for a murderer but rather anyone who might possess information that could shed even a glimmer of light on the case.

He printed the list and left the Mac on Sleep. Staring abstractedly at the seventeen names of total strangers, he was aware that reducing them to a half dozen or fewer was tantamount to drawing straws. After some thought he decided on a simple method of selection: He would divide the names into three groups. In the first — his A group — he would include those who he felt might be the most likely to provide useful information. In the B group, the next-best candidates; in C, those he would eliminate for the time being. Even then, he knew the process was based on nothing more than part intuition, part probability, and a lot of guesswork. It was an exercise that was completely foreign to him and ran counter to his customary modus operandi, which relied mostly on the power of deductive reasoning and the application of logic.

He picked up a pencil and drew three columns — A, B, and C — on a piece of paper, then started to allocate names into the columns as he saw fit.

After a first pass, he wrote "Molly Henshawe" and "Bridget Morley" in the C column. If anything was to be learned from the interviews, he somehow doubted it would come from two relatively young women, each of whom worked and presumably lived over a hundred miles from where the crimes took place. After some thought, he placed the young naval officer, James Morley-Lytton, in the C column. His parents would surely be more than willing to discuss their serviceman son. He pondered the three wives, deciding they belonged in the C column, too. Julian Heywood's name was next. Kingston wrote him in the A column. His reasoning was simple: Julian knew Simon Crawford, had been at the estate, and worked within an hour's drive from Sturminster.

By now he'd finished his scotch and he looked at his watch. It was almost seven and he was hungry. Somehow he didn't fancy the idea of cooking. A glance out the window confirmed that it was one of those rare balmy London evenings when it seemed that the denizens of the city had decided to take to the streets and parks en masse, spilling onto the pavements and roads outside pubs in shorts and shades, as if they were on the Côte d'Azur or strolling the Via del Corso in Rome. Why not join the madding crowds, he decided, and walk to the Antelope for dinner? He could continue to work on the list there.

He picked up Morley's list, folded it, and went into the kitchen to get the unfinished *Times* crossword. Ten minutes later, he was sitting at a corner table in the Antelope's upstairs bar/dining room — usually quieter than the one downstairs — with the list of names in front of him, the *Times* on the seat beside him, and a glass of Côtes du Rhône at his elbow. Waiting for his pasta with smoked salmon, he took a long sip of wine and started in on the list again — this time, given the dearth of information, with a less inferential attitude. By the time his check arrived, there were nine names on his A list. Nine people were still more than he would ideally like, though.

By breakfast the next morning, he'd win-nowed the A list down to six: Sebastian Hurst, Julian Heywood, Bryce Lytton, Vanessa Decker, Roger Bartram, and Jessica Henshawe, Oliver Henshawe's ex.

He was still in the kitchen, cleaning up, when the phone rang. For a moment he considered not answering it, then changed his mind on the third ring — it could be Andrew. Kingston hadn't heard from him in some time and was feeling guilty about not having called.

"This is Kingston."

"Glad I caught you, Doctor."

The Midlands accent — it was Inspector Wheatley again. What did he want this time? Kingston's mind flashed on what Morley had said, about giving up their inquiry and talking with the police. Was that why Wheatley was calling?

"Lord Morley tells me you're still working on the Sturminster murder case."

"I am," Kingston replied.

"Good. I'll come straight to the point, then. I'd like to talk to you about what, if anything, you've learned."

"I'd be glad to answer any questions —"

"Not on the phone, Doctor. I think the

time has come when you and I should have a face-to-face. I'm suggesting that you take a leisurely drive to Stafford in the next few days and we can — shall we say — compare notes. When can you make it?"

They settled on the coming Monday, four days hence, at eleven A.M. Wheatley provided the address, phone number, and directions — once in the city of Stafford — and the call ended on a somewhat more cordial note.

Kingston didn't spend time thinking about the call; he'd been expecting that sooner or later Wheatley would want to talk to him personally. Instead, he went about setting up some meetings of his own: interviews with his A-list people. He started with Bryce Lytton, for two reasons: First, there was the chance that he could also get to talk to his partner, Sebastian Hurst, and learn about Roger Bartram at the same time, and second, he was the only one who didn't require a contact number; he should be easy to reach by calling Windrush Racing Stables. Getting to Lytton was easier than he'd expected, and the man seemed happy enough to talk and agreed to see him.

Two days later, with the top down, despite a forecast of rain later in the day, Kingston was on the A4 approaching the village of Lambourn on his way to meet with Bryce Lytton at Windrush Racing Stables. When Kingston had made the appointment on the phone, he'd asked Lytton if it would be possible also to interview Sebastian Hurst, Lytton's partner. But Hurst was in Ireland looking at a horse and wouldn't be back until the following week. Instead he gave Kingston a phone number where Hurst could be reached in Wexford. Kingston had also inquired about Roger Bartram, to learn that a month earlier he'd been severely injured in a light aircraft accident when his Cessna had crashed on landing during a heavy rainstorm when returning from a race meeting in Scotland. He was currently in a rehab center in Reading. Lytton had offered the address, but Kingston had told him not to worry.

He was looking forward to his visit to Lambourn. He'd never been to a racing stable before though, in aggregate, he'd left a princely sum at dozens of racetracks over the years. What had been a three- or four-times-a-year flutter in his married years had become a regular happening since he'd befriended Andrew.

Following Lytton's directions, Kingston turned off the main road and headed west on a lane crossing the rolling Berkshire Downs. The surrounding countryside couldn't have been more English: lush pastures and wheat fields stretching to the horizon, separated by dense woods and hedgerows; leaf-canopied lanes, old stone bridges crossing streams arched with willows; flint-and-brick villages tucked into the folds of the gently sloping land, each with its omnipresent church steeple reaching to the white-clouded sky. Now and then Kingston spotted horses with helmet-clad riders cantering across the brows of the hills. In one village he had to come to a stop to allow exercising horses to trot by. Boning up on the area before he'd left, he'd read that more than thirty racing stables were situated in and around Lambourn and that fifteen hundred racehorses were based in the valley.

Fifteen minutes later he drove up the white-fenced chalk lane to Windrush Stables and parked alongside a half dozen cars up against a large wooden building. The place was both spotless and attractive. In the middle of the courtyard, a circular raised bed was filled with perennials and annuals. Other equally colorful arrangements spilled from wire baskets attached to the surrounding walls. As he got out of the car, he saw three men in conversation across the graveled courtyard. The tallest of them, wearing a Barbour vest and peaked cap, waved him over.

"Dr. Kingston?"

"Yes. And you must be Mr. Lytton."

"Bryce, please."

The two shook hands, then Lytton introduced him to the other men, one a trainer, the other a veterinarian. They talked for a while and when the others had left, Lytton asked Kingston if he would like a quick tour. He didn't need asking twice. The tour started with the stables, where Kingston was introduced to several of the racehorses by name. Next was the exercise complex, where, to his surprise and amusement, one of the horses was being exercised in a doughnut-shaped equine pool. Last they walked a short distance to the ten-furlong track where two of the horses were being put through their paces.

During this time Kingston had had the chance to size up the horse trainer. Lytton seemed to be genuinely friendly and — from the couple of quick asides he'd made on their walk, one about the horse in the pool being a regular Michael Phelps — there was no doubting his sense of humor. In appearance he fitted the role: lightly tanned, leathery skin associated with men who spend much of their time outdoors, gray-streaked hair, thinning on top, and deep-set blue eyes that, at first glance, appeared black in the shadows cast by his bushy eyebrows. His voice belied his somewhat rural appearance; it was cultivated but with no affectation of class.

When they returned to Lytton's office, the phone was ringing. Lytton took the call, leaving Kingston to look around the spacious, light-filled room, which was furnished with mostly built-in contemporary fittings and up-to-date electronics, including a sixty-inch wall-mounted plasma TV. The wall behind Lytton's desk was filled with framed photographs, various horse-racing awards, and memorabilia. Lytton appeared in many of the photos, more often than not alongside racehorses — presumably winners — sometimes in sailing situations and, in two photos, with collector cars in the background.

Lytton ended his call and they got down to the business at hand. To begin with, Kingston was pleased to hear that Lytton was already aware of his credentials. Whether it was Morley who had told him was moot; more important, it meant that he didn't have to waste time explaining to Lytton how he had gone from botanist to investigator.

For five minutes, in his methodical professorlike way, Kingston summarized the events that had taken place during the past three weeks, starting with Endicott's murder. Lytton listened without comment. Even though some of the incidents had not yet been reported, Lytton showed no signs of surprise to what Kingston said. He could only assume that Crawford or Morley had given Lytton a thorough briefing.

"How's Francis taking it?" he asked when Kingston was done.

"Hard to say," Kingston replied to the unexpected question. "Doing his best to keep Sturminster out of it and doing his damnedest to get to the bottom of it. Seems to be handling it well, everything considered. The main reason he hired me was that he was frustrated by the lack of progress with the official inquiry."

"I see."

"I wonder if you'd mind answering a few questions?"

Lytton smiled diffidently. "I'm not a suspect, I hope?"

"Not yet." Kingston smiled back.

"That's good." Lytton nodded.

"I'll start with the obvious one. Have you

ever had contact with, or know of anyone who's had contact with, either William Endicott or Tristan Veitch, a historian who lived near Stafford?"

Lytton shook his head. "No."

"I've heard people refer to a so-called Morley family feud that's said to have started centuries ago but persists to this day. Know anything about that?"

"I've heard about it, sure. Who hasn't? It's a legend of sorts around these parts. It makes for good dinner conversation every once in a while. It usually depends on how much wine's been consumed. It goes back a couple of hundred of years after the two Morley brothers built Sturminster — with a rift between them over the alleged missing fortune."

"But there's no animosity, disagreements, grudges among the family, now?"

"Not that I'm aware."

Kingston leaned back, meeting Lytton's incurious gaze. "Do you and your wife spend much time with other members of her family?"

"Not so much anymore. I don't want to be accused of telling stories out of school, but it's no big secret really. Truth is, nowadays we get to see her relatives only at the holidays — Christmas, mostly. Even then, it's only a couple of them. Daisy, my wife, goes down to Devon when she can, to see her brother Graham and his wife, Victoria. She and Daisy have always been close. But there are never big family gatherings, reunions, if that's what you mean." He shrugged. "They're just not that kind of family."

"Do you or members of your family visit Sturminster from time to time?"

Lytton shook his head. "I can only speak for Daisy and me. The last time we were there was probably five years ago." He paused and tapped his forehead. "I apologize. I never asked if you wanted something to drink. Tea, coffee, a 'sharpener' of some kind, perhaps?"

"Thanks for asking but I'm fine," Kingston replied.

"Go on, then."

"Any of the family interested in gardening?"

Lyttton chuckled. "If you ask me, Napoleon had it all wrong when he called us a nation of shop keepers. He should have called us a nation of bloody gardeners. Seems like everybody and his brother gardens these days."

Kingston smiled. "You're right. Let me rephrase that. Anyone in the family who belongs to a garden club, exhibits flowers, that sort of thing?"

Lytton thought for a moment. "My ex-wife. But you don't want to hear about her, I'm sure."

"I very much doubt it. How long is it since you were, er . . . parted company?"

"Nineteen eighty-four."

"A long time." Kingston shook his head. "I'd have no reason to talk to her."

Lytton frowned. "Francis told me you were formerly a botanist, but why the horticultural interest?"

"The main reason Lord Morley hired me was for my experience with criminal investigations, but oddly it happens that in this case there's a horticultural angle."

"Really?"

"Tristan Veitch was poisoned using a highly toxic plant by the name of aconite. Ever heard of it?"

"I haven't, no."

"It probably grows freely around here, and most nurseries carry it. It's become a useful drug medicinally but at the same time its root contains the deadliest poison in the plant world."

"You'd think they'd ban it."

"You would."

Neither spoke for several seconds, Kingston making a mental tally to determine if there was anything further he should ask.

"I ran into your stepson a couple of weeks ago," Kingston said offhandedly.

Lytton expressed surprise. "Really? Julian?"

For a nanosecond, Lytton appeared to have been taken off guard by Kingston's comment. His eyes narrowed imperceptibly but quickly returned to normal. "How was he? Did you talk to him?"

"I didn't. It was at Sturminster. I'd been getting a briefing from Simon Crawford, the manager. I was just leaving when Julian arrived. He had a quick chat with Crawford and left."

"He was probably trying to sell Crawford another car. He works for a car company up north. A car salesmen."

There was no mistaking the pejorative way that Lytton had said "car salesman."

"Sells Aston Martins, Mercs, Jags, high-performance cars."

Kingston nodded. "Crawford told me he owned an XK120."

"Nice car."

"Your other son is in the navy, I believe?"

"He is. We're proud of him. He served with the coalition fleet in Iraq a couple of years ago."

"We all owe him a debt."

"You're right at that."

Five minutes later, they shook hands and Kingston drove away from Windrush Stables with a small gold horseshoe stamped with the stable's name in his pocket.

Leaving Lambourn, he thought back on their conversation. He'd learned more about the sport of kings but as far as gaining any information relevant to the case, it had been a wasted effort, except for Lytton's reaction to his stepson, Julian. What was that about? he wondered.

SEVENTEEN

Back at his flat, he was pleased to see that another e-mail from Crawford had arrived. It was what he'd been waiting for: contact information for the people on Veitch's list. He scanned it quickly. There were addresses and phone numbers for all, with two exceptions. Jessica Henshawe and Vanessa Decker had neither a phone number nor an address.

He decided to focus on two other men on the A-list: Julian Heywood and Sebastian Hurst. He glanced at his watch: a little after four. A car dealership should still be open, he figured. He picked up the phone and dialed Julian Heywood's work number. The woman who answered with a chirpy "Performance Motors" said that Heywood was in the showroom and that she would page him. Within a minute he was on the line.

"Good afternoon, Mr. Heywood. This is Dr. Kingston. We met briefly at Sturminster, recently. I was with Simon Crawford at the time."

A lengthy pause followed, suggesting that Heywood's recollection was blurry.

"I must confess, I don't remember. Are you calling about a car?"

"I'm not. No. It's regarding the recent murder there."

Again, Heywood was slow to answer. "I see. What makes you think I can help?"

"I'm not even sure you can. Lord Morley has asked me to look into it, and with his permission I'm familiarizing myself with a few family members. We're collaborating with the police, of course. Have they talked to you about it?"

"No, they haven't."

"I plan to be near Nottingham in the next few days and wondered if I could stop by and ask a few questions — when you're not busy, of course. Among other things there are a couple of people local to the area you might be able to help me identify."

"You'll be wasting your time, but that's up to you. The best day would be Tuesday. Where are you coming from?"

"London," said Kingston, glancing at his diary. That was the day after he was seeing Inspector Wheatley. It would be convenient to fit the two meetings in the same day. "Any chance of Monday?"

"Sorry, that's out."

"Tuesday it is, then. How about noon?"

"That'll be fine. We're on the south side of Nottingham on the A52. Performance Motors."

"I'll find it, don't worry."

Kingston put down the phone thinking about the call. Heywood had sounded apathetic, but that was to be expected. Anyone being asked to answer questions about a murder case wouldn't be jumping for joy in anticipation. Speaking of which . . .

Looking at the list again, he decided that while he was at it he might as well try to get hold of Sebastian Hurst, Bryce Lytton's partner at Windrush Stables, as well. Like Inspector Jonathan Whicher, Scotland Yard's first great detective, who claimed he could see people's thoughts in their eyes and that in faces he could always find something readable, Kingston didn't trust the telephone when it came to interviews. He would far prefer to question Hurst face-to-face, but for the sake of expediency he decided to make an exception. He'd call Hurst, introduce himself, explain how he was involved in the murder case, and ask if he would mind answering a few simple questions. If Hurst appeared receptive, Kingston would conduct the interview on the phone. If his reaction was otherwise — if he seemed reluctant or resented the implication — Kingston would further explain and request an appointment to interview him in person.

Kingston needn't have bothered with Hurst, as it turned out. Hurst answered Kingston's questions succinctly, saying that he didn't know and had never met Endicott or Veitch and knew little or nothing about the rumored Morley family feud. Asked about members of the Morley family, he said that he'd only met Francis Morley on one occasion and, except for Daisy, he'd never met any of the others Kingston mentioned. A question about the poison aconitine and another inquiring if Hurst had any interest in gardening were both met with negative answers. There was nothing to be learned here, Kingston decided. He thanked the man for his time and crossed his name off the list.

In bed that night — he'd turned in early deciding he wanted a clear head before facing Inspector Wheatley — he thought about the case and what little progress he'd made. He still had no idea who had killed William Endicott and why, which was the reason he'd been hired. Instead, he'd become inextricably entangled in another murder case and a completely unexpected turn of events brought about by Veitch's supposed discovery alleging that the centuries-old Morley legend could be factual and could also have a bearing on the Sturminster case. To complicate matters, there was the question of Amanda. How did she fit in to all of this? Had she been working with her brother more closely than she'd claimed? Did she know more than she'd professed? Or was he being overly suspicious? There was no evidence whatsoever to suggest that she hadn't been honest with him all along and wasn't genuinely concerned for his well-being. After thinking on it for another minute or so, he concluded that he was trying too hard to connect the dots and it was starting to cloud his judgment. It had been a long time since he'd even come close to a friendship with anyone of the opposite sex and he wasn't accustomed to it and should really be flattered. He closed his eyes and let it go at that.

EIGHTEEN

By ten A.M., the entire Midlands was under a blanket of sullen gray stratus. Now and then Kingston could hear the mutterings of thunder over the steady drone of the exhaust. Not the cheeriest of beginnings for what could turn out to be a stressful day, he thought. He spotted the Stafford exit signs ahead and moved to the inside lane. Since leaving London on the M1, he'd seized the opportunity to open up his prized TR4 and give the old gal a long-overdue workout. For him, an hour of Motorway driving was fifty-five minutes too long, so he'd planned ahead to exit early and take the less-traveled roads to Stafford and the Staffordshire police headquarters.

Half an hour later he arrived at the police station, a three-story yellow-painted building on the northeast side of the city. At the front desk, the duty sergeant said that Inspector Wheatley was waiting for him. Kingston presented his ID, signed in, and was given directions to the interview room.

Kingston knocked on the door and heard a muffled, "Come in." When he entered,

Wheatley rose from the couch where he'd been writing and crossed the room to meet Kingston.

"Thanks for coming, Doctor," he said with a firm handshake and a spare smile.

"Lawrence is fine," Kingston replied with a more generous smile. "I only use the handle when I need to impress someone — which is hardly ever these days."

"That's fine." Wheatley gestured to an upholstered armchair by a low table. "Please sit down."

Kingston sat and crossed his legs, observing the inspector. He shuffled his notes, preparing to sit on the opposite side of the table. Kingston reckoned that Wheatley was about ten years younger than he and looked to be in good physical shape. He was unexpectedly well dressed compared with most of the policemen Kingston had encountered in his travels: gray flannel suit, crisp white shirt with French cuffs, and tightly knotted tie — not regimental, thank goodness. There was a scrubbed look about him, as if he'd just had a hot shave, which emphasized his eyes, which were watery gray and red rimmed, giving him the appearance of being perpetually tired. He got right down to business.

"The reason we wanted to talk to you

personally, Lawrence, is that we would like to know what, if anything, you've uncovered since you've been working for Morley. We only know what Morley has told us. What we don't know is how up-to-date his information is, or how selective he's been in, shall we say, withholding information. If you know anything that we don't, I want to hear it now."

Wheatley's use of the majestic plural, as it's often called — the use of "we" to refer to a single person — gave Kingston pause for an inner smile. He recalled the admonishment stating that its use should be restricted only to kings, poets, or people with tapeworm.

"I'd be most surprised if Morley would be guilty of that," he replied, thinking on the question. From his previous jousts with the police, Kingston was no stranger to the methodology of police interviews and with what barristers termed "discovery," the sharing of sensitive information.

"One of the things Lord Morley and I agreed on from the beginning was transparency, Inspector. That anything we discovered would be shared with you, that he would report my findings to you."

"A good try, Lawrence, but it won't wash. What concerns me is how much are you disclosing to *him?* Are we getting the whole story or just what suits you?"

Wheatley's abrupt manner was becoming a mild annoyance, but Kingston restrained himself from replying in kind. "It's been barely a month since I started working for Morley, and in that time I've spoken to him four times at the most. What I'm trying to say is that I don't report to him daily, so there have been and will in the future be times when he's not fully informed."

"Very well. Have you been working on the case these last few days?"

"I have."

"Tell me what you've been doing."

Kingston cleared his throat. "I spoke yesterday to a man named Bryce Lytton, Morley's brother-in-law."

"Regarding . . ."

"When you and I talked on the phone, the time before last, I told you what Veitch had said when I was at the hospital: that he'd uncovered what he termed heinous crimes involving members of the Morley family, crimes of such magnitude that when his story became public it would expose not only one of the biggest cover-ups in our history but also crimes involving staggering amounts of money."

"Yes. We know all about that. No need to

rehash it. So why speak to Lytton?"

"I found a list of names in Veitch's notes. Lytton's was one of them."

"Who else was on the list?"

"Mostly Morley's relatives."

"I see. And where did you find this list?"

"On a flash drive."

"A what?"

"A computer storage device."

"And this was where?"

"At Veitch's house."

"I see." Wheatley scratched his cheek, obviously not fully understanding what Kingston was talking about. "You were at the house *before* the break-in?"

"No. I was at the hospital when it happened — staying in a hotel, in the hopes of seeing Veitch again, to be more accurate. I told you that when we talked on the phone — the James at Lichfield."

For the first time Wheatley looked confused. "Let's get this straight. You found this device containing Veitch's notes after the break-in, and *after* our people had gone through it?"

Kingston could see why the consternation. Why hadn't the police found it?

"Yes."

"We missed it. Is that what you're saying?"

Kingston was tempted to say, "It rather

looks that way, doesn't it," but instead simply nodded.

"I'd like a copy of that list."

"Of course."

"So you're planning to interview all these people?"

"Only several of them, to start." He filled Wheatley in on what he'd learned from Lytton and Hurst, which boiled down to absolutely nothing. When Kingston explained that they both felt the Morley family feud was nothing but a legend and could have little bearing on the murders, Wheatley nodded his head impatiently.

"I must say I agree with them." Wheatley shifted his position on the couch, which didn't look as if it were made for comfort. "So what else was on this drive thing? Anything we should know about?"

"Several pages of historical facts and figures about people living at the time the admiral and his brother were alive: Walpole, the prime minister; his son Horace; Thomas Gray, the poet. Not much else."

"Why them?"

"I haven't the foggiest. He was a historian, I suppose."

"I'd like to see them anyway."

"I'll send everything."

"Good. And what about Endicott's

mother? Did you learn anything from her?"

The sudden change of subject threw Kingston for a second. He supposed that was Wheatley's intent.

"Nothing, other than that her son was an accomplished gardener. He'd won some awards growing dahlias."

"Then he probably belonged to a garden club. Being a botanist, that would interest you, of course."

"Yes. Tristan Veitch was a gardener, too."

"I gathered as much when we were at his house. The garden was quite impressive. Can't say that much for the house, though."

Kingston nodded.

Wheatley smiled. "I don't need to tell you, everyone is a gardener in this country. Anyway, we explored that connection and found nothing."

An uneasy silence followed, as Kingston waited for the next question or comment, but none came. Wheatley appeared to be immersed in thought and Kingston wondered if he'd run out of questions, but that wasn't the case.

"How well do you know Amanda Veitch?" Wheatley asked phlegmatically, tilting back his head slightly, chin resting on his forefinger.

The question surprised Kingston and he

scrambled to find an answer that was non committal. "Not well at all, really. As I explained, I happened to come into her life at the worst possible time — for her, that is. I simply did what I could to help her deal with the tragedy, that's all."

"What do you know about her? Her background, her relationship with her brother? Were they friendly?"

"As far as I know," he replied. "Nothing she's said or done has given me the slightest reason to suspect that there was any animosity or conflict between them, if that's what you mean. After all, they lived together."

"So do married couples — and we hardly raise an eyebrow when a quiet-mannered hubby slips arsenic into his abusive wife's Ovaltine, or vice versa."

"Are you suggesting that Amanda might have murdered her brother?" As soon as the words had left his mouth he knew that he should have phrased it differently. It gave the impression that he and Amanda were closer than he'd intimated, that he was leaping to her defense.

Wheatley remained impassive. "Not necessarily. We're simply interested in knowing how someone managed to poison a man who rarely wandered far from home and had few visitors. In this business we sometimes get too hung up with the small details — I'm not saying that they're not important — but sometimes it's what's staring you in the face that gets overlooked. That said, we'll be talking with Miss Veitch again in the next couple of days."

Kingston was impatient to move on and forget Amanda for now. "I understand your reasons for suspicion and the need for diligence, Inspector," he said. "All I'm saying is that, in all of our conversations, she has appeared deeply and genuinely disturbed by her brother's death and the way it happened."

"We'll see, won't we?" Wheatley got abruptly to his feet. "Thanks for coming, Doctor. And you won't forget to send me a copy of that list and the other papers you mentioned."

"I won't. And from now on I'll make sure that you're informed of new developments as they happen and not after the fact."

"That would be appreciated," said Wheatley. The way he said it, Kingston couldn't be sure whether he was being sarcastic or not.

With that, the interview ended.

NINETEEN

On the short walk to his car, Wheatley's last words were still swimming in Kingston's head. Did the inspector really suspect Amanda? Kingston harked back to the day that the two of them spent together. She had been so adamant and convincing in denying knowledge of the poison, aconitine, or how it could have been administered. She appeared to have been as perplexed by it all as he was. Could he have misjudged her? If Wheatley were right — which Kingston prayed would not be the case — Kingston would end up looking mighty foolish.

Settling into the bucket seat of the TR, he managed a smile. He wondered how he was going to explain all this to Andrew. He wasn't good at baring his soul and had gone to great lengths all his life to avoid doing so. He inserted the key in the ignition and turned it on. Amanda was still the only thing on his mind, and it took several seconds before he realized that the starter motor was still grinding away. He waited for a half minute, then tried again — still no ignition. He sighed, got out, and opened the bonnet. On top of his skirmish with Wheatley this was the last thing he needed. He looked into the engine compartment to make a visual assessment, to see if he could spot any obvious problems. Then he noticed it.

Balanced atop the chrome-plated valve cover was a package the size of a small book wrapped in brown paper. His name was typed on the plain white label. "What the hell . . ."

He picked it up and studied it, turning it over. He wondered if he should open it, keeping in mind letter bombs, booby traps, and the like. He decided that he was being excessively cautious and that no conflagration or such could result by simply tearing off the wrapping. Even so, he removed it slowly and methodically. He tossed the wrapping paper into the car and looked at the book: *Countryside Flowers of Britain.* He took a quick look to see if a note was tucked inside or anything was written in the opening pages: nothing. More confused than ever, he tossed it carefully onto the passenger seat, on top of his blazer, and went back to see why the car wouldn't start, how it had been disabled. A quick check of the obvious located the problem. The distributor cap was open and the rotor had been removed. He let out a deep sigh, knowing that he was either going to have to call for a tow or phone around to find a parts company that might have a replacement in stock — the latter most unlikely, he knew.

He closed the bonnet, slipped behind the wheel, and flipped open his mobile. He stared out the windscreen at the row of parked cars opposite, wondering whom to call first. Then he saw the rotor, sitting on top of the leather cowling above the instrument panel to his left. He was surprised that he hadn't noticed it earlier.

A minute later, he was on the road out of the city heading home, more perplexed than ever as to why someone would want to disable his car as a way to leave a book on wildflowers in the engine compartment, of all places. Surely there had to be an easier way. It was absurd — or was he missing something? He couldn't help thinking back on what Wheatley had said: "Sometimes it's what's staring you in the face that gets overlooked." Kingston hoped that it wasn't an omen.

After an uneventful but rainy drive home, Kingston placed the book on the coffee table and went to the kitchen to rustle up something to eat. He made a mental list of the things needing action in the coming hours and days. First was to continue the interviews — Julian Heywood tomorrow, then Jessica Henshawe. He must also find a way to contact Vanessa Decker. If she was still living abroad, that could be difficult. Then there was the gardening connection. Despite Wheatley's dismissal of a possible relationship, he wanted to sniff around some of the Staffordshire garden organizations — or, better, try to locate dahlia societies, to establish whether Veitch and Endicott were members and, if so, if they'd belonged to the same garden club. He should call Andrew, too. It had been some time.

Picking up the phone in the living room, he noticed that the flashing answerphone light showed one message. He must have missed it before. He pressed Play.

"My name's Tyler Holbrook. My wife and I own Winterborne Manor."

Kingston listened more closely. New England accent, he thought.

"I was talking with my builder, Mike Kennedy, last week. He said that you'd called him about the frieze in the dining room. There's probably not much more that I can add that he hasn't told you already, but I reminded him of something that cropped up during the demolition. He thought it might interest you and gave me your number. If you'd like to give me a call, I'll be happy to explain." Kingston jotted down the phone number.

Ten minutes later in his study, with a cup of just-poured tea at his side, Kingston made the call. A young child answered. With engaging candor she volunteered that her father was in the garden trying to start a lawn mower, without success, and that she would run and tell him right away that "Dr. Kingston was returning his call."

In less than a minute, Holbrook was on the line.

"I hope it's not a bad time?" said Kingston.

"No, not at all. Glad to take a break, actually. Libby probably told you — the damned lawn mower?"

"She did."

"Let me tell you why I called you, Doctor. Mike Kennedy said that when you and he talked he'd neglected to tell you what we found when we started to dismantle the frieze in the dining room. For what it's worth, I thought it might add a nice touch of interest to your story."

"I haven't finished the piece yet," Kingston fibbed, "so I'd love to hear about it."

"When I first told Mike that we were taking out the frieze, he was not only horrified but reluctant to do the work. Through a mutual friend we'd sold the tiles to an antiques dealer and, naturally, he insisted that each and every one be in mint condition. We were concerned at first that, being porcelain and old, too, it mightn't be possible. Mike didn't want to take responsibility for it, and I can't say as I blame him. Eventually he called in a guy from an architectural salvage company who was expert in that sort of thing. Even then, it turned out to be a painstaking process that took several days to complete. Anyway, getting to the reason for my call — behind one of the tiles they discovered a small cubbyhole cut into the wall. Inside was a letter — three sheets of handwritten notes."

Kingston's pulse quickened. "Really?"

"Yes. They were yellowed with age but in remarkable shape, all things considered."

"What were they about?"

"They referred mostly to the history of the house. I was prepared to include them with the frieze, as part of the sale, but Mike insisted that they belonged with the house."

"So you still have them?"

"We do. As a matter of fact, we had the pages professionally preserved by an archive specialist in Oxford, chap called Lewellyn-Jones — they're now the centerpiece of a scrapbook we've put together on the property. A historical record of Winterborne."

"Would it be possible to see them?"

"Sure. I have copies, would those do?"

"That would be fine."

"If you want to take a look at the originals later, you're welcome to, of course."

"Thank you."

"I'll have my wife, Cassie, mail them."

"You don't have a scanner by any chance? If you do, perhaps you could e-mail copies."

"I do, but the computer crashed on me yesterday. It might take a couple of days."

"That's fine. I appreciate your going to this trouble, Mr. Holbrook."

"Tyler's fine — happy to be of help. We're still a long way off from moving into the house, but when we do, I'll give you a call and you can come down and see it."

"I'd like that," Kingston said, and they bid each other good-bye.

Interesting, Kingston thought — handwritten notes hidden inside the wall. Mostly about the history of the house, Holbrook had said, but still . . . interesting. Winterborne must have been mentioned in Veitch's notes for good reason, but had he known about the papers? Had Veitch managed to obtain copies of the notes? He could have asked Holbrook if he'd given copies to anyone else, he supposed. He decided he would if the notes proved to contain anything of interest.

He was about to get Veitch's list from his study, to determine whom to interview next, when the doorbell rang. It was Andrew with a sheepish look on his face. "Sorry to bother you, Lawrence, but I seem to have locked myself out. Can I borrow the spare key?"

"Come in," said Kingston, smiling. "Where have you been, anyway? Spent all that money you won at Kempton Park on another trip? That was a great evening, by the way. I don't think I thanked you."

"I sold the Lagonda."

"You *did?* You said you'd never part with it."

"I know. But it's been garaged for twelve years and in that time I've driven it at most a couple of dozen times. The good thing is that its value's kept climbing. I got an offer I couldn't refuse, as they say. A chap down in Plymouth of all places."

"You drove a Concours 1937 Lagonda Rapide down to Devon?"

Andrew nodded. "On the back of a flat-bed lorry."

"You continue to amaze me."

"Good news is that I'm filthy rich again, bad news is that I got some kind of bug when I was down there and ended up in a hotel room, sicker than a dog for two days."

"You mean you overcelebrated?"

"Wish that had been the case."

"I'm not going to ask what you sold it for."

"Six figures." Andrew grinned. "About ten times what I paid for it."

"I can see why you recovered so quickly. Care for a drink?"

"Why not?"

They went into the living room, where Kingston poured a vodka and tonic for Andrew and a whisky for himself.

Andrew slumped back on the sofa. "So," he said with an impertinent smile, "how's the case going? Make any sense out of those notes of Veitch's?"

"Not as much as I'd hoped, but I'm following up on a couple of things."

Kingston gave Andrew a blow-by-blow account of what had happened, finishing with the news that Amanda was now, of all things, a murder suspect.

Andrew finally stopped shaking his head in displeasure and took a last gulp of his drink. "What can I say, Lawrence," he said with a sigh.

After a moment's silence, the conversation turned to the upcoming Open Garden day. Andrew had decided to make a long weekend of it, with a blowout brunch on Monday, to which they would invite mutual friends. Andrew mentioned Henrietta's name, which brought moans of protest from Kingston. She was a bohemian artist type who had a habit of becoming brazenly amorous after a couple gin and tonics and for some reason always targeted him. They chatted for another five minutes, after which Kingston left to get Andrew's key, kept on a hook in the kitchen.

When he returned, Andrew was leafing through the British flower book that Kingston had left on the coffee table, planning to look at it later.

"Nice," Andrew said, getting up. "Someone's pressed a flower in it."

Kingston placed the key on the table and looked over Andrew's shoulder to see what he was talking about. His scalp tightened and tingled. The pressed flower was blue and the title on the page opposite was AC-ONITUM.

After Kingston had described the deadly properties of the plant, Andrew went to the butler's table, where he refreshed their drinks — this round as much for palliative reasons. The look on his face and lack of his usual exhortations were clear signs that the threat implicit in the pressed flower had shaken him as much as it had Kingston.

"What do you plan to do now, Lawrence?"

he asked soberly.

Kingston paused before answering. "I don't know. I need time to think about it." His eyes darted around the room as he weighed the disturbing new development.

"What the hell is there to think about? Whoever sent that is deadly serious. If you ask me, they murdered Veitch and Endicott to prevent them from revealing this big secret that they'd stumbled on and now it seems you're in their way, so —"

"I'm not so sure it's that simple. What if it turns out that Amanda poisoned her brother? How would that square with your rationale?"

"I thought you said that was almost out of the question."

"I did, but now I'm wondering . . ."

Andrew sighed. "I never thought I'd ever hear myself say this, but I'm beginning to think that I should get a little more involved in your ill-advised activities. Which doesn't mean to say that I'm going to risk life and limb, chasing criminals down dark alleyways, though."

"Are you actually offering to help?"

"Up to a point, yes."

"I appreciate that, Andrew, it's not like you. All right, then, here's what I suggest we do. First, we continue with the inter-

273

views. I want to talk with some of the gardening clubs and societies as well. There's also the outcome of Wheatley's interview with Amanda we may have to contend with. If she's charged with murdering her brother — heaven forbid — that could change everything."

"Do you plan to tell Inspector Wheatley about this?"

"You mean the pressed flower?"

Andrew nodded.

"Sooner or later. It's really up to Morley. I'll tell him first."

"There's something else you have to do, too." Andrew stood and glanced down at the book one last time. "Install one of those peephole security gizmos in the front door."

"I'll think about it," said Kingston.

Andrew nodded, then spoke again, in a more serious tone. "Lawrence, I've learned by now that, regardless of what I think, you'll plow straight ahead anyway and do what you believe is best, despite the inherent dangers. But this time, it's obvious you need to take extra care."

"I will. That's a promise."

TWENTY

Kingston was up before daylight the next morning, having spent the night tossing and turning, thinking about the most recent turn of events, including the implicit warning in the flower book and wondering who sent it. No question, it must be someone who wanted him off the case. Although Morley was getting impatient, it was most unlikely that he — or Crawford, for that matter — would want that. Amanda was the only person he could think of who was dead set against his continuing the investigation, but for her to have sent it seemed utterly absurd. He couldn't imagine her doing such a thing.

After breakfast, he began by Googling *Dahlia Societies UK.* The first listing was the National Dahlia Society. There he found a link to the Midlands Dahlia Society. On that site, he wrote an e-mail message, requesting information on William Endicott and/or Tristan Veitch. He went on to say that he'd been told that either or both had won awards from the society in past years and he was interested in knowing which garden clubs the two men represented. He did not mention that both men had been murdered. Doubtless all the club members would be more than aware of the double tragedy by now. He signed off using his full title: Professor of Botany, University of Edinburgh (Ret.).

He was going to make more calls, but he didn't want to be late for his midday appointment with Julian Heywood. He shut down the Mac and went to get dressed.

Performance Motors was more upmarket than Kingston had expected. On any other occasion he could easily have spent an hour ogling the spit-polished Mercedes-Benzes, BMWs, Audis, Porsches, Aston Martins, and the odd Bentley and Roller that paraded their distinguished marques on the showroom's black granite floor as if jewels on velvet. The rare display of automotive pulchritude engendered no feelings of ambition or envy in Kingston. Though he could afford a few of the entry-level models, owning such cars was no longer the temptation it had been in the past. His doughty TR4 served him well, and the only way they would ever part company would be when either or both became too infirm to continue the trusty relationship.

When Julian Heywood approached, after being paged, it took Kingston a few moments to recognize him. He wore a gray chalk-stripe suit that smacked of Savile Row, with white-collared pink shirt and a neatly patterned dark blue tie. His hair appeared shorter and better groomed than when they'd last met: just the kind of person you would want to negotiate the sale of a £50,000 Jag.

"Let's go into the showroom," said Heywood, after introductions. "My office is a little claustrophobic."

They settled into comfortable leather swivel seats at the end of a long modern-design table.

"I must say, your collection is impressive," said Kingston. "Outside of the London Motor Show, I don't recall having seen so many beautiful cars under one roof."

"It's the biggest in the country, actually."

"I won't take too much of your time — is it all right if I call you Julian?"

"Of course."

"You're no doubt familiar with the murder of William Endicott at Sturminster and the subsequent homicide of a man named Tristan Veitch, who is now believed to have been a friend or an associate."

Heywood nodded. "I am. I'm surprised it hasn't received a lot of press. We don't get too many murders around here."

"I'm told that was a police decision. I'm

not privy to the reasons why but I imagine that it has to do with shifting attention away from Sturminster. You probably know about the disaster that resulted after the ill-advised Arcadian monument–Bletchley Park public relations debacle a few years back."

"I do. I was working there at the time. Not for long, though."

"What were you doing?"

"General dogsbody, I suppose you'd call it."

"That's how you came to know Simon Crawford?"

Julian nodded. "The only decent one in the bunch."

"By bunch, you mean —"

"The Morleys. Particularly that creep Francis."

"Your uncle, I believe?"

"Uncle. Don't make me laugh. The man's a liar and a cheat, and he treats his staff like peasants."

"I've heard stories to that effect." Kingston cracked a sardonic smile. "So you quit?"

"I was fired. Morley accused me of theft."

"Were you innocent?"

Julian nodded again. "Of course. If it hadn't been for Simon, Morley would have filed criminal charges. That's the kind of thing he does. One moment he's as nice as pie, the next, a sadistic bastard."

"Do you see much of Crawford?"

"Very little. From time to time I've tried to get him interested in a few of our cars — that's about it. He always maintains that he can't afford nice cars anymore. Maybe Sturminster's going through a rough patch financially. I don't know."

For the next ten minutes Kingston asked Julian Heywood much the same fundamental questions as he had Bryce Lytton and Sebastian Hurst. Heywood's answers were quick and terse, mostly yes or no. It reminded Kingston of his interview with Simon Crawford. The similarity in response was striking. It was time, Kingston decided, to start asking questions to which yes or no would not be adequate answers.

"How long have you known Simon Crawford?"

Heywood thought for a moment. "Must be six or seven years. Soon after he came to work for my uncle."

"He told me that he owned an XK120." Kingston smiled. "One of yours?"

"No. I've been trying to get him to part with it. It's in Concours shape — a convertible, worth a bundle. Jaguar made three versions — roadster, convertible, and coupé."

"Yes, I remember. Is that why you were at

Sturminster the day we met?"

"Er . . . yes. As a matter of fact, it was."

"Did Crawford ever discuss either of the murders with you?"

"We'd discussed Endicott's. For a while it was the only thing everyone at Sturminster was talking about."

"Did he offer any opinions?"

Heywood shook his head again. "Not that I recall." He blinked restlessly, then looked away briefly. "Do you think Simon knows something about it . . . is he involved in some way?"

"No. I'm only trying to establish the relationship between some of you Morleys and other people close to the family or Sturminster itself. Lord Morley provided me with a list," he said, taking it from his jacket pocket. "Mind taking a look at it and telling me who you know and who you don't?"

Heywood studied the list for a minute, then looked up. "I know who most of them are. Not to say that I know much about them."

"Who are you unsure of?"

"I don't know a Vanessa Decker, or Roger Bartram."

"Morley seems to think she's a distant cousin, living abroad."

Heywood shook his head. "I don't know her."

"Roger Bartram is an associate of Bryce Lytton, your stepfather, I believe."

"I wouldn't know that."

"You sound as if you don't want to know."

"Let's just say that I'm persona non grata as far as Lytton is concerned. The feeling's mutual."

"I see," said Kingston, remembering Lytton's reaction when Julian's name was mentioned. "You wouldn't know his partner, Sebastian Hurst, then?"

"Only by name," he said.

"You do know Oliver and Jessica Henshawe, though?"

"I've met them only a couple of times — years ago. He's related to Lord Morley, a cousin, I believe. They live in Leicester, as I recall."

"What does his wife, Jessica, do?"

"Does she work, you mean?"

Kingston nodded.

"Not that I'm aware."

"Did you know they were divorced?"

"I didn't, too bad. As I said, I met them quite a few years ago." He handed back the list.

Kingston gazed over Heywood's shoulder, his eyes resting on a "previously owned" silver Jaguar XK8 convertible. It was distracting to be asking such probing questions surrounded by many millions of pounds' worth of seductive cars. He wondered for a moment if Heywood had chosen the showroom for that very reason. He shrugged off the idea as overreaching and turned his attention back to Heywood who, if nothing else, was at least exhibiting patience and proper respect for the grave circumstances warranting the interview. Kingston felt uncomfortable having to ask probing personal questions but proceeded anyway.

"Forgetting Lytton, how well do you get on with your family, in general?"

Heywood swiveled his chair to and fro, pondering his answer. "Rather an odd question, since there are so many of us. With the exception of Francis Morley and Lytton, all right, I suppose. If you've talked with some of the Morleys already, you'll have no doubt gathered that we may be typically British in that sense. We treat each other with respect in some cases, tolerance in others, and avoidance occasionally. Speaking for myself, I try to maintain distance and only minimal contact, enough to be considered acceptable. My late grandmother summed it up well. She used to say that families are like fudge — mostly sweet with a few nuts."

Kingston smiled. "Any Morley nutty enough to get mixed up in this mess?"

"Not that I know of."

"Tell me something, Julian. It seems that with almost every family member I've talked to these last weeks — other people, too — the rumor of a lingering family feud surfaces. You're a younger member, I know, but have you ever heard anything that would provide evidence or give credence of such a rift ever existing?"

"Sure, I've heard about it. But I've always been given to believe that it took place centuries ago — when Admiral Morley accused his brother with walking off with money that was supposed to be used exclusively for improvements at Sturminster."

"Yes, we know that already," said Kingston, perhaps a trifle huffily, having heard the same refrain a half dozen times. "But what I keep asking myself is whether this feud has anything to do with recent events, whether there's a connection of some sort — perhaps a secret that has lain dormant for two hundred and fifty years and has now been uncovered?"

"And that's why people are being murdered?" A restrained expression of amusement passed over Heywood's good-looking features. "Sounds positively Gothic. You

283

think a living family member might be involved?"

"I don't know. Let's just say that it's my job to find out."

"If I hear anything, I'll certainly let you know." Heywood reached in his back trouser pocket and took out his wallet. Glancing inside, he said, "I seem to be out of business cards. I have some in the office. I'll give you one before you leave."

Kingston was out of questions anyway, so he rose, at the same time handing Heywood his card, which he'd put in his shirt pocket in anticipation. They left the airy showroom for Heywood's office.

While Julian was taking out a box of business cards from his top drawer, Kingston looked around the cramped space. Several framed pictures of cars and a couple of plaques adorned the wall behind the desk. For the most part the room was tidy; the desk bore the usual stacks of folders, papers, computer, and two trophies, which Kingston guessed to be for sales performance. Accepting Julian's card from across the desk, he glimpsed something that gave him pause. Next to the box of cards in the still-open drawer, among the pens, pencils, paper clips, et cetera, he wouldn't have noticed it if not for its shiny color. It was a small gold horseshoe identical to the one that Bryce Lytton had given Kingston.

TWENTY-ONE

Driving home, Kingston spent the first ten minutes speculating as to how a gold horseshoe trinket from Windrush Stables had ended up in Julian Heywood's drawer. After having just made it eminently clear that he had no time for his stepfather, it begged the question as to how Julian had come by it. If Lytton had given it to Julian, which would be the most logical answer, it could have been a long time ago, before he and his stepfather had a falling-out. The other implication — an intriguing one — was that Julian had lied, but if so, why? Could several Morleys be in on this together? Was the whole idea of a family feud nothing more than a cover-up?

The brake lights of the lorry in front of him went on suddenly. He jammed his foot on the brakes just in time to avoid what could have been a nasty crunch. "Forget the bloody Morleys," he muttered. He turned on the radio and concentrated on the road.

He was on the straight stretch of the A4 between Newbury and Reading when he realized there was a car following him.

It was a gray BMW, with a man at the wheel. It had maintained a comfortable distance for the last half hour or so, which in itself wasn't necessarily unusual but there had been many places where passing would have been possible, and in his experience BMW drivers were usually the first with lights flashing and foot to the pedal. He thought no more of it, and by the time he'd passed through Reading, ten miles later, the car had gone.

But an hour later, crossing the Chiswick Flyover, making a quick lane change, he swore he caught a glimpse of the BMW again, several cars back. He dismissed the thought, reminding himself that there must be hundreds if not thousands of gray BMWs on the roads. Ten minutes later he arrived at his garage with no further signs of phantom gray BMWs. The TR4 safely locked up, Kingston headed for the King's Road, where he planned to stop at Partridges deli to pick up dinner and a bottle of port.

Crossing Sloane Square, he passed the central fountain and waited at the traffic light to cross to the Sloane Street side. Out of the corner of his eye he caught a glimpse of a man in a dark windbreaker. The nondescript middle-aged man had just stopped and taken a seat on a nearby bench, where he unfolded the newspaper he was carrying and started to read. The signal changed to green and Kingston crossed. On the other side of the road, directly ahead, was Peter Jones. Turning past a large window displaying their Hugo Boss men's summer clothing, he saw a clear reflection of the square. He was puzzled to see that the man in the windbreaker was now standing at the same traffic light — that had since turned to red — waiting for it to change. After the episode with the BMW, Kingston was beginning to question his judgment. He was imagining things, he told himself. But why, he wondered, had the man sat for such a short time if he'd planned to read the paper? Kingston kept walking, tempted to sneak a backward glance. Fifty yards farther along, now on the King's Road, an opportunity presented itself that gave him a plausible reason to look back. Two kids on skateboards were rolling toward him, and though there was no danger of collision, Kingston stepped adroitly to one side, turning as he did, to let them pass. About fifty feet back, he saw the man stop suddenly and look at a store window.

That put it to rest, then. There was no question anymore that his first instincts had been correct. Why was he being followed? To find out where he lived was the first reason that came to mind. On second thought, that didn't make too much sense because nowadays there were many ways of obtaining personal addresses. The other reason, which he preferred not to dwell on, was that if the man shadowing him had anything to do with the people who'd killed Endicott and Veitch, he could be in danger, too.

Thinking hard how he could shake the man off, Kingston picked up his pace, doing his best to conjure movie scenes where the good guy had outsmarted a tail, trying to recall an evasive measure that might work. A mad dash along the crowded pavements of the King's Road was out of the question, and he didn't know of shops where he could casually enter and quickly slip out the back door into an alley, to leap over the convenient fence and vanish. When he saw the number 11 double-decker bus ahead, taking on passengers, the answer was staring him in the face. Timing would be critical, he knew. He was about twenty feet away and only one passenger remained to board the bus. The moment the elderly gentleman was safely on the bus's platform, Kingston would start his dash. If he gauged it just right, he could reach the bus and jump on before it gathered too much speed. It had been a long time since he'd done it, but he would soon find out if he still had it in him.

At the back of the bus, not even winded, Kingston looked back to see the man in the distance standing on the pavement, newspaper dangling at his side, watching the bus disappear. Kingston's smile was short-lived. He had a distinct feeling that it was only a temporary reprieve.

Hopping off the bus three stops later, he backtracked and made a hurried and wary shopping stop at Partridges. Ten minutes later, back at the flat, he closed the door behind him with his back and a sigh of relief. Andrew was right. He was going to have to be very careful indeed from now on. He picked up the post.

In the kitchen, Kingston put the Partridges bag on the counter, then went to the living room, dropping the post on the coffee table. Standing to one side of the window, he pulled the curtain back slightly and looked down onto the street. All appeared normal, no sign of the man with the newspaper.

He sat on the sofa and riffled through the post. Among the usual smattering of bills and junk mail was an envelope with a return address he didn't recognize at first. From Holbrook, he realized. It must be the copies of the three pages found behind the frieze. He pulled out the sheets of paper and the brief cover note from Holbrook, unfolded them, and flattened them out on the table.

He was pleased to see that the copies were clear and that the handwriting, which had a graceful calligraphic quality, was legible. He was amused, as always when he read early writings, by the spelling of many of the words and the letter "e" added to words, making "downe" and "halfe"; the flourish resembling an "f" in place of "s," making the "professor" appear as "profeffor."

The first page described the site and orientation of the house with respect to the surrounding land, conditions of climate, and its relationship and significance to neighboring villages and towns. *"The land was highe of no particular shape and, with nothing in the way of trees, walls or hedges, was frequently windswept. The soil was described as heavy and not suitable for the purposes of agriculture."*

He learned that the land around the house was developed as the house itself was still under construction, a practice that many of today's builders might well be advised to adopt, he mused. The various designs and layouts of driveways, paths, walls, fencing, gates, ornamental and kitchen gardens, and planting of trees, hedges, and borders were described in great detail.

The next page referred to the house itself, how it was designed and constructed. He was starting to get a sinking feeling that this and the remaining page would be much of the same. By the time he'd reached the bottom of the page, he was even more discouraged, now worried that the papers would prove to be of no help whatsoever to his investigation

He turned to the last page, running his forefinger down, reading slowly though knowing that odds were that it would be no different from the others. Near the foot of the page, he almost missed the word "frieze." He stopped and reread the paragraph:

The dining room is to be embellished with a decorative frieze embracing its foure walls. The quotation chosen will be rendered in decorative porcelain tile worke. Each tile, approximately one-foote square, is to be individually designed to display a letter of the alphabet. At the recommendation of Architect, Matthew Seward, the highly respected designer Godfrey Upjohn has beene commissioned to undertake design and fabrication of the tiles. Seward is noted for his interpretations of classical Hellenic architecture as ably demonstrated in the Grecian-inspired monuments at the Sturminster estate in Nottinghamshire, commissioned by Samuel Morley; and at Aspinhill Court in Leicestershire. Seward and Upjohn have created designs for several places of business, private residences, and follies, including those of the Right Honorable Jeffrey Wylde, Lady Marchfield, and the statesman, writer Horace Walpole.

Seward. Sturminster. Morley. Names that Veitch would have been very interested in, though what relevance they — or the frieze — had to the matter at hand wasn't clear. Still, Veitch was interested in them, so . . .

He slowly shook his head. It was all so infuriatingly confusing.

He folded the pages and placed them back in Holbrook's envelope. He was about to put them in a drawer of his tansu — until such time he could take another look at them, if he ever did — when he paused, staring at the envelope in his hand. He tried to recall Holbrook's exact words but couldn't.

Kingston was sure that he'd said something to the effect that they'd found a letter and it was three pages. But knowing that it would be sealed up behind a wall for God knows how many years, wouldn't the person hiding the letter have placed it in an envelope?

He put the envelope in the top drawer of the Japanese chest and started for the bedroom. He knew why the absence of an envelope nagged him. It was the outside chance that the envelope itself might offer further elucidation: whether it was addressed to anyone; if it noted the contents, dates, anything that might help. He was grasping at straws again, but he was getting used to that. He stopped, went back and picked up the phone. Why wait? he asked himself, as he entered Holbrook's number.

He was surprised when Tyler answered after the second ring.

"It's Lawrence," he said. "Sorry to bother you, but perhaps you could answer a quick question?"

"Sure."

"Were you there when the papers were discovered behind the frieze?"

"I was at the house that day, yes."

"Do you recall if there were just the three sheets, or were they in an envelope?"

"They were in an envelope. I remember

because it was an unusual shape."

"Do you still have it?"

"I believe so. Why?"

"I don't know. It's sheer speculation on my part. Was anything written on the envelope? Was it addressed to anyone? Dated? Anything else?"

"Odd you should ask, because we wondered what they meant."

"They?"

"The letters written on the inside flap of the envelope."

"What do you mean by letters?"

"A long sequence of letters of the alphabet, separated by a vertical line with an arrow pointing to another, longer, sequence. Gibberish. We made a scan of it. I could send it to you."

Kingston couldn't hold back his exuberance. "Absolutely. Please."

"Do you mind telling me what the hell's going on here, Lawrence?"

"It's a long story, as they say, but I've every reason to believe that those letters you've described could be some kind of code. They could be the key to solving a riddle that goes back more than two hundred years."

"You're kidding? Only in England!"

"I really appreciate this, Tyler . . ."

"I happen to be on the computer, so I'll send it right away."

Five minutes later, Kingston's Mac *dinged*. He opened Holbrook's e-mail with the attachment and read his note:

Dr. Kingston,

I guess I should have mentioned the envelope before. It was larger than a standard one and the face of it was blank. We thought nothing of it 'til Libby noticed the writing inside in black ink. We had no idea what it all meant other than it could have been some kind of secret message, so we saved it. Do you think that's what it is?

Tyler

Kingston opened the attachment and smiled. The scan showed two long lines made up of random letters of the alphabet. Underneath them was a vertical arrow pointing to seven more lines of jumbled letters below. All told, he figured there could be as many as two hundred characters. For a moment he flashed back to the letters on the monument at Sturminster.

It was a code of some kind. It had to be.

TWENTY-TWO

Kingston printed it out. He was relieved to see that all the letters were readable, though some had faded somewhat. He studied them closely. With the nine lines separated by a vertical arrow, he reasoned that there were probably two separate codes and that solving the first would provide information that unlocked the key to the second. To begin, he decided to focus on the first two lines:

HEPYEVUAOTJGOTNPGVITUGINICHUM
ZCGIPYHUAUASJUYIGUVVEARGUOXH

↓

HMFCZBTZUXDCINGFGXLJVIURSGWMKNLF
BSKAWTHERZFBYPTIXILJIMAEOMGGIUZA
XNQYTNOMDXMJBEGMYYQXNCIMPXGYCVXX
PBWZZTOLPKFSRGJQFEJAUYVTHIUEUIUC
QWWPSVDAXOUONCQMOBDFBUFWHOBNTILQ
YZHVRPMFTBUFBGATLUIBJWYOJDVFSRMC
OVUGMYTZWNGYWAZWCIMFINKICCNAYOWXWD

There was no longer any question in his mind that it was a cipher, a code of some kind. If so, what sort of message? Short sentences? Places? People? Geographic coordinates? Directions? He closed his eyes for several seconds, dredging up what he knew about codes, the fundamentals he'd been taught in army intelligence. Cryptography generally, he knew, could be divided into two branches, known as transposition and substitution. If this were a transposition cipher, the letters of the message would have been rearranged systematically, effectively generating an anagram. If it were a substitution cipher, each letter of the Roman alphabet would have been paired with a different letter.

There was only one problem, and it was significant. To decipher the code, the receiver must possess what is commonly referred to as a "key," a shift pattern that specifies the exact details of how the encryption or code was devised.

The Winterborne code, as he'd decided to call it, represented a huge potential breakthrough but, as it stood, the string of letters meant nothing without the key. He thought of calling the man at GCHQ who had looked at the message found on Endicott's body, knowing that he could probably make faster progress, but he decided against it for now. In any case, without the key, he doubted that even the most expert cryptanalyst could do anything with the letters on the envelope.

About to close down the computer, there was a *ding* announcing another e-mail. It was from Muriel Williams, secretary of the Midlands Dahlia Society. A response to his query, he hoped.

Dear Dr. Kingston,

In answer to your inquiry regarding Mr. William Endicott and Mr. Tristan Veitch, I am sad to report that both men were victims of recent homicides. I can provide the following information, which we sent recently to the Nottinghamshire police who made a similar inquiry:

Both men exhibited and won awards in several local dahlia shows in the years between 2002 and 2005. Mr. Endicott won prizes at the National, Royal Bath & West Show at Shepton Mallet in 2003 and again in 2005. Mr. Veitch won similar local awards and a National award at Harrogate in 2004.

Both were members of the National Dahlia Society and the Brookside Garden Club in Derby.

I hope this helps in your inquiry.

Sincerely,
Muriel Williams
Secretary, Midlands Dahlia Society

Kingston printed the letter and read it a second time, always a habit. For starters, it confirmed that Wheatley had followed through on the garden connection between Veitch and Endicott. "Interesting," he muttered, recalling Wheatley's saying that this thread had led nowhere. Nevertheless, he still intended to follow up. The police were not always right.

Establishing a direct relationship between Endicott and Veitch represented a critical step in the case. Apart from anything else, it meant that the probability of Endicott having worked with Veitch on his project had increased exponentially. But something puzzled him. It was logical to assume that Veitch had been killed to silence him and to steal the volatile information that he'd dredged up, but what motive could those same people have for killing Endicott? It seemed far-fetched that their both belonging to the same garden club held the answer.

Putting the letter aside, he decided to call Ms. Williams sooner rather than later and try to arrange for a meeting with one of the officers of Brookside Garden Club. Perhaps he could arrange for a visit with Amanda as well, since he'd be in the area anyway.

Later that evening, he and Andrew met for

dinner and a couple pints in the upstairs bar at the Antelope. While they were waiting for their food, Kingston reached in his pocket and took out the sequence of letters copied from Holbrook's envelope. He placed the paper on the table in front of Andrew.

"What do you make of this?" he said.

Andrew studied it for a few seconds, then looked up, frowning. "What are those letters supposed to be? Welsh postal codes?"

Kingston smiled. "Good try. No, I believe they're ciphertexts — codes of some sort."

"Really? How did you come by it?"

"They were written on an envelope that contained historical papers found concealed in the wall of an old house near Banbury — behind a frieze, actually."

"This has to do with the Sturminster case, I take it?"

"I've reason to believe it does. The house dates back to the early part of the eighteenth century, so it's reasonable to conclude that the envelope could have been placed there a long time ago."

"Over two hundred years?"

"Maybe."

"How did you find out about all this?"

"The house and the frieze were mentioned in Veitch's notes. No details, just a brief comment. The frieze was also mentioned in the hidden historical papers."

"So how are these cipher things decoded, deciphered, whatever the word is?"

"It requires what is called a key phrase. It's like a PIN, in a manner of speaking. Only two parties have access to it, usually the sender and the receiver. Though it could be composed of numbers, it's invariably a series of letters, a word or phrase that can be committed to memory."

"How do you know all this stuff?"

"I thought you knew — courtesy of Her Majesty. I took intelligence courses at JSSI, Joint Services School of Intelligence, in Ashford, back in the fifties."

"Like Bletchley?"

"Somewhat. Let me show you the basic methodology." He took a pen from his inside pocket and wrote the alphabet in capital letters on an empty space on the paper place mat.

ABCDEFGHIJKLMNOPQRSTUVWXYZ

"All right," he said. "Cryptography 101. First I'll show you a substitution cipher used by Julius Caesar. As you might guess, it's referred to as the Caesar shift cipher or simply the Caesar shift."

"Cipher meaning . . . ?"

"In simple terms, a system of substituting letters or symbols. A secret way of writing or a code."

Andrew nodded, looking only mildly interested, and sipped his beer.

"One type of substitution cipher our friend Julius used — and it's well documented, by the way — was to replace each letter in the message with the letter three or more places farther along the alphabet. Like this," he said, writing under the plain alphabet. "This is referred to as the cipher alphabet."

```
ABCDEFGHIJKLMNOPQRSTUVWXYZ
DEFGHIJKLMNOPQRSTUVWXYZABC
```

"So if the message to be sent — the plaintext, as it's called — is 'Key is under mat,' the cipher text would be: NHB LV XQGHU PDW." He wrote a check mark above the paired letters to further demonstrate.

```
  ✓   ✓✓   ✓ ✓ ✓✓    ✓✓✓✓    ✓
ABCDEFGHIJKLMNOPQRSTUVWXYZ
DEFGHIJKLMNOPQRSTUVWXYZABC
```

"Even I can understand that," said Andrew, now appearing more interested. "To decipher the code you'd have to know how many letters to shift."

"Exactly. However, therein lies a small problem. If the sender and receiver keep the shift number or cipher alphabet written on a piece of paper, enemies could capture it or someone could steal it, discover the key, and immediately read any communications encrypted with it." He put down the pen and looked at Andrew. "You're a high-tech sort. Think of it much in the same way as today's passwords. Rarely are they numerical, they're nearly always a word or name, or a combination thereof — one that's easy to remember." He paused to take a sip of beer and continued. "So the emperor soon realized that a key phrase, easily committed to memory by both the sender and the receiver, was essential. Here's what he did."

Kingston quickly scribbled another plain alphabet on the place mat, then glanced at Andrew to make sure that he wasn't losing interest, which he wasn't. "To make it easy," he said, "I'm going to use the emperor's name as the password — the key phrase, or key for short." He wrote JULIUS CAESAR on the corner of the place mat, then continued. "For it to function as a cipher, we must eliminate any letters in the password that are duplicated, which leaves us with JULISCAER." He looked at Andrew again. "Are you with me, so far?"

"Yes, Professor." Andrew smiled.

"Good. Instead of the simple three-letter shift we used before, we substitute our key phrase followed by the remaining letters of the alphabet after the R, making sure not to repeat any that already appear in our key phrase." He wrote quickly as he spoke. "Like this."

```
ABCDEFGHIJKLMNOPQRSTUVWXYZ
JULISCAERTVWXYZBDFGHKMNOPQ
```

Andrew leaned closer, studying the two rows of letters. "Clever," he muttered. "The lower row contains all the letters of the alphabet with no duplicates."

"Exactly," Kingston replied, handing Andrew his pen. "Now let's see if you can create the ciphertext, the code for our original message: 'Key is under mat.' "

"Piece of cake," said Andrew, starting to pair off the letters. Within thirty seconds he'd written, VSP RG KYISF XJH.

"Excellent," said Kingston. "You've earned another beer."

"Much obliged, but I see the problem already."

"You do, eh?"

"You now have a Winterborne ciphertext but no key. No password. Right?"

"Go to the top of the class."

"How can you . . . we find it?"

"I wish I knew. If I were to hazard a guess, I'd say it has something to do with Winterborne Manor or, more specifically, the frieze, since that's where it was hidden."

"What does this frieze look like?"

Kingston described the alphabet frieze and what little he knew of its history, mentioning the Holbrooks and how co-operative they'd been. By now, each had consumed two pints of Chiswick Bitter and had finished a bottle of Muscadet with dinner. Kingston recognized that it was now pointless to go on talking about Winterborne and the basics of cryptography. This was borne out when he looked up from signing the credit card slip to see Andrew trying to make eye contact with a redhead seated across the crowded room with another woman. Kingston smiled, wondering what Andrew's reaction was going to be if they turned out to be partners and not just friends. Ten minutes later, they left the warmth of the Antelope, feeling no pain, braced for the walk back to Cadogan Square. Kingston opened the pub's door to face a howling gale and drenching rain.

"I have a key phrase for this," Andrew yelled over the tumult.

"I don't want to hear it," Kingston shouted back. "Let's call for a cab."

TWENTY-THREE

At breakfast the next morning, after working on the *Times* crossword for twenty minutes, Kingston had managed to pencil in half a dozen answers. One clue struck him as being particularly ingenious in its brevity: *Happy with what's inside.* The seven-letter answer was *content.* Feeling pleased with himself and clearheaded, he put the puzzle aside and picked up Holbrook's envelope, looking abjectly at the sequences of letters that had been written on it more than two hundred years ago. It was as if they were taunting him. Nine lines of scrambled letters of the alphabet — a couple of hundred at least, he estimated — stood between him and, in all likelihood, the incriminatory secret Veitch had uncovered. Without divine intervention or his discovering something that he'd overlooked in Veitch's notes, he knew that finding the key was next to impossible. By now he'd dredged up every possible word, phrase, and sequence of letters he could think of that might be the key to reading the first of the two encrypted messages. He'd tried the letters found in Endicott's pocket, the sequence of letters on the Arcadian monument, and a dozen others, all without success. He got up and made a fresh pot of tea.

Staring abstractedly out into the small, walled garden, he watched a gray squirrel scamper along the blackened brick wall and recalled the philosopher Heroux's words to live by: "There is no trouble so great or grave that cannot be much diminished by a nice cup of tea." Spooning the loose Darjeeling into the warmed pot, he decided to start at square one, to conduct yet another overview of the case, making notes as he went. Back at the kitchen table, cup of tea at hand, he began by jotting down dates, random thoughts, questions, reminders of conversations, and people's names — some connected by lines and arrows — in an attempt to refresh his memory on all the information he'd accumulated since starting on the case.

By the time an hour had passed he'd filled out a dozen sheets of paper. He went slowly through his disorganized notes, then reread them, hoping to find details or minutiae that he'd overlooked: a slip of the tongue, conflicting facts, contradictions, anything that could point to duplicity or guilt, or provide a clue to revealing the key phrase to the Winterborne code. He found nothing.

He poured himself some more tea and thought harder on it.

While he'd focused mostly on who was behind the murders, those trying to suppress Veitch's putative bombshell, he hadn't considered how much his antagonists might know about Veitch's discovery. Whoever had rifled Veitch's house and taken all his notes, writings, and everything related to his research might already have found out what the secret was, what impact it would have, and what repercussions might follow. That supposition, if correct, meant that they would also know about the Winterborne cipher, would have found out what the key phrase or phrases were, and could already have decrypted one or both codes. Kingston seriously doubted the last — solving the second code would certainly require expert help, but it couldn't be ruled out entirely. He was convinced, too, that it was they — whoever they were — who had been following him and had sent the pressed flower to warn him off, knowing that he was getting closer to the truth and bent on exposing them.

There was an easy way to find that out, he realized. He needed to call Holbrook anyway. He reached for the phone, then hesitated. Was he making a nuisance of himself? he wondered. All these calls must be making the man wonder just what Kingston was so persistent about. He brushed aside the thought and picked up the phone.

His misgivings were unfounded. Holbrook seemed to welcome the call.

"You've got us all excited about the secret code now," he said. "It's all Libby talks about these days. What can I do for you?"

"Other than yourself, the architectural restorer, and the people at the archives company, Tyler, how many other people know about the existence of the letters on the envelope?"

A pause followed. "Well, no one . . . other than my wife and daughter. Why?"

"It's not important," Kingston answered quickly. "Just curious, that's all."

"Someone else did call asking about the frieze, though."

"Really?"

"Yes. A woman. She said she was researching listed buildings in the county."

"Did she leave a name?"

"I didn't speak to her. My wife did. The name, though . . . I think it was Baker or

Barker, maybe —" He hesitated. "Erase that. Just to be sure, I'd better ask Cassie. She'll remember, but she's not here right now. I'll have to call you back."

"Did your wife tell the woman about the papers?"

"I'm not sure. She might have."

Kingston could hear a note of puzzlement in Holbrook's voice and decided he'd let things go at that. Any more questions, he might start to get truly suspicious.

"I promise not to bother you again for a while, Tyler. Thanks for being so cooperative. It means a lot to me."

The conversation ended there.

Standing at the kitchen counter, looking out the window, he thought about Winterborne and Holbrook's disclosure. A woman researching listed houses would not be unusual, but nevertheless her interest could have been more than purely architectural. As he thought about it, "researching listed houses" was a rather vague job description, but those may have been Holbrook's wife's words. How many women were on Veitch's list? he asked himself. He went to his study, retrieved the list, and brought it back to the kitchen. He laid the list on the table and wrote the names of the women only on a separate piece of paper, making a brief note alongside each name to remind him who was who. He quickly eliminated the two young women, Bridget Morley and Molly Henshawe, as he'd done before, and for the same reasons. Five names remained:

Victoria Morley: Graham Morley's wife. Active in local politics and community issues.
Nicole Morley: Wife of Adrian Morley (retired).
Daisy Morley-Lytton: Lytton's wife of 25 years. Antiques dealer.
Vanessa Decker: Distant cousin. Living abroad?
Jessica Henshawe: Oliver Henshawe's ex-wife.

After studying them, he eliminated Victoria Morley as being too elderly and also living too far from Staffordshire, in Torquay. Then he crossed off Nicole Morley's name for much the same reasons. He wrote a question mark by Daisy Morley-Lytton's name and circled the remaining two, Vanessa Decker and Jessica Henshawe. Locating Jessica Henshawe shouldn't be difficult. Her former husband would surely be able to help in that regard. Vanessa Decker was another problem entirely. If an Internet search came up empty, he would have to drop her from the list.

He cleaned up the kitchen and went to his study. After checking for new messages in his mail program — there were none — he turned his attention to Vanessa Decker. As he'd expected, Googling her name brought up pages of Facebook and Myspace listings, nearly all of them teenagers or young women. As a shot in the dark, he tried "Vanessa Morley," getting the same results. He might have to give up on Vanessa Decker, he decided. That left one last person to contact, Oliver Henshawe, who should know the whereabouts of his ex-wife.

Later that afternoon, Kingston called Amanda. Dialing her number, he was embarrassed to realize that he'd been so consumed with the unexpected and unsettling events of the past days that a week had passed since they'd last talked. While he didn't want to give her the impression that he was being oversolicitous, neither did he want her to feel that he'd forgotten her. Mostly because of the questions that Inspector Wheatley had asked about her, his guarded suspicions, Kingston had thought about the call and what he should say and had even toyed with the idea of asking her to Andrew's lunch. She picked up after several rings, sounding out of breath.

"I'm sorry, Lawrence. I was out in the garden."

"I won't keep you long," he said, trying to be as genial as possible.

"Just wanted to see how you're doing. I've been meaning to call all week, but Andrew returned from a trip, and between spending time with him and a wasted drive down to Berkshire for an interview, the week just disappeared. Added to that, Andrew's Open Garden is coming up and I try to help him with it every year."

"Yes, I remember. You told me about it."

Her tone was noticeably lackluster, but Kingston remained upbeat. "Perhaps you'd come down for the day. I know you would enjoy it and Andrew would like to meet you — I've told him about you, of course. You could stay overnight if you like. The house has four bedrooms and he's doing a special brunch on Monday."

"That would be nice — if I'm not behind bars."

"Behind bars?"

Kingston winced. Wheatley had told her, then?

"Inspector Wheatley called me a couple of days ago. He wants me to go to the police station for questioning. Frankly, I'm beginning to dislike the man. I insisted that I've told him everything I know and it would be a waste of time, but he got very snippy, said 'that remains to be seen.' "

"I met him this week. I was about to tell you. He wanted to compare notes, as he put it, and I must agree, he's not exactly the most civil of civil servants. You've nothing to worry about, Amanda. It's what they call a routine inquiry."

"That's hardly how he put it."

Kingston tried to ease the conversation away from her upcoming interview with the inspector, but he knew by now that, despite his reassurances, her mind was elsewhere; she wasn't the same Amanda he'd spent time with two weeks ago. He could only assume that Wheatley's call had upset her more than she was ready to admit. She ended the conversation abruptly, promising to call Kingston after she'd met with Inspector Wheatley, to let him know how the interview went. Lowering the phone, Kingston wondered if inviting her to Andrew's event had been a good idea. He wouldn't tell Andrew he had done so, he decided. He thought no more of the call, and though the sun was not quite yet over the yardarm, poured himself a glass of Macallan and settled down with the crossword for a half hour or so.

That evening, after watching BBC News,
Kingston took out the Winterborne cipher
again with the faint hope that simply looking at it long enough might trigger a
thought, a subtle clue, or an epiphany that
would lead to finding the key phrase. He
was still convinced that the arrow had been
placed there to signify that there were two
separate codes. For now, though, he would
ignore the last seven lines and focus on the
first two. Logically, the key phrase would be
connected in some way to the frieze itself.
He thought of the Ecclesiastes excerpt. That
would certainly make sense. He pulled out
the folder that contained everything connected to the case, took out the quotation
and read it aloud:

Through wisdom is an house builded;
and by understanding it is established;
and by knowledge shall the chambers be
filled with all precious and pleasant
riches.

He studied it, trying to imagine which
words or phrase he would select as a key
phrase if he were encrypting the message.
After a minute, he concluded that at least

eight stood out. He took a sheet of paper and wrote down his first choice, WISDOM, followed by the remaining letters of the alphabet, excluding those that already appeared in WISDOM, as he had done when he'd demonstrated the Caesar shift to Andrew. He then placed this cipher alphabet under the plain alphabet. Under those two lines, he wrote the first two lines of the Winterborne code using a red pen.

```
ABCDEFGHIJKLMNOPQRSTUVWXYZ
WISDOMNPQRTUVXYZABCEFGHJKL
HEPYEVUAOTJGOTNPGVITUGINICHUM
ZCGIPYHUAUASJUYIGUVVEARGUOXH
```

He then tried to decode the Winterborne code using WISDOM as his key phrase. He started by matching the first red letter of the Winterborne code, H, to the H on the second-line cipher alphabet. It resulted in the letter W on the upper, plain alphabet, line. This wasn't an encouraging start because to make an English word, there were only six letters that could follow W: four consonants and the letters H and R. If the next letter in the code was none of these, then the key phrase was incorrect.

The next letter of the code was E. He ran his fingers across the second line to find that

316

E matched T in the upper, plain alphabet. He leaned back, disappointed. No English words started with WT. He checked his cipher alphabet to make sure he hadn't made an error, then tried decoding it with each of the seven other words he'd chosen earlier, including ECCLESIASTES. None worked.

TWENTY-FOUR

In his study the next morning, Kingston took out Morley's updated list with the contact numbers. Yesterday, he'd obtained an e-mail address for Oliver Henshawe from the Leicestershire County Record Office and dashed off a note to him, asking how he could get in touch with Jessica, his former wife. He'd explained that he was working with Lord Morley on the Sturminster case, making sure to put Henshawe's mind at rest by stressing that it was only a routine inquiry.

He started to think about Vanessa Decker. Tracking her down was proving to be far more difficult than he'd anticipated. Why was she the only one who was so elusive? He was going to have to start spending more time trying to locate her.

Soon after receiving the Dahlia Society's

letter, Kingston had spoken with the Brookside Garden Club's secretary, who had provided the name and phone number of their club's president, Stephen Meeke. A couple of hours later Kingston reached Meeke at his home in Derby. He was familiar with Kingston's reputation, as both a botanist and an amateur investigator, and was more than happy to meet with Kingston, to the point of insisting. Since the club had no office, it was decided that they would meet at Meeke's house in Sunnyhill on the south side of Derby. Andrew, true to his promise, agreed to go along.

Kingston still had no word from Amanda, so that part of his planned excursion didn't seem as if it would happen. This was more of a disappointment than reason for concern. When they'd talked, she hadn't said when Wheatley would interview her, so the meeting might not yet have taken place. On the plus side, not having to make the fifty-mile detour to Abbot's Broomfield would make the day more manageable.

The next afternoon, with clear blue skies for a change, Kingston and Andrew arrived punctually at the modest semi-detached brick house on Waddesdon Way, Derby. There was no need to double-check the

318

number; it was the only house on the street that could possibly be owned by a dedicated gardener. Oddly enough, though, Kingston couldn't spot a single dahlia among the painterly mix of plants and shrubs that filled the length and breadth of the front garden. Perhaps they were showcased in the back, he thought.

A smiling woman in her midfifties answered the doorbell. She introduced herself as Steve's wife and led the two of them down the hall, through the kitchen and a conservatory, to the garden, where her husband and a slender well-dressed lady were chatting under a large dogwood tree. After Meeke introduced Muriel Williams, the club's secretary, they all settled down at a teak table under a striped awning.

Meeke leaned back and smiled. "I must say I was surprised when you called, Doctor. As you know, we're a small club, and when I told a couple of the members including Muriel, here, that you were coming to Derby, the entire club wanted to meet you."

"To a lot of us gardeners, you've become a somewhat legendary figure," Muriel added. "We could have sold tickets."

Ignoring Andrew's quickly raised and lowered eyebrows, Kingston smiled and shrugged. "Someone once said that 'All

319

news is an exaggeration of life.' But I have found the challenges rewarding."

Meeke's expression clouded. "You're aware that both the men you're inquiring about are recently deceased?"

"I am, yes. That's why I wanted to talk to you. Several weeks ago, I was retained to conduct an independent inquiry into William Endicott's murder. Now, with Veitch's homicide, I discover that they both belonged to your club. I grant you the connection might be flimsy, but sometimes the most mundane and seemingly normal associations eventually turn out to be significant factors in solving crimes."

"What would you like to know about them?" asked Meeke.

"How long had they been members of Brookside?"

Meeke glanced at Muriel, as if to say *You may know better than I.*

"I believe William joined in 2000 or thereabouts," she said. Then, after a pause, "And I'm pretty sure that Tristan Veitch joined in 2003. I remember because we were all amazed when he walked off with the best-of-show award at Harrogate in the summer of 2004."

"Did they know each other well?"

"I would say so," she replied.

Meeke nodded. "Yes. They invariably sat together at meetings, and I know they'd visited each other's gardens."

"How many members are there in your club?" asked Kingston, pulling on his earlobe.

Meeke looked up at the awning briefly, thinking. "Currently, about sixty."

Muriel nodded.

"And your meetings are monthly?"

"Yes," she replied.

"I've been told that Tristan Veitch was something of a solitary person. His sister said he kept pretty much to himself. Is that how you'd describe him?"

"That would be reasonably accurate, I suppose," said Meeke.

"Not antisocial," said Muriel, "but hardly the life-and-soul sort."

"How about Endicott?"

"He was friendlier," she replied. "Speaking as a woman, I found him a bit nosy. I'm told touchy-feely, too." She hesitated. "I suppose I shouldn't speak ill of the dead — but he always wanted to know everything about you." She looked at Meeke. "Was that your impression, Steve?"

Meeke shrugged. " 'Inquisitive,' would be the right word, I guess."

"In conversations, did either of them ever

321

mention Sturminster?"

Both shook their heads. "No," said Meeke emphatically.

"I'd like you to look at a list of names, if you would," said Kingston, taking out Veitch's list from his inside jacket pocket. He passed it to Meeke. "Let me know if any are familiar."

Kingston and Andrew sat admiring the garden while the two studied the list. Kingston smiled. "Never seen so many dahlias," he said sotto voce to Andrew. After a minute Meeke handed the list back to Kingston. "Sorry," he said. "I don't recognize any of them."

"Same here," said Muriel.

"Thanks." Kingston put the list back in his pocket. "I'm particularly interested in the two women on the list — Vanessa Decker and Jessica Henshawe."

By their expressions and silence Kingston knew that he was at another dead end. He was about to thank them both when Mrs. Meeke arrived with a large tray, bearing a plate of scones, cups and saucers, and a pot of tea. This helped ameliorate both his disappointment and his rumbling midriff, since he'd eaten very little for breakfast. Over tea, they were talking about more mundane matters when Muriel interjected.

"I just thought of something. We did have a member whose name was Vanessa. But her name wasn't Decker." She glanced at Meeke. "Do you remember her? Tallish, Scandinavian-looking blond woman."

"I do," he replied. "That was quite some time ago. Did she ever give a reason for leaving?"

"I believe she was moving," said Muriel.

Kingston tried to suppress his eagerness. "Was she cozy with either Endicott or Veitch?"

Muriel chuckled. "Not with Veitch, that's for sure. As for Endicott, it's hard to say. Like I said, he fancied himself as a bit of a ladies' man. Is it important?"

"It could be, possibly. If they were at all close, it would fit with a theory I have. Do you remember her surname?"

Meeke looked to Muriel again. "It escapes me right now," she said. "I know it wasn't Decker. But it'll be easy to go back through some of the newsletters or the minutes of meetings to find it." She eyed Kingston knowingly. "You're thinking that she might be the Vanessa you're looking for?"

"It's a distinct possibility. Women have been known to reassume their maiden names after divorcing."

"Maybe that's why she was moving,"

Meeke interjected.

Another fifteen minutes passed while they toured the garden and chatted about things horticultural and significant gardens in the area that Kingston or Andrew might not have visited — Haddon Hall, Biddulph Grange, and Elvaston Castle being three. Kingston thanked them all and he and Andrew departed.

They were at the curb, about to drive off, when Kingston saw Muriel out of the corner of his eye, hurrying down the garden path to the gate, waving. He wound the window down as she approached.

"I remembered the name of the lady you were asking about: Vanessa Carlson. I'll go through the records for an address and phone number, but can't make any promises. It *was* a few years ago."

Kingston thanked her and, with a quick wave, he and Andrew drove off.

"Well, that was worthwhile," said Kingston, looking pleased.

"It must be the same woman, don't you think?"

"I'd say the odds are very favorable. Hopefully, before long we'll find out."

For a while, rather than chat, Andrew seemed content to enjoy the passing Derbyshire scenery, occasionally glancing at the rearview mirror.

Passing a familiar brown National Trust Gardens road sign, Kingston thought about Andrew's Open Garden, which was now two days away. Earlier, they'd agreed on a plan: Kingston would arrive at the house in Bourne End early tomorrow prepared to tidy and spruce up the garden. He would stay overnight and act as co-host during the open house on Sunday, from ten to four, then stay overnight again for *La Grande Bouffe* brunch on Monday.

"Have you finalized your guest list for the lunch yet?" he asked.

"I think so, why? Anyone else you want to invite?"

Kingston shook his head. "No. Just being nosy."

"You're sure?"

"Yes. Did you invite Henrietta?"

"No. I decided to save you the embarrassment. Personally, though, I think she's fun."

Kingston was going to mention that he'd been thinking of asking Amanda but thought better of it. "Don't get me wrong," he said. "She is fun and witty, but she doesn't drape herself all over you."

"I wish she would. I might enjoy it."

"You were very quiet today, Andrew. I'm glad you came, though."

"There wasn't much for me to say or do. As someone once said, 'It's better to keep your mouth shut and be thought a fool than open it and remove all doubt.' "

"I can guarantee you it'll be more fun when we track down this Vanessa Carlson woman and get to talk to Jessica Henshawe. As a matter of fact, you could do the interviews. Right up your street."

"Be glad to."

Thinking about the two women reminded Kingston that he hadn't heard from Tyler or Cassie Holbrook. He'd promised to call back about the mystery woman who was so interested in the frieze.

Waiting at a traffic light, Andrew took another furtive glance in the mirror.

"Why do you keep looking in the mirror?" asked Kingston, finally curious.

"Just checking to see if we're being followed, that's all."

Kingston just shook his head.

Back at his flat at five o'clock, he found a note on the coffee table from Mrs. Tripp.

Dear Doctor,
I left a little early today to take Tinker to the vet. I left a Cornish pasty in the fridge, thinking that you might not want to cook

tonight after being gone all day. I'll see you next week.

Underneath was scrawled a large G, which stood for Gertrude — a revelation that Kingston had discovered only recently, though she'd charred for him for over five years. It mattered little because he'd never be able to call her Gertrude.

After inspecting Mrs. Tripp's pasty — it looked authentic and appetizing, with a nice golden crust — and checking his mail, he poured himself a drink and sat on the sofa to call Tyler Holbrook. Their young daughter, whose name he recalled was Libby, answered, in the same polite manner as on his last call, saying that her daddy was not home but her mommy was and that she would go find her.

Kingston thanked her, telling her who he was.

"I remember you," she said. "You're the man with the nice voice."

Cassie came on the line. "Dr. Kingston. Good to hear from you." Kingston found the Southern drawl melodious and pleasing, much as many Americans find the English accent charming. "How's that investigation of yours goin'?"

"Not making as much progress as I'd like,

sorry to say."

"Tyler's back in Boston for a few days. Should I have him call you? I'll be talking to him tonight. Pity you're not closer to Banbury. I could have him bring you back a couple of lobsters, too."

"That would be nice. Thanks for the thought. Actually, it's you I wanted to talk to — to ask you a question about the frieze."

"Don't tell me you've solved the mystery of the letters on the envelope."

"I wish I had. No, it's about the woman who called you some time ago, inquiring about it. Your husband mentioned her. He thought it was around the beginning of the year."

"Yes. I remember her well. She was very persistent, wanted to see it."

"I take it you never actually met her?"

"I didn't. She called initially asking about the house, saying that she was a freelance writer working on an article about historic houses in Oxfordshire and had found that ours was listed and could she see it. I told her that it was impossible because we were in the middle of restoring it and that there wasn't much to see. I went on to say that we'd be happy to show it to her when we were finished — that's when she asked about the frieze. I told her it had been taken down and sold."

"Did she say how she'd heard about it?"

"No. I didn't think to ask at the time. I assumed that it must have been from a history book or something of that sort."

"Your husband said that her name was Baker, or a name sounding like that."

"I think it was Blakely. Anne Blakely. I wouldn't be sure, though. There was no reason for me to remember it."

It was probably insignificant, Kingston thought. It could have easily been an alias.

"Did she leave a phone number or any way to contact her?" he asked.

"No. And I didn't think to ask."

"Was there anything else?"

"There was. She wanted to know if our contractor had removed the frieze or if it had been someone else, like a specialist. That's when I started to get suspicious. It seemed an odd question for a writer."

"Did you tell her about the secret compartment, finding the hidden envelope?"

"Odd you'd ask that, Doctor. It was as if she knew the frieze might have concealed something — she might have even mentioned 'some papers.' She didn't say it in so many words, but I remember wondering at the time if she didn't know more than she was letting on." She paused, and Kingston

329

could hear her daughter's voice in the background. "Sorry about that," she said. "Libby was asking if you were coming to see us." She chuckled. "I've taken the liberty of telling her that you're a private eye."

"I'd best remember that, should I get to meet her."

"In answer to your question, just to get rid of the woman, I told her that we did find some papers but they contained only historical notes related to the house and nothing else. She asked if she could get copies of them, saying that the information might be of great help to her work. I simply told her that I didn't have them, because we were compiling a scrapbook of Winterborne, and they were with a company that was preserving them. By this time a little red light was flashing in my head warning me not to tell her anything more — to end the conversation."

"And you did?"

"Yep."

"Earlier, you said, 'when she called *initially.*' Did she call a second time?"

"She did. I was surprised. She said that she'd like to see Winterborne when it was completed and it was convenient, but meantime she was still anxious to learn as much as she could about the frieze. I told her that

I'd told all I knew, but she wouldn't take no for an answer. She wasn't exactly rude — just determined. She said she was calling back because she'd like to talk to the people we'd sold it to so that she could take a picture of it, if it was okay with us. She also asked if I would give her the name and number of the company that had dismantled it. Why she would want to talk to them, I have no idea. I told her that if she left her phone number I would ask the buyer and have him call her."

"She didn't leave a number, I take it?"

"She didn't."

"I'm not surprised. Anything else you can remember about what she said, an accent?"

"Not really. No, wait. Her voice."

"Her voice?"

"Yes. It was husky. Like she might be a smoker. That's all."

At least that was something, Kingston thought, making a mental note.

"I thought Tyler had told you about all this?" Cassie said.

"No, he said he'd get back to me."

"He must have thought I'd called. Sorry. He's usually so dependable in that sense."

"Not to worry, he's a busy man by the sound of it. I do have one last question, if that's all right?"

331

"Sure."

"The cubbyhole that held the letters. Do you recall which letter tile covered it?"

Another pause followed. "Gracious me, I can't remember. Is it important?"

"I'm not sure."

"You know who might know? Libby. She's been making up mystery stories about it and helping her dad with the scrapbook. They're having a great time with it. Hold on and I'll ask her."

In a minute she returned. "Libby is sure it was the letter 'P' — as in 'Precious.' She remembered because she thought something precious should have been hidden behind it."

"Smart girl."

"She said her dad thought it was for 'Proverbs.' "

"Proverbs? Why proverbs?"

"The quotation, it's from the book of Proverbs. I thought you knew that."

"I was told it was from Ecclesiastes."

"No. We looked it up. The Kings James version."

Kingston felt like a damned fool for not having verified it in the first place, rather than relying on the memory of the bloke in the pub. He thanked Cassie, saying that what she'd told him could turn out to be more valuable than she might realize and that he would let her know if he tracked down the mystery woman. He asked her to thank Libby, too, but thought it premature to tell her that her daughter's remembering the letter of the tile could become a factor in helping solve the riddle of the Winterborne frieze.

Kingston topped up his drink and went to his study. He took out the Winterborne code from his file and a notepad from his desk drawer.

He wrote the alphabet on one line and, underneath, PROVEBS, the key phrase, with the single repeated letter R removed.

ABCDEFGHIJKLMNOPQRSTUVWXYZ
PROVEBS

Then, after the S, he added the remaining letters of the alphabet, skipping any that were already in PROVEBS. He checked to make certain that all the letters of the alphabet appeared on the lower line, with none repeated. One simple slip and the ciphertext would not function. It appeared to be correct.

Next, he placed the Winterborne code below the two lines and started to transpose the matching letters of the code from the

lower line, cipher alphabet, to the plain
alphabet above.

```
ABCDEFGHIJKLMNOPQRSTUVWXYZ
PROVEBSTUWXYZACDFGHIJKLMNQ

HEPYEVUAOTJGOTNPGVITUGINICHUM
ZCGIPYHUAUASJUYIGUVVEARGUOXH
```

The first letter of the Winterborne code
was H. On the second-line cipher alphabet
it was paired with S on the plain alphabet
above. The second letter, E, became E, and
P became A. As he wrote the letters SEA on
his pad, his pulse quickened. The next letter
would be critical. He took a deep breath,
and when he saw that the next letter, Y, was
paired with L, he exhaled loudly.

He was on to something.

Within seconds he had three words: a
complete phrase. SEALED IN CHURCH-
YARD.

He'd done it. He'd broken the first part
of the code.

He looked up at the ceiling, punching his
fists in the air. He wanted to call Andrew —
somebody — but restrained himself. He
went back to finish decrypting. Another two
minutes and it was done. He leaned back
and studied the full message:

```
HEPYEVUAOTJGOTNPGVITUGINICHUM
SEALEDINCHURCHYARDTHIRTYTOSIX

ZCGIPYHUAUASJUYIGUVVEARGUOXH
MORTALSININGUILTRIDDENBRICKS
```

He read it again:

Sealed in churchyard thirty to six.
Mortal sin in guilt ridden bricks

As he stared at it, trying to make out what it meant, his euphoria abated. After all this, he'd been expecting the message to provide specific information or, at the very least, some kind of direction or clue telling how to proceed.

Instead, he was looking at a damned riddle.

TWENTY-FIVE

Saturday evening found Kingston and Andrew, limbs aching and fagged out, sitting on Andrew's terrace at Bourne End, each with a gin and tonic. The sun was dipping across the river, burnishing ripples of gold on the slow-flowing jade water. Only the twitter of aerial-feeding martins and nightjars broke the stillness as they swooped and dived along the river at lightning speeds.

They'd both worked in the two-acre garden from early morning until six, with a short break for a boxed lunch that Andrew had ordered from a local café. Necessary watering had been completed first thing, a good soaking. The long lawn leading down to the river had been raked and mowed; gravel paths weeded, roses deadheaded, and beds given a fresh layer of mulch. Paint-work was touched up on the long arbor and planter boxes, colorful annuals had been planted to fill bare patches here and there, the terrace had been swept and hosed down, and sun umbrellas set up in seating areas. They'd also positioned a long table under an umbrella on the terrace for iced and hot tea, soft drinks, Pimm's Cup, and a variety of biscuits and cakes.

When they'd first sat, Kingston had pulled out the decoded Winterborne message, determined to keep trying to find out what it meant. He'd shown it briefly to Andrew when he'd arrived so he was now familiar with it, too. "Damned thing's infuriating," said Kingston. "All this time and trouble to decrypt the code and what do we get? A blasted riddle."

"I don't get it either. If they wanted to make it almost impossible to solve, why bother with a code in the first place?"

Kingston nodded. "If we knew who 'they' are — or were — it might help in trying to read their minds."

"Someone from the distant past — the 1700s, I suppose."

"We know that, Andrew. Who exactly, though . . ."

"According to what Veitch said, one of the Morley family. Yes?"

"In all probability. But not necessarily."

Andrew downed the last of his gin and tonic and placed his glass on the wicker side table. "The way I read what you've got there, back then someone buried something in a churchyard — around Sturminster, probably. The reference to 'mortal sin' and 'guilt-ridden' makes it pretty clear that whatever they buried under 'bricks' was something that they didn't want to 'fess up to, or would be ruinous if discovered."

"Yes. That's all rather obvious. And it leads us to conclude that the 'someone' would be one of the two Morley brothers who, in their aberrant partnership, had created Sturminster only to regret it later." Kingston realized that he was being uncharacteristically patronizing, so he switched to a friendlier tone. "But that doesn't help solve the conundrum, does it, Andrew? It doesn't tell us unequivocally who the 'someone' or the 'something' is."

Andrew swatted a mosquito buzzing his ear. "If we were to think like them, it might."

"Oh, come on. Think like them? How are we supposed to do that?"

A brief silence followed that seemed to suit them both.

"Any theories at all?" asked Andrew, his tone lacking enthusiasm.

"I don't deal in theories. I gather facts. I keep gathering as many facts from as many people as I can, then I sift through them. I compare them to see if a statement — or what's been sold as a truth — contradicts another one, either from the same person or someone else. You see, people with nothing to hide speak the truth without having to think. It's those who are hiding something who must be extremely careful how they answer questions. It can be the tiniest mistake but, sooner or later, chances are one will slip out."

"I must remember to buy you a briar pipe," said Andrew with a straight face.

Ignoring Andrew's sarcasm, Kingston swirled the ice in his glass and took a long sip of gin and tonic. "When I was helping the police in Hampshire, a suspect had stated that a man, a stranger to him, had come 'up' to London to see him. We knew that the man in question had indeed traveled to London from Brighton, but the suspect had no way of knowing where the man had started his journey. A two-letter slip eventually forced him to admit full knowledge of the man who was, in fact, an accomplice."

"Very clever. This case of yours, though, it always seems to be at an impasse."

"You needn't remind me." Kingston sighed. "Over the last weeks I've interviewed and talked to more than a dozen people with hardly anything to show for it. I'd really hoped that breaking the code would have changed all that. It's damned dispiriting."

"I know I said I'd help you, but I'm at a bit of a loss as to how."

"I understand, but having second eyes and ears is a big plus, Andrew, believe me. My success rate on this one has been pretty miserable so far."

Kingston rested his glass on the arm of the chair and stared out at the river, contemplating Andrew's offer. "If I could only find this damned Decker or Carlson woman, we might be able to make some headway. I just know she's somehow mixed up in all this."

"What about your friend Amanda?"

"What about her?"

"I mean, how is she doing?"

"I'm not sure. The last time we talked she was about to be interviewed again by the police, this time at the station. I tried to make her feel better, reassuring her that it was a routine procedure, but she was clearly upset."

"I'm not surprised, considering the pain and suffering she's been through already."

"I know." Kingston sighed, shaking his head. "I didn't want to tell her, but it's about the poisoning. Wheatley told me so when I was up there. He has no suspects and he's asking how a man who lived with his sister and rarely ventured out of the house managed to get poisoned."

Andrew frowned. "You don't think she did it, though?"

Kingston sipped his drink and lowered his glass and looked down into it, introspectively. "I don't know, Andrew. I just don't know what to think anymore."

After a pensive moment, Andrew spoke again. "I've been thinking about this code business."

"What about it?"

"It's so complicated, so convoluted. You're obviously proficient in that department, but even you are having limited success. How come Veitch didn't have the same problem?"

"I'm not sure I follow you."

"From what you told me, Veitch implied that the coded messages were involved in his exposé."

"Correct."

"So how did he decode them?"

"We don't know for sure that he did."

"Granted. But let's assume for a moment that he managed to. He wasn't a cryptology expert, was he?"

"Not from everything I've been able to determine. At least he wasn't in any of the armed services or involved with any security organizations, because the same thought had occurred to me and I quizzed Amanda about it."

"Then he must have had help. Another thing — we don't know for sure if he'd also broken the 'churchyard' riddle."

"With help, he could have broken the first code, which was rudimentary, but I wouldn't be so sure about solving the 'churchyard' riddle," said Kingston. "That's another matter entirely."

"It raises yet another question: How did he get his hands on the Winterborne code in the first place?"

"I've asked myself that same question. According to Mrs. Holbrook, the only people who knew about the hidden code were her

341

family, the archive preservation company — oh, and the architectural salvage people — and they didn't know what the envelope contained. I can't answer your question."

"How would you learn about code breaking? Where would you go? Whom would you talk to?"

"Books have been written about the subject, of course, but other than the intelligence branches of the military and the government agencies, frankly I don't know."

"What about Endicott? We know he was a friend of Veitch's. He could have also been working with him."

"To what end?"

"Think about it. He might have known about cryptology."

"He couldn't have learned it in the services. Conscription had ended long before then. The bottom line is that, from everything I know, Endicott seems to have had no knowledge of codes. So we've come full circle."

They sat in silence for a moment. The sun had gone down and the temperature with it. Andrew was about to suggest that they go inside when Kingston muttered something, speaking to himself.

"The archive company."

"What?"

"The people doing the preservation."

"What about them?"

"It's the only possible way that Veitch could have known about the Winterborne papers."

"How, though?"

"Through the woman inquiring about the frieze — Blakely, whatever her name is."

"I thought you said that Tyler Holbrook's wife claimed that she didn't tell the woman anything."

Kingston put a hand to his forehead. "As I recall, all she said was that the papers were with a company that was preserving them. Granted, it's not much to go on, but it could have been enough for the woman to have tracked them down and persuaded them to let her see the papers. I wouldn't think there are too many companies of that kind around."

Andrew didn't look convinced. "Surely no company handling clients' historical documents, private papers, what have you, would ever allow a complete stranger to go near them. Lawsuits would be fast and furious."

"Unless they had the client's permission."

"That's not true in this case, though. Is it?"

Kingston shook his head. "I don't know."

"Think about it. If the Holbrooks had

given permission, the archive people would have shown the woman the papers, but it would be highly unlikely that they would have shown her the envelope. Why would they?"

"You're right."

"Sorry to throw cold water on your theory. It's just not plausible."

Kingston stared intensely across the lawn to the river, now a band of gray, the graceful willows alongside silhouetted in black. When he was in one of his deep-thought moods, Andrew knew not to interrupt. Kingston suddenly turned to him. "I must pay the archive people a visit," he pronounced, as if it must be done that very minute.

"*We* must pay them a visit. Remember?"

"Yes."

"Why?"

"I must be getting sloppy. I should have thought about it before."

"Thought about what?"

"How Tristan Veitch learned about the Winterborne papers."

"I thought we just settled that."

"No. We've been focusing too much on the code and how Veitch managed to break it. We're forgetting that Veitch knew nothing whatsoever about the codes until the papers were discovered. And we've been assuming, wrongly, that it was the Blakely woman who told him about the papers and also the code."

"You've lost me."

"It had to be someone from the archive company who told Veitch. An inquisitive employee perhaps, or even the manager or owner — someone who not only knew Veitch but also knew that he would be highly interested."

"To the point of selling the information?"

Kingston nodded. "Maybe."

"You could be right. I can't see any other possibility."

"There is none. I suggest we take a run up to Oxford on Tuesday, if that's okay with you."

"I don't see why not. One of my favorite places."

Andrew stood and picked up his glass, intimating that the subject was closed. "How about another before dinner?"

"Why not?" Kingston replied. "It's going to be a long day tomorrow," he added, regretting the cliché.

The Open Garden at Bourne End exceeded all expectations. Unlike the previous year, when it had been gray and cool, the skies were cloudless and by noon the temperature was close to eighty — a heat wave to most, but nobody complained. Despite no official visitor count, based on food and drink consumption, Andrew guessed it at approximately two hundred — substantially more than last year and surprising for such a small village. Many guests stayed in the garden longer than usual, just to have a chance to chat with Kingston, who looked quite the Colonial gentleman in a navy linen jacket, cream slacks, and black-banded Panama.

Brunch the following day was a huge success, too. The weather continued much the same, calling for thirst quenching with larger than anticipated quantities of champagne, wine, Pimm's, and Schweppes before, during, and after Andrew's extravagant catered lunch. Kingston was glad when the last guest had departed and he and Andrew were able to relax at last in deck chairs on the lawn in the still of a summer's evening and just drink soda water and make bland comments now and then. Kingston hadn't had to spend much of the day trying to evade or repel Henrietta, for which he thanked his friend.

Arriving home just before dark, Kingston

was in no mood for anything other than to glance at his mail and check his phone and e-mail messages. After that, he planned to spend an hour or so trying to finish the rest of the Oxbridge-Bell book before retiring early. In the last three days he'd eaten too much, drunk too much, talked too much, listened too much, and slept too little. He also made a mental note to remind Andrew to retire the mattress in the guest room that he'd occupied. It was like trying to sleep on a sack of tennis balls.

Finding nothing in the post that required immediate reading, he played back three phone messages. The first was from Francis Morley, asking Kingston to call. The second was from Muriel Williams, the dahlia club lady, saying that she had more information on Vanessa Carlson. And the last was from Amanda asking that he call her. From the tone of her voice and brevity of the message, he got the impression that the news wasn't good. The e-mails could wait until morning, he decided, but returning her call was essential. It wasn't too late and he saw no reason why she shouldn't be pleased to hear from him.

Amanda answered after the second ring. "Thanks for calling, Lawrence," she said.

Kingston was relieved, if only for a mo-

347

ment, that her voice seemed a little more sanguine than it had on her recorded message. "Just got your message. I was gone for the weekend. Andrew's a big do at his house on the river. I arrived home literally ten minutes ago."

"Sorry I missed it. Was it fun?"

"It was, but rather exhausting. More important," he said in a comforting tone, "how are you? Did you meet with Inspector Wheatley?"

"Yes, I did. Last Friday. That's why I'm calling."

While they'd been talking, he'd been trying to gauge her mood, but the tone of her voice gave no clue. "How did it go?"

"Not at all well, I'm sorry to say."

"Tell me what happened."

"First, I have an apology to make — a confession, if you will."

"To me? A confession? For what possible reason, Amanda?"

"I haven't been completely truthful in some of the things I told you when you were here. I omitted facts I didn't think significant, only to protect Tristan, but somehow Wheatley knew of them or is very good at guessing. He's accusing me of withholding evidence."

"These facts, what were they? What,

exactly, did you withhold?"

"When I'd said that Tristan hardly ever went out, that wasn't quite true. I realize now that it was a stupid mistake on my part. I really don't know what I was thinking at the time. I probably thought that it might help shield him from further scrutiny. I didn't know if what he'd been researching — this Morley family thing — had got him into some kind of trouble."

"But Tristan didn't exactly have a social life, did he? Lots of friends?"

"Heavens no! He preferred to keep to himself and generally shunned visitors, but he was by no means misanthropic. Occasionally he went out, and sometimes he wouldn't tell me where or with whom. It didn't bother me. He wasn't the sort to get into trouble in pubs, excessive drinking, that sort of thing — and I never stayed up waiting for him to come home. It was an unspoken arrangement that might seem unusual to a lot of people, but we weren't married. If we were, I'm sure I would have felt differently."

"I'm a little confused, Amanda. If Tristan went out occasionally, which would entail meeting someone or other people, surely that would help substantiate your case. It would open up the possibility that someone else could have poisoned him. It shifts the burden of guilt away from you."

"I offered the same argument. Wheatley agreed in principle, but he maintained that it still didn't change matters that much, that I could still have done it."

"Did you ask him what your motive was, if you had?"

"I did, as a matter of fact. He said he could think of several. That's when he told me they were launching an investigation into our financial affairs: our respective savings, inheritances, wills, debts, and so on. I've grown to dislike the man. He has no social skills or tact whatsoever."

"I don't think they're part of the job. But in my experience, not all policemen are like that. What else did he say?"

"He pressed me about a possible relationship between Tristan and the man who was murdered at Sturminster. Had I ever met him? If he'd been to the house at all, or had phoned?"

"William Endicott."

"Yes."

"Had you met him?"

"No. I hadn't."

"While we're on the subject, do you know if Tristan did business with an archive preservation company, in Oxford, I believe?"

"No. I'm afraid not. Even if he had, I doubt that he would have mentioned it anyway. Is it important?"

"I'm not sure. It's probably just another dead end."

During the lull that followed, Kingston debated whether he should tell her that he had indeed established a connection between her brother and Endicott through the Brookside Garden Club. He decided to wait for now so as not to open up the issue for even more speculation. Then Amanda spoke again.

"I didn't have anything to do with Tristan's death, Lawrence. That's the truth. The very thought of it is . . . repugnant." Her voice quavered on the word "repugnant" and she paused momentarily, probably to regain her composure, Kingston guessed. Then she continued. "There was no deep brotherly-sisterly love between us — if he were with us still, he would readily admit that — but we were good friends and generally speaking got along well. We shared most things, respected each other's needs and space, and in no possible way would either of us ever have considered harming the other."

"I believe you. Wheatley is just trying to coerce you. Now he knows that you weren't truthful on that one matter, he's asking himself if you could be lying about other things, too. I doubt that he has one iota of evidence to prove your culpability."

"You may believe that, Lawrence, but Inspector Wheatley's last words, before we parted, were that he now considers me a prime suspect in Tristan's murder."

TWENTY-SIX

After Kingston put down the phone, he sat staring into space, trying to weigh the significance and implications of what Amanda had just told him. Was Wheatley simply applying undue pressure in the hope that he might get her to divulge more information about her relationship with her brother, or did he really have sound reason or plausible evidence to consider her a prime suspect? Kingston was unclear on the legal procedure but thought that, as a prime suspect, she would have been informed of her rights and been advised that she could have a solicitor present. From what she'd said, none of that had taken place. Kingston was still convinced that she was innocent, but he couldn't do much about it other than to find out who had really murdered Tristan and Endicott.

He realized that he'd been so absorbed in Amanda's plight that he'd forgotten the other two phone messages, particularly the one from Muriel Williams, which had sounded encouraging. He dialed her number. Her husband answered, and soon she was on the line.

"Sorry, Doctor, I was out in the garden," she said.

Kingston smiled. It seemed that everyone he called these days was in or had been in the garden at the time. "I got your message," he said. "You have some information on Vanessa Carlson, I believe?"

"Yes. She left the club in 2005 because she was leaving the area."

"Was she moving abroad?"

"She didn't say so. At the time, she wanted us to continue sending the club newsletter, and I have the forwarding address and phone number that she gave us."

"Excellent," said Kingston.

"If you're ready, I'll give it to you."

"Go ahead."

"It's The Tithe Barn, 43 Magpie Lane, Linslade, Bedfordshire, LU7 2MR. The phone number is 01525-973-214. That's all the information I could find. I hope it will help."

Kingston thanked her, telling her he

would let her know how it worked out. "I have a question, Muriel," he said. "Do you remember if there was anything memorable about her voice? Anything unusual?"

"Not really. It was lower than most women's, perhaps."

"Husky, maybe?"

"You might say that, yes."

He thanked her again and the call ended. With the phone still in hand, he dialed the Linslade number. A man answered, an elderly man by the sound of it.

"I'd like to speak with Vanessa Carlson, please," Kingston asked in the most congenial tone he could muster.

"Vanessa Carlson?"

"Yes. I was told this was her phone number."

"Her phone number?"

"Right. I'd like to talk with her if she's at home, please."

"You'd like to talk with her?"

Kingston knew by now that the man was either deaf or senile — or both. "Vanessa Carlson," he said, raising his voice.

"Sorry, she don't live here no more."

"Do you know where she went? Maybe an address?"

"Let me ask Mildred."

The man had obviously abandoned the

phone in search of his wife or caregiver, so Kingston stared at the wall and waited.

This time a woman's voice. "Sorry about that. Dudley's lost his hearing aid — third time this week. You were asking about one of our tenants, I believe?"

"I was, Vanessa Carlson. I'm trying to locate her, related to a police matter."

"Lord, she's not in trouble, I hope?"

"No. No. It's a routine inquiry. Nothing serious. Did she leave a forwarding address?"

"She did, but I believe she's moved again since then. Always on the go, that woman. I know where she works, though. A friend of mine ran into her a couple of weeks ago. She told me. It's Stratford Estate Agents in Milton Keynes."

Kingston made note of it on his pad by the phone. "Is she a single woman?"

"Yes, she is. Divorced."

"About how old?"

"Ooh . . . fiftyish, I'd say."

"Anything unusual about her voice?"

"An odd question."

"It is, I know, but I don't have a photo or a good description of her and I'm just trying to make sure that she's the woman I'm looking for."

"I never thought too much of it, but now

you come to mention it she sounded as if she was a heavy smoker at one time, though I never saw her smoke. A bit like that American actress — her name escapes me — she was married to Humphrey Bogart, I believe."

"Lauren Bacall."

"That's her. Sort of a gravelly voice."

"Good. That's the same description others have given me. It must be her. I'll give Stratford Estate Agents a call. And thanks for your help. Give my regards to Dudley, too."

"I will. Good luck."

Kingston was pleased. It looked like his persistence in tracking down the elusive Vanessa Carlson had paid off. Once he'd verified with the estate agent's office that she was still working there, he would pay her a visit. That would have to wait a day or so because tomorrow was spoken for. He and Andrew would be in Oxford for the best part of the day, not that it should take that long to chat with the archival people, but Andrew would never let an opportunity pass for a leisurely lunch in a good restaurant and Oxford had many.

He returned Morley's call next. The woman who answered said that Lord Morley was in London for a few days and that she would make sure he got the message the next morning.

In bed at last, Kingston spent an hour finishing Oxbridge-Bell's book, long overdue. Toward the end, the subject of the putative Morley "feud" was discussed. The upshot was that the author had uncovered no evidence in his considerable research to support the persistent speculative claims of serious malfeasance on the part of Samuel Morley. Despite this, it was known that while Samuel was benefiting from his brother's largesse, he was diametrically opposed to the methods by which the moneys had been obtained. His pacifist sentiments and his association with people of like views, among them many intellectuals and liberal thinkers of the time, were well known. While hardly a revelation, this provided another possible reason for Samuel Morley's acquaintance with Horace Walpole and Thomas Gray, both of whom seemed to fit the bill in that context.

Another curious tidbit in the closing pages concerned Matthew Seward, the architect who had designed Sturminster's monuments and was also chummy with both Horace Walpole and Thomas Gray. Seward had disappeared soon after Sturminster's monuments were completed, and no reports of his death had ever been presented or registered. One explanation offered for this mystery was that Seward had been a frequent traveler to various parts of Europe and the Middle East, and it has been speculated that he might have died while on one of these journeys.

Kingston wondered why this wasn't mentioned in Veitch's notes. Given that Seward had played only what appeared to be a supporting role in the events of the time, Kingston shrugged it off as irrelevant.

Staring at the shadowy coved ceiling before dozing off, Kingston thought back on his discussion with Andrew on Saturday evening. Andrew had raised a good point when he'd questioned how Veitch had managed to get his hands on the Winterborne papers and, even more puzzling, how he'd acquired the special skills to decipher complex codes to reach his conclusions. If it hadn't been Veitch or Endicott who'd solved them, then who? Nobody on Kingston's list or anyone he'd contacted since working on the case appeared to have such capabilities, though he had no way to know for sure, without more questioning. The more he thought on it, the more he kept coming back to Endicott.

Because of the garden club he had gotten

to know Veitch fairly well. But what reason could have persuaded Veitch to enlist Endicott's help? Why would he want to share the potentially dangerous knowledge he'd uncovered? Kingston tried to envisage possible scenarios: Endicott had found out what Veitch had discovered and threatened to expose him to the Morley family if he didn't share in the potential rewards? Had Endicott been blackmailing Veitch? He came up with a couple of less likely explanations before returning to Andrew's original thought: Endicott could have been the code expert — without him Veitch could have gone no further in his investigation.

Kingston pulled the sheets up under his chin and turned on his side. Closing his eyes, he thought about tomorrow's trip to Oxford, but not forgetting that he had to make three important phone calls, too. First, was an exploratory call to Stratford Estate Agents; next, one to the archaeology and art institute, to ask the dean if Endicott had ever exhibited any interest or skills in cryptology; and the last, to pose the same question to Mrs. Endicott. He couldn't think why he hadn't asked her during his visit.

TWENTY-SEVEN

When Kingston and Andrew arrived in Oxford it was close to noon. Being a particularly bright and cheerful morning, with promise of a warm day ahead, they'd chosen to drive in the TR4 with the top down, taking the more scenic route through the Thames Valley towns of Maidenhead, Henley-on-Thames, and the ancient market town of Wallingford — coincidentally, once home to mystery writer Agatha Christie — where they would stop for lunch on their way back.

Shortly before leaving, Andrew had announced that he'd made a reservation at a three-star restaurant that served small dishes, taking delight in describing certain items on the menu and telling Kingston that the chef recommended that diners allow at least three hours to savor the meal.

Aubrey Lewellyn-Jones, Library and Archive Conservation, was located on Blue Boar Lane, a narrow passage tucked behind Oxford's bustling High Street, somehow fitting for such an esoteric enterprise, thought Kingston. They entered through a nondescript door, inside of which was a brass plaque on the wall directing visitors upstairs. At the top of a narrow, perilously steep staircase covered in Oriental carpeting with brass runners, they went through the plate-glass door. Andrew muttered something about being in a Dickens novel, which Kingston ignored.

They were in a spacious, high-ceilinged workspace, naturally lighted by four sky-lights and a bank of iron-framed windows running the length of the far wall. Several oversize workbenches were positioned around the room; map chests and wooden file drawers circled two of the remaining walls, and in strategic areas, green-shaded lights were suspended from the ceiling by steel rods. The overall effect struck Kingston like being in the inside of a Victorian greenhouse sans plants.

As they entered, a lanky, bookish-looking man aptly attired in a dress shirt and bow tie under a tan smock stood, returned a document that he'd been studying to its cellophane sleeve, and walked over to greet them.

"How may I help you," he asked.

"My name's Kingston and this is my colleague, Andrew Duncan. Are you Mr. Lewellyn-Jones?"

"I am, indeed."

"I was talking recently with a gentleman named Tyler Holbrook, who told me that you helped with preservation work on certain historic papers of his that were found concealed in a wall of his house in Banbury — Winterborne Manor."

Lewellyn-Jones raised his eyebrows and squinted at the ceiling over the wire rims of his glasses. "Ah, yes. I remember those. An American fellow."

"That's him," said Kingston, nodding.

"Interesting documents — remarkable condition, considering their age. So what brings you here?" he asked with an ingratiating smile. "Perhaps you have a restoration or preservation project that you'd like to discuss?"

"Not exactly. We're here concerning the Winterborne papers."

The archivist gave them a quizzical look.

"Don't worry," said Kingston. "If it's privacy issues you're worried about, Tyler knows me well. As a matter of fact, I've been helping him with the content of the papers — educating him about the significance and relevance of the luminaries mentioned in the pages. He probably told you, he's compiling a historical record of the house."

The archivist looked flummoxed. "Yes, he did," he mumbled. "So what is it that you want to know about the papers?"

"We need to know if anyone, other than

you or your employees, has mentioned or shown the documents to anyone."

Lewellyn-Jones gave a wounded look and was quick to reply. "Of course not. All customers' documents and materials in our safekeeping are considered sacrosanct, much in the same way as with information that passes between you and your solicitor or bank manager. I can assure you, Mr. Kingston, that nobody had access to them."

"Is it possible that another customer might have chanced on them, or that one of your employees might have become intrigued by them, then mentioned them to someone else, perhaps?"

"It seems I'm not making myself clear. We've been in business for twenty-five years, and not once during that time has anyone ever questioned our work or our integrity. Nothing belonging to our clients is ever left untended or placed at risk. *Nothing.* We simply cannot afford to do that. Most of the items left in our care are not only valuable but also irreplaceable."

Andrew chimed in before Kingston could get another word in and make the man more offended than he already was. "I think we'd best be on our way, Lawrence," he said, quietly. "I think you've provided the information we were seeking," he said to

Lewellyn-Jones with a smile, giving Kingston's sleeve a subtle nudge.

Lewellyn-Jones appeared to be placated as he walked with them to the door. "Please give my regards to Mr. Holbrook when you next see him."

"I will," said Kingston.

They were walking past an open roll-top desk that Kingston assumed to be Lewellyn-Jones's, when he stopped. A bank of framed photos and diplomas artfully arranged on the wall above the desk had caught his attention — one in particular.

"Beautiful car," he said.

Lewellyn-Jones joined him, looking at it, too. The color photo showed three men standing in front of a shiny blue vintage car.

"It's a 1937 Alvis Speed Twenty-Five," said Lewellyn-Jones. "It originally belonged to Nigel Packenham, a well-known actor at the time. I was the third owner. That's me on the right. Had a little more hair in those days." He chuckled.

"What a beauty. Do you still have it?"

"Sadly, no. I had to sell it — about six years ago, long story."

"That's a shame."

"When you have no choice, it makes it even worse." He gave a grudging smile.

"Anyway, it went to a good home," he added.

At the door, Lewellyn-Jones bid them good-bye and they descended the stairs into Blue Boar Lane.

Walking down the street, Andrew looked at Kingston. "Well, that was a waste of —"

"Sometimes you get lucky," said Kingston, smiling as he interrupted Andrew.

"Lucky? What do you mean? You were really starting to upset that poor man."

"That poor man was lying through his teeth, Andrew."

"What are you talking about?"

"The photo."

"What about it?"

"The man in the middle. Guess who that was?"

"You tell me."

"It was a younger Tristan Veitch."

"You're kidding. How do you know?"

"Because it's the same car as the one in the picture I saw in Veitch's office. Veitch was standing by it. I don't think I told you about it. In that picture the only recognizable part of the car was the bonnet mascot, the eagle — used on some Alvis models. It's the same car. There's no doubt about it."

"So that's how Veitch got to know about the Winterborne code?"

Kingston nodded. "It makes sense. Veitch was a historian and, for the best part, Lewellyn-Jones's business deals with restoring and preserving historical documents. I'd say that that rules out the possibility of coincidence, wouldn't you?"

"You could be right," said Andrew after thinking on it for a moment.

"I'd bet the farm on it," Kingston replied.

TWENTY-EIGHT

Lunch at the Landing, on the banks of the Thames in Wallingford, was much as Andrew had described it: a seemingly never-ending succession of small dishes accompanied with sommelier-recommended wine pairings, that dragged on over three and a half hours. Afterward, Andrew had judged it one of the best restaurants that he'd visited in the last year or so, while Kingston had found the food above average but the overall experience too labored and pretentious. Though Kingston would never dare say so — it would start an impassioned debate ending in his being labeled a culinary purist with no sense of gastronomical adventure — he would have far preferred a perfectly grilled Dover sole or perhaps Steak Diane. All that aside, he was in an especially good mood throughout the afternoon, still chuffed with the results of their chat with the mendacious Lewellyn-Jones.

On the drive home, Andrew started to complain of a toothache, saying that if it persisted, he would call his dentist's emergency number that evening.

When Kingston rose the next morning, a near gale was buffeting the trees in the square and rain was chattering on the window-panes. By the looks of the rivulet coursing along the gutter on the street below, the storm must have blown in several hours ago. He was planning to drive to Milton Keynes to confront Vanessa Carlson this morning and he couldn't have chosen a worse day. Andrew had called the evening before to tell Kingston that he'd managed to get a dentist appointment at noon and wouldn't be able to accompany Kingston, as they'd arranged. He'd reasoned with Kingston to put the trip off for one day, but Kingston had prevailed, assuring his friend that he was only going to see a woman in an estate agent's office on Milton Keynes's high street, and that Andrew's presence — though he would enjoy the company — would make no difference one way or another.

Kingston planned to spend the first part of the morning catching up with phone calls — in particular to Dorothy Endicott — and taking yet another look at Veitch's notes and the baffling Winterborne riddle. After that, depending on the storm and before it got too late, he would decide whether or not to make the journey. He figured, with normal traffic, Milton Keynes to be no more than an hour and a half's drive, so he would still have plenty of time to do the roundtrip and be back at a respectable hour. Doubtless the interview would be brief.

His call to the institute the day before had drawn a blank. The dean was as solicitous as before, regretting that he had no knowledge whatsoever to indicate that Endicott had skills in cryptography. He assured Kingston that he would inquire with all members of the faculty if Endicott had discussed anything of that nature with them and, if so, would let Kingston know.

Breakfast finished, he dialed Dorothy Endicott's number. When he'd called yesterday, he was told that she was gone all day on a trip to London but would be returning late that evening. It was a couple of minutes before she was located, but when she answered, she sounded in the same good humor as before.

"Dr. Kingston. What a pleasant surprise. I didn't expect to hear from you so soon. Are you coming up to see me again? I hope."

"Not yet, I'm afraid. I'm still spending all my time on your son's case. But I'll have to meet with the police in Stafford sooner or later. When I do, I'll let you know. That's a promise. If the timing is right, I'll take you out for a nice lunch."

"I'd really enjoy that. Are you making any progress?"

"Very little, sad to say. Whoever said that 'it's the drudgery and boredom of police work that eventually solves cases' knew what he was talking about. I called to ask you a question, Dorothy. It's something that I should have asked you the last time."

"Of course. I told you I would tell you everything I possibly can, if it means finding out who killed William and why."

"At any time during William's growing up, schooling, career path, did he ever show an interest in codes or code breaking?"

"Cryptology. Oh, yes. He was very good at it."

"He *was?* When was this? When he was younger, at school?"

"He first became interested when he was at County Grammar School. He used to do the cryptic puzzles, the ones in the newspaper. Then he started studying it more seriously. His interest continued when he went to university. I remember his telling me one day that he was considering pursuing a career where cryptology skills were required. I believe he was looking into civilian jobs with intelligence and national security agencies. I wouldn't be sure, though."

"That never happened, I take it?"

"No. It was a good idea at the time, but the more he learned about the modern technology involved and all the advanced computer stuff that goes with it these days, the less he liked it. He finally gave up, to pursue his original goal, which was archaeological studies, as you know."

"Well, Dorothy," Kingston said, trying to rein in his elation, "what you've told me answers a question that's concerned me for some time."

"I hope it helps in a good way."

"It does."

"Are you saying that he might have been killed because of his interest in cryptology?"

"Not necessarily." Kingston hesitated for a moment, not knowing how much to tell her.

"You're a nice man, Doctor — clever, too. I won't ask any more questions. There's not much point because I know that you wouldn't say anything that could cause me more stress. Perhaps the less I know for now is for the best, but eventually I would like to know the real reason for William's murder. To set my mind at rest."

"When we know the full story, you will, Dorothy. I promise you."

"Don't forget to call me when you know you're going to be in Stafford."

"I won't. I'm sure it will be soon."

Kingston put the phone down feeling exuberant. At last another piece of the puzzle had fallen into place. Studying the science for that long, Endicott must have been exceptionally accomplished at cryptography, he thought.

Two hours later, Kingston was on the A5 approaching the sprawl of Milton Keynes, Buckinghamshire. He'd decided to make the drive when the rain had stopped at ten thirty and the somber skies had magically, but not atypically, transmuted into a hazy blue with a ragged layer of low clouds. Before leaving, he'd called the estate agent's office and had been assured by the woman who answered that Vanessa would be there most of the day.

Passing the off-ramp sign to Bletchley, he

smiled. In Britain's darkest days of the war, the little town served as headquarters of the illustrious World War II code-breaking masterminds. "Pity you couldn't be of help," he said to himself. He would love to have been on the team responsible for breaking the Nazis' Enigma code and thereby shortening the duration of the war. In about fifteen minutes he would come face-to-face with the elusive Vanessa Carlson. He was rather looking forward to it.

The estate agent's office was in the heart of town and Kingston had no trouble finding it. He opened the plate-glass front door and entered a small room that looked like every other estate agent's office he'd seen. The lone occupant, a man Kingston guessed to be in his midforties, was seated at an empty desk. Seeing Kingston, he stood. He was a large man, with large features on his florid face, dressed in a brown leather jacket, black T-shirt, and tan jeans. Immediately Kingston sensed that something was off-kilter. Surely, even in Milton Keynes, estate agents would never dress in this fashion, he thought.

"Can I 'elp you?" he said. His voice matched his attire and wasn't overly friendly.

"I'm here to meet Vanessa Carlson. I was

told she was working today."

"She ain't 'ere and she's not expected back today. Who shall I say was looking for 'er?"

Kingston was thinking fast. "Dr. Kingston. I doubt she'll know me, though."

"Funny. Because she told me to expect you."

"I don't follow you," said Kingston, his suspicions now confirmed.

"Harassment's not a laughin' matter. I've 'alf a mind to call the police," the man replied, sizing Kingston up with clear intent.

Kingston was now thinking of making a hasty retreat. He eyed the door, wishing it were a little closer. "You've got it wrong. I only want to talk to her," he said. "I've never met the woman in my life."

The man started moving closer to Kingston, arms dangling by his sides, fists half clenched. "You made a big mistake by coming 'ere, chum," he said menacingly.

They were now separated by no more than three feet and Kingston was thinking of making a run for it. He started to inch back toward the door, about to speak, when the man's huge fist lashed out at him. He managed to spin at the last moment. The fist missed his jaw and slammed, full force, into his left shoulder, hurling him off balance into a desk by the window, knocking a table lamp and a telephone to the floor. Half on, half off the desk with no possible means of defense, his shoulder throbbing with pain, there was little he could do as the big man loomed over him, his right fist raised. "It would give me the greatest pleasure to put you in hospital, mister. But I've been told not to do that. You ain't gonna get a second chance, though. You stay away from Vanessa, or you'll end up on a slab. Now get out of here before I change my mind," he growled, kicking Kingston in the shin. "Bugger off and don't come back!"

In the Pay & Display car park, Kingston sat in the TR nursing his shoulder, wincing in pain at the slightest movement. His shin hurt, too; it was bloodied but nothing serious. It would be several days of aspirin and sleepless nights, he knew, before his shoulder improved. He stared at the dashboard thinking about what had just happened. Mistake number one was not bringing Andrew along. But how was Kingston to have known he'd be meeting a gorilla instead of Vanessa Carlson? He also wondered what to make of the man's saying that he'd been told not to mess Kingston up. What reason could they have — whoever *they* were — for not giving him a real going-over? Was it possible that they'd also reached an impasse in solving the code and were now forced to count on him to do so? At least he knew that he had the right woman, no question now that Carlson was the woman who had masqueraded as the researcher, quizzing Cassie Holbrook about the house and the frieze. The incident also implied that he was still under surveillance: The only way that Vanessa Carlson could have known that he planned to show up in her office was from the couple in Linslade. Even though he hadn't left his name, Kingston's calling the estate office to ascertain if Vanessa would be at work that day would have confirmed any suspicions she might have had.

Driving out of the car park, his thoughts turned to the Brookside Garden Club and its three members: Veitch, Endicott, and Carlson. How did each fit into the picture? he wondered. Somehow he couldn't see them working in concert with the common cause of solving a centuries-old mystery. So what role did each play? He'd gone over this ground before but knew that if he could establish their relationships — whose side each was on — it would help answer a lot of questions. At least there was no need for more speculation on Endicott's relationship with Veitch. Little doubt remained that they'd become partners, because Veitch needed Endicott's cryptography skills. But something had happened, and whatever that something was had most likely led to Endicott's murder. And what about Vanessa Carlson? How did she fit into the puzzle? Today's fiasco left little doubt that she was implicated with the people who had been trying to prevent Veitch from publishing his discovery. Or had they been simply trying to find out exactly what it was that he'd uncovered in order to find the supposed hidden money? Maybe it was both? She had been the only one remaining who might have provided answers, but now that door had been slammed shut. Between the pain, the disappointment, and the humiliation, Kingston had had quite enough for one day. He slipped a disc into the CD slot determined to forget today's misadventure, soon calmed, if in spirit only, by Sarah Chang's Brahms Violin Concerto in D.

When he arrived home, there were no phone messages. He found it curious that Morley had not called. They'd been playing telephone tag for several days, and thus far in their dealings Morley had always been quick to respond. A letter from Oliver Henshawe was among the day's post. He sat on the sofa and read it, before tending to his shoulder.

Dr. Kingston,
Regarding your inquiry about Jessica. I regret to say that six months ago she suffered a stroke and is now a resident at Larkmead Woodlands Nursing Home near Leicester. Prior to that, she had been in declining health and living with a friend in Market Harborough for a year. The address is Larkmead Woodlands, 28 the Lanes, Wynton Bassett, Leicestershire, LE3 9LH.

I wish you success in your endeavor to bring the guilty parties to justice for the terrible crimes committed at Sturminster. I'm familiar only with what I've read, having lost touch with Francis over these last several years.

Yours sincerely,
Oliver Henshawe

He put the letter aside, feeling a modest sense of pity for Jessica Henshawe's misfortune but glad that he wouldn't have to conduct another interview. Hers would have been the last, but he was tiring of asking the same questions over and over and getting little for the effort. He took two aspirin and

377

spent the next twenty minutes applying a makeshift ice pack to his shoulder while watching the BBC News. After a supper of leftovers and two glasses of Burgundy, he went to bed early, reading for an hour before dozing off. All things considered, he managed to get a decent night's sleep, waking once in the small hours, in the middle of a dream in which he was at an elegant party at a house that resembled Winterborne. Among the guests, in eighteenth-century attire, were Robert Walpole, Horace Walpole, and Thomas Gray. He never had the opportunity to talk to any of them, being forcibly removed as persona non grata.

Twenty-Nine

The next morning, after soaking in a hot bath for twenty minutes, Kingston felt greatly improved, though he couldn't stop thinking about yesterday's punishing incident. In the kitchen at eight thirty still in his pajamas, reading the *Times* and waiting for the toast to pop up, the doorbell rang. He padded along the hallway and opened the door, surprised to see Andrew standing there. Surprised, because Andrew was an admitted late riser known to boast that he didn't consider dawn to be an attractive experience, unless he was already up.

"Come in," said Kingston. With the Milton Keynes humiliation uppermost on his mind and his aching shoulder, he'd forgotten that Andrew was taking his Mini in for servicing at nine thirty and Kingston had promised to follow him to Hendon and bring him back home. After that, they were lunching at a newly opened brasserie in Richmond followed by a walk through Chiswick House and Gardens. "Would you like a cup of tea before we leave?" he asked.

"No thanks."

"How's your tooth, by the way?"

"It's fine now. I need a crown, though." Andrew was sizing up Kingston's attire. "You hadn't forgotten, had you?"

"No," Kingston fibbed. "I wasn't watching the clock. I'll be ready in less than five minutes."

An hour later, when they were heading back to Chelsea in Kingston's TR4, Kingston decided it was as good a time as any to tell Andrew what had happened in Milton Keynes. He'd barely started when Andrew shook his head and interrupted. "I thought there must be another reason why you were moving like a tortoise with a hangover this morning," he said.

Kingston chose not to answer right away

but eventually continued, keeping his eyes on the road.

From then on Andrew listened silently. Save for several shakes of the head, his expression and posture showed neither surprise nor the usual exasperation. He waited for Kingston to finish before saying his piece.

"What do you expect me to say, Lawrence?"

"That it was stupid of me, that I should never have gone alone, that I should throw in the towel before it's too late — that I never listen to a word you say?"

"I couldn't have said it better, except I might have added that you deserved what you got and you're damned lucky it wasn't a hell of a lot worse."

"You don't have to remind me," said Kingston, weaving through the everyone-for-himself snarl of traffic at Marble Arch.

Andrew shook his head for the umpteenth time. "I give up. A few days ago, we sat in the garden at Bourne End and agreed — if I recall correctly — that if I were to help you with this damned case, you wouldn't go off on these trips of yours alone. You assured me that, from now on, we would work to solve it together. Either your memory is failing you, or you must have since decided that it wasn't such a good idea after all."

"You're right. You're right. I should have waited. My only excuse is that there was a sense of urgency to it — the opportunity to corner this Vanessa Carlson woman while I had the chance. Afterward, I knew I'd made a big mistake going alone. I've got a bruised shoulder and a painful shin to remind me."

"Seriously," said Andrew, "why don't you consider giving it up? I know I sound like a cracked record, but why not turn everything over to the police and just walk away from it, go back to leading a normal life?"

Kingston glanced at Andrew and nodded. "I should take your advice, I know, but we're so damned close to solving it."

Andrew sighed. "There's that 'we' again. If you ask me, I don't think you really want me to help you. I'm too old for all this stuff, anyway." He looked at Kingston, who was keeping his eyes on the Knightsbridge traffic. "And you're way past it."

The rest of the trip was spent mostly in silence, both knowing that further discussion about the Milton Keynes incident would serve no purpose.

The following morning, Kingston was up earlier than usual. He'd been up half the night, unable to erase from his mind the galling events of the last couple of days and driven to distraction by the Winterborne riddle. In the seven or so years that he'd been involved in criminal cases, he'd never felt so frustrated. He sat in the kitchen now, the riddle in front of him and next to it a list that he'd compiled of people's names, places, incidents, and events mentioned in Veitch's notes. He'd gone through the list several times but had been unable to find even the remotest connection to the riddle.

He topped up his tea — his third cup — and glanced at his watch. In seven minutes, not a second more or less, Mrs. Tripp would be at the front door and, as was his practice, he would make himself scarce for a while.

Hearing the doorbell at the appointed time, he pushed aside the papers and went to let in his ineffable and indispensable charlady. She was starting to busy herself in the kitchen, picking up his breakfast plate, asking if he'd finished with his tea, when, out of nowhere, a thought struck him.

"I've been trying to solve a riddle of sorts, Mrs. Tripp," he said, picking up the two sheets of paper. "Perhaps you'd care to take a look at these. I'm trying to find a connection between the riddle and something on the list — a person, a place, an incident, anything. You may spot something I've overlooked." He handed her the papers. "You know that old saying about being too close to the forest to see the trees?"

"Oh, yes, I do." She beamed. "I'd be more than pleased to take a look. I must say I'm not very good at puzzles, though, and if you can't solve it, I don't know who can."

Kingston had a last sip of lukewarm tea and took his teacup to the sink counter, leaving her to study the riddle. He thought about going to his study but had a feeling that it wouldn't be long before she handed the papers back to him — and he was right.

"Sorry, Doctor." She looked genuinely disappointed that she'd been unable to help. "It really is a strange riddle, isn't it?"

Kingston sighed. "It certainly is."

"The Walpoles? Weren't they politicians?"

"They were, yes. Back in the eighteenth century."

"And Thomas Gray? Would that be the poet Thomas Gray?"

"Indeed," Kingston replied.

A brief moment of silence followed. Then, to his amazement, Mrs. Tripp gazed up at the ceiling, as if straining her memory, and started to recite Gray's *Elegy,* in a voice that had a poignancy that was unfamiliar to him.

"The curfew tolls the knell of parting day,
The lowing herd wind slowly o'er the lea,
The ploughman homeward plods his
    weary way,
And leaves the world to darkness and to
    me.

"Now fades the glimmering landscape on
    the sight,
And all the air a solemn stillness
    holds . . ."

Her voice trailing off, she regarded Kingston with a pleased look on her face.

He was shocked momentarily by her recollection of the poem and her eloquent recital. "That was amazing. Wonderful," he said.

"We learned it in school," she said. "Didn't you?"

"I did — I suppose we all did back then — but I certainly can't remember it like you. Can you recite the entire poem?"

Now she looked bashful, as if she wished she hadn't got carried away. "I don't think so. It's awfully long, you know. It is lovely, though. For me it's still the most beautiful poem ever written."

"I would have to agree."

"Did you ever visit Stoke Poges?"

384

"I should have, but living in Scotland most of my life, I never had the opportunity."

"It was written in the churchyard there. He lived in the village —"

Kingston held up his spread hands, as if to say *Stop.*

A few seconds of silence passed, while Kingston was frozen in thought and Mrs. Tripp looked most bewildered.

Then, slowly, Kingston moved his hands up to clasp his head on either side, and a smile spread across his face.

"Mrs. Tripp, I do believe you've done it," he said, now clearly elated.

"Done what?"

"Solved the riddle."

She regarded him, a blank expression on her face. "I did?" she said.

"I'm almost certain. What's the title of the poem?"

She frowned and looked at him as if to say *What kind of question is that?*

"The title?" he said.

"Why, it's *Elegy Written in a Country Churchyard.*"

He was about to hug Mrs. Tripp but thought better of it; she might think he'd lost his mind. Instead he gave her a huge smile and said, "You're brilliant, Mrs.

Tripp." He knew that would embarrass her, which it did.

"I believe," he continued, "I'm almost sure, in fact, that the churchyard mentioned in the riddle is not really a physical churchyard at all. It refers to the poem. 'Sealed in Gray's poem' — that's what it means."

"Well, goodness me," said Mrs. Tripp, beaming. "I'm glad I was of help."

"You don't know just how much." He was about to say that it would mean a nice raise, when he bit his lip. He would give her a generous bonus, he decided, if it turned out that he was right.

THIRTY

In his study, Kingston got *The Oxford Book of English Verse* off a shelf. Even though it was only a couple of minutes since Mrs. Tripp's stroke of serendipity, he now had a good idea what "thirty to six" in the riddle meant: They were seven lines of the poem, the thirtieth to the thirty-sixth. Studying the *Elegy,* he saw that it was constructed of thirty-two stanzas, each of four lines. Kingston found the eighth stanza, which started with line twenty-nine. Lines thirty to thirty-six were:

Their homely joys, and destiny obscure;
Nor grandeur hear with a disdainful smile,
The short and simple annals of the poor.

The boast of heraldry, the pomp of power,
And all that beauty, all that wealth e'er
    gave,
Await alike the inevitable hour;
The paths of glory lead but to the grave.

So this was it, he said to himself. Exposing the long-dormant dark secret of Sturminster could be close at hand. All that was necessary now was to solve the code hidden in the seven lines of Gray's *Elegy:* the seven lines of the second ciphertext on the envelope, under the arrow. Problem was, solving it wasn't going to be anywhere as easy as the first code. It wasn't so much a question of it being beyond his knowledge of cryptography as his ability to remember the process essential to decrypting a cipher embedded in the lines of a book or a poem. He had a vague recollection that it required a separate shift for each letter, as opposed to just the one shift in the codes that he'd demonstrated to Andrew, but that was about all. He leaned back, pondering this new dilemma.

Kingston read the spare and powerfully

moving lines several times, even knowing it would be of no help in solving the riddle within. He opened his file cabinet and pulled out the Sturminster file, quickly finding a copy of the Winterborne code. He started to transfer the characters in the Winterborne ciphertext underneath each character in the seven lines of the poem. He had every expectation that both the poem and the key would have the same number of characters, which they did. The first two lines completed — no punctuation and no spacing — he studied them to make sure he'd made no errors.

THEIRHOMELYJOYSANDDESTINYOBSCURE
HMFCZBTZUXDCINGFGXLJVIURSGWMKNLF

NORGRANDEURHEARWITHADISDAINFULSMILE
BSKAWTHERZFBYPTIXILJIMAEOMGGIUZAXNQ

Satisfied so far, he continued until the seven lines were completed. He then went to work, putting his memory and perseverance to the test, buoyed by an unfounded sense of optimism that, by plugging away at it assiduously, the methodology would come back to him and he would succeed in unlocking the code. After an hour and a half, he put his pencil down and, with great reluctance and humility, admitted defeat.

After thinking for a minute or so, he decided that if he were to seek expert advice, the best place to look for it would be GCHQ. Though he preferred not to, that would mean calling the chap Morley had mentioned. He would surely be able to offer advice. Kingston riffled through the Sturminster file and found the copy of the report that Harry Tennant had submitted to Lord Morley. He then reached for the phone and called Directory Enquiries for the number.

Kingston's call was transferred to Tennant's office. Miracle of miracles for a government department, Tennant was on the line in seconds. Kingston introduced himself, mentioning his brief stint with intelligence in Ashford and further explaining that he was conducting an inquiry into the Sturminster murders on Lord Morley's behalf.

"Morley told me that some time ago you examined what was suspected as being part of a coded message," said Kingston.

"Right. Have you found the other half?"

"No. Somehow I don't think we will, either. I'm calling about another matter, this time it really is a cipher."

"You sound sure of that."

"I am certain of it. The problem is, it's hidden in the lines of a famous poem and I've completely forgotten the method of deciphering it. It's been so long since I've done that sort of thing. I have the cipher-text, of course."

"Be happy to help. Do you want to e-mail me the information?"

"If it's not asking too much, I'd prefer that you walk me through the methodology on the phone. The information contained in the decoded message could be of a personal nature and extremely sensitive and I don't want to put you in what could be a vulnerable position."

"I understand. That's usually why codes are necessary: to protect critical information."

For the next ten minutes, with Kingston writing notes, Tennant went through the steps enabling Kingston to decipher the second part of the Winterborne code. Satisfied that he could now do it, Kingston thanked Harry — as he'd asked to be called — and they chatted for another minute or so.

"I have one more request, Harry, if that's all right?"

"Of course."

"Two, actually. For several reasons it's

extremely important to the investigation that nobody learns of our conversation. The second is equally imperative. If anyone should happen to inquire about decoding ciphers related to the Sturminster case — no matter whom it might be — I would ask that you find a way to decline such a request. It's a lot to ask, I know, particularly for someone in your position. All I can say is that the code in question could very well be crucial to solving the recent crimes committed at Sturminster and perhaps some from the past. If the information falls into the wrong hands, it could have nasty repercussions, even endangering more lives."

Tennant paused. "I'll take your word for it, Lawrence," he said. "And you have mine. I wish you luck and you must promise to tell me about it, if and when it's solved."

Kingston put down the phone and immediately picked it up again to call Andrew with the good news, but the line was engaged. After closing the door, to silence the drone of Mrs. Tripp's vacuum, he returned to his desk and, with Harry's instructions next to him, started anew trying to solve the message concealed in the lines from Gray's *Elegy*.

Five minutes later, still struggling with the code, there was a knock on the door. He got up and opened it to see Mrs. Tripp. "Mr. Andrew is here to see you, Doctor," she said. "He's in the living room."

"Tell him to come in, if you would, please." He left the door open and returned to his desk.

"I called you a few minutes ago," said Andrew, entering the study. "Your line was busy."

Kingston spun his chair around. "I was talking to a code expert," he said.

"I was on my way out, so I thought I'd stop by. A code expert? Anything happening? You look like the cat that just swallowed the canary."

"Happening? Might be an understatement." Kingston pulled on his earlobe. "Pull up that chair and sit down. Mrs. Tripp and I just solved the Winterborne riddle."

Andrew frowned. "Mrs. Tripp?"

"That's right. Turns out she's a Thomas Gray aficionado. She can practically recite the entire *Elegy*."

"Really. Gray's *Elegy*?"

Kingston went on to explain how it had all happened just a few minutes earlier and of his conversation with Harry Tennant.

Andrew looked wide-eyed. "Are you close to solving it?"

"I'm not sure. It sounded easy when Tennant described the methodology, and I wrote it all down, but it's not as easy as I'd hoped. Instead of a simple shift of the alphabet, like the one I showed you, this involves a shift for each individual letter."

"I see."

"Are you in a hurry to go somewhere?"

"No. I was going to the bank and the post office."

"Then you might want to stay, because this could be a moment you'll remember for a long time. If you want some coffee or tea, go ask Mrs. Tripp."

With Tennant's instructions beside him, and Andrew sitting alongside, Kingston went back to work on the code, focusing on only the first two lines of the ciphertext:

```
HMFCZBTZUXDCINGFGXLJVIURSGWMKNLF
BSKAWTHERZFBYPTIXILJIMAEOMGGIUZAXNQ
```

For the next ten minutes, assiduously matching the cipher characters against those of the poem and double-checking to make sure there were no transposition errors, a coherent message began to unfold. Kingston knew that he'd succeeded in breaking the code. When the two lines were completed, he and Andrew read the decrypted lines, below, in awestruck silence, soon broken by boisterous high fives.

```
THEIRHOMELYJOYSANDDESTINYOBSCURE
NEATHTEMPLESTONESTHECOLDTRUTHSTA

NORGRANDEURHEARWITHADISDAINFULSMILE
NDSTESTAMENTTOBLOODIEDHANDSANIGNOBL
```

With the technique now down pat, Kingston went back to work feverishly, and in another ten minutes they were looking at an eight-line printout of the decrypted message that was hidden in the seven lines of Gray's *Elegy:*

Neath temple stones the cold truth stands
Testament to bloodied hands
An ignoble life of sin and lies
Moulders in shame from worldly eyes
Five north of centre oer column tall
The epilogue is writ upon the wall
Auriga awaits a judgment day
His four spoked wheel points the way

"The 'temple' must be the Athenian Temple monument at Sturminster," Kingston muttered. "And all the time I was focused on the Arcadian monument."

"It's another damned riddle. And who or what is Auriga?" Andrew asked, frowning.

"It's a riddle, all right, but it also gives

directions, tells how to solve it. Auriga, as I recall, is one of the constellations in the Milky Way. It's the Latin word for chari-oteer."

Andrew was shaking his head. "So what does it all mean?"

"Give me a moment, Andrew," Kingston replied impatiently. "I need to think about it."

Kingston studied the eight enigmatic lines for a minute or so, reading the words carefully, eventually looking up toward the ceiling. The 'stones' must be those on the floor of the temple," he said, staring into space. "I only saw them from a distance, but they appeared quite large. We need to determine the center point of the floor, which is simple. Then, in a northerly direction, count off five stones. That should position us next to, or near, one of the inner columns. 'O'er column tall' suggests that above the column, in all probability on the bas-relief frieze — most Greek temples have them — there should be a chariot or the figure of a chari-oteer. Most likely it will be the former because the 'judgment day' — or revelation, if you will — is to be found in the wheel of the chariot."

"Something hidden behind the wheel?"

"No. My guess is that the chariot wheel

itself conceals a device that activates a mechanism of some kind that raises one of the stones."

"Under which we'll find the answer to all of our questions — the secret of Sturminster?"

"I'm sure of it, Andrew. It leaves little doubt. There's a problem, though."

"What do you mean? I thought you just said we'd solved it?"

Kingston was pulling on his earlobe. "A different kind of problem. We obviously can't go barging around the temple during the daytime, with all those visitors and staff people around. They can get as many as two thousand visitors on a good day." He paused, looking aside, then said, "We must go in at nighttime."

Andrew looked startled. "You're not serious, surely?"

"What do you mean?"

"Are you suggesting that we break into Sturminster's grounds in the middle of the night and start chiseling away at their temple? We'd probably be arrested before we got past the gates. You *must* hand this over to the police."

"We're not going through the gates. They'll all be closed anyway. And this is far too complicated to involve the police at this point. Before we do that, before anything, we must find out if we're right about the riddle."

Andrew looked anything but convinced. "Surely they must have a security system."

"They do. Crawford told me."

"How do you plan to deal with that?"

"He also said that it was impossible for them to monitor every inch of their fifteen hundred acres twenty-four/seven."

Andrew shook his head. "Count me out," he said.

"I thought you insisted on accompanying me from now on," said Kingston.

"Not if it means breaking the law."

"Come on, Andrew. We're this close to what could be a huge discovery. Why do you think someone went to all the trouble of devising such complex codes and riddles? The only possible explanation is that what he was hiding was either — as Veitch was convinced — to cover up a crime of historical proportions or to conceal something of incalculable value . . ."

"Or both."

"Possibly."

"Forget the crime part, Lawrence. We both know it's all about the loot."

Kingston didn't hear Andrew's last comment. He'd gone to the window and was staring out at the square, chin cradled on his clenched fist, deep in thought. Suddenly, he turned and came back to face Andrew. "We must drive to Sturminster tonight," he said with underlying urgency.

"*You* must drive to Sturminster tonight," retorted Andrew, starting to get up.

"I need to think more about their security. How far do you think it is from the main gate to the Athenian Temple?"

"Lawrence, you know damned well I've never been there. What's got into you?"

"Sit down," said Kingston. It was more a command than a polite invitation.

Andrew slumped in the chair, grudgingly, facing Kingston. In situations like this, he knew better than to argue and remained silent, glaring at his friend.

"If I were to guess, there could be two or three layers of security at Sturminster. Figuratively speaking, let's call them circles of increasing diameter, like ripples caused by a pebble thrown into a pond. The first circle embraces the house and the adjacent garden — not a large area. The next covers all the land surrounding the eight monuments — a substantially larger area." He paused and closed his eyes briefly, as if trying to recall the topography. "Last, there's the open land, with no structures, stretching to the outer perimeter, by far the biggest part of the estate." He paused and looked at Andrew. "Are you following me?"

Andrew nodded petulantly. "Go on," he muttered.

"It stands to reason that the innermost circle around the house and its immediate surroundings would be monitored with more vigilance, probably by a combination of nighttime patrols, closed-circuit cameras, and perhaps other electronic devices. This doesn't concern us, though. It's the next two circles that we must deal with. Of the two, the inner one will present the bigger problem. That's where the Athenian Temple stands. As for the parkland to the outer perimeter, my guess is that surveillance there is minimal or there's none at all. It's all open land with nothing to steal or vandalize. Besides, the perimeter is huge. You must get it into your head, Andrew: Sturminster is about five times the size of Kew Gardens."

"Okay. But you're not suggesting we hike in, are you?"

Kingston shook his head. "For heaven's sake, can't you come up with something more constructive?"

"I'm simply trying to find a way of going in there without ending up in jail."

"What do you think I'm trying to fathom?" Kingston shot back, with a hint of impatience. "We must get a map, get to know the lay of the land, find out what other roads access the property — such as trades-men's entrances, and we need to establish the exact location of the temple and the sec-tion of the perimeter that's closest." He raised a pointed finger, wagging it. "And — let's not forget to check the phase of the moon."

Andrew's sigh of resignation was self-evident as he shook his head. "And our horoscopes, while we're at it," he muttered.

"I'll ignore that."

"Let me make sure I understand what you're suggesting. All we are doing is a reconnaissance, nothing more. Right?"

Kingston nodded, holding up his hand. "However, if all goes well, and providing we're not interrupted, we could test our theory — to see if I'm right — that there's a mechanism in the frieze that raises a stone in the floor, revealing what's underneath."

Andrew sighed. "I still don't see why we can't just turn this over to Lord Morley and the police. Isn't that what you were hired to do? Your assignment is completed. Let them do the heavy lifting and mopping up. Be-sides, what you're suggesting is patently asking for trouble. It could be dangerous, Lawrence. Dangerous."

Kingston drew himself up to full height, commanding Andrew's attention. "Look, Andrew," he said forcefully. "This is my last attempt to convince you why we must do this at night — that there's no other way. First, we will have the place all to ourselves. Second, if we're successful in finding out what's under the floor of the temple, it could — and I say could — also lead to solving the murders. Why don't we go to Lord Morley and the police, you ask? I'll tell you why. Because I've reached the point in this investigation where I don't trust anybody, least of all any of the Morley family, with all their damned secrets. I keep asking myself why I've been shadowed and threatened, but more important, by whom. As far as I'm concerned, everyone's suspect now." He drew a breath, looked around the room, then continued. "If we tell Morley that we've solved the riddle and tell him everything we know, what's to prevent him and his people from going in alone, finding what's under the floor of the temple, and then denying the presence of anything, covering the whole thing up? As for Wheatley and the police, Morley could quite easily dissuade them from investigating the temple. He could simply remove all evidence, saying that he'd gone over it already and had come up empty-handed. Don't forget it's on private property, and unless Wheatley were to suspect that the temple contained evidence concerning the murders, he might take Morley's word for it that nothing out of the ordinary was found. If push came to shove, Morley could easily show them to prove it. No. I've come this far, Andrew, and I'm damned well going to finish it, with you or without you."

"All right, Lawrence. I somehow didn't expect you to change your mind." He got up and walked toward the door. "I'll call you in the morning," he said, holding it ajar. "Maybe thinking about it overnight will make you see reason," he added, closing the door quietly behind him.

THIRTY-ONE

Shortly after eleven the next night, a red Mini Cooper, with Andrew at the wheel and with lights off, backed into a rutted lane off one of the roads bordering Sturminster and parked a dozen yards in, up against a wooden farm gate. Kingston and Andrew, both dressed in dark clothing, got out and closed the doors quietly. As far as the moon was concerned, they had lucked out. It had just entered its new phase and the night was about as dark as it could get.

Since ten thirty, after dinner at a pub some fifteen miles away, they'd been driving around the public perimeter roads encircling the estate looking for a suitable place to park off the road, in a concealed spot, as close as possible to the estimated location of the Athenian Temple. Earlier, Kingston had studied a Google Earth view of the house and park on the Internet and had printed out a single map that showed the three private roads crossing the estate, each leading to the house. As Andrew had surmised, all three entrances were closed, blocked by wrought-iron gates at least thirty feet wide and half as tall. A brief examination had revealed CCTV cameras mounted high on both sides. As expected, no service roads were marked. Fortunately, the map showed the location of the eight monuments and, though not to scale, it seemed that the Athenian Temple was about three-quarters of a mile in from the road and, as luck would have it, was the closest of all the monuments.

They had decided earlier, but only after Kingston had employed every single weapon in his arsenal of verbal skills, logical thinking, and powers of persuasion, that their first foray would be considered exploratory. Andrew had agreed to Kingston's caveat that if, by luck, they encountered no difficulties and managed to reach the temple undetected, they would keep going and attempt to uncover the temple's secret. Additionally, Andrew had stipulated that he would agree to take part in what he called "this madcap adventure" only if it involved no physical risks, that they didn't push their luck, and that, if confronted with a situation where even the slightest chance of being accosted or apprehended seemed likely, they would beat a hasty retreat.

After a brief confab and waiting silently for at least fifteen minutes, to determine if there were patrols of any kind in their section of the perimeter — there were none — they embarked on phase two of their mission: to walk briskly across the open parkland to the Athenian Temple. Equipped with just a builder's tape measure, a stick of chalk, a flashlight each, and no tools except Kingston's trusty Swiss Army knife, they set off into the dark and the unknown.

Well clear of the park's roads, the land was easy to traverse, even at night. Occasionally they passed small herds of cows — some with wickedly long horns — that grazed the grassy slopes and hollows where spreading canopies of ancient oak, beech, and chestnut trees shaded them from the heat of the daytime sun. Reaching the crest of a knoll, they saw sprinkles of light in the distance. "That's the house," said Kingston, whispering, unnecessarily. From all appearances thus far, it was doubtful that a living soul knew of their presence. "My guess is that we've come about half the way, so according to the map, we should head slightly to the left." He pointed the way.

They continued in silence across the open land, prepared at any moment to dive for the nearest cover or fall flat on their bellies at the first sign of security personnel or vehicles. Twenty minutes later, their progress still unimpeded, it seemed that they would reach the temple unnoticed. Kingston was now trying to envisage what to expect: the stone being raised, no doubt revealing steps descending into some kind of underground chamber. A phantom shiver ran through him. It dredged up long-forgotten memories of Wickersham Priory, in Somerset, and a case he'd helped solve several years ago. That investigation had culminated in a deadly face-off in the catacombs beneath the ruins of a medieval priory in which he and Jamie Gibson, heiress of the estate, had come close to being buried alive. It was one of the most frightening experiences in his life, and he found himself praying that nothing like that would happen in the events about to unfold.

They reached the terraced steps of the Athenian Temple and stood for a moment next to its stone-columned façade, waiting and watching silently for anything that appeared out of place. They then made a visual search of the structure for signs of surveillance or security devices. Finding none, they ascended the steps and walked onto the platform, paved in stone slabs three feet square. Kingston estimated the space to be at least thirty feet wide and twenty deep. At the top of the columns above the square stone abacus, a bas-relief frieze circled the four walls above the architraves that supported the ceiling and roof. Already Kingston could see a problem. If, as the decoded message instructed, the mechanism to raise the floor stone were concealed in the frieze, it would be beyond their reach. It was well over twelve feet above the platform, he estimated. While pondering the dilemma, he took out the tape measure and, with Andrew holding one end, laid it out diagonally across the floor, first in one direction and then the opposite, to establish the center point. He marked the center stone with a small chalk cross. He then pulled out a piece of paper from the inside pocket of his parka. Using his flashlight, carefully shielded by Andrew's parka, he unfolded it and read the last four lines of the decoded message sotto voce:

"Five north of centre oer column tall
The epilogue is writ upon the wall
Auriga awaits a judgment day
His four spoked wheel points the way"

Kingston checked the compass on his old Swiss Army watch and studied the fluorescent arrow to establish north. Handing the message to Andrew, he counted off the stones as instructed, marking the fifth with another faint chalk cross. The stone was next to one of the rear columns: The instructions seemed accurate. He then looked up at the elaborate frieze and studied the relief scene depicting horsemen preparing for a chariot race. With the flashlight shielded by one hand to dim its light, he scanned the elaborately sculpted images of horses being coaxed into position; young warriors, some wearing body armor, others with crested helmets; ranks of horses, four and five deep, side by side in festive procession. Directly in line with the column's horizontal center point, his eyes alighted on a chariot manned by a warrior. "Auriga," he muttered. Fortunately, the four-spoke wheel, approximately a foot in diameter, was low on the frieze, where he could see it more clearly. With a glimmer of light steadied on it, he studied the pictorial details. Though not knowing quite what to expect or search for, he was discouraged to see that it appeared no different from the rest of the frieze's design. If it was the essential part of the mechanism that raised the stone, revealing whatever was below, it was certainly ingeniously disguised, he thought.

"Do you think that's it?" Andrew asked.

"It must be. The chariot's lined up perfectly with the column."

"How do you propose to reach it?" Andrew asked. "Even if I stand on your shoulders, it looks like we'll come up short. We should have anticipated this."

"Sure. We should've lugged an eight-foot ladder with us. That would've raised an eyebrow or two if we'd been caught, eh?"

Kingston turned off the flashlight and looked around the temple as if hoping for divine intervention, realizing that this setback would be difficult, if not impossible, to resolve. They were in the middle of nowhere, as it were, and the chances of finding something nearby that would help them reach the frieze were next to zero.

"We could always come back," said Andrew, breaking the long silence.

"No," said Kingston, tugging on his earlobe. "There has to be an answer."

"We could bring in a cow to stand on. That might do it."

"Very funny."

"Sorry."

Kingston raised a pointed finger. "Wait a moment. You may be on to something."

Andrew simply frowned, obviously deciding to remain silent after the last rebuke.

"The last herd of cattle we passed, the ones lying under the trees. If I'm not mistaken, there was an old trough alongside the fence."

Andrew nodded. "There was."

"About six feet long, as I recall."

"Longer, maybe."

"Let's take a look."

Fifteen minutes later, muscles and backs aching, they were back at the temple carrying a mud-spattered galvanized trough, square on both ends and about six feet long. It weighed a ton, but they'd managed by lugging it short distances at a time.

Kingston thought it best not to mention it

to Andrew, but he was starting to wonder why everything so far had happened so easily, without even the slightest indication that they might have been spotted or were being tracked. Dragging a cattle trough a couple of hundred yards across open land had been a huge risk, even in the dark — close to comedic, when he thought about it. Maybe he'd misjudged the sophistication of Sturminster's security systems. Too late to worry about that now, he knew. They had to keep going.

They stood the trough on end and pushed it up against the column directly below the frieze where the chariot wheel was located. Taller by at least five inches, Kingston insisted that he should climb up and activate the mechanism, if indeed it still functioned after two hundred–plus years — another possible setback he hadn't considered until now.

Andrew wiped the algae and mud off his hands on his trouser legs and positioned himself, feet spread, back pressed against the trough, hands clasped in front of him to form a step on which to raise Kingston as high as possible. Neither had tried anything like it before, though they seemed to know instinctively how it was done. The only concern now was Kingston's weight and whether Andrew, who was on the slight side, had the strength to lift him high enough to enable him to clamber onto the top of the trough.

The first attempt failed because Andrew's hands were clasped the wrong way. Kingston had trouble gripping the trough's slippery surface, fell and stumbled, but managed to keep his balance. On the second attempt, with a grunting and puffing Andrew supporting him, Kingston finally managed to get sufficient traction on the slick surface of the metal to haul his body to the top of the trough, where he stood upright. With one arm partly circling the column to maintain his balance, he reached up to the frieze. Andrew watched from below, fingers crossed, making sure that the trough was stable.

"Here goes," said Kingston. He placed his right hand, fingers spread wide, on the chariot wheel and pushed.

THIRTY-TWO

Kingston waited for half a minute. Nothing happened. All was silent save for the occasional rustle of leaves from the beech trees whose lower branches brushed against the temple roof.

"Any joy up there?" Andrew asked in a stage whisper.

"No. When I press the wheel, nothing happens."

"Press harder."

"I have."

"It's probably stuck after all these years. Try thumping it with the heel of your hand."

After several vigorous thumps, Kingston gave up. "Still nothing. Any other bright ideas?"

"Let me think."

A half minute of silence passed before Kingston spoke again. "Maybe you should come up and try — I doubt you'll be able to reach it, though."

"Try one more thing."

"What's that?"

"It's a wheel, right?"

"Of course it's a wheel."

"Then try turning it."

"Why didn't I think of that?"

Kingston placed his spread fingers against the wheel of the chariot, on the four spokes evenly spaced around the hub, applied pressure, and turned counterclockwise. To his astonishment and relief, the wheel moved. He heard a series of muffled clicks from somewhere inside the wall. More sounds followed — grindings, scrapings, and knockings, as if some gigantic primitive clock mechanism had been activated. He looked down, eyes fixed on one of the stones below, about ten feet away. The thin ribbon of mortar around its edges was starting to crumble as it inched slowly upward. It continued to rise, as if lifted by an invisible hand, leaving a thin layer of powdery dust on the surface of the surrounding stones. Kingston half slithered and half jumped off the trough, and landed near Andrew, who appeared mesmerized by what was happening.

They looked at each other briefly, nothing more. Words seemed superfluous as they waited for the mechanism to complete its job. A minute later all movement and noise stopped, and the temple fell silent again. They moved closer to examine the result. The thick slab of stone now appeared suspended in air, its base three inches above the surface of the floor. A foul, musty odor wafted from the hole, making them cover their mouths and noses. On closer inspection they could see that the stone was supported in one corner by a thick metal rod.

"It must pivot on the rod," said Kingston, grasping the stone in his large hands.

"Ingenious," Andrew said admiringly.

Kingston pulled on the stone and it swiveled effortlessly, perfectly balanced on the rod. He brought it to rest clear of its original position. They moved in closer and saw a primitive wooden ladder attached to the wall of the three-foot-square opening — beyond that, pitch-black. Kneeling, Andrew turned on his Maglite and pointed it into the hole. All they could see below was a dirt floor. They looked at each other momentarily, as if to say *You go first,* then, without a word, Kingston bent down, gripped the rails, stepped gingerly onto the second rung of the ladder, testing its sturdiness, and glanced at Andrew before descending. "Here goes," he said. His foot was on the next rung, supporting most of his weight, when suddenly it slipped. Immediately he knew why, cursing his stupidity. Mud from the cow pasture had wedged between the heel and sole of his shoes. He should have scraped it off. Gripping the rails with all his might, he dangled, his other foot searching for the rung. He managed to get a toe on it and found his footing.

"For Christ's sake, be careful," Andrew said, keeping his voice down.

Kingston glanced up at Andrew. "I'm okay."

The words had barely left his mouth when an ominous crack and sound of wood splintering echoed in the space below. Andrew watched, helpless, as Kingston fell backward into the dark of the hole.

Andrew was already climbing down the ladder. "Are you all right? I'm coming down there," he said.

"A bit shaken up. My ankle doesn't feel good, though."

Using the edge of the rungs, close to the rails, Andrew made his way carefully down and turned on his flashlight. Kingston was lying on his side by the wall, a few feet away, gripping his ankle.

"Bugger!" he said, looking up at Andrew.

Andrew knelt beside him, knowing there was little he could do other than to help alleviate the pain and make Kingston as comfortable as possible while he went to get help. "All we can do right now is to try and stabilize it and help reduce the swelling," he said. "And don't try to take you shoe off. That'll make it worse." He unzipped his parka, took off his scarf, and wrapped it tightly around Kingston's ankle, cinching it as best he could. "That should help a bit," he said, standing. "Just stay put, and don't try to stand or move around. We'll get you in a more comfortable position, then I'm going to the house to get help."

Kingston nodded, knowing that Andrew

was right. The pain was starting to set in, and he guessed that his ankle was badly sprained or even fractured. With Kingston propped against the wall with Andrew's jacket as a pillow, Andrew ascended the ladder, leaving Kingston alone.

"Hang in there, and whatever you do, don't try anything dumb," he said at the top. "The cavalry's on its way."

For a minute or so, not wanting to use up the flashlight batteries, Kingston sat in the semidarkness of the hole, only meager starlight coming from the opening above. He now wished that it were a moonlit night. He flicked on the flashlight and shone it around. He was in a rectangular room, roughly twelve by fifteen feet, with old brick walls and a crudely plastered ceiling. Despite his pain, a hollow sensation was welling in his gut, a surge of mounting disappointment. The room was empty.

He turned the flashlight off. It doesn't make sense, he thought. Why go to all the ridiculous trouble of keeping it such a guarded secret — the elaborate mechanism, those complicated codes? It must have been built to conceal something. It was like Howard Carter finding an empty pyramid. The obvious explanation was that it had once held a cache of some kind that had been emptied long ago. After all, the temple was built in the mid 1700s. The more he thought about it, though, the more convinced he was that he and Andrew were the first to discover the vault since it had been built. He remembered when they'd watched, spellbound, as the stone had risen, disturbing the dust of centuries, the fetid stench that had filled the air. Until proved otherwise, he would cling to that opinion.

For no reason, he shone the flashlight hastily over the space once more. He thought he saw a movement in the opening above. He fixed the light on it and left it there for a moment. He must have been wrong, he concluded, turning off the Maglite, returning to his thoughts.

He was trying to calculate how long it would take Andrew to reach the house and return with help. He would likely be intercepted by security when he got close to the house. That would speed things up, thought Kingston. He started to wonder how long it had been since Andrew had left. He mouthed the thought to himself. "Must be at least —"

His words were suspended in air. The muffled thud of a silencer was unmistakable. The bullet struck Kingston in his upper chest, slamming him hard against the wall. The flashlight rolled away out of reach. In seconds another shot followed. It passed over Kingston's head and thudded into the soft brick wall above him.

Lying on his side on the dirt, he placed a grimy hand inside his parka against his right chest just below the shoulder. It was wet with blood. Trembling with the shock and excruciating pain, the realization that some-one was trying to kill or maim him brought on a wave of nausea. He tried to turn, to look up to see who was there or what might happen next, but he couldn't. He stared up at the wall waiting, in dread. Then he saw it. One of the bricks a few feet above him was fractured and part of the surface shat-tered by the impact of the second bullet. He caught a tiny glint of steel, guessing it was the edge of the bullet that was still embedded in the soft mortar. Underneath the muddy ocher of the bricks, he saw yet a different color.

Gold.

THIRTY-THREE

Kingston huddled in the corner of the dark room, his hands pressed hard against his chest. Despite the gnawing pain, he couldn't block the chilling thought of what must

surely follow. He had no idea of time —
were minutes passing, or seconds? He
thought he heard voices in the eerie silence
but couldn't be sure. He wanted to look up
but couldn't move and could barely open
his eyes or focus them. His mind loosed its
moorings, castigating itself as though already detached, summing up a life that was
about to end.

*What a fool you've been, Lawrence Alastair
Kingston — stubborn, conceited, and, yes,
even reckless. You wouldn't listen to Amanda's and Andrew's warnings, would you? And
now look where it's got you. I only hope
Andrew hasn't been shot too. I'd have never
forgiven you for that. I know what you're thinking, though: So far, you're the only one who's
suffered but you've achieved your goal, solving the mystery of Sturminster — or, at least,
believe you have. But was it worth it? I can
only hope so, because it looks like —*

He jolted himself from his delirium,
wondering how much blood he was losing.
Feeling more and more light-headed, he
guessed it must be plenty. All he could do
now was keep pressure on the wound and
pray. He was past wondering who had shot
him and why he hadn't finished the job. The
next shot — if it came — would certainly
be lethal.

419

Merciful even.

He stared up at the opening — a black square specked with stars — determined to keep his heavy-lidded eyes open and not drift away again.

More time passed. How much, he had no idea.

Voices.

Were they real?

Yes. No, wait —

He must be imagining them.

He looked through filmy eyes at the opening again. Someone was descending the ladder; others followed, carrying a stretcher.

A face loomed close to his. It was Andrew, he was certain. "Hang on, Lawrence. We're getting you out of here," he said in Kingston's ear.

Kingston reached out to Andrew; he had to tell him, before the others discovered it. He found Andrew's arm and held it for a moment, gaining strength from the simple act. The other men, three or four of them, gathered nearby, talking quietly among themselves, a stretcher off to one side. One of the men approached and kneeled beside him. It took him a moment to realize that it was Simon Crawford, Sturminster's dapper manager. It was the casual clothes, he realized. Over a black turtleneck, his Barbour jacket had seen better days. "We're getting you to a hospital," he said. "Your friend'll be with you. You're going to be fine."

With Andrew at his side, he was lifted onto the stretcher, a blanket laid over him, then strapped down. Crawford went up the ladder first, then called down orders. As Kingston was lifted, he tugged on Andrew's arm, dragging him alongside the stretcher. "It's all right, Lawrence," Andrew comforted. "It won't be long now."

"Listen to me," Kingston said in a hoarse voice, pulling Andrew close.

"What is it?"

"It's the bricks," Kingston whispered.

"What bricks?" Andrew whispered back.

"On the walls. I think they're filled with gold."

"Gold?"

"Keep your voice down. Find a way to slip back. Look at the wall behind where I was shot. You'll see it — the gold. There's a bullet there, lodged in the wall. Get it and keep it. Understand?"

Andrew squeezed his hand tight. "Don't worry, I will," he replied.

Now Kingston felt himself being raised into a near vertical position. The blood rushed from his head, the light-headedness and nausea returning. Then he was lying flat again, looking up at stars, being hurried across an open space and lifted into a vehicle. It cheered him that Andrew was nowhere to be seen. He breathed a deep sigh and closed his eyes.

He slipped into a dream: floating slowly down a river, on his back, like Millais's *Ophelia* before she drowned. But unlike her, he wasn't singing. Far off, a chorus of muted voices was singing a cappella. He was being lifted again, as if by invisible hands, carried upward toward a blissful golden light that beckoned. Yet as he drew closer, the light's radiance dimmed and he slid into a velvety blackness, soothing and soporific.

The pain was gone. He was asleep.

THIRTY-FOUR

Seven hours later, Kingston awoke to find himself staring at a white ceiling, a blinding white that made him avert his eyes. He soon realized that the assault on his retinas had less to do with the white paint than the bright light flooding the room through a picture window. He glanced sideways, shielding his eyes, to get a better view, seeing what appeared to be the environs of a small town. He rolled his head slowly on the pillow to take in the room: He was in a hospital ward. Glancing upward, he saw the IV bag with its clear liquid hanging from the stand beside the bed, the tube taped to his arm, and various monitoring devices. It didn't seem to be a critical-care ward, which was comforting.

His chest was painfully sore, as he discovered when he tried to slide upward on the pillow. His ankle ached, too. He vaguely remembered falling from a ladder and ending up on a dirt floor, immobilized. As embarrassing and bathetic as that had been, it was nothing compared to what had followed. He started to reconstruct the chain of events in the subterranean room.

Slowly it all began to fall together, scene by scene, like trying to recall a particularly bad dream, his mind blanking on the details. He remembered being shot in the chest and lying helpless on the dirt, drifting in and out of consciousness while Andrew went for help. Then he recalled seeing the bullet lodged in the brick and spotting what, at the time, he was sure was gold inside the shattered brick. Could he have imagined or invented it in his delirious state? Where was Andrew, for that matter? Had he been able to retrieve the bullet? Kingston chided himself for not having instructed him to somehow cover up the exposed gold. He should have warned him about the unknown shooter as well. Too late now, he said to himself, returning to his memory of the catastrophic night.

His thoughts were interrupted by a man's voice. "How are you feeling, Lawrence?"

Kingston turned toward the door to see that two men had entered. One was young and tall, with a mop of ginger hair flopping over one eye. He was wearing a tan summer suit with a loosely knotted tie. Kingston recognized the man behind him immediately: Inspector Wheatley, looking as sartorially correct as ever.

"I'm Dr. Anderson. I believe the inspector needs no introduction."

"Good morning, Doctor," said Kingston. He gave a perfunctory nod to Wheatley. "Inspector."

"Well, I've got good news for you," said Anderson, standing over Kingston. "I can't say you dodged a bullet, but metaphorically you did. You're a lucky man. Apart from tissue damage and some minor issues, you're none the worse for wear. A few inches lower and it might have been a very different story, though. We'll keep you here for a couple of days, and if nothing changes, you can go home."

"That is good news."

"If you feel up to it, you can see visitors, but don't overdo it," said Anderson, patting Kingston on his "good" shoulder. "It's a cliché, I know, but for the next forty-eight hours you need to rest as much as possible."

Kingston nodded. "Thank you, Doctor."

"If it's all right with you, Inspector Wheatley would like to have a word, but I've cautioned him to go easy on you and to keep his questions brief. How long he stays will be up to you."

"That's fine," said Kingston, eager to know what had happened in the missing several hours — if the police had found out who'd done the shooting.

The doctor departed and Wheatley pulled up a chair.

"I'm genuinely sorry for what's happened to you, Lawrence, and glad for your sake that it wasn't a lot worse," said Wheatley in his customary terse and expressionless manner. "I won't waste your time right now inquiring about what exactly you were doing at the temple — we can get into that later. If you don't mind, though, perhaps you could tell me what happened from the time you and this Andrew friend of yours trespassed on Sturminster's grounds."

Kingston smiled at the "trespassing" accusation. He found it hard to believe that

Wheatley would let him and Andrew off so
lightly. Figuring that the inspector must be
feeling sorry for him, he thought no more
of it and, for the next few minutes, he
related what he could remember, reminding
Wheatley that most of the time he was in
the subterranean room he was in and out of
consciousness. Though reconciled to the
fact that his involvement in the case was
now a thing of the past — that from now
on it was in the hands of the police — he
made no mention of his suspicion that the
walls might contain gold ingots. Nor did he
reveal that he'd asked Andrew to retrieve
the bullet. If push came to shove later, and
Wheatley accused him of withholding evidence, he could claim amnesia or his inability at the time to determine fact from
fantasy. Unlike their first face-to-face meeting, Wheatley was patient and considerate
of Kingston's ordeal and injuries, and
listened without interrupting. Kingston had
expected at least a few questions after
finishing his account and was surprised and
thankful when Wheatley stood, as if to signal
his leaving. He must have taken the doctor's
caution about brevity to heart, thought
Kingston.

"I've spent enough of your time, Lawrence. Thanks for your patience. I'll leave

you to get some rest. We'll be talking again, of course. There's still that small matter of your trespassing that needs to be addressed."

"I have a question, if you don't mind," said Kingston.

Wheatley nodded. "Go ahead."

"Do you have any idea who shot me?"

"I was going to ask you the same question. The answer is no. As yet we don't have a suspect. That's about all I can tell you."

"What about the bullet? Did the doctor retrieve it?"

"Don't worry, that'll be for ballistics to worry about."

"What about Amanda Veitch? Is she still a suspect?"

"For someone who almost went for a Burton, you certainly have a lot of questions. As for the Veitch woman, let's just say that we haven't decided to file charges yet."

"I understand."

Wheatley nodded and managed a decent smile. "Get well, Lawrence," he said. "And leave the rest to us. You've done enough . . . for now."

Kingston knew the inspector wanted to say "enough damage" and respected Wheatley for resisting the temptation. "One last thing, Inspector. On your way out, could you ask the nurse if she can rustle up a copy of the *Times*. I'd appreciate it."

"Be happy to."

Kingston closed his eyes. The encouraging news about his gunshot wound had made him feel much better already, both physically and mentally. On several occasions in the past he'd been lectured by his now dear departed physician in Scotland about the importance of understanding and respecting the symbiotic relationship between the health of both the body and the mind — that they were interconnected, that one affects the other, and that neither can be separated. He was the person who had recommended that Kingston do the *Times* cryptic puzzles.

This newfound burst of enthusiasm and optimism made him start thinking about the case again. His alter ego was telling him to forget it, that it was prideful, ill advised, and could well delay his recovery. On the other hand, the compulsion to bring matters to a close was unexpected and, given the trauma of the last several hours, much stronger than he would have thought possible. With the conflicting emotions tugging at his leathery conscience, he stared out the window at the pleasant view. After more staring at the ceiling and more thought, he reached a compromise. He reminded himself that, like it or not, he was confined to a hospital bed for at least two more days and that there was little or nothing he could do, anyway. In a few minutes, he drifted off to dreamless sleep.

THIRTY-FIVE

Someone was touching his shoulder. He heard a voice — a woman's. He opened his eyes, squinting against the bright light. A nurse in a blue tunic was standing next to him, a glass of water in one hand, a pill bottle in the other.

"The doctor wants you to take your medication."

"What is it?"

"Something for the pain," she replied with a coaxing smile.

Kingston managed to shift himself up on the pillow into a half-sitting position, his arms outside the blanket. He looked at her more closely. She was quite tall and not unattractive, had a pleasant expression on her face, and was waiting patiently.

So why did he suddenly feel apprehensive? Nothing unusual about the pain medication; it would be expected after surgery.

"What time is it?" he asked.

"About noon."

Kingston took the glass, sipping from it, trying to understand his unease. She *was* rather abrupt — was that it? Aren't nurses usually a trifle more cheery, more sympathetic? After all he'd been through, he certainly deserved a little more, like a comforting "Well, how are we doing, Mr. Kingston?" or "Starting to feel better, are we?"

She smiled again, opened the bottle, and shook out two small pink pills. He sipped more water.

"Sorry, I'm parched," he said. "Give me a moment." He took another small sip. "By the way, what's the name of this hospital?" he asked. "No one has told me."

"It's the Staffordshire Memorial Hospital."

"And my doctor's name?"

Her smile vanished, replaced by an unsettling look she quickly tried to cover. "Everyone in the hospital's here to help you, Mr. Kingston," she said brusquely.

Instantly, he knew.

It's her voice. The huskiness. That's why she said so little.

"I understand," he said.

He held out his free hand for the pills, then suddenly threw the water in her face

430

and grabbed her wrist. The motion, though short, sent a searing pain through his chest, but he was determined not to let go.

"Vanessa Carlson, isn't it?" he shouted, tightening his grip. "Or would you prefer Decker?"

"Let me go, damn you," she sputtered, pulling back and struggling desperately to wrench herself free, dragging him across the sheet with her. Yanked by the tube in his left arm, the IV stand and bag on the other side clattered down against the bedrail.

His eyes darted about the bed, searching in vain for the nurse's call remote.

"Help!" he bellowed. *"Help!"*

Now half off the bed, Kingston's chest was stabbing with needles of pain; what little strength he had was draining fast. Any minute, he would fall to the floor and it would be all over.

She realized it, too. She fumbled in her tunic pocket with her free hand.

A wave of panic, nausea, and raw adrenaline coursed through Kingston as he saw what she'd pulled out.

A syringe.

He let go of her arm and crabbed back across the bed. Immediately, she came at him, pointing the needle like a dagger. He felt for the chrome IV pole with both hands, gripped it, and shoved the bag end into her stomach. She howled and staggered back. He rolled off the bed, almost falling but managing to stay on his feet. As she recovered and came around the end of the bed, he yanked the IV catheter out of his arm, flipped the bag off its hook, and hoisted the IV stand off the floor to a horizontal position, the four-legged base away from him. The opened vein in his arm was bleeding, but he ignored it. With a primal strength and fury coming from someplace in him he didn't know existed, he whirled and swung the stand at her. Her reflexes were quick and she dodged the first swing. But she didn't count on it continuing full circle. Kingston was gripping the pole like an Olympic hammer, and on the next rotation the heavy base crunched into her back below her neck with a sickening thud. She collapsed like a rag doll; the syringe spun across the floor into the wall. Kingston dropped the IV stand and collapsed on the bed. He leaned over, picked up the dangling remote, and pressed the button to summon the nurse.

THIRTY-SIX

Kingston sat on the bed staring at Vanessa Carlson's body, waiting anxiously for the nurse and for his heart to stop thumping. He was sweating profusely and the pain in his chest was returning with a vengeance. What a surprise was in store for the poor nurse, he thought. Not to mention Andrew. Where the hell was he? Kingston wondered.

The door opened and a nurse entered. She stopped dead in her tracks and put a hand to her mouth. "Good God! What on earth — ?" she exclaimed, wide eyed, kneeling by Carlson's body.

Kingston explained briefly what had happened, pointing to the syringe, and the nurse left immediately to get help. Within minutes she returned with a doctor and two orderlies and a gurney.

They all waited silently while the doctor examined Vanessa Carlson. Kingston's sigh of relief was audible when the doctor finally announced that she was alive. Even though she had tried to murder him, the idea that he might have killed her — even in self-defense — was repugnant to him. The doctor went on to say that the extent of her injuries wouldn't be determined until they'd made a thorough examination, but Kingston had heard all he wanted to. The pain in his chest had subsided somewhat and he lay back gingerly on the bed, his head sinking into the crumpled pillow, and stared at the ceiling, his mind numb.

The orderlies lifted Vanessa Carlson's body onto the stretcher with practiced efficiency and departed with the nurse in tow. The doctor remained and turned his attention to Kingston, removing the dressing and examining the wound for tearing or damage. Satisfied that Kingston was none the worse for wear, the doctor said that the police had been informed, then offered a few cautionary words about "behaving" and resting, before giving Kingston a sedative and leaving.

Kingston was dozing when he heard a man's voice. He opened his eyes and saw Andrew. "About time you showed up," he muttered, still groggy. "Where the hell have you been?"

"With the police mostly. After they whisked you away, Sturminster's security people put me under house arrest, I suppose you'd call it. After spending the best part of the day locked up at the house reading magazines and napping, the police interviewed me. Inspector Wheatley."

Kingston managed a nod. "He was here.

Doesn't seem that long ago, but I've lost all track of time."

"Hardly surprising."

"He didn't tell me he'd spoken with you. Anyway, have they told you what happened here? It was bloody awful."

"They have."

"Is that all you have to say after that woman almost killed me?"

Andrew looked away. "I don't know what to think or say anymore, Lawrence. I know I should be thankful and relieved that you've survived, but at the same time I'm pissed off at you for being so damned reckless and thoughtless, ignoring everyone's advice — all in the name of your blind ambition with this lousy case."

"I can't argue with you, Andrew. Everything you've said is true. But you might give me — or us, I should say — credit for solving it."

Andrew looked back at Kingston. "Partly solving it would be more accurate. It looks like you and Veitch were right about a fortune being buried somewhere at Sturminster. And it's safe to assume it's the money purloined by Samuel Morley, as we expected. We still don't know for sure — unless I'm out of the loop — who killed Endicott and Veitch, or how this Carlson woman fits into the picture. As for the gold, sooner or later the police or Sturminster's people will discover that the walls of that place are filled with gold ingots — if they haven't already. Even when they do, I still have an uneasy feeling that's not the end of it. What's more, I don't think we can assume that they — whoever *they* may be — are going to give up just yet."

"I have some answers —"

"No more, *please*."

Kingston held a hand up. "I know. I know. This is not the time to discuss it. You'll only get angrier. When I get out of here then we can talk about it more."

"As long as it's just talk, that's fine."

Andrew reached into his pocket and pulled out a misshapen bullet, holding it up for Kingston to see. "It was where you said it was. I covered up the damaged brick as best I could, and unless someone goes over the wall inch by inch, they won't find it."

"Good. I was hoping you might."

"Here," he said, flipping it to Kingston.

Kingston's reaction was slow. He dropped the bullet and it slipped off the blanket and bounced to the floor. Andrew knelt to look for it. After a few seconds he stood with the bullet in one hand, a mobile phone in the other. "Someone's missing a mobile," he said. "It could be that woman's."

"We should be so lucky," said Kingston. "Check the voice mail."

Andrew spent a few moments tinkering with the unfamiliar mobile. "There are two messages," he said. "Hold on."

Andrew listened to the playbacks. In less than a minute he looked at Kingston again, his expression unreadable. "The first is from a garage, reminding her that her BMW is due for servicing next week."

"And the second?" asked Kingston impatiently.

"I think you'll like this one better."

"Who is it?"

"Here, you can listen for yourself." Andrew cued up the message and handed the phone to Kingston.

Kingston took it, glanced at the display and pressed Play.

"It's Morley. Kingston is still alive. He's in Staffordshire Memorial Hospital. We can't do anything more now. I'm afraid you'll have to take care of it, as quickly as possible. Whatever you do don't try to contact me — wait until I call you. Sorry."

Kingston closed the phone and stared at

it. "Well . . . I'll . . . be damned," he said, shaking his head.

Thirty-Seven

Kingston put the phone down on the blanket, his eyes fixed somewhere in middle space as the full force of Morley's words soaked in.

"What are you going to do?" Andrew asked.

Kingston pulled himself together and shifted his perceptive gaze to Andrew. "I had it all wrong," he mumbled.

"I don't understand."

"Well, partly wrong."

Andrew shook his head. "Do you mind telling me what you're trying to say?"

"It was Simon Crawford who tried to kill me down in the pit. But I never thought for a moment that Morley was involved in this mess. Crawford and Vanessa Carlson, yes — I'm sure that we'll find out that they were hand in glove all the time — but Francis Morley? Was that why he hired me? Good God!"

"How do you know for sure it was Crawford at the temple?"

"The security system was my first clue. At the time I wondered why it was so easy: We could not only waltz halfway across Sturminster to reach the temple but also drag that trough across the park, take all the time in the world trying to find the key to the secret room, and not be spotted. It had to be something to do with the security system. We knew from the cameras at the gates that a security system was in place."

"Are you saying that the system was deactivated?"

"Not necessarily, though that might be a natural supposition."

"What else, then?"

"I'm sure now that it was functioning all the time and we were being watched from the moment we entered the park to the end."

"So why weren't we apprehended?"

"Because Crawford and Morley knew that we were probably on to something that might lead them to the hidden money. That's what's been driving them all along, from the very beginning."

"Because they couldn't solve the riddle or figure out the Gray's *Elegy* part of the code."

"Either or both."

"I'm confused. It would mean that Crawford would have had to sneak away to the temple, take a couple of potshots at you, and then return. Surely, if the system was on and the cameras were running, he would have been captured on tape."

"He could have done it several ways, and whether Morley was with Crawford when they had us under surveillance is irrelevant. Having given it considerable thought, here's how I believe Crawford pulled it off. He knew the system intimately — it was no doubt installed under his supervision. More often than not, I believe that surveillance cameras continually pan sensitive areas; they are cycled to complete one pass from left to right, say, and then back in the opposite direction. In the case of the camera covering the area surrounding the temple, Crawford knew exactly how long that cycle was and could have easily adjusted it, to slow it down. He would then know exactly how long he had to get to the temple, get his shots off quickly, and return to reset the system."

"So when the police looked at the tapes all they would see would be us?"

"Right. I'd been wondering all along why Crawford didn't fire more shots. He simply didn't have the time. And he had no way to know if he'd actually shot me."

"He had to leave quickly or risk being caught in the act."

"That's what I think. We'll know fairly soon, I'm sure."

"Is that going to be enough to nail him? It's still supposition."

"There was something else."

"I somehow thought there might be, knowing you."

"It was when I was being lifted out of the room on a stretcher. I was woozy and it took me a moment to recognize Crawford when he knelt to talk to me. You see, I'd never seen him out of his dapper business clothes and I distinctly remember that he was wearing a Barbour jacket, black turtleneck, and dark trousers that night. He looked uncharacteristically shabby. Not only that, his trousers and the lower front of his jacket showed traces of powdery dust on them — the very same dust that had been disturbed and had settled on the floor where the stone slab was raised. None of the other men had dust on their clothes."

"Very observant of you, considering the shape you were in. Of course, to shoot at you he probably had to kneel or even lie down to peer into the hole."

"That's what I figured. And unless he's had his clothes dry cleaned, traces of that dust will still be in the cloth fibers, even if he gave them a good brushing afterward."

"Have you told any of this to the inspector?"

Kingston shook his head. "Not yet. See if you could reach him for me, Andrew — Staffordshire police headquarters, in Stafford. Tell them it's urgent."

Five minutes later, Kingston's bedside phone rang. It was Wheatley.

"Thanks for calling, Inspector," said Kingston. "I have some rather startling news for you . . ."

THIRTY-EIGHT

Bourne End, ten days later

It was an agreeable summer's day at Andrew's house. All morning the sun had been playing cat and mouse, dodging in and out of the white clouds, but had finally gained the upper hand and since noon the temperature had crept up to the low eighties.

Since Kingston had arrived at eleven, he and Andrew had been sitting on the terrace with drinks, talking, of all things, about the Sturminster case. Oddly, though, it was as if each would prefer to discuss something else. Andrew, more than Kingston, had made a couple of creditable efforts to change the topic only to have the conversation eventually wind back, as if tugged by an inexorable external force, to where they'd begun. Though they'd been talking about the case on and off for the last ten days, it seemed that there was always another recollection, another revelation, and more questions arose constantly, some with no cut-and-dried answers.

Only in the last couple of days had the murders slipped from the front pages of the nation's newspapers and from the TV headlines. To the best of Kingston's knowledge, Vanessa Carlson was still in the hospital recovering from the internal injuries and broken bones caused by Kingston's punishing blow. Wheatley had told him that they'd run a check on her mobile and home phones. Billing records listed dozens of calls between her and Crawford in the last six weeks.

In light of the overwhelming evidence, both Simon Crawford and Vanessa Carlson had confessed to and been charged with the murder of Tristan Veitch and the attempted murder of Lawrence Kingston. Francis Morley, who had also confessed, had been charged with being an accessory in both the murder of Veitch and the attempt on Kingston's life. All had been arraigned and were in jail awaiting preliminary hearings.

"Are you getting hungry?" asked Andrew,

after Kingston declined a second gin and tonic.

"I am. Knowing your inclination for — shall we say — generous helpings and courses, I had only tea and one slice of toast for breakfast. Were you able to get the wild salmon, by the way?"

"Of course. Flown down from Scotland yesterday."

Andrew picked up the empty glasses and started for the kitchen. "Why don't you camp out here while I get things started. Give me about ten minutes. There're some new magazines in the rack over there."

"Sure I can't help?"

"You've been ordered to relax," Andrew said over his shoulder.

Kingston was engrossed in a *Gardens Illustrated* article about Harold Peto's Italianate garden at Iford Manor when he thought he heard the faint ring of the doorbell. He thought nothing of it until he heard voices. He looked up to see Andrew step onto the terrace. He had a wide grin on his face. "Someone here to see you, Lawrence."

Kingston was, bewildered. As far as he knew, not a soul knew he was at Bourne End.

"Hello, Lawrence," said Amanda, smiling, as she joined them on the terrace.

For a fleeting moment he was lost for words as he rose from his wicker chair. She looked lovely: the white linen dress, the straw hat, her wide-set sparkling eyes and winsome smile. "Well, I'll be — !" he sputtered. "What a wonderful surprise."

"It was Andrew's idea," she said.

"Please sit down," said Kingston, smoothing the tablecloth unnecessarily as a way of giving himself a few extra moments to think. Seeing Amanda was like a ray of sunshine, but now an unwelcome cloud was moving in, already casting a shadow over what, for him, had been a joyful moment.

"I'll get you a drink, Amanda," said Andrew. "What would you like?"

"Something bubbly would be super, if you have it?"

"Absolutely. Well, I'll leave you two alone for a moment," said Andrew, departing.

As they were talking, Kingston had been thinking hard. Several days had passed since he'd last talked to Inspector Wheatley. Among the many things they'd discussed related to the case, Kingston had explained his theory about William Endicott's death, which understandably had taken a backseat following the headline-grabbing events at Sturminster. As for Amanda, he'd only talked to her twice — once from the hospital, a call cut short by the nurse, and again a couple of days later, so he had no idea how much she knew about the most recent developments.

By now Wheatley would have called to tell her that she was no longer a suspect in Tristan's death. As a point of courtesy alone he would have surely done that, given his punctiliousness. This prompted Kingston to wonder whether Wheatley had also broached the subject of Endicott's murder. Suddenly, with Amanda sitting there, it had become important for Kingston to know the answer to that question.

In one of his several conversations with the inspector in the days following the incidents at Sturminster and at the hospital, Wheatley had told him that Crawford, Morley, and Vanessa Carslon had all sworn in their respective interviews that they had nothing to do with Endicott's murder. Wheatley had expressed doubt, but it fitted with Kingston's theory: that Endicott had been their pipeline to Veitch's activities, and the last thing the three of them would want would be for him to be silenced. Kingston had been harboring a suspicion as to who had killed Endicott for some time. He'd even ventured that opinion to Morley early on. In the past weeks he'd gone over it at least a half dozen times and kept coming back to the same answer — it must have been Veitch. When he'd told the inspector this, a long silence had followed. He'd taken it to indicate that the police hadn't considered that possibility, which he found surprising. In their conversation he'd been careful not to say "murdered" because it was more self-serving to think that Endicott had been killed accidentally during a struggle and not with premeditation. For Amanda's sake, Kingston would naturally prefer that to be the case.

Kingston's rationale was straightforward: Early in his research Veitch had told Endicott about his suspicions and growing certitude about wrongdoings at Sturminster, and the more Endicott learned, the more intrigued he became in the project. Endicott was still infatuated with Vanesssa Carlson, whom he'd met at the garden club. Though theirs was probably an on-and-off relationship, Endicott made the mistake of mentioning to her that he was helping Veitch, telling her what they were working on. Unbeknownst to Endicott, she was dating Simon Crawford and — as she had since admitted under oath — had been for some time. As Endicott learned more, so did Crawford, and he eventually told Morley about Veitch's discovery. Unlike Crawford, whose main interest was the hidden money, Morley's concerns were twofold: finding the money for himself and Crawford and preventing the information from becoming public, which would result in irreparable damage to the family name and to Sturminster. It could spell the end of the dynasty and the entire estate.

When Veitch got his hands on the Winterborne code from Llewellyn-Jones, it was a huge break, but it also created a new problem: He needed someone he could trust to decode it. Though he might not have known to begin with, it was a fortunate stroke of serendipity when he learned of Endicott's cryptography skills. With Endicott's expanded role and growing realization that Veitch was really on to something and the vast amount of money that could be at stake, he figured that he should be entitled to a generous share of the proceeds. If he could crack the codes, he was certain that it would lead them to the money.

Kingston's theory was that Endicott had given Veitch an either-or proposition: Cut him in for a sizable share or he would go to Morley and tell him everything. Exactly what happened next would, most likely, never be known. But a terrified Veitch had a body on his hands and had to dispose of it. As a historian, he knew everything there was to know about Sturminster. That included not only the Arcadian monument and its mysterious unsolved da Vinci–like inscription, but also the pathways and tiny dirt roads. Linking Endicott's death to Sturminster by dumping his body close to the Arcadian monument was a devious move. To make it appear even more related, Veitch scribbled a few letters on a piece of paper, ripped it in half, and placed the written part in Endicott's pocket. It achieved its intended purpose: to raise all kinds of speculation of more sinister implications.

Kingston had met Veitch once and only briefly, but having learned more about him — how he thought, what he'd discovered, and how potentially hazardous that information might be — it was just the kind of thing he would have done faced with the horror of knowing that he'd killed a friend and could never prove it was an accident. In a perverse way, it was almost admirable. If he did become a suspect and the accusation of blackmail surfaced, he knew that it could be tantamount to a murder conviction.

Kingston looked at Amanda, realizing that he'd better say something intelligent soon or she could start to think that his injury and harrowing experience had somehow impaired his mental state. He was glad when she spoke first.

"How are you feeling?"

"Quite well, all things considered. Healing faster than I'd hoped for — actually, more a bruised ego and embarrassment than anything else. How about you?"

"I'm managing to come to grips with it, and sleeping more than three or four hours a night for the first time since the day Tristan died. I still find it impossible to believe everything that's happened, though."

Kingston knew that the polite conversation couldn't last. One way or another, lingering questions had to be asked and answered by both of them. "Did you hear from Inspector Wheatley?" he asked without ceremony.

"I did. Yes. He called when you were in the hospital. He told me what had happened. He said that the Carlson woman had confessed to poisoning Tristan and that I was no longer a suspect. I can't describe what a relief that was. He also told me briefly how she did it. Unknown to me, Carlson and Tristan knew each other through the garden club. According to her statement, it was something of a surprise to Tristan when Carlson had called, because they hadn't been in contact for a long time. She told him that she had revealing information about Sturminster's missing money and arranged to meet him at a pub not far from Abbot's Broomfield. Apparently, she slipped the aconitine into his drink with an eyedropper. It helped that Tristan had ordered whisky, which made the poisonous tincture undetectable. She claimed that she hadn't meant to kill Tristan, only to give him enough poison to require hospitalization. Their intent was to get both of us out of the house so they could steal all of Tristan's papers, everything he'd discovered."

"A likely story."

Amanda nodded. "One more thing. The inspector said that Carlson has nursing credentials and once worked at a hospital in Coventry."

"That would explain a lot."

"Inspector Wheatley even apologized for the anguish that he knew it must have caused me — being a suspect. He was actually nice for a change."

"Anything else?"

She brushed her fingers across one eye. "You mean his and your theory about Tristan having killed William Endicott?"

Kingston wished he could be somewhere else. "It's only an educated guess," he said, "but we both thought it important that you should know about it. If it were to be proved later that that's what happened, it would come as less of a shock. Not to dismiss or make light of it, but I believe that when all's said and done, Endicott's death will remain unsolved and soon forgotten, overshadowed by the other, far more sensational crimes. I seriously doubt Tristan's name will ever appear in the newspaper, other than as the historian who laid bare Sturminster's secrets."

"You're a clever man, Lawrence — thoughtful too, even if a little headstrong," she said, smiling quixotically. "The way you explain it, I almost believe you. Don't worry, though, I'm learning to live with lots of stressful things these days. You, too, I imagine. I think I can handle it, if that's what concerns you."

Kingston was about to reply when Andrew arrived with the champagne.

"Sorry it took so long, but I'm sure you two weren't lacking for things to talk about. Perhaps you'd do the honors, Lawrence, while I finish in the kitchen," he said, putting the ice bucket and glasses on the table and departing.

Kingston poured them each a glass of Veuve Clicquot and they continued discussing the Sturminster case. About five minutes or so later Andrew reappeared announcing that lunch was finally ready in the dining room.

Throughout the meal, Kingston and Amanda were content to let Andrew do much of the talking. It was almost as if, left out of the early conversation, he was determined to make up for it. By now he was privy to most of the details of the Sturminster case, but Kingston was impressed by some of Andrew's questions. Clearly he'd absorbed a lot more information than Kingston had given him credit for.

"I'm curious, Lawrence," said Andrew, sipping his wine. "Did you ever figure out who was shadowing you? Was it Morley's people?"

"You mean the man on the King's Road and the one in the BMW?"

"Right."

"They were Wheatley's tails. He told me that with the case at a standstill, it might be a good idea to know where I was going and whom I was talking to. That's how he knew I'd gone to see Dorothy Endicott, among other things."

"And what about the gold horseshoe, the one Lytton gave you?"

"What do you mean?"

"How come Julian Heywood had one in his drawer? You'd said that he and his father-in-law were not on speaking terms."

"Ah, yes. For a while I thought there might be a connection between Julian Heywood and Bryce Lytton, that they might be involved somehow in Endicott's murder. It really made no sense, but I eventually called Julian and asked him how he came by the horseshoe. Apparently his mother had given it to him years ago. That's all there was to it."

Soon the conversation drifted to more pleasant matters: Amanda admiring Andrew's Georgian house, commenting on the furniture, décor, and the garden, wanting to know more about it. Andrew was only too glad to oblige, launching into a lengthy explanation of its history: built for a famous Shakespearian actor around the mid-nineteenth century and the garden laid out much later by a theater-set designer. He finished by giving Kingston most of the credit for the way the garden looked today.

Some forty minutes later they'd finished Andrew's sherry trifle and were having coffee when Kingston seized the conversation in a rather unexpected way.

"I hesitate to bring up Sturminster again," he said, "but with everyone, including myself, naturally focused on the events and crimes of the present, we've tended to overlook the past. We shouldn't forget that it was what *actually* took place at Sturminster two hundred and sixty years ago that got Tristan interested in the first place."

Andrew frowned. "I'm not sure that I'm following you. Hasn't the, quote, 'Sturminster legend' been laid to rest? Don't we now have a pretty good idea of what happened in those days?"

"I believe we still have only partial knowledge. I could be wrong, and I hope I am, but in the coming weeks the nation will be shocked again when it's revealed what else might have happened back then. It's incomprehensible how it's remained such a guarded secret all these centuries and it also provides a clearer understanding of why Samuel Morley went to such lengths with the complicated secret codes to protect his ill-gotten fortune and other crimes."

Andrew shrugged and glanced at Amanda. "He does this occasionally. It's the professor coming out."

Kingston ignored the flip comment. "I'll explain," he said. "It was something that Tristan said that day at the hospital that stuck with me. He talked about 'damning information' and 'heinous crimes.' It took me time to realize that while we were focusing on the hidden cache of money, there could be another, more macabre, secret that Samuel Morley had to live with —"

Amanda interrupted. "The 'heinous crimes' part?"

"Exactly. And 'guilt-ridden bricks.' "

"That was a clever play on words," said Andrew.

Kingston nodded. "Lying in that underground room, after I'd noticed the gold inside the brick, I started thinking: How could Morley have built the room under the temple without others knowing that the bricks were filled with gold ingots, if indeed they all are?"

"Are you talking about the workers, the bricklayers?" asked Amanda.

"Mostly. There was someone else, too — a man who played a big part in Morley's grand design for Sturminster. The man who had designed and overseen construction of his monuments and had undoubtedly helped construct the room under the temple *before* the temple was built — Matthew Seward, the architect."

Andrew looked confused. "Where is all this going?"

"I'm getting to that." Kingston glanced about the terrace while gathering his thoughts. "Oxbridge-Bell's book on the history of Sturminster gives passing reference to certain deaths on and around the estate during the period in question, oddly enough all male. Though lacking specifics, the author concluded that most were either accidental or job related — no mention of homicides. What is more telling, however, is a single paragraph concerning Matthew Seward. It states that Seward disappeared soon after he'd completed Sturminster's monuments, and no reports of his death have ever been presented or recorded. He simply disappeared. One explanation offered was that Seward had traveled often to various parts of Europe and the Middle East, and it has been speculated that he might have died while on one of these journeys."

"So what are you getting at?" Andrew frowned.

"I'm suggesting that when the time comes to dismantle the room under the temple to find out exactly how much gold it contains, further excavation will reveal that it also served as the tomb of one or more workers and possibly Matthew Seward." He paused, as if to underline the gravity of what he'd proposed. "I believe that's what Tristan had in mind when he said 'heinous crimes.'"

Amanda grimaced. "You're saying that they knew too much and had to be . . . silenced?"

"Either that or they'd resorted to black-mailing Morley. If you think about it, he'd have had little choice — a fortune amassed over several decades was buried under that temple."

"Grisly. The tabloids are going to have a field day with that," said Andrew.

Kingston nodded. "They will, I'm sure. And you know what? I wouldn't be at all surprised as the days pass if even more transgressions surface, when the tattered pages of Sturminster's sordid past come under closer scrutiny."

"I trust you won't be part of that inquiry, Lawrence," said Amanda.

"Not on your life. I'm done with it."

"Then let's talk about something else."

"How about more coffee?" Andrew inter-jected.

Amanda said yes. Kingston declined, and Andrew left for the kitchen.

Alone again, a silence fell between them, as if each was waiting for the other to say something first. Finally Amanda spoke.

"I've been making quite a few changes to the house," she said. "I've cleaned out Tristan's office and painted it, and I may get the floor refinished. I'm also getting rid of a lot of stuff." She paused, fingering the string of amber beads resting on her blouse. "I was thinking it might be . . . well, I wondered if you'd like to come up to Stafford again. There are two things in particular that I wanted to tell you about."

He smiled. "You make it sound quite mysterious."

"I had planned to surprise you, but I see no reason why you shouldn't know now." She stopped fidgeting with the beads and dropped her hands into her lap. "The first is the wine cellar." After a pause, she went on, her voice more upbeat. "I've really no need for it and I could use the space. Before I start dismantling it, I thought you might like to go through the bottles and pick out those you'd like."

"My goodness. Are you sure?"

She nodded. "If you don't take them, someone else will. I'll keep a few, and what remains I'll either sell or give away."

"That's extremely generous of you. Wait 'til I tell Andrew."

"Bring him with you when you come up. We can make a day of it. Lunch and a wine tasting."

"It sounds delightful. When he comes back we'll set a date. You won't have to ask him twice."

Kingston picked up his water glass, draining what little was left in it as Amanda started to rummage in her purse. "You mentioned two things," he said.

"Yes. The other has to do with Charlie. I want you to meet him," she said, appearing to have found what she was looking for.

Who on earth was Charlie? he wondered. Perhaps she'd hired a gardener — she'd talked about that possibility. It couldn't be a new boyfriend, surely?

She closed her purse, looked up at him, and slid a small photo across the table. "Here," she said. "He's two months old."

Kingston was looking at a close-up of a black puppy with its tongue hanging out.

"You'll love him. He's adorable. I got him from the animal shelter last week — part Lab, part sheepdog."

Kingston grinned. "Well done. I can't wait to meet him. That reminds me, I should return your Pet Tag."

"No, you hang on to it, as a keepsake. He already has the old-fashioned kind."

Kingston handed her the photo and leaned back, measuring his next words carefully.

"Amanda," he said, pausing, "I want you to know . . . to know how much I've admired your courage and composure during these last horrendous weeks. There's no point in dwelling on the past, other than to think about the irony of it: Were it not for all that misery, we'd never have met."

He waited for her to say something, but all she did was return his gaze with an amused look, as if sympathizing with his struggle for words.

Kingston shifted in his seat, wondering whether to continue. "Maybe that didn't come out right. What I'm trying to say —"

"You don't have to say anything, Lawrence," she interrupted, shaking her head. "It won't change anything. We survived, didn't we? And that's all that matters."

"Yes, I suppose it is."

"I'll go on loving and missing Tristan, and being forever thankful for what you've done. As for the future, I'm going to do my best to erase all thought of these last wretched weeks and, as the cliché goes, simply get on with my life." She stopped herself, as though wondering whether to leave it at that, then continued. "There's one more thing I'd like to say, and then we'll drop the whole thing before we both become mawkish. And that *would* be embarrassing."

Kingston nodded.

"I'd like it if we could remain friends. As you know, I don't have too many, and at least you'll have seniority — I mean that in a positive sense, of course," she finished with a mischievous grin.

"In that case, I accept."

"That makes me very happy."

Kingston smiled and leaned back. "For a single rose can be my garden . . . a single friend, my world."

"That's nice. Did you make that up?"

"No. I stole it."

Ready with the coffee, Andrew could hear their laughter from the kitchen.

A FEW WORDS
ABOUT THE CODES

From the beginning it was clear that encoding and deciphering codes would play a pivotal role in my story and it was imperative that they be accurate. To achieve this, I was privileged to obtain methodology from the science writer and author Simon Singh, MBE, and Cary Davids at the American Cryptogram Association.

After a rudimentary self-imposed course to make sure that I understood the process, there remained the task of compiling the two riddles. The first was easy, based on a simple shift of letters as described by Kingston to Andrew on page 188. But devising the second (Winterborne) riddle took considerable time and racking of my nonmathematical brain. First, the riddle required the exact number of characters as those in the poem's seven lines. Next, it had to give the solver not only exact but also cryptic instructions on how to open the secret chamber. Last, it had to have relevance to the frieze and the chariot and be couched in language believable enough to have been written in the eighteenth century. I have no idea how many days passed before I'd managed to compile the riddle, but I know that in the end, few empty pages remained on my notepad.

For readers interested in knowing exactly how the Winterborne code (ciphertext) was created (enciphered), following is the mathematical formula:

First, the letters of the poem (the key) were assigned a number (shift) based on their numerical position in the alphabet. Thus, with the first word of the poem, THEIR, the first letter T = 20, H = 8, E = 5, I = 9, and R = 18. The next step was to shift the letters of the MESSAGE (plaintext) using the same process. Thus with NEATH, the first letter N = 14, E = 5, A = 1, T = 20, and H = 8.

Creating the code (ciphertext) can be done in two ways: the first, by manually shifting each individual letter, which I experimented with using two separate strips of the alphabet, sliding one under the other and counting off the letters to determine each coded letter. A far less laborious method was provided by the ACA:

Winterborne Code

1st plaintext letter (message): N = letter 14 of the alphabet

1st key letter (poem): T = letter 20 of the alphabet

1st ciphertext letter (code): H = letter 8 of the alphabet

The shifted letter (code) is determined by adding the numerical positions of plaintext and key letters. In this case, the code number would be 34 (20 + 14). But since there are only 26 letters in the alphabet, the code letter (H) is arrived at by deducting 26 from 34.

2nd plaintext letter (message): E = letter 5 of the alphabet

2nd key letter (poem): H = letter 8 of the alphabet

2nd ciphertext letter (code): M = letter 13 of the alphabet

In this case, the shifted code letter (M) is 13 (5 + 8). Note that this is determined by addition, not subtraction, if the total of plaintext and key letters do not exceed 26.

Following this formula, the first five coded letters of the Winterborne code are HMFCZ, which when decoded = NEATH.

Enciphering Rule

Number of ciphertext letter = number of plaintext letter plus number of key letter. If the number of the ciphertext letter is greater than 26, subtract 26 to get the correct letter number.

Deciphering Rule (reverse of enciphering)

Number of plaintext letter = number of ciphertext letter minus number of key letter. If the number of the plaintext letter is less than 0, add 26 to get the correct letter number.

Applying the deciphering rule to the Winterborne code, the first letter of the message is obtained by deducting the numerical position of the first letter of the poem (T = 20) from the numerical position of the first letter of the code (H = 8). 8 minus 20 equals minus 12. Since this is less than 0, add 26 to get the answer 14, the numerical position of letter N (first letter of the message).

ABOUT THE AUTHOR

Anthony Eglin is the author of four English Gardening mysteries, and lives in California.

The employees of Thorndike Press hope you have enjoyed this Large Print book. All our Thorndike, Wheeler, and Kennebec Large Print titles are designed for easy reading, and all our books are made to last. Other Thorndike Press Large Print books are available at your library, through selected bookstores, or directly from us.

For information about titles, please call:
(800) 223-1244

or visit our Web site at:
http://gale.cengage.com/thorndike

To share your comments, please write:
Publisher
Thorndike Press
10 Water St., Suite 310
Waterville, ME 04901